G000043712

The Girl On The Half Shell

Susan Ward

Cover Design by Sara Eirew
Copyright © 2014 Susan Ward
All rights reserved.

ISBN-10: 0615975925
ISBN-13: 978-0615975924

All Rights Reserved. In Accordance with the U.S. Copyright Act of 1976, the scanning, uploading, and electronic sharing of any part of this book without the permission of the publisher or author constitute unlawful piracy and theft of the author's intellectual property.

This is a work of fiction. Names, characters, places, and incidents either are the product of the author's imagination or are used fictitiously. Any resemblance to actual persons, living or dead, events, or locales is entirely coincidental.

DEDICATION

For my bugs

Author's Note

Thank you for downloading The Girl on the Half Shell. To find out why **USA Today HEA Blog** recommended The Series as a summer sizzling read, please continue the journey with books 2,3,& 4. The entire series is free in Kindle Unlimited.

The Girl on the Half Shell

The Girl of Tokens and Tears

The Girl of Diamonds and Rust

The Girl in the Comfortable Quiet

At eighteen I could not see the future. None of us can. What I didn't know at eighteen is that none of us really see the present. It is full of random moments and others we think significant, but we can't tell at the time, not really, which is which.

Table of Content

Chapter One

People would have stared at my father even if he had not been famous. He is just that kind of man, but it has taken me until the age of eighteen to understand that. In my younger years, when I hated Jack in fleeting spurts, I thought fame was like a suit; he could take it off for me if he wanted to. Now I know better than to have childish expectations of what my father can or can't do for me. Life with Jack is what it is. It is enough that he showed tonight, even if he did miss nearly the entire senior class spring recital.

I carefully conceal myself in the stage curtains as I watch Jack slipping into the auditorium and fading back into his customary seat in the far left corner. I can feel him in the darkened theater though I can only make out the hazy detail of his shape with my eyes.

Any other parent making that entrance would have had no impact on the audience. It is soundless. But my father is Jackson Parker, an icon of the sixties, forever part of the music and voice of a generation, and the entire chemistry of the room instantly alters.

Rene drops her chin on my shoulder as she stares out at the audience. "So, Jack did come," she says. She frees my fingers from the shabby velvet and tosses a harsh glare at the curtains, their age-beaten elegance a thing she finds preposterous since the private Catholic boarding school we reside at costs a small fortune in tuition each year. The shabbiness of the facility she is certain is nothing more than deliberate proletarian punishment for children of non-proletarian families. "He said he would come and actually showed. Chalk one up for team Jack. That's more than my dad ever does. Some girls just don't know when they are lucky. It could be worse, Chrissie. Your dad could be my dad."

Criticism with a joke chaser: a typical Rene-ism that might have made me laugh if it didn't remind me that even Rene didn't fully get me at times. In fairness, I don't always get myself. I like my dad. I really do. Everyone likes Jack, but the first emotion I always feel when I see my father is an intense desperation for him to leave.

I brush at the little balls of dust on the formerly flawless black of my dress. "I should have practiced more."

Rene gives me the look. "Practiced more? That's all you've done since your audition for Juilliard was scheduled. You couldn't have practiced more if you tried. Besides, I don't think it's possible for you to disappoint Jack."

Another nails on the chalkboard moment: *Jack*. I hate when my friends call my dad Jack, the easy familiarity they manage with him when my own relationship with my father has never been anything close to easy.

As I wait for the music director to introduce me, icy nerve bands tighten my stomach. It is so stupid to want the floor to swallow me whole, but for some reason since scheduling my audition for Juilliard I have worked into my mind the notion that my future would be foretold by this performance. I've never known what I want to do with my life and the decision to audition for Juilliard seems the first decision I've made about who I am and who I want to be.

"Please, help me welcome our final performance tonight, our featured soloist, Miss Christian Parker, who we hope will soon depart us for Juilliard." I nearly miss my introduction and, after hearing it, I wish I had. It seems an impossible to fulfill expectation since I know that my talent isn't Juilliard gifted standard.

Focus. Sit on chair. Adjust instrument. Nod. Breathe, Chrissie, breathe. I start to move the bow and my fingers in a sheltering cocoon of Hayden's Cello Concerto No. Two in D Major.

The music finishes and the music director comes to my chair offering his hand. I bow amid the thundering applause as Jack slips quietly from the theater before the ovation dies down. In and out of my world like a shooting star. This shooting star I know where to find next. It is a familiar routine to minimize the bullshit of other parents interfering in our father-daughter time. Exit scene left, reappear next scene in the privacy of my dorm room.

Backstage I start to carefully put my instrument into the case. Out of the corner of my eye I see the school's three most popular girls closing in on me.

Crap, not Eliza and her mob. That's the last thing I need tonight.

Eliza has that breezy confidence and overt sexuality of a girl who comes from money and knows she is pretty. Money somehow provides her a wash that her prettiness is more than it is, that she is more than she is, that she is somehow more in the room than anyone else could ever be. I am never in the room as much as Eliza is.

These girls are all from money, and they wear it like goddesses preparing for dazzling futures. Their confident prettiness makes me feel like there is something wrong with me. I never feel I fit with them.

It is Rene I identify more with, a girl genuinely suffering in her emotional convolution, no matter what she projects on the surface, no matter what people say about her. Still, it would be nice to know once what it felt like to be Eliza.

Her red, pouting lips curl into a cat-like smile directed at me. It should piss me off. It has the opposite effect: it diminishes me.

Eliza tosses her hair back over her shoulder, a signature move. "Hey, Parker, everyone is meeting up at Peppers and we're having a party tonight. Sort of a kick-off before we all tailgate down to Palm Springs. Why don't you come?"

Rene gives me a sharp look as if I need to be warned what they are up to. They are messing with me, obviously out for a little human sport tonight. Pick on the weak girl; make her feel inferior before going off for their super-duper plans. I hate this game, but even knowing they are messing with me I am stupidly flattered by the invitation.

I say nothing and Tami smiles at me. "We can pick you up at your house in about an hour. You are on your way home with Jack, aren't you?"

The mention of Jack helps me find my voice. These girls are so obvious at times. How did they manage never to appear pathetic? They are still superior even in their obviousness.

"I can't go. Rene and I are leaving early in the morning for New York," I say.

"Ah, that's right. You're not off to Palm Springs with the rest of the seniors." Eliza smirks.

"God no, we're not off to Palm Springs. Why would anyone want to be anywhere you are?" Rene says.

Eliza lifts a perfectly waxed brow. "Because anyone who is anyone will be there. And that doesn't include you, Rene. I don't recall you being invited."

I look up at the circle of girls. I hate that phrase: anyone who is anyone. Eliza works it into every conversation. Rene calls them perfectly wretched. They are strangely seductive in their artificial charm and downright meanness. Life looks so clearly defined and easy for Eliza.

"Come on, Rene, we really need to hurry," I say quickly, trying my best to be cutting with icy civility. "I don't want to keep my dad waiting."

Eliza flicks a shiny black curl over her shoulder. "Don't run home, Parker. It's the last Friday before break. Everyone is going to be there. It's not like you have to run home and practice for your audition. It's not like they're going to turn you away. You could play chop sticks with your toes and Juilliard would accept you."

"You know what your problem is, Eliza? You don't take anything in life seriously if it doesn't involve you," Rene snaps in quick defense.

In a moment the girls are surrounding Rene all angry and superior. Jeez! Not again. Eliza shoves her face into Rene's. "I wasn't talking to you. You know with her connections she doesn't have to worry about anything. It's clear that she doesn't get the right kind of support from you. If you were a real friend you'd back off and stop pulling her down with you."

"You'd be a lot more popular if you dumped Rene," Jane says intensely into my face in a way that makes me want to slap her. "She's a very odd girl. Everyone likes you, Chrissie. They just don't like her. Too mean. Too messed up."

"Too ready to mess around with everyone's boyfriend," Tami says snidely.

That should have humiliated Rene. It is cuttingly cruel partly because it is true. I stare at Rene, hurt for her.

Rene just glares. "It's not my fault that the guys you date all get bored with stupidity and narcissism."

"And being a slut makes you a genius?" Tami coolly lifts a brow.

"No, the sixteen hundred on my SATs makes me a genius. The sex I do for fun. You'd know that if you had sex for fun instead of to hide your lack of intelligence."

"I don't have sex at all," Tami says.

Rene gives her a nasty smile. "God, what a phony you are. Lying about it is almost as bad as using your body for power. Both are self-depreciating. That's what makes you not a genius. You don't screw for fun and you lie about it."

Eliza is wide-eyed staring at me. It is clear this isn't going the way she wants and that she doesn't know what to do with Rene's comment. I watch as it seems to take Eliza an excessively long time to formulate her response.

"Look, Chrissie, we can pick you up in about an hour so long as Rene doesn't tag along," Eliza says firmly. Then, fake sweet face in place: "Look, you have to swear not to tell Brad that I told you, but he's going to be there. He really wants to see you. I think he wants to patch things up."

And there is the hook. There is always a hook with girls like these.

"It's going to be a killer party," Jane says enthusiastically. "Eliza's dad booked the private room at Peppers. Everyone's going to be there. Brad got some really, really good coke for his birthday. He wants to celebrate with you."

I realize that Eliza is watching the change of my expression and enjoying it in some sort of sick way. Stupid and cruel. I turn my focus back to packing up my stuff. "Enjoy your party." I snap the cello case closed.

Eliza gives me an impatient frown. "God, Chrissie. Do you have to be so touchy about everything? There's no rule that says you have to do the drugs. You won't end up like your brother just by going to a party and having fun. Don't you think you need to get beyond your brother, Parker? I'm sure they have parties at Juilliard. Are you going to ditch those too?"

My face burns and my stomach turns. That easily Eliza can diminish me into something small and inadequate. Get over my brother? Where does a girl get the nerve to say such a thing to someone? It is insensitive and cruel and ugly. Why didn't it make her look ugly? She still looks Eliza perfect. I stare at her. There is a sudden, painfully heavy quiet all around me.

"Back off, Eliza," Rene screams in a voice that shakes the rafters.

Father Morris looks up from the first row of the theater. He locks eyes on me and I lower my gaze because I know what he is thinking. Father Morris sees too much, too much of the time, though he's kind of cool in that young priest, reformer sort of way where he tries to work the problems one-on-one with the students. I'm one of his favorite projects and I know his reaction to this. He didn't hear Eliza. He's thinking I shouldn't be friends with Rene. He's thinking he should call my father even though I've begged him not to. He's thinking I lie every time I tell him I am OK and everything is just fine.

I look back up to see if Father Morris is still watching and focus back on Rene's tirade. "...And I hope someday you get everything you deserve in life."

Rene says that with just the perfect amount of bite. I hate that I didn't say something to defend myself. I rush offstage and set off across campus with Rene following, praying that Father Morris doesn't follow to the dorm room as well. I've told Father

Morris things I haven't told anyone. Things I haven't told Rene. Things I doubt I'll ever tell Jack.

I look down at the ground to hide my face, wondering how Father Morris got me to open up to him. I never talk about my issues to anyone, but somehow Father Morris got into my lockboxes. Maybe it's a guy thing that makes it possible for him to break through my wall of protection. Or maybe it's a priest thing. I don't know. He just wormed right through my wall.

Father Morris is young and attractive, and when I find myself comfortable in the company of someone other than Rene they are usually male. A strange contradiction in my personality, but I feel more comfortable with guys than girls, though that isn't saying much, and honestly Father Morris is a poor example of that theory because I know he can't talk about what I tell him.

I never intended to talk to him, and the next thing I knew, I was telling him all kind of things. It was comfortable to tell him some of the things in my "lockboxes," those compartments inside where I bury things about my family members that I don't want to deal with. Father Morris was genuinely reassuring and didn't look at me as though the things I told him were really messed up.

"Now I've seen everything." Rene gives me a fleeting angry look. "You wouldn't have gone with them, would you have, Chrissie?"

I flush and my heart rate inexplicably increases. I bite my lip, feeling guilty that, for a moment, I wanted to ditch Rene and go with Eliza's group.

"I'm sorry."

Rene looks at me startled in that way that makes me worry that she is pissed at me. But I can see that she isn't and that she's completely unruffled by her confrontation with Eliza—one of the things that I so admire about Rene. She is immune to the meanness of others. Rene is Rene, and she is completely comfortable in that.

Rene looks away first.

"I can't believe that Brad used Eliza as a go-between," she says in disgust. "Only a moron would think sending Eliza would get you to Peppers. Do you think he dumped you because you don't party? You know a lot of guys won't date a girl who won't party."

I shrug as if the issue of Brad doesn't matter to me. "I don't put out. That's why he dumped me."

"I know that."

"Then why did you ask?"

Rene frowns at me.

"I don't know why you let the wretched talk to you that way. They'd put up with anything to be your friend. And really, Chrissie, I think we should re-evaluate our rule pact before college. It was a good idea to create a list of rules our freshman year, but we've almost graduated and the rules are silly, especially since I broke all of them the first year of high school. Now I understand why you put no drugs on your part of the list. But don't you think it's time you take sex off the list? Really, I don't understand why you have such a hang-up about sex. It's just sex. It's better to do it the first time in high school when the guys last about a half of second. It really does hurt the first time, Chrissie. I understand all your hang-ups, but not the sex. Can you please explain the sex to me…?"

I tune out Rene's voice and focus on how pleasant it is to be out of the stuffy auditorium. It is my favorite kind of Santa Barbara night, fogless with a full moon, slightly cool but not enough for a sweater. There is certain predictability to the world here, constant temperature approximately seventy-four degrees and the only deviation a month of fog and occasional days of

9

light rain. Time moves slowly here and it feels as though the world beyond can't intrude through the natural protective barrier of mountains and ocean and affluence.

What does Rene's father call our hometown? A transplanted New Yorker, he calls it fantasyland. *You don't live in the real world girls. You girls live in fantasyland. Happy people. Happy traffic. Even happy palm trees too stupid to know they don't belong here.* The world and its problems seem so far from here, or so Mr. Thompson always says, but they seem very real and very close to me.

One of my problems Rene is dissecting: my difficulty with intimacy that has evolved into almost a phobia about sex.

My other major life problem I find in my dorm room when I enter. I see my father standing in front of the far wall, studying the pictures I have pinned up. The second I close the door, he whirls to give me that much famous smile that has seen more glossy than a Milan runway model.

"You were spectacular, Chrissie. Your mother would be so proud of you."

Why does he always do that? Why can't he just tell me what he thinks? I set down the cello case and begin to pull the pins from my hair. I start to gather a change of clothes: a pair of jeans, my UGG boots and a t-shirt. "I just need to change then we can go."

I dart into the bathroom and quickly shut the door. I should have been able to manage a better response to Jack. I didn't even say hello or give him a hug. Just a fast retreat. Why are our connects so rough and abrupt? Why did Jack let them be? I can hear Jack conversing with Rene and their flow is easy and friendly and it hurts me.

"So you're going to New York with Chrissie?"

"Yes, she's stuck with me for spring break. Dad is doing a trial in DC, but he wants to have dinner one night while we're there, if that's OK with you."

"Whatever Chrissie wants."

Whatever Chrissie wants. OK, Jack, stop with the nonparenting for parents crap.

I pull my long hair into a ponytail, grab the gown from the performance and go back into the dorm room. Jack is studying the wall again and Rene gives me that look, the be nice to your dad look, and darts into the bathroom to change. There is an uncomfortable stillness in the room now that Rene is gone. Well, uncomfortable for me, but Jack seems not to notice. I drop before my suitcase to finish my packing, watching as Jack goes from picture to picture before pausing at one.

He turns from the wall and I can feel his eyes on me. "I thought you were done with Brad."

Direct hit. Vulnerable spot in under five minutes. "I am. We move out in a month. There didn't seem a point to taking the wall apart since we have to do it in May anyway. I don't think I can take down his picture without ruining the rest of the wall."

Before I can move away, Jack laughs and ruffles my hair, the golden-brown wisps that are the exact same color as his. "Come on, Chrissie. Lighten up."

"I'm sorry, Daddy. It's not you. I'm just uptight about everything these days."

I can feel Jack watching me and I stare at my bag, making awkward movements to close it. I finally look up at him and Jack smiles, the one he always does when he seems to silently take stock in the similarities between us: golden hair, deep blue eyes, and the ivory-tone skin, lightly tinted apricot from the sun. It pleases him to take note of our similarities. He does it often. It has the exact opposite effect on me; it confirms for me that while genes are passed on they don't always work out with the same success from generation to generation. What is a spectacular combination on Jack is much less spectacular on me.

Nice as my features are, I know that I am no beauty. On a good day I am willing to concede that I have a nice body and a pert face. I can't think of another adjective that more aptly applies than pert. At five foot three, I certainly didn't get my father's height. Jack is well over six feet. I didn't get his charisma either.

Jack grins, his blue eyes twinkling. He's done taking stock of me and he's in a good mood. It's a loving look. I can't feel it. I know in his way my father loves me. I just wish he had more time for me, enough time in any one time to connect.

I stomp out that train of thought and drag my suitcase to the door. I want to have a good vacation in New York with my dad, three weeks. Next fall I'll be in college. This could be my last chance to work through whatever is wrong between us.

"Do you want to stop for dinner on the way back to the house?" Jack asks.

My stomach knots. Jeez, I have three miserable weeks off in the spring. Couldn't he keep those weeks free just for me? I try to contain my disquiet. "Who do you have at the house this time?"

Jack is unruffled by the question. "Just the same old gang." He says it as though that explains everything and makes it all right. "I expected them to be long gone before this week, but here we are." He gives me that famous smile. "Don't be mad at me, Chrissie. Do you want to stop for dinner or not?"

"Let me ask Rene what she wants."

Jack fixes his eyes on me. "What does Chrissie want?"

Like that really matters, mocks the pouting child inside of me. Jack could say a thousand times whatever Chrissie wants but that wouldn't once make it real. When are things ever the way I want them? I stare at my dorm room. I never wanted this, but I've been here eight years.

"I don't care. I'll leave it up to Rene."

I'm not hungry, so it was stupid to leave it up to Rene. Rene always wants to go out. She loves walking in to a crowded restaurant on a Friday night with Jack and getting a table without waiting. She loves how special it makes her feel to be in public with him. But then Rene doesn't live with the awareness that perfect strangers know the most painful parts of her life.

That thought makes me angry at Rene and I don't want to be angry with Rene. She is my best friend, and to be honest, my only friend. Rene can be irritating as hell, but Rene never lets me down and I can always depend on her. Rene is a good person no matter what people say about her. And Rene knows who she is and where she is going in life.

Rene knows exactly what she wants, having mapped out her life in microscopic detail since practically kindergarten. I pretend that I feel that way about Juilliard, but I don't. And shouldn't I know what I want to be by now? I bet a therapist would have a field day with me.

I tear up and stare out the car window trying to focus on the shops we're passing. It's nine o'clock, but even on a Friday night on State Street there isn't much happening in Santa Barbara. Most days nothing much is happening and the streets usually roll up at eight.

I can feel Rene watching me as Jack chatters away. Does he even notice I'm nearly crying? Does he notice or does he ignore? Is it easier to pretend not to see that I am totally messed up than to ask me about it? Has he ever even noticed that the only friend I have is Rene?

Jack turns the car into a parking lot and I turn in my seat to look at him. "Really, Daddy, do we have to go here tonight? Can't we just go through a drive thru or something? We never get fast food. That would be a treat after dorm food. Or we could just eat at home. I'm sure Maria has something for us to eat at home."

Jack smiles. "You know how I am, Chrissie. Buy local. I'm not going to Burger King or a Taco Bell just to save a few minutes."

"Burger King and Taco Bell are franchises privately owned so it would be buying local," I insist.

Jack shakes his head. "It would still be feeding the corporate menace."

"Record companies are corporations, why are they OK?" Rene asks innocently. "Don't you own a label?"

A smile starts to tug on my lips. We're not little girls any more, Jack. Rene isn't the least bit intimidated by you.

Jack stares as if deeply offended. "For the same reason Dukakis is OK and Bush isn't though they are both politicians."

"I voted for Bush," I inform my dad and the expression on his face goes through several rapid changes.

I bite my lip to keep from smiling. I'm not just messing with Jack. It is the truth. I turned eighteen before Election Day and my first vote was for a Republican. I felt an almost rebellious sense of glee when shoving the ballot into the box. I can't say that I was enthusiastic about Bush. But I did like Reagan, the feeling of having everyone's granddad in the White House watching out for us all, and he just seems like such a nice man. I don't know if Reagan's policies were good or bad. I'm not political and Jack is political enough for any one family. But I liked the quiet certainty the world seemed to hold when Reagan was President and Bush was his Vice President, so I voted for Bush.

"Enough." Jack makes a comical gesture as though a dagger has just gone through his heart and I know he is only half joking. "Next you're going to tell me that you don't want Juilliard. You want law school."

I make an exaggeratedly sheepish face and Jack freezes in mid-step. "Really?"

I climb from the car.

"It's your fault, you know, that she is the way she is," Rene says. "It's every parent's fault. We are all destined to be the opposite of our parents. So don't blame Chrissie for voting for Bush. It's your own fault."

The look on Jack's face is priceless. I laugh.

I loop my arm through my dad's. "No, Daddy. I definitely don't see law school in my future."

A smile teases at the corner of Jack's lips. "You can be anything that you want, baby girl. I was only teasing. Anything you want so long as you're happy."

He means it, but for some reason comments like that from Jack always piss me off. It makes me feel like there isn't anyone guiding me through life. If I said I wanted to be a ditch digger, Jack would probably only say *The world needs ditch diggers too*. How are you supposed to make major life decisions with parenting like that?

Jack opens the heavy wood door, Rene darts ahead of me, and with a hand on the small of my back Jack guides me before him into the packed, dimly lit entrance. The restaurant Jack selected is a Santa Barbara landmark, dark with red carpet and red leather booths, dated in décor and known for its Italian food and generous drinks. The walls are lined with pictures, pictures of the famous, the political and the historic. There is a picture of Jack here with the owners, and one of my mother.

As I drop into our booth I notice in the center of a cluster of celebrity photos above Jack's head there is a picture of President Reagan on his ranch in riding gear. I laugh. I stare at it until Jack turns to look. Jack frowns. I give him a smile. The frown lowers and he turns the photo so poor Reagan can no longer stare at the back of his head.

I laugh and I'm in a good mood again. Nothing in my life is certain, I'm still a mess, I don't know why I feel the way I feel most of the time, and I don't know where I'm going, but I do know that I am not my father's daughter. And that's OK.

Chapter Two

I feel sick, like I want to vomit. "What do you mean you are not going to New York?"

Jack leans back in the booth and stares at me. I must have said that too loudly. Even Rene looks uncomfortable. I don't check to see if people are listening. People are always listening. I start to play with the paper from my straw.

My cheeks redden. "You promised," I snap irritably since no one says anything.

Jack sighs. He leans ever so slightly forward with his elbows on the table. "I've had this thing going on," he says quietly and I feel that rapid flash flood of emotion in me again. *Thing*. I hate when Jack blames "thing." It could be anything. It could be nothing. But it is an old excuse, his things that ruin our time together, his schedule, things that take precedence, things I know nothing about, things he will never share with me. "…it can't be helped, Chrissie." That famous smile flashes at me again. "Besides, you girls are eighteen. I thought you would prefer New York without me. Who wants their dad along on spring break?"

I feel again that strange pressure of time running out. It is an odd thing to feel when you are only eighteen. All my desperate hopes for New York are that easily demolished. He doesn't want to spend time with me. It is not my imagination. For some reason, he doesn't want to get close to me. I dash a hand across my eyes. If I cry I'll feel even more stupid than I do right now.

Silence descends at the table and I know it is my fault. We were having such a lovely dinner and I ruined it. Even knowing that, I am angry at Jack because I hate the silence. Jack says nothing when he thinks there is nothing to say that will help. I would prefer if he just said anything, got angry with me, said something pointless. That would suggest an effort, a note of caring, a note of something, a clue that we are father-daughter, irrevocably and undeniably connected in a way that neither of us can ignore.

From the corner of my eye, I see the cocktail waitress closing in on us again. Her shirt is cut too low, she has that pretty girl sort of obviousness that looks so pretty even when she is obviously flirting with my dad in that irritatingly phony way. She probably never thought she'd end up working here. Oh no, she was supposed to work somewhere better than slinging drinks in a locals' haunt, she was supposed to end on a happy bed of stars like Eliza. I fix my eyes carefully on my father's glass, the discreetly disguised mineral water filling the cocktail glass.

More drinks. Where does she think she's going to put them? An endless stream of Jack Daniels has arrived since we sank into our booth, forgotten, cluttering the table to the point it was hard to fit our dinner plates on it. The waitress must be new since she thought it perfectly normal to interrupt our meal continually with bits and pieces of paper asking if Jack would autograph them and bringing every drink sent by a fan.

"Jeez, enough with the drinks already. Can't you see he doesn't want them? He's been sober for ten years. I would have thought you were the type to at least read a tabloid."

Oh god! Did I say that out loud? The sudden shock of Jack's expression tells me I did. And darn, the waitress looks like she's about to cry.

It is a horrible moment, that kind of earth-quieting, horrible moment that will only get more horrible rapidly. The owner of the restaurant is closing in our table. He must have heard. *Be honest with yourself, Chrissie, everyone heard.* In the commotion around me I start to grow smaller and smaller and more inadequate. I started this and I can't get a word out of my mouth, not even to apologize to the poor cocktail girl who is shaking with mortification. Tom, the owner, is flustered and apologetic. Jack is charming and reassuring. Rene is fascinated and watching with a sharply arched brow. Fascinated by what? Oh, the poor pretty waitress. How pretty she looks now that she is crying.

"I'm sorry, Jack. Truly, my apologies. She's new..." those are the only words I catch in the ensuing drama. The owner apologizing for the waitress. No one apologizes for me, and I was the bully here, a dreadful Eliza wannabe hurting people I think insignificant. I stare at the waitress. There are no words from my mouth, but I hear them in my head: *It's me! I'm the awful one. I didn't mean to be mean. I'm just pissed off. It's been a really trying day.*

I can't take any more. I say nothing, not even to Rene who is still absorbed in watching and I slip from the booth. Getting out of the restaurant is more of a hassle than getting into it had been. Someone must have put the word out that Jack is here. The sidewalk is packed with retro throwback sixties types, all waiting patiently their turn to see him, the voice of a generation. They would be happy if they only got to see him. I brush at my face and realize I'm crying and it doesn't matter because I'm not with Jack so no one notices me.

I push through the bodies feeling small and inadequate and—unfortunately—mean. I'm used to working free of the crowds that sometimes spring around Jack unexpectedly like a flash fire and I am an expert at disappearing. Though not tonight. I was not invisible tonight. They'll talk about tonight at *Harry's* for a while. Perfectly wretched. I was perfectly wretched.

I lean against the car to wait and realize I am hyperventilating. I can't feel my limbs, and I know that the car I lean against is damp but I can't feel that either. Everything looks so strange, the near empty streets, the cluster of people outside the restaurant in the all-but-vacant strip mall, and the way the world looks beneath the bleak fluorescent light of the parking lot. I probably look strange, too.

I sink to the ground, angry with myself for the senseless drama I created tonight. I am not a dramatic girl. Everyone always says I'm sensible. I am not a mean girl. Everyone always says I'm good. But tonight I went postal over a cocktail.

I really hate that I'm crying. Time loses the feel of realness when you cry. Seconds can feel like minutes, minutes can feel like seconds, and it is hard to tell which because it is the cry that determines that. Sometimes after I cry I check my watch and I'm always surprised. Sometimes it's only a few minutes, but it was a really bad cry that feels like forever. And other times its half a day, and it felt like nothing at all, like a dripping faucet, an irritating sound punctuating otherwise normal sound. An irritation, no more significant than that.

Jack and Rene step off the sidewalk and into the parking lot. I take a deep, steadying breath and stand up. How long have I been waiting? It feels like they've left me out here an eternity.

I watch them cross the parking lot to me. They don't look strange in the bleak fluorescent light of the parking lot. Jack looks like Jack, perfectly normal, and Rene has that glow about her as if she's just left the best party and is thoroughly pleased with the world. I curse Rene in my mind for forcing me through the fiasco of dinner, but then, it really wasn't her fault, and no one is more surprised than I am, that I went postal over a cocktail.

Postal over a cocktail. It is all very stupid, especially now that I put it that way. They both smile at me as if everything is normal. No one says anything and we climb into the car to make our way home. I am committed to my silence during the car ride to the house and no one disturbs that, and I am grateful that they don't, though I wish Jack would.

It is a short drive home, and five minutes later we are on Marina Drive making our way down the dimly lit narrow road into Hope Ranch, the neighborhood I've called home since birth. The familiar sights make some of my gloomy mood wane. I love the neighborhood I live in. It is private and quiet and wooded and protected. It is home.

Marina Drive is lush with woods: sycamore, oak and eucalyptus trees flourish among the richly green vegetation. On one side of the road are the cliffs above the beach. With the windows down and the music off you can hear the crashing surf as you drive, and I love that sound, sounds of home. On the other side is low rising hills with stunning homes upon them. Wayward, paved arteries flow through the thicket, private pockets of modest ranch homes and massive estates.

My father's house has been in the family for two generations. It is a rustic, chicly humble Spanish style single story stucco and red tile structure. There is a main wing with two wings jutting off that gives it the shape of a not fully completed square. It sits on a cliff above the ocean, the modestly landscaped five acres left as close to natural as possible, and is only partially enclosed for privacy so as not to intrude on the equestrian trails that cut through Jack's land.

No one owns the land or the beach, Chrissie. We are only caretakers. I was five when Jack said that, I was sitting in the yard watching as he pulled down the fencing with his own hands that my grandfather had put in place with his own hands. The house had transferred to my dad when grandpa had gone into the nursing home, but the fence had stayed until after Jack Senior passed away. We didn't live here full time until I was five. It was the year Mom got sick.

Now I feel teary because I've thought of Mom. There are more emotional punches inside, but in the driveway tonight the first emotional punch is Mom.

Jack climbs from the car. "You girls are going to have to share your room, Chrissie. There is not a spare room in the house, I'm afraid. And stay away from the pool house. Its current occupant doesn't need you bothering him."

That's it? That's what he has to say to me after I created that enormous scene? I nod and focus on pulling my cello case from the trunk.

Rene smiles and takes her bag from Jack. "Maybe I'm exactly what your pool house guest needs."

I start to laugh. That comment I didn't expect, but it effortlessly lifts the mood. Even Jack seems to be unbending, I notice, which is strange, because before the unbending I didn't even notice he was tense. Rene probably saw it and I didn't. Too close to the problem is what she always tells me. Perhaps she is right.

Jack's smile this time is pleasant. He ruffles Rene's dark hair. "Not on your life. I want you somewhere I can keep an eye on you."

I watch and follow them into the house. Jack's relationship with Rene is more father-daughter normal than it is with me.

The house smells good, Maria cooked dinner tonight, and for about the hundredth time I wish we hadn't gone out to dinner and had just come home. It smells like enchiladas and I love enchiladas made at home.

We find Maria in the kitchen busily tidying the mess created from feeding a house of guests. She has been with us forever, a refugee from Somoza, whom we all pretend is legal, but isn't.

Maria carefully rinses a used paper towel. Everything has value to her. Nothing is ever thrown away after a single use. We have adjusted to living with her—the used paper towels, the giant balls of foil, and the wrapped half-finished meals in the refrigerator.

I watch her flatten the Brawny across the twenty-thousand dollar marble counter.

Maria's round, matronly face softens when she sees me. "Chica. You are home. I have missed my beautiful girl. ¿Cómo está mi niña"

The feel of Maria's embrace is familiar and warm, but I slowly grow agitated because it lasts longer than I am ever comfortable with, and the perfume on her flesh is slightly smothering.

I disengage and step back quickly. "Is Daddy being good to you? You tell me if he's not."

Maria looks aghast. Jack laughs. I stare at the used paper towel spread neatly on the marble.

"Señor Jack, he is no trouble. Never. It is good when there are people in the house. Señor Jack's band is like family. I don't mind the extra work. It is never work for family. And the new one, the young one, he is like a ghost. A sad ghost. Four months he's been here and so sad and no trouble. It is good he is here with Señor Jack."

She crosses herself in silent prayer for her sad ghost and I struggle not to laugh because I am really a very bad Catholic and

Jack is an atheist and no one prays at the drop of the hat faster than Maria. And whoever Jack has tucked away in the pool house is most likely not sad, most likely an atheist, and most likely just a burned out musician in need of a crash pad.

Rene sticks her finger into the guacamole, loudly sucks it off the tip, and makes a popping sound as she pulls her nail through her lips. "A sad ghost in the pool house. I am intrigued."

Jack squeezes Rene's shoulder. "Be intrigued some other time. I mean it, little girl. Stay away from the pool house. Now go away."

Chiding, parental and smoothly charming. Jack can be so multifunctional with Rene.

"Before you disappear, go out on the patio and say hello to the guys," Jack says to me. "Just a smile and a hello, Chrissie. Then you two can run off and do whatever you two do."

Just a smile and a hello. I feel her again, the small child in me. I didn't talk from 1975 until 1977. One morning, I just lost my words and they all stopped. Mom was alive when this phase of me started, and the way each of my parents handled it was so very different.

It was mom who forced me to play the cello, to take the lessons that would force me into public recitals and get comfortable speaking before people and hopefully end my silence. I remember my first recital. I was five. I had to give my name and the piece I selected to play. I didn't want to talk. The words were painful in my throat and made me sick in my stomach. I had to force them out which didn't feel good and I hated that people were watching me. When the performance was over, I ran to my seat beside my father, promptly threw up and cried in his lap. Jack was a good dad that day. He said nothing, let me cry, and I remember those gentle fingers stroking my hair even though Mom was humiliated by me.

Jack's solution was to pretend I had no problem. He would take me with him to those places in town he could go comfortably, he would hold my hand, and before we entered a store or restaurant he would say: *Smile and say hello, Chrissie. It makes people happy when you smile and say hello.* And he would smile his stunning smile and I would want to make him happy so I would force myself to smile and say hello to each stranger we met.

I still smile and say hello to every stranger I meet. I can't seem to stop myself, and sometimes I have these really long, involved conversations that are more comfortable and significant because I don't know these people. It is just easier to let out the words when the people are not people active in my life. It really annoys Rene, because while I can't manage a reasonable conversation with the kids at school, I can talk thirty minutes with the gas station attendant.

I don't want to please Jack tonight so there will be no smile and hello from Chrissie. I lean across the marble breakfast bar and grab Jack's keys. "I can't get my car out of the driveway. Do you mind if I take yours?"

Jack lifts a golden brow. "You just got home, Chrissie. Where do you want to go?"

It's not a reprimand and not words that precisely express that I can't leave, just a query I can do what I want with. There is a hint of disappointment in Jack's voice, that is all, but it is not enough to make me stay. I feel a familiar desperation to get out of the house.

"I want to go sit at the beach and have some dessert. We won't be late," I say, smiling.

I can tell Jack doesn't want me to leave, but he won't say it. "You have an early plane in the morning. Drive carefully. There isn't any fog now, but it's been rolling in every night so be careful."

"Let's go, Rene." I drop a fast kiss on my father's cheek, push away from the kitchen counter, and go quickly to the front door without bothering to look if Rene is following. I know she will eventually.

I wait in Jack's car a handful of minutes before Rene comes bouncing out front. She sinks in a disgruntled way into the seat next to me.

I turn on the ignition and put the car in gear. "What took you so long?"

"Since you're dragging me away, I wanted to at least be sociable and say hello to everyone. Are we really going to get dessert? I can't eat another bite."

"No, I just wanted to go to the beach for a while. Get some air."

"You're pissed off about dinner aren't you?"

"I'm not pissed off about anything."

"Then why are we at Hendry's Beach hiding from Jack?"

"I'm not hiding from anyone."

Rene stares at me speculatively, but I ignore her, pretending to focus on the short drive to the beach. I pull into the empty beach lot and park in a space close to the walkway to the sand. I quickly climb from the car.

Please, just let her let this go. My trusty lockboxes feel all shaky at present, I don't want Rene to probe and for some reason I am afraid for them to open. I just went postal over a cocktail. I don't want to know how I will feel, what I will do if a lockbox is opened. Not tonight.

I make a hasty retreat toward the beach. I am sitting on the bottom of the narrow, short flight of steps from parking lot to sand, pulling off my UGGs, when Rene sinks beside me in her loose limb way. The beach is nearly deserted: a couple walking, a man with a dog, and us, spoiled brats from the Ranch as the public school kids like to call us.

We leave our shoes by the steps and Rene takes my hand, dragging me across the sand to put distance between us and the restaurant on the rocks.

"Why didn't your father come tonight?" I ask.

"He's in DC on a case. Remember?" I flush. I know that, but in my desperation to make any conversation, rather than conversation of why we are here at the beach, I foolishly blunder into sensitive territory. Rene is studying me. Then she shrugs. "He's going to be gone four weeks. Remember?" Then making a face: "One week trial. Four weeks screwing young law associate. Maybe you'll get to meet his fembot thirty-seven at dinner."

Fembot: Rene's term for her father's pretty young girlfriends. *They* are pretty. *They* are young. I loop my arm around her shoulders and sing: "Sometimes I feel like a motherless child..." and because we are alone I sing louder, letting my voice flow from that place deep inside of me that makes it bluesy and throaty and pure like Jack's.

Rene instantly laughs and when I am done I can hear someone somewhere clapping. We collapse into each other, laughing harder as Rene pulls me farther away from my secret admirer.

"Why don't you ever sing? You have a beautiful voice."

"Too close to home. I prefer the cello."

"That's close to home, too. Only it's your mother not Jack, that's why you prefer orchestra." She says it in that knowing way, as best friends do.

We lie back against the sand. Above us the moon is a hazy blur and the sand feels good. A light fog is rolling in; the air is slightly damp and heavy with the mist, and the white bed beneath me is inviting, moist and slightly chilled. Behind me is the sound of the restaurant, to the left a dog barks from the sandy stretch beyond the slew where dogs are permitted to run unleashed, and in front of me there is only the sound of waves. The sounds are familiar and calming.

Rene pulls from her pocket a pack of Marlboros and pops one into her mouth in a careless way as she rummages in her pocket for a lighter. I watch the smoke swirl around Rene's face.

I turn on my side to face Rene. "Why do we call this beach Hendry's? The sign says Arroyo Burro, but I've never heard anyone call it that. It's always been Hendry's."

"I don't know. Why does it matter?"

"Why don't we just stay here? Let's not go off to college, Rene. It all seems so pointless. Does it seem pointless to you?"

Rene seems to give it thought. Then, "You know what our problem is, Chrissie? Why everything seems so pointless? We are the generation of nothing. There is no war. There is no grand social struggle. There is no political wrong to right. There is nothing. We have everything we want and nothing we need. Even the music isn't good. We live in empty houses. We have too much time to think only of ourselves. It would be better for there to be a little strife than to be a generation with too much time to think only of ourselves."

And just like that out of nowhere Rene can say something profound and tap into exactly what I'm feeling. How does she do it? That comment is the first thing that has made sense to me today. 'We are the generation of nothing.' And of course, nothing is pointless. Whatever I do it will be pointless. It's the times we live in so I should just surrender like Rene.

I watch her, thankful she is my friend. The silence is comfortable and I lie there watching Rene smoke.

She hands me the cigarette. I focus on the cherry-flame. "Where did you get these?"

"They were on the table on the patio. I snaked them. What is it about Catholic girls sneaking cigarettes to sneak a smoke? It's so cliché."

I take a puff. I don't like to smoke, but tonight I want to be me more like Rene, less like myself than ever before.

Rene sits up and pulls from another pocket a small bottle of scotch. She takes a long swallow and then says, "I wish my dad was like Jack."

"I wish my dad was more like your dad. I wish once Jack would just yell at me like your dad does. But he never yells. He never just says *You screwed up, Chrissie. I'm disappointed in you.* He never tells me what he really thinks."

Rene takes another drink, longer, more. "Then come to my house and next time my dad starts yelling, stay in the living room instead of running off and hiding. Why would it be better if Jack yelled?"

"Then I would know what he thinks. What he expects. That he cares. He never says *I'm disappointed in you.* He never says he's proud. Sam was always his favorite. It feels more like he's just stuck with me and doesn't know what to do about that."

Oh crap, one of my lockboxes is opening. No, Chrissie, not tonight. Don't let yourself dwell on your brother tonight. Don't think about how Jack was after he died. Don't think about how Sam looked laying blue and cold in his bedroom. Don't think of how his flesh felt. Don't think about how everyone loved

Sammy, how much he screwed up, and how remarkable he was. Don't think of Jack's months of drunkenness. Jack's rage. The days of being forgotten by Jack. All the bad days. So many bad days. Before those days of boarding school, Jack's recovery and second run at sobriety.

I lift my cheek from the sand to find Rene staring at me.

"Jack said he was proud of you tonight."

"Oh, no he didn't. He said, 'Your mother would be so proud of you,' but not a word about what he thinks. Never a word about what he thinks."

"At least Jack tries, Chrissie. I'm not saying he's perfect. I'm not saying he's even good at it. I'm saying he tries. Cut him some slack if he's not doing it right."

"He's not doing it at all. We are going through life tiptoeing around each other."

Rene takes another drink. "Jack tries."

Jack did try, but somehow it makes it all the more awful.

Rene springs to her feet and begins to brush the sand from her legs. "We should go back."

"You just want to party on the patio with the rock geriatric ward."

Rene laughs. "That is a terrible thing to call your dad's band. Jesus, your dad is young and hot. You just can't see it because he's your dad. And why not hang with the rock geriatric ward since we won't be at Peppers with the rest of the seniors?" Rene closes the scotch bottle, almost puts it back in her pocket, and then buries it the sand. "We'll leave something for the bums instead of tossing it. I am sure Jack would disapprove of that since I took it from his bar."

I stand up, brushing the sand from my backside. Rene loops her arm around my neck and we walk toward the car. I can smell the scotch on her breath, and I like the smell, though

I should hate it, just as I hate the endless glasses always sent to our restaurant table.

"I have a rule pact for New York," Rene announces out of nowhere.

I start to laugh. "When did you come up with it?"

"Just now. I make your rules. You make mine. And Doctor Rene thinks what Chrissie needs is to do one crazy thing a day until we are back at school."

I laugh harder. Only Rene could float between profound and ridiculous in an hour. "And how will I know if it's something crazy to do? Do I ask you?"

"Oh, you'll know. Did you think what you did to that poor waitress was crazy? Well, you're right. It was crazy. But it was a good thing to do. I loved watching you do it, Chrissie. You let some of it out for once. When the voice insides you says no, just do it. Be bad. Be young. Be wrong. Lose your virginity. It's OK."

Rene takes my cheeks in her hands and does a fast friendship kiss on my lips and suddenly this isn't silly but deadly serious to her.

Oh crap, why tonight? Another of Rene's sneak attacks on all my little issues.

I fumble in the dimly lit parking lot to unlock the car door. "Fine. One crazy thing each day. But here's your rule pact, Rene. You can do anything you want and I won't tell, but you have to spend one day with your dad and be nice to him even if he's with fembot thirty-seven."

That was a really bitchy thing to say. She leans with her arms on the roof of the car. Then she points at me. "You stay sweet."

Now I want to cry again. "You stay cute."

It is our ritual, how we prop each other up or how we say hello and goodbye to each other as we pass on campus on our way to class. I can't remember how I became sweet and Rene became cute, but it is how it is, how it has always been.

I pull the car from the parking lot and I am there at the intersection to Cliff Drive. I feel all shaky and loose inside again. If I go left I drive into the fog and back home. And right—where will right take me?

I turn right toward the city and away from home and Jack.

* * *

The parking lot is packed and thumping with the sounds of a live band. We are on State Street on a Friday night about to enter a club at midnight. I know this is not a good idea, but this is where the car has taken me: To Peppers and Eliza's private party and Brad. For some reason I feel pissed off enough to come here and do...do what?

I unbuckle my seatbelt and climb from the car. I look at my modest t-shirt and worn jeans. Jeez, I'm wearing UGG boots. Not exactly club gear. I haven't any makeup on and my hair is a ponytail. Rene is waiting, staring at me from the other side of the car.

"We are not actually going to crash Eliza's party, are we?"

"We're not going to crash the party," I say quickly.

"Then what?"

I stare at the giant tote Rene hauls everywhere with her. "What do you have in your bag? You must have something cuter than this t-shirt. I look like a lost school girl in UGGs."

Rene makes a face. "That's because you are a lost school girl in UGGs. If you're going to go postal again tonight, warn me in advance." She dumps the contents of her bag onto the passenger seat as I come around the car.

Rene's giant tote is a very, very odd thing. She carries everything she might need, I mean *everything*, absolutely everywhere she goes. It used to worry me. I used to call it the 'everything I need to book bag.' And I was afraid Rene was just going to take off and disappear one day. Then I wouldn't have anyone. A selfish thought, but it used to worry me because without Rene I wouldn't have anyone.

"Well, do you have anything I can change into in there?" I ask.

Rene rummages through her junk. "No shoes, but this should be cute even with the UGGs."

She pulls out a gold blouse and a jean mini-skirt. She tosses them to me. They still have Saks Fifth Avenue tags on them. They are slightly wrinkled, but they'll work better than what I have on.

I change in the parking lot behind the car door. The blouse is too tight, Rene isn't busty, but the skirt works even though I have to roll it once to make it short.

"Stand still."

Rene has eyeliner, mascara and lip gloss in hand.

"You should let me do your makeup more often," Rene says. "I like it better when I do your eyes."

"You use too much mascara. The lashes fall out in the morning."

"It looks better." She is putting the lip gloss on my lips. She reaches for a brush. "Toss your hair over."

The brush goes through my hair in a couple of hard jerks. She sprays it with hair spray. I toss my hair back. She sprays again.

"I love your hair. It just sort of floats back into an 'I've just been fucked' kind of look."

I touch it. It feels stiff to me.

Rene looks up as she shoves her junk back into her bag. "So now what?"

We walk from the parking lot onto the sidewalk.

Rene stops and throws her everything bag onto the concrete. "Well, this is a bust. We'll never get in. Not tonight. It's packed. What the heck is going on here?"

There is a line down the street, turning the corner to the club entrance. It is the first Friday of spring break, so of course there is a line. I grab Rene's hand and pull her along with me past all the pretty girls staring. The line is flush with rich, pretty girls and I can feel *the stare*, the stare that screams from their impeccably made-up faces that they think we are not the kind of girls who can line jump.

For once, getting into a downtown club on Friday will be my problem. We won't even have to drop Jack's name, which is part of a bigger secret I haven't shared with Rene. I spent a lot of time in this club in December during our winter break. Had a lot of my "gas station attendant" moments with the staff.

I shake my head, not wanting to think of winter break. Jack was gone almost the entire month, *one of his things,* and Rene was in the Cayman's with her mother. I hated being in the house alone with no one to hang out with. It made the hours drag painfully slow with no one to hang out with. So in the evenings I would pretend to Maria I was off on some super, Eliza-type plans and just come to Peppers alone.

Nightclubs are good places to be alone. Always new people. Always laughter and music and other people alone so you don't feel so pitiful that you are alone.

At the front of the rope line, I am relieved. I know the bouncer. "Randy." I shout over the blaring music from within to get his attention.

Randy looks, does a thorough security type scan of the crowd, sees me, smiles, and the rope is pulled back. Rene and I are pulled quickly into the courtyard in front of the door. The front of the line is pissed.

I can feel Rene watching me as if she wants this explained, but I ignore her. Randy keeps his eyes on the front of the line, but leans in to hear me.

"It's really packed."

"Some group from Seattle is booked tonight. It's crazy inside, Chris. Crazy. Not cool at all. Not the usual scene." He starts pushing back against the line. "Hey, behind the line or I boot you to the end." He's stressed. The crowd is enormous and I can feel the pulse in the air that this is a happening. I didn't know there was a special event tonight, but I bet Eliza did and that's why she had Daddy book her a private room.

Randy grabs my arm. "Are you packing? I can't let you in if you're not packing. ABC has been a real pain in the ass lately."

I pull from my purse the fake ID Rene appropriated for me. She takes them from her father's fembots under the pretense she has a right to check their age. There is an entire shoe box of stolen IDs in our dorm room. Rene is the go-to girl for ID, but I think the box means something else to her, though she hasn't told me.

I hold the New York license beneath Randy's nose. He checks it, then Rene's. "Any trouble, Chris, and you run out the back," he whispers in a low, fierce tone. "A fight. Police. Anything. You run. You get caught in here tonight it'll make the papers and we'll lose our liquor license. That fucking whore with the band will make sure it makes press."

My entire face colors. I nod before Randy lets me walk into the club with Rene. The ground level bar is a crush of bodies. I fight my way to the railing above the dance floor below. The music is ear-splittingly loud. I can feel Rene watching.

At the railing she leans in and stares at me. "Chris?"

No one calls me that. I shrug. It's the nickname I prefer, who I am here, in this little bit of bad. I'm glad Rene doesn't probe further. She is caught up in the band on stage. A young, blond shoeless singer. He's very hot, in that grunge sort of way Rene likes, loose jeans, bare feet, stringy hair, and lean body hopping on stage.

"God, I'd love to go home with that tonight," Rene purrs, fanning herself with a hand. She looks at me. "OK, now what? We didn't come here just to watch Eliza, did we? That would be so pathetic, Chrissie."

Downstairs in the private party room with the mirrored window is Eliza and her mob. On the floor by the stage Tami is dancing with Johnny Ramirez, her public school boyfriend that she kept even after Eliza ended their year of *oh, it's so cool to date boys from the public school* phase.

The smart thing to do would be to leave before they see us, but I just want to do something and I don't know what I want to do. Rene is waiting, trying to ignore the guy beside her, who is working really hard to get her attention.

She shakes her head in aggravation and looks at the pest at her side. She arches a brow. *"You're—"* heavy exaggeration on you're—"talking to me?"

She says it in a perfectly bitchy, rich girl sort of way, a superior put down well done, and the guy just stares at her. She shakes her head and grabs the cocktail waitress passing by. "Two Kamikazes."

I'm not really much of a drinker, I don't know what's in a Kamikaze, but it sounds like the right kind of drink for tonight. I grab the rail and pull myself up to see down below. It's really packed in here. It's easy to pick out the hot girls in the crowd. They are always dancing. Always laughing. Always drinking. Always tossing their hair.

I take a hefty swallow of my Kamikaze and realize it's just a fancy name for a vodka drink. Hmm… the drink isn't bad at all. I scan the crowd, watching the hot girls. What would Eliza do if I were the hot girl in the private party room with her ex-boyfriend? I take another hefty sip of my drink, hoping some kind of inspiration will come.

Rene is on her second Kamikaze. She can out drink a sailor. First, scotch at the beach, then two cocktails in under fifteen minutes. She stares at the glass. "How many of these do you think make a set? Six? Eight? They're so cute. They'll make a cute set in my apartment in Berkeley."

I frown. "What?"

"The glasses." She holds one up then slyly tucks it into her everything bag.

"You're stealing the glasses?"

Rene nods and smiles. "I have to drink one more. You have to drink two. Or is eight a proper set? I am never sure how many of anything should be in a set. Perhaps I should call my mother. Mom would definitely know that."

I roll my eyes. I finish my drink, motion to the cocktail girl for another, which really pleases Rene since I hand her my glass, and now there are three rattling around in her everything bag.

What would Eliza do to me? She'd want to make me feel small, insignificant. As if my party wasn't the happening. As if her party was the happening, which is exactly how I feel now. How would she do it? How would she do it?

I look at Rene. I know what Rene would do. "Who's the hottest guy in here?"

Rene doesn't answer. The pest is gone and there is a new guy beside her and this one she's talking to. I tug on her shoulder. I repeat my question.

She holds up a finger to her latest conquest, a superior gesture of be silent and wait. "Why, Chrissie? What are you going to do?"

I give her a hard look. "Just answer me."

"You are not going to do anything stupid?"

I give her another look. It takes Rene only a moment to zoom in on a guy standing on the other side of the upstairs bar. "Him, Chrissie. Him. Definitely hot and just the right amount older."

I look in the direction of her stare. I whirl to put my back to the bar and slouch down slightly. Oh no, not him! Another secret I haven't told Rene: In December I had a near fuck experience. Jack flew off the day after Christmas, and it had made me really angry in that way I never handle well. I went to Peppers, got drunk, and before I knew it was with Mr. Incredibly Hot across the bar having a near fuck experience. I don't even remember how I got to his house, I was that drunk.

I can feel my face scrunching up tighter as my eyes tightly close to a foggy picture of ending up on a pool table with my shirt up and this guy snorting lines off my stomach. There is nothing attractive about a man who snorts coke, not even off your stomach, and I couldn't seem to stop what was unfolding...and then the panic: *How did I get here? What have I done? How do I get away? Is he just weird or dangerous?*

I still can't believe I did it, let myself get fuzzy drunk, unable to figure out how to get out of the house with some guy I don't know who wants to bathe me and shave me *there*. It was being drunk that saved me, because I was enough drunk to vomit all over his tile, but not so drunk as to pass out.

As it was, he wasn't dangerous, just weird, and pretty OK about everything in the morning. He gave me some sweats to change into, drove me back to my car and probably burned my number, which wouldn't have matter because I didn't give him my real number or name. Rule number one of Rene: *never give your real name and number to a guy you meet in a bar.*

I cringe. Oh no, I am definitely not making contact with Mr. Near Fuck Experience. I'm beginning to feel nauseated, my head is spinning, but not from the alcohol because I really haven't had that much. Please, don't let it turn into a full blown panic attack.

"Chrissie? What the hell's wrong with you?"

"Nothing! That guy is too old."

"Old for what?" Rene turns to her new guy friend. "Oh crap, I've got to get her out of here. I think she's drunk. She doesn't drink much. I can't take her home drunk. It will be a total shitstorm if I do."

"Rene, I'm OK," I reassure her rather feebly. When I turn to look at her I realize we are being watched by her latest male conquest and another guy who looks like he is with him. Jeez, he's really cute. Maybe twenty, with blond streaked light brown hair and big green eyes. A really cute surfer/rocker sort of guy. Cute and probably clueless. *He'll do…* just as I think that, something flashes in his eyes.

"Hey Rene, is there something wrong with your friend," he says, but his eyes never leave me.

Rene frowns. "She's a lightweight. Like I said she doesn't drink much. Do you need to go outside for some air, Chrissie?"

My cheeks burn. *Can you embarrass me even more, Rene?* I ignore her and lean over to speak to the cute stranger. "Hi. I'm Chris."

The guy stares at me, and then shrugs as if to say, *OK I'll play.* "Hi. Neil. Neil Stanton."

I can feel Rene watching.

"How would you like to be a really, really cool guy and do me a really, really big favor?" I ask.

OK, what's up with all the 'really.' So Valley Girl. How lame is that? Like, really, really lame. I take a steadying breath.

This can go one of two ways. It can be a *Breakfast at Tiffany's* moment or the last scene in *Butch Cassidy and the Sundance Kid*: the firefight in Bolivia scene. Probably Bolivia. I pound the last of my drink and turn my head so I can lock eyes on Neil. He's watching me, amused and a little wary in that way guys have when they are unsure if there is something wrong with a girl. I put the glass on the bar. Here goes nothing.

"I want you to go downstairs to the dance floor and wait for me," I say.

"Wait for you?" He stares at me. OK, what did I say that was wrong? Those pleasant green eyes are staring at me really pissed. He takes a long drink from his beer. "Hey, if this is a brush off, it's unnecessary. You don't need to make a fool of me. I wasn't trying to hit on you."

It takes me a moment to figure out why he is mad. He thinks I'm messing with him, in that bitchy rich girl way, and for some reason my confidence soars even knowing he's thinking I'm a total bitch. I'm never the one who gets to experience the feel of pretty girl power and I certainly didn't expect to with super-hot guy. He thinks I'm a bitch.

I start to laugh.

"Screw you," Neil says. He turns to his friend. "We're out of here, Josh."

His temper focuses me. I grab his arm. "No, no, no. It's not like that, really. Please, let me explain. I'm not that kind of girl."

Now the look he gives me is just plain insulting. I look to Rene for help. Not a chance, her eyes scream at me. She's going to leave me alone in this.

This has gone from bad to worse. How do I dig out? The truth. Just tell him the truth. It can't get worse than this. He already thinks you're a bitch and probably a crazy bitch at that.

I stare up into those angry green eyes waiting expectantly. "I wouldn't mess with you because I'm the girl who usually gets messed with. You see, there's a girl down there having a party and she invited me, but I know it's just because she wants to do something to humiliate me. But at some point between dinner and now I just got pissed. You know, like when you've had enough of someone messing with you and you're just angry. Fed up pissed, and I thought, what would piss her off more? Show up here, have a hot guy meet me and look like I don't care about her stupid party. That would piss her off more, because she enjoys having people care when she's really, really mean to them."

Damn. Really, really again. The whole speech makes me come off pathetic. The air in my lungs forces its way out in sharp, rattling spurts.

Neil stares at me. "Are you telling me the truth or is this some other bitch game?"

"The truth," I insist, totally embarrassed now.

After a few seconds I force myself to look at him. He's frowning, but...*is that a smile in his eyes?*

"You think I'm hot?"

I refrain from rolling my eyes at him and start to laugh. "You're OK."

He shakes his head. "You better not be messing with me." He takes Josh's beer and downs it. "You want me just to wait by the dance floor?"

I nod. "All you've got to do is wait for me. Pretend like we're together. Dance a dance and walk out with me. That's all."

He looks undecided. Neil looks at his friend. Josh shrugs, but shifts his eyes to Rene who is too busy watching me to notice. His friend wants him to do this. He thinks it will get him hooked up with Rene for the rest of the night.

Neil orders another round of drinks. When his beer comes, he grabs it. "Don't keep me waiting or I walk."

I nod. Rene looks at me in a way that makes me a little less brave, like she thinks this is a childish stunt and pathetic and just plain not going to matter.

I walk down the steps. It's just bullshit, but knowing there's this cute guy down there waiting for me gives me a little extra swagger in my step.

Then I touch the bottom step and in a flash I know I've read this guy all wrong.

Chapter Three

The kiss is hard, fast and burningly intense. Neil is all around me, strong and unfamiliar and in command with his maleness. He forces my mouth apart and he fills me with his tongue. I feel panic, that shattering panic I felt in my near fuck experience. I don't know this guy. I didn't know Mr. Near Fuck Experience. Neil is messing with me now that he thinks he's in control.

I struggle in his arms and try to break free. "Stop it. I didn't say you could touch me."

Neil ignores me and his hands flatten against my back. He must still be pissed off and somehow I didn't see it. Did Rene see? Is that why she gave me the look?

I feel like I'm going to freak out and make a fool of myself in Peppers. Oh how Eliza would love it if I freaked out on the steps of Peppers.

I jerk as his hand takes hold of my ass to lift me up into him and this time I use my hands to try to put a little space between us.

"I thought you wanted this believable," he whispers as his mouth moves to my neck.

"Believable yes. Insulting no," I snap, still struggling in his arms.

"Haven't you ever been kissed before? Stop wiggling. I'm only doing what I would do if you were really my girlfriend and I was waiting for you."

"That explains why you are alone," I counter. "Stop mauling me."

He steps back and rakes an aggravated hand through his tousled waves. "God, you had better be at least eighteen. You feel like you've never been kissed before. You're not thirteen or something, are you?"

"Of course, I'm eighteen. I just don't kiss perfect strangers."

"You don't kiss anyone. I can feel a girl who doesn't like to kiss. Why don't you like to kiss?"

This guy is just doing me a pathetic favor so why does he have to go all Dr. Ruth on me? Who would have thought this guy would be sensitive enough to pick up on anything? Neil's got me all worked out in under five minutes.

I ignore the question. He shrugs. "Forget it. You don't owe me any explanations."

He takes my hand and starts pulling me through the crowd. I look over my shoulder and thankfully see that Rene has followed with Mr. New Conquest. Halfway across the room I realize lots of girls are looking at Neil, he is pretty hot, and he slaps hands here and there, stopping to talk when his name is called as he continues to work through the room. Neil is known in this crowd and popular. Most of the people don't look local, but they know him, and it feels good to be pulled along with him in that "this girl's with me" proprietary way and to feel unexpectedly a part of whatever is happening in this club tonight.

He stops when we're at the far side of the room at a standing table beneath the stage. In between songs, the lead singer leans over to say something to Neil. Neil laughs, says something back. I can't catch it, the room is too noisy.

I look across the room. Rene is still several feel away. "You're not from Santa Barbara, are you?"

Neil isn't really paying attention to me. His eyes are locked on the guitar on the stage. I lean into him and repeat my question louder.

"I'm a local," he says, not shifting his eyes to me, his head moving in tempo with the music. "I just live in Seattle now." He sets his beer on the table. "Different kind of scene. Less bullshit than SB. Most everyone here is from out of town. A few locals. But most everyone is here to see him."

The band is good. The sound is different. But what is so special about *him?*

Neil leans forward into me, his elbows on the table. "This is one of those nights you'll remember. You don't know it now, but it is. You are here, in a no-name club, watching Kurt before he becomes famous, before he becomes iconic, as he's just there changing music forever."

Oh, crap. Way to go, Chrissie. This guy is a musician, probably with some struggling, no-name band in Seattle. That's why he's part of the happening here. He's one of them. Leave it to me to find a musician in the crowd. That's all I need.

I force a smile. "If you say so."

"You can't hear why they are so great?"

There was something insulting in the way he said that. I start to critique the band in my head: *Three guys. Guitar, bass and drums. Sort of a little heavy dirge rock, mixed with punk and metal. The music is too angry for mainstream popularity. I hear a little bit of the Ramones and a twinge of Black Sabbath. Three cords, simple arrangement. Kurt has an interesting voice. Rene thinks he's hot. The drummer is the one with the talent.*

I bite down hard on my lip. *Oh no! Did I just say that out loud? Crap!* Neil fixes his gorgeous green eyes on me. I feel something. I'm not sure what. It's sort of a strange thing. His eyes are hard to read, and then finally he starts to laugh. I feel some of the tension leave my body.

"You are an ignorant girl when it comes to music. You can't kiss and you don't know music." Neil takes a dollar from his pocket, rips it in half, and hands a piece to me. "We'll see who's right."

I hold up my half of the bill. "What am I supposed to do with this?"

"Keep it. Someday we'll know which one of us is right and the winner gets the other half of the dollar."

There is something cute and boyish and challenging in him. The corners of my lips tease with a smile. "What makes you think I'm ever going to see you again?"

Neil shrugs. "You have to. I'm a really cool guy who just did you a really big favor and you have half of my last dollar."

Rene and Josh finally join us. Neil sets down his drink and takes my hand. "What took you so long?" he asks Josh.

"Andy's over there." Guy stare. Serious guy stare. Then, Josh sighs heavily and asks, "Are we staying or hitting it?" He looks at Rene. "You want to go somewhere to party?"

Neil's mouth presses into a hard line. "I'm supposed to dance with you, right?"

I don't like how he says that. "You don't have to if you don't want to."

Neil rakes a hand through his hair. "It's not you. There's just someone here I don't want to see. Get it?"

"Ex-girlfriend?"

He gives me a quizzical look. "No. Just some asshole I don't want to see."

Josh says, "Neil, you're really going to have to get over it someday."

"He screwed us over. Fuck him."

I'm in the middle of a heated argument between the guys, and Neil's fingers tighten on my hand as he leads me onto the dance floor. The dance floor is large, but I can see that Eliza and her mob have left the private party room and are mixed through the crowd. Eliza is dancing with Brad. She pretends not to see me and I pretend not to see her.

Unfortunately, my eyes connect for a moment with Brad's. He looks away quickly as though I were nothing. I feel weak, mortified, and pathetic. With that touch of eyes I am forced to admit to myself that being here is only half about Eliza. I wanted Brad to see me with someone else, so he would think he didn't matter, so that maybe he would stop mattering to me.

I'm being consumed by an array of emotions. I can't process them. They are too quick. And the lights in the club are casting strange color across the crowd, making Eliza and Brad harshly gleaming figures, and the music is angry, the way I feel inside, angry, angry, angry.

"You OK?" Neil shouts.

He's watching me intently. I lean into Neil. "We don't have to dance."

He shrugs. "I don't want to lose my really cool guy standing."

I wonder if I've just been obvious over Brad and if Neil saw my obviousness.

"What was that all about," I ask wanting to change the subject.

"I don't want to talk about it. Just a friend who screwed me over. It happens."

The heat of the room and the press of bodies around me suddenly feel too close. I can feel that Neil is annoyed and doesn't really want to do this, is just following through because…I don't know why he's following through on being a really cool guy.

As a group, we roll into another song. The floor is packed, the music loud, Rene is in her element, and Neil and Josh are drinking, holding us, somehow still moving and somehow still arguing. Everyone around me seems drunk. They all look so into the moment, so into the scene. I don't feel connected with the mood at all. I'm no longer in the room. I stop being in the room the second Brad touched me with his eyes and looked away as if not seeing me. I feel awkward and small as people near me slam into me and every so often Neil's body presses up against me.

I stare up at him to keep myself from looking again at Eliza and Brad. Neil is staring at something across the room. There is a sudden internally contained tension that he didn't have before.

I look over my shoulder. That must be Andy. Neil's friend-enemy. There is something very odd in the way Andy is taking stock of me and staring at his friend.

I turn back to find Neil's eyes on me. I don't know what he sees on my face, but his expression softens. He leans into me. "You are not enjoying this at all, are you, Chris?" He frowns. "You don't like to kiss and you don't like to dance. You are a very strange girl. You don't like this at all."

I flush. This guy can see just enough, but not too much. He can't see the part where I grew smaller and smaller because some jerk that dumped me doesn't care that I am here with another guy.

Tears threaten behind my eyelids. I sway into Neil.

"Hey! Are you OK?" He sounds genuinely concerned.

I nod. He steadies me with his hands, his body moving in a matching rhythm with mine and he takes more care that people don't crash into me. I look once away and then back at him.

He scrunches his nose. "Not helping, is it?"

I shake my head.

"I've got an idea." Quickly he puts his drink down. Before I know what he is doing he's lifting me from the floor until my arms are on his shoulders and my thighs against his chest. "Do you know what they do in Europe? They don't crash into each other like we do in America. They bounce. Do you want to bounce, Chris?" He makes a hop. God, this is embarrassing. People don't bounce in downtown clubs in Santa Barbara. I make a move with my hands to put me down, but Neil doesn't. The look in his eyes changes into something sweet and gentle and kind. Jeez, this guy has beautiful eyes. I feel them all through my limbs. Another bounce. "Do you want me to make you bounce, Chris?"

That is said sweetly, teasing. I start to laugh and his arms tighten their hold of my body against him as he continues to bounce on the beat. God, this guy is so hot. I didn't notice how hot until he started to laugh and smile. I feel my heart accelerate.

Josh lifts up Rene, and we are bouncing and laughing. Out of the corner of my eye I can see Eliza watching, and she looks really irritated.

Neil bounces me until the end of the next set, and I love it even though Rene and I are the only girls being bounced.

The music stops and I can hear thumping on wooden stairs as the band rushes off stage to the dressing room outside of Les's office. Neil is still holding me off the floor, but I am being lowered down to earth in front of him.

"Why don't we bounce, Chris?" His mouth is against my neck, stirring the sensitive flesh beneath my ear, no longer playful. "Let's go back to my place."

Jeez, when did this change from being a favor between two strangers to Neil thinking I'd go home with him? I look frantically around the bar, but Rene is nowhere to be found.

Somehow she's already disappeared with Josh. *Crap, she's just left me alone in this.*

I bite my lower lip. "I need to find Rene. I need to go."

He stares down at me, then shrugs and puts an arm around me holding me in a casual, friendly way. "Come on. We'll go talk to the band for a while. Give Rene and Josh a few moments, if you follow my drift."

I follow him up the stairs. There is security at the top of the stairs and Neil leans in to say something. The big, burly bouncer smiles at me.

We're let into the private party and I can't help but look to see if Eliza is watching. She is staring and furious. She starts moving toward me. Oh, crap. I realize why she invited me to Peppers tonight. She wanted Jack's daughter to get her into the private party that Daddy's money couldn't seem to do. I push my body against Neil, hoping he'll hurry before Eliza catches me. I don't care about this band, this party, but Eliza does and it is enough to make me walk through the door.

* * *

The minute I'm in the room I want to get out. The upstairs private party is not my type of scene. The tiny room is packed. Neil has my hand and starts to pull me through the bodies. There is a raw kind of energy all around me. The girls here are not pretty girls. They are the other kind of girls that I never seem to fit in with, the fringe, wild, counterculture types. They are snorting lines of coke off a table, laughing, kissing, touching.

Everyone is wired, into the moment, and I know I look different, that I am different from them in my *oh so Santa Barbara* UGG boots and Saks Fifth Avenue mini skirt, and the one carat diamond studs in my ears that I never think about, but for some reason I remember them now.

A few feet from the singer, Neil says, "Wait here."

I stand alone in the room feeling strange and out of place without Neil beside me. My frantic gaze locks on Neil talking with the band. They talk, smile, laugh, and then talk some more and I'm wondering if he's going to leave me here alone forever when Neil takes my hand and pulls me into the conversation. The band is really nice, kind and friendly and for some reason really inclusive in the way they talk to me. They instantly engage me in conversation and seem really interested in what I have to say, not at all like the guys at school.

As we talk I see flashes. Someone is taking pictures and the last thing I need is a picture of me with this crowd making the rounds. I look around frantically trying to find the camera. Then I see the girl on the couch with the Polaroid and I feel foolish for being paranoid. I steady my breathing and tell Neil I have to go.

The club is empty as we walk out the back entrance. The windows to my dad's car are all steamed up and I can see Rene and Josh in the back seat. *Jeez, Rene, in my dad's car? Did you really just screw a guy you met in a bar in my dad's car?*

"Hey Josh. Let's roll," Neil shouts.

I stop a few cars away. "Thanks, Neil. You've been a really cool guy tonight."

He smiles and it's sort of like he's disconcerted, not knowing how he should deal with me.

"It's been OK, Chris. I had fun with you tonight. If you're ever in Seattle look me up. Maybe we can hang out sometime."

I brace myself. "Maybe I should give you my number in case you come back to Santa Barbara this summer."

Neil's smiles at me quizzically. I feel instantly stupid. If the guy wanted my number he'd have asked for it.

"I leave next week on a six month tour. I don't plan to be back in Santa Barbara."

God, why did I have to offer him my number?

Josh and Rene climb out of the car. She starts giving him her number and I wonder if it's her real number, if she gives her real number to guys she screws in parking lots.

All and all, it hasn't been a completely disastrous night. I'm feeling kind of OK even though Neil did give me the brush off. I sink into the driver's seat and wait for Rene to climb in.

I turn the ignition and put the car in gear. There's a tap on my window. I roll it down. Neil says, "Drive carefully. You've had a few drinks. Not enough to be legally drunk, but they could pick you up anyway."

I nod. That was a really sweet thing to say. "I'll take it really, really slow."

Neil laughs at the really, really. He turns to leave and then pauses. It's almost like he's debating with himself. His fingers curl over the top of my open window. "Hey, I know I'm just some guy you just met, but nice girls with rich, famous daddies shouldn't be in bars trying to play games with guys like me. The guys you meet in bars play cruel games that hurt. Fuck! Didn't Daddy teach you anything about how the world works?"

Oh crap! I know, I suddenly know. "You used me. You were a cool guy so you could use me to get into the party."

I'm furious now.

He shrugs.

"Everyone uses everyone, Christian Parker."

I roll up my window and pull from the parking space.

* * *

"God, Chrissie! Do you have to drive so slowly? I want to get home, get a shower and get some sleep."

Rene is slouched in her seat trying to adjust her panties. It's 2a.m. and the fog is really thick.

"I don't want to get pulled over. If I get popped for drunk driving in my dad's car it will make the front page of the NewsPress."

"If you keep driving so slow the first cop that sees you will know you've been drinking." She pulls down the visor and starts to touch up her lip gloss with the lighted mirror, which is really irritating because it makes it harder to see out of her side of the car. "You should have let me drive."

"Oh yeah, that's a great idea. What are you on, anyway? You guys didn't do drugs in my dad's car, did you?"

Rene glares at me. "I wouldn't do that. I can't believe you asked me that."

"Really. Oh, really. You screwed a guy in my dad's car."

Rene shrugs. "He was cute. Neil was cute too. He was really into you, Chrissie. Did you give him your number?"

"No. And he wasn't into me. Just another user. Why is the world so full of jerks?"

"Because half the planet is male."

I change the subject. "Did you see Eliza's face as Neil and I went into the private party. She was pissed."

"Jeez, you'd think it would have stopped being about Eliza as soon as you had that hot guy bouncing you on the floor. Bounce. Bounce. Bounce. You should have bounced him back to his place."

"I couldn't. You were bouncing my dad's car."

"What was the private party like?" Rene asks, rummaging through her bag.

"It was awful. Smoky. Packed. All kinds of freak girls there doing drugs."

Rene laughs. "Why do you have half a dollar bill stuck in the fold of your UGG boot?"

"Neil made me a bet. He thinks that band is like the Second Coming or something. If he's right, I have to give him back the half of the dollar."

I see the high metal arch on Marina Drive that signals we are officially off the city streets and back into the safety of Hope Ranch. I increase my speed.

"See, he does want to see you again," Rene says shoving her junk back into her bag. She sprays her mouth with breath spray. I park the car as close to the front door as I can manage. Rene grabs my arm. "You go in first. See if I can make a clean shot to the bathroom."

"Why?"

Rene's eyes widen intensely. "I smell like sex. I don't want to get caught by Jack smelling like sex."

"You can smell sex?"

"God you are ignorant. Guys can always smell sex. Go check the house for me."

"Slut." I only say it because it's a joke and it seems to fit.

"Prude." Fiercely back at me.

Rene grabs my cheeks and gives me a hard kiss. "Do I kiss better than Neil?"

I push her away. She is laughing at me folded over in her seat. She looks up. "Run and check. Hurry. I have to pee."

As I walk to the front door I can hear the sound of rowdy men floating over the roof. The noise makes me think of my brother. Sammy and his friends used to fill the house with laughter and music. As a little girl I would hover, hidden, just enjoying watching my big brother, knowing if I got caught all Sam would do is ruffle my hair, toss me over his shoulder, and send me back to my room with a stern warning not to tell Jack.

I peek into the empty entryway and step in. I should have told my dad about the parties. I knew that Sammy's parties were bad. I didn't tell because I didn't understand why I was supposed to. I loved him. Sammy said don't tell. That I understood.

I go as far down the hallway as Sammy's room and turn around and go back for Rene. When I get outside, she's hopping beside the car like she's about to pee. God, she is really messed up. I didn't notice in the car that she is all crumpled and ratty haired, and acting wired.

She is more than just drunk. She did coke with Josh in my dad's car and lied to me about it. I can see it in her agitated movements and the way she is standing. She's coked up. Josh got her coked up and screwed her in a car.

I put my hands on her arms to stop her hopping. "It's OK. Everyone is on the patio and Maria is asleep. Just run. Clear shot to the bathroom."

Rene runs into the house. I hear my bedroom door slam. The shower turns on. I go to the kitchen and I fill a glass with ice water even though I'm not thirsty, but if I don't drink it I'll have a headache in the morning because of the alcohol.

I toss Jack's keys back on the breakfast bar. I lean against it, sipping my water. The patio door opens and Jack steps into the kitchen.

"I'm glad you're back. I was worried about you driving in this fog."

He smiles, then goes to the refrigerator.

I watch him over my ice water. *I'm wearing different clothes, Jack. Don't you even notice? And my hair is all puffed out and sprayed like a heavy metal chick.*

Jack leans an ear up toward the ceiling. "Is someone taking a shower?"

Ours is an old house. Large, solidly built, but the plumbing groans all through the adobe.

"Rene. She doesn't think there will be time in the morning."

"Oh, that reminds me. I'm taking you to the airport at nine, only a half hour earlier than we planned. I've got this thing."

"Sure, Daddy. No problem."

"Are you OK, Chrissie?"

I put down the water glass. "I'm fine."

"You should turn in too, baby girl."

He drops a kiss on my head.

"I think I'm going to practice for a while."

"Well, don't stay up too late. You have an early plane."

I watch Jack disappear back onto the patio. If he had asked one probing question I would have crumbled. There is so much I want to talk to Jack about. I want to tell him about Rene. I want to tell him about me. I just don't know how to start it and Jack never tries to start it.

In my bedroom I find Rene curled atop the covers of my bed, hair still damp, my mother's quilt wrapped around her. I sit down beside her and I close my eyes. I'm exhausted, but not the kind of exhausted that gives way to restful sleep. If I go to sleep now, the way I feel, I will only have dreams, dark dreams, the kind that scare me.

I tuck the blanket in around Rene, and then I make my way down the long hallway to the back of the house where the studio is. The recording studio walls are lined with gold and platinum records, but I stop at the pictures of my mother to pay homage to how beautiful she was, how elegant she appears in the photos of her during her career with the New York Philharmonic.

My parents were such a strange couple. Opposites. I've never understood how they locked in place together.

I go through the soundproofing door into the studio and I sink to my knees before my cello case. I pull free the instrument and bow, and I switch off all the lights except a single dim spotlight above my chair. I settle in the chair and go through my routine, adjusting the instrument, clearing my mind and preparing to play.

It feels good to play. The music is soothing in its beautiful precision. It is not angry and confused like the music in the club tonight. I focus on the controlled moves of my fingers. The music is not like me. I'm angry and confused most of the time. But Bach is beautiful and precise. Slow, and then building, then pulling back. I wonder if that's why I still play the cello even though I'm not very good at it.

I am almost through the prelude when I sense someone is watching me. The room beyond is almost pitch black. I can't see anyone, yet somehow I feel them, the presence of someone beyond the soundproof glass when that should be impossible to feel. I try to lose myself in the music. I can't. I halt the bow above the strings. I stare.

"You're very good."

The voice floating in on the intercom is male, low, raspy and accented. So it isn't my imagination. I'm not alone. I strain to pick out detail at the dimly lit console behind the soundproofing glass. I am only able to see a figure, large and casually reclined in a chair, bare feet propped on the table. Jeez, how long has he been watching me? He looks settled in.

Why doesn't he say something? Oh, it must be my turn to talk.

"*That* was mediocre. It's my audition piece for Juilliard, but I'm waffling and I think I should play Kodaly's Sonata for Solo Cello Opus Eight. Bach seems just a little too predictable. What do you think?"

OK, that was rotten. This guy probably doesn't know Bach from Bon Jovi.

"The Bach. It suits you. The Kodaly I think too dark, too dramatic, too aggressive for you. Stay with the Bach."

Jeez, it's a sexy voice. British and raspy. I don't recognize the voice. Who is this guy? I struggle to pick out more detail of my companion. He rises, and I can see that he tall, muscled, and graceful of movement. I wish I could see his face.

"Close your eyes," says the voice on the intercom.

"Why?"

"Just do it."

I close my eyes. There is something so imperative about his manner that disobeying doesn't seem an option. The studio door opens. There is the sound of bare feet against floor. The warm presence of a body moves into me.

"Don't open your eyes. I'm not going to hurt you and if you open your eyes this will do you no good."

"It won't?"

My fingers tighten around the neck of the cello.

"No." I feel the displacement of air that follows movement and then the heat of him even closer. "You are a very beautiful girl."

"What?" I don't know what to say to that.

I start to ease back but he stops me. "You are a very talented girl," he whispers. "You are going to be remarkable at your audition. And you should most definitely play the Bach. It was flawless."

I try to speak. His fingers touch across my lips to silence me. He leans forward and I am paralyzed just feeling his body near me. I haven't even seen his face and I'm wondering what it would be like to be kissed by him. His voice is a seduction. His words. The way he turns them on his lips.

He takes a deep breath. On my cheek there is the whispering touch of a fingertip. The skin is rough and hardened.

The kind of harshness you get from years of working the metal strings of a guitar. But somehow he knows how to touch with them so they are like a velvet seduction. Like his voice. A little raspy. A little rough. A velvet seduction. His touch moves down my face to trace my lower lip. The play of him leaves me frantic and weak. He puts a light kiss on my forehead and then I feel him moving away.

NO! That's wrong. All that just to kiss me on the forehead?

"Open your eyes. Don't hit me. It was a kiss for luck."

"I wasn't going to hit you. It was a peck, not a kiss. Downright…"

Oh my god! He is crouched down in front of me and only inches from me is a face I've seen a thousand times from a poster hanging on my wall in my dorm room. He doesn't look at all like he does in his music videos, and stepping out of the TV definitely improves him. I like him better this way: simple jeans, a loose fitting t-shirt and what is surely one of Jack's worn long-sleeve flannels. Even if I didn't own every scrap of music he's ever recorded, even if I hadn't seen every video, I would have been blown away just looking at his face.

Alan Manzone is beautiful. He has lustrous black, unkempt shoulder length hair. I don't really like long hair on guys, but oh, on this guy it is perfect. It frames his face and softens the features that would have been too strongly carved without it, especially with those dangerously intense black eyes. God, they are true black. I've never seen such a thing before, and they've got giant iridescent irises flecked with shimmers.

He doesn't move. I don't move. He doesn't speak. I don't speak. OK, whatever game this is it is working very well.

I fight to recover from the shock of finding him, and realize he's watching me and expecting some kind of reaction. He knows exactly what he is doing to me with his little drama and he's enjoying it. His smugness reminds me of Neil and that makes my temper flare. Oh no, Mr. Sexy British Rocker, I am not going to play your game and make a fool of myself. Some other guy has already made a fool of me tonight.

I adjust my cello in front of me as I fight for something to say. It's not easy. Those intense black eyes make it nearly impossible to string together words. "Well, well, well. Not what I expected. The voice was hard to read, but the kiss. Definitely confusing. It made me think you were old. But you are a surprise."

"A good surprise?"

My heartbeat quickens. "I don't know. We just met."

Alan remains crouched before me. "Why are you so nervous about your audition for Juilliard? You must know that you are extraordinary."

Am I really in my dad's studio with Alan Manzone telling me I'm extraordinary? I swallow nervously and I think he is suppressing a smile.

I tuck a stray lock of hair behind my ear. "Just life jitters. I'm not sure of what I want to do. I'm not sure if I want to go to Juilliard. I'm not sure about anything. Today, I'm not even sure about the cello and it is my favorite instrument."

"Well, you should be certain about the cello. You are remarkable."

I blink at him, unsure what to say. There is something in his voice I can't decipher at all. Is he being gracious, or mocking me? Toying with me or just making small talk?

I swallow as I stare into his gorgeous face. I search for words and then smile at him. "Are you an actor?"

Something flashes in his eyes too quickly for me to be certain of his reaction.

"Why?"

"This has all been very theatrical. You seem like an actor."

His smile is rueful, but he looks vaguely disconcerted. "Sorry about the theatrical. I'm working on getting rid of that."

"I didn't suggest you should. Especially not if you're an actor. I would think that would hurt your craft."

"You can set aside your worry. Not an actor. A musician."

I set the cello down in the case and hold out my hand. "How do you do? I'm Christian Parker."

"The introduction is unnecessary. You look just like your dad. He likes to brag about you, in case you don't know that."

It's just a lie, but it makes me happy that he went to the effort of giving me that. "You are not doing well getting rid of the theatrical. You seem almost committed to continuing it. When one introduces themselves the other usually does the same. Introductions are generally considered polite. Would you like to try again?"

He laughs. "I'm British. You do realize the absurdity of lecturing me about politeness?"

"Sure I do, Mr. Whoever You Are. But I don't know who you are," I lie.

"Really?"

His reaction is very odd. Maybe I shouldn't do this.

I nod and struggle to maintain a deadpan expression. "Really. Nothing personal, but I've been locked away in a dark cell for eight years."

"Prison?"

"Worse. Boarding school. I only get parole three times a year. Two months in summer, one month Christmas, three weeks Spring. It makes it really hard to keep up with the world. The last time I was out Reagan was President."

"You haven't missed anything. Not much has changed."

I smile. "That's good to know. I like Reagan. I'm going to miss him."

"Well, any friend of Maggie's is a friend of mine."

"Maggie?"

"Margaret Thatcher. A great lady."

"A great lady, but you shouldn't say that in front of Jack. I don't think I've heard any of my dad's friends compliment Thatcher and Reagan on the same day. Interesting. And you must be someone to be sitting in with Jack's gang on the patio."

He shrugs and extends a hand. "I'm Alan Manzone. It's a pleasure to meet you."

"Well, Alan, it's a pleasure to meet you. So what instrument are you extraordinary with?"

"Guitar. With this gang I play the drums. I don't know if I'm extraordinary. I was just here when this started. No drummer. I was here."

"Are you naturally self-effacing or is it just being British?"

"I'm not self-effacing at all. I'm generally considered arrogant, flamboyant, obnoxious and completely self-absorbed. At least in the American press. They are less kind in the UK."

That comment made him sound tired and annoyed with himself. I study his face, not sure how to respond.

"I've had a tough year," he adds.

"Why tough?"

"I'm very good at fucking up. In fact, I excel at it."

"It can't be that bad," I say.

"Oh, yes. That bad. Hardly anyone is speaking to me. The label is pissed. The promoters won't touch me. I'm being sued by everyone."

Wow, I never expected to hear that. There was something in the papers about him walking out on his US tour, but nothing that suggested it was as bad as all that.

"If not for Jack I'd probably be in a cell in the Chicago area," he mutters, exasperated and shaking his head.

Jack? What does Daddy have to do with this? All this is news to me so my surprise is genuine and I can feel inside of Alan a strange pressure, a sort of not completely contained internal need to talk. But why is he here with me when Jack is only a patio away?

Now that I'm over the shock of finding him, I see details that I missed. He looks emotionally beat up. Under the theatrics, confidence and charm, he seems a very troubled guy, soulful and tired. Troubled, soulful, and tired at twenty-six. In real life he seems younger, nearer to his age. What the hell has happened to this guy?

A little lightness seems like it would be a good thing. "Jack puts me in a cell and keeps you out. That doesn't seem fair since I'm his daughter," I tease.

He laughs and pushes his hair from his face. "Well, you're out of your cell tonight, but I'm still working free of mine. Forgiveness is a tough road."

"Do you want to go for a walk? I like to take advantage of freedom and fresh air every chance I get. Or do you have to get back to the geriatric ward?"

"Sacrilege. Some of the greatest musicians in the world are sitting on your dad's back patio."

"But for some reason you're here sitting in a studio with me. Why?"

"Feeling a little shaky tonight and even when I'm not I usually prefer solitude when I'm not working."

"Is that how you ruined your career? You're one of the twelvers?"

I wait. I already know the answer. I can see it. But that is another shock tonight. I hadn't read anything about *this*. How did they keep it from the press?

"Twelvers?"

"Twelve step buddies of Jack. What's your poison? Booze, pills or coke?"

He eases back on his heels as his eyes comb my face in a searching way that is uncomfortable. He shakes his head. "God, do you have any idea how strange that sounds coming from you?"

I flush. "Why is that strange from me?"

"Because it's like being questioned about my substance abuse by a Disney character. When I look at you I half expect animated, chirruping birds to appear."

That was insulting. I feel my temper stir. "Well, if you don't want to answer, you don't have to be rude."

He looks puzzled for a moment. "Ah, the Disney character comment pissed you off. I didn't mean it as a pejorative."

I roll my eyes. "I'm sure from you it's a compliment."

I stand up.

"You're not leaving are you?" He cocks his head to one side as though he doesn't want me to.

I feel the color in my cheeks rising again.

"Are you going to stay pissed at me all night for that?"

All night? How did this turn into all night? He rubs his chin with his long index fingers as he waits for my answer.

"No," I say with false sweetness, "I'm going to go to bed and forget all about you."

I start for the door.

"Heroin," he says from behind me. "I didn't mean to be rude earlier. You know, with the Disney comment. I'm still learning how to have normal conversations with real people."

I stop. It's the first thing he's said not packed with confusing theatrics. An honest statement that's left him looking very exposed, very vulnerable.

"Real people? As opposed to...?" I ask.

"Everyone else in my life. I'd been clean eight years, but a year ago I had what they benignly call in Rehab a set-back."

I'm intrigued by his honesty, in spite of my early irritation with him. "Eight years is a long time. Why did you relapse?"

He smiles wryly. "There are no whys. Only using and not using. Why is not allowed in the Rehab halfway house of Jack's. Only the why nots."

Yes, that sounded like Jack. "For what's it worth I would never have guessed heroin."

"Really? Why?" His voice is low and he's gazing at me intently.

"I don't know. It doesn't seem to fit you. You seem more elegant than that."

He laughs. "Elegant? That's a first for me."

"You're a tough guy to read, Alan. But you are elegant. It's all mixed up in that strange sort of British rocker, messy jeans, t-shirt, shoeless, grunge sort of thing you've got going on. But definitely, somewhere in there, elegant."

He grimaces. "If that's how you see me then I have an image crisis to contend with and I'm spending too much time with Jack. I'm definitely not going for a shoeless grunge sort of thing. Your dad doesn't let people wear shoes in the house. Remember?"

He looks down at my feet and I realized I am still wearing my UGGs with Neil's silly half dollar sticking out of the fold. "Oh, I forgot our coastal customs. See what being in prison can do? Do you want to go for a walk or not?"

I don't know why I change my mind about going to my room, but I just do. Not waiting for his answer, I leave the studio quickly. I don't look to see if he follows. I bypass the patio off the kitchen and go down a long hall at the other end of the house to another patio exit. The yard is dark and woodsy here. I slow down, and then stop on the side of the house near the edge. I look back over my shoulder to find Alan standing patiently behind me.

I put a finger over my lips, and shush him. Carefully, I peek around the corner of the house.

"Why all the subterfuge?" Alan asks, whispering. "Will you get in trouble for taking off to the beach with me?"

My fingers do a fluttering motion for him to lower his voice.

"No. Of course, not. Jack approves of everything. Well, everything but booze, drugs, Republicans and the Government." I point to a set of wooden stairs at the far end of the property that disappear over the cliff. "We have to make it there without them seeing you. If Jack sees you, he'll keep you talking for hours. And I don't like to walk alone on the beach at night. Stupid, but it scares me."

"It should scare you and you shouldn't do it alone. Not even here. You're a very beautiful girl."

The compliment this time irritates me because I know that I'm not beautiful. He says it very blandly in that *be nice to Jack's daughter* sort of way that I really hate.

"Do you always compliment girls that way? Sort of randomly, out of thin air? And all very matter-of-fact?"

"No, not usually. I never compliment anyone. I'm self-absorbed. Remember?"

I make a face, grab his hand and tug him along with me at a running pace to the stairs. I am laughing by the time it's over and I lean against the rail, hardly able to talk through my laughter. I look up to find him staring at me. He's annoyed by my laughter. Why should he care what I think? His eyes burn into me as if trying to figure out what's up, and I'm nearly compelled to confess that I know perfectly well who he is and I've just been behaving crazy and lame all day.

"I'm going to check tomorrow, but I have to know today. Are you really, really famous?" I ask.

Now he's suspicious. "Why?"

"Because us sneaking from the house to the beach was really, really lame. We didn't have to do any of that. I just wanted to see if you'd do it."

Those beautiful black eyes shift rapidly to annoyance. "I am really, really famous."

I make a nod. "Good."

Even though it is dark, the way only lit by moonlight, I trot down the wood steps built into the cliff, the pattern of unevenness known to me and not the least bit intimidating. I'm sitting in the sand, UGGs already off, by the time Alan joins me.

He stares down at me and holds out his hand. "Now what?"

"We just walk, until we find somewhere we want to cop a squat where the tide isn't too high."

"Do you do this often?"

"Only when I'm home."

He rolls his eyes. "Talking to you is like playing Ping-Pong. Are you always so cheeky?"

I laugh. "Cheeky? Alan, that is a first for me and what did you mean by 'this'?"

"I didn't mean anything bad. You know, kidnap musicians you find at your dad's house, make a fool of them, then take them for moonlight walks on the beach."

"You followed willingly."

"Thank you for not saying I willingly made a fool. Do you have a boyfriend? Are you involved with someone?"

Whoa! My heart turns over. Where did that question come from? "Why do you want to know?"

"You're very confusing and definitely a challenge to talk to."

Me? Confusing? For a moment I wonder if he's making fun of me. I kick the sand with my feet. "Nope. I don't have a boyfriend."

"That surprises me. Something in that nope tells me you used to and the story is not good."

"Nope. Not good. Not bad, just sort of nope." I tilt my face to look up at him and I can see that he's waiting for me to explain that answer. For a fraction of a second he looks really interested, though I can't imagine why any guy would be interested in my dating history. Maybe he's just making small talk. "I don't date that much. I just can't seem to connect with the right kind of guy. I met someone I sort of like tonight but he is what I call my classic type A jerk so I won't be seeing him again. Just to let you know there are four types of jerks who usually try to date me: Type A, type B, type C, type D."

He nods, his eyes bright with amusement again. "Very organized. A good system. What's a type A jerk?"

"Guys who pretend to be interested in me because of Jack. Usually musicians with a band they've failed to tell me about or just a really big fan."

The teasing glint vanishes in Alan's eyes and there is a sympathetic heaviness to his gaze. His mood shifts so suddenly it catches me off guard, and then I realize that this is something about me that Alan Manzone would get without even an effort.

"What was really disappointing about this guy was that he slipped right under my radar. I'm usually really good at spotting A through D."

"So what are the other types of jerks?"

"B's are guys who date me because of money. C's are guys who date me because of how I look. And D's are guys who assume because of who my dad is that I'll party and be wild. Wild as in sexually easy. My last boyfriend was a type D jerk. I should have dumped him instead of waiting for him to dump me."

"You need to rearrange your list. C's should be money. Cash. And the B's for how you look. Beautiful. More logical. But the D is appropriate. Just plain dumb."

"So, that's the whole story of me and why I don't have a boyfriend and why the answer is just nope. I can only find A through D jerks. I'm hoping if I get into Juilliard it will be better in New York."

"Don't count on it. I live in New York. Lots of jerks. Lots of guys like me."

I laugh. "Thanks for the warning. What kind of jerk are you? I don't think you fit in A through D. Is there a new type jerk in New York?"

He ignores the question.

"Do you like living in New York? I've spent hardly any time there," I say.

"I do. I don't know how it will work for you. Very different from California. And certainly different from Santa Barbara."

"There is that."

"You seem pensive again."

"It's hard to plan a future. To know if it's right. I've worked toward Juilliard my entire life. My mother went. She wanted me to go. It doesn't seem right to change the plan now."

"You have to live for yourself. Not your mother or your dad."

"Yes, but I'm afraid what I would prefer is too normal. Not interesting at all."

"Normal is interesting. I don't even know if it still exists."

"I don't even know if what I want is normal. I don't want to be anything. I don't want to spend my life absorbed in trying to be anything. I just want to go to UC Berkeley with my best friend Rene. Study something. I don't know what. Maybe meet a nice guy. Maybe get married. Maybe have lots of kids. And just be. Be more focused on living than trying to be something. Why is it so important to 'be' something? I just want to be and be happy."

"I was almost ready to sign up. It sounded charming right up to the point of 'lots of kids.'"

"I take it you don't like kids."

Something in his face changes, a sudden harshness and something else. "If I had my way there would be an abortion clinic on every street corner."

"That's an awful thing to say."

"Why lie? We don't know each other well enough to have to lie."

"It's still awful. You shouldn't say things like that."

To make a fast shift in conversation, I point at two logs touching in a V-formation. "Do you want to sit down for a while?"

He shrugs and sinks down on a log. I settle beside him and stare out at the ocean. He doesn't seem to want to talk anymore so I respect the silence. I look at him and a single laugh escapes me. There is something in how Alan sits that tells me the beach is not his thing and that he's a little uncomfortable with whatever it is we're doing.

After a few minutes I slip from my perch and lie back in the sand. I stare into the fog above the ocean, seeing the gleaming tinge of the moon. He watches me and then follows, copying my posture, lying on his back, arms crossed beneath his head as a pillow, staring at the sky.

I fight not to look at him. "Isn't it beautiful? Every so often the fog pulls apart and you can see a star. Then pouf it's gone. One minute a star, then nothing."

I glance over at him. Holy crap that was a really dumb thing to say to an international superstar in crisis who thinks he's trashed his life and career.

Change the subject quickly. "I want to stay here until morning."

"Why?"

He's suspicious again.

"I want to see the sunrise," I explain.

He relaxes.

"Don't you have an early plane? Jack said he was taking you to the airport in the morning. I leave tomorrow too. I offered to let you travel to New York with me, but Jack didn't think that was a good idea. I don't blame him. I wouldn't want my daughter in a private plane with me."

His head turns fractionally toward me and my heart rate goes through the roof as my head spins. I could be winging my way to New York with Alan Manzone if Jack hadn't killed the offer. It's a lot to absorb, especially with him lying beside me in the sand.

"I do have an early plane," I explain to cover my shock. "But I want to stay awake until the sunrise. If I stay awake all night I'll sleep on the plane. I really hate flying. Being shut in, surrounded by people. And don't take Jack refusing your offer personally. A private jet would violate his ideology. We always travel commercial. Proletarian normalcy. Jack is committed to proletarian normalcy."

Alan gives me a small laugh. "This is proletarian normalcy?" he mocks playfully. "You live on a beachfront estate in Santa Barbara."

"Jack is committed to the ideal. He is not always philosophically consistent. If you've spent enough time with Jack to be worried that you're spending too much time with Jack you should have picked that up by now."

Alan laughs. There is silence again for a long while. I chance another look at him and I wonder what he's thinking. He glances at me from the corner of his eyes.

I bite my lip and study his face. "Do you know what?" I ask. "We're doing my favorite thing. Lying in the sand, talking through the night, and waiting for the sunrise. Everything wonderful in life is free, but most people never get that."

His eyes fix on me intensely and too hard to meet for any length of time. *OK, what stupid thing did I say now?* He looks a touch irritated and a touch troubled again.

I turn my head and stare at the moon. "Sorry to get all serious on you," I whisper. "I have a habit of doing that. My friends get really annoyed with it. Do you want to hear something stupid?"

A pause. Then laughter again, soft and textured. "Sure."

I sit up and point at the ocean. "Jack hates the oil derricks. Don't even mention the Santa Barbara oil spill in 1969. He will go all Greenpeace on you. But I love the oil derricks. When I was a little girl and we'd drive home from Los Angeles along Highway 101, I couldn't wait until we reached the coast so I could see them. They looked like pirate ships to me. It made me so happy to see them. It meant I was almost home. It still makes me happy to see their lights at night. It is the favorite part of my drive home from Los Angeles. The oil derricks that Jack hates. Isn't that stupid?"

I am laughing when I look over to smile at him. I quiet and freeze. He is crying, not overtly, but there is moisture on his face and a shimmer in his eyes. I don't know how to handle this, especially since I haven't a clue what's going on with him. His expression changes and he looks embarrassed.

"That is not a stupid story at all."

I smile because there is no way to force the words through the lump in my throat. My hand moves toward him. I can't stop it. I begin to touch his tears away. His eyes flash, and I am embarrassed and totally confused by what prompted me to do that. I lie back into the sand beside him.

He says nothing and I'm quiet as I silently debate with myself whether to ask. I stare at the fog, not brave enough to look at him. "I know this is rude of me to ask, but what happened? What happened to make you so sad? And that's what you are. Underneath everything. Very sad."

His eyes are harsh as he studies me and I tense, wishing I could slap my mouth and take back that question. I can feel those black eyes combing the taut lines of my face and when I peek at him from the corner of my eye, his expression softens and is no longer hostile.

"I lost someone important to me," he says quietly. "It's been just over a year."

"I'm sorry. I thought it was something like that. Were you very close?"

That question Alan ignores. He seems surprised by his honesty and uncomfortable in it. I don't press, but I still feel the need to say something.

"I've lost my mom and my brother. I'm not going to say anything cliché like 'time heals all wounds.' I used to hate it when people said crap like that. Do you know it's been ten years since my brother died and people still say crap like that to me? It is worse when they think I can just snap out of it. This wretched girl said to me tonight 'Don't you think you need to move beyond your brother?' How would she know? She's never lost anyone. I think we heal when we heal and that's the end of it. Cut yourself some slack. Be sad until you're not. It's allowed."

Quiet again. *Crap, maybe that was the wrong thing to say.*

"You're not like any eighteen year old girl I've ever met." His face, even smiling, is so intense, half in shadow and half touched in moonlight. "Do you always talk this way?"

There is something in his voice that I can't quite read. It makes me tense. "Unfortunately. People always say I need to lighten up. I think I'm worse than usual tonight because you started with that whole theatrical thing."

He gazes down at me. "Then I'm glad I was theatrical. I didn't plan to be. I had an entirely different scene in my head. It just seemed to fit the picture you made sitting in the dim light playing Bach. None of this is what I intended."

Intended? I don't know what to make of that.

I let out a ragged breath and search for something to say. "This is the weirdest date I've ever been on."

His eyes are now angry and intense.

"Date? Is that what you think we're doing?"

That was a stupid thing to say. The date comment is definitely a clunker. The adrenaline spike leaves my body making me feel cold and humiliated.

"Sorry. Stupid joke. But don't think you need to explain the difference. I'm not a little girl. I know what this is. That's an entirely different section of my journal."

That kicks his anger up a notch. "Stop it. Stop with the playacting."

I bite my lower lip. He is really pissed off and I don't know why. "I can't. It a nervous habit. I don't do it intentionally."

He stills. The emotion leaves his face. He stares down at me.

"Nervous with me. Why?" He is sitting above me, on bent knees, carefully watching my reaction. "Why are you nervous with me?"

"I don't know. Everything got just a little too real."

"Me or the mood?"

"Both."

"Are you cold?"

"Why?"

"You're shaking." He holds the flannel long sleeve shirt out from his t-shirt. "Do you want my shirt?"

I shake my head. It is hard to keep up with the pitching conversation and the changing currents of the mood.

"May I kiss you?"

Every part of me freezes all at once. *Oh my god, where did that come from?*

My head spins as my eyes round so much it is painful. Alan's long index finger lightly traces my jaw and he smiles. "I'm going to take your silence as a yes."

I tense from head to toe in anticipation of his mouth and take a deep breath as he starts to lean toward me. I feel his fingers first, lightly on my cheek, nothing more, and my muscles start to calm. He is all around me, balanced on his arms, not touching, but the feel of him is like a ghost all across my flesh. The first touch of his lips is just a touch, gentle, a whispering hint of eroticism and tenderness. Everything about him is nerve-poppingly quiet. I've been kissed, and Neil is right, I don't like to kiss, but I've never been kissed like this. Not in this sweetly gentle way that has instantly made me melt into his mouth.

"Don't close your eyes," he whispers.

I open them as his mouth comes back to me and now he is giving me the feel of him in slow degrees, inch by inch until I'm surrounded by all of him, until it feels as though there is nothing on this earth but him. His mouth leaves to touch my hair, the sensitive flesh beneath my ear, the slope of my cheek.

He traces the outline of my lips with his kiss, then across my brow to my temple before he slowly leaves me.

I find him staring down at me. He looks the same: cool, calm and in control. I feel like I'm about to melt within my skin.

"Why did you stop?" I whisper.

"I shouldn't have done that."

His expression betrays nothing. It's hard to speak. "Why?"

"I owe Jack a lot."

"Oh."

He lies back in the sand. His face is tense. "After all the rotten things I've done this year I don't need to do one more. But I wanted to meet you and I now get why Jack didn't think that was a good idea."

My head spins. This was no accidental encounter. Alan Manzone wanted to meet me. He searched me out in the house. He wanted to meet me. But why?

I stare at him. I don't know what to say.

"Listen, it's not you," he says.

I blush.

"You're a very lovely girl."

I crinkle my nose. "Lovely? Is that the British equivalent of an American guy saying you have a nice personality?"

"I'm not sure. What's nice personality a code for?"

"Friend material. Not attractive, but likeable."

"Oh, it is definitely not a code for that." He stands up. "If you weren't Jack's daughter I wouldn't have stopped and you'd hate me in the morning. I don't want you to ever hate me."

I hug my knees and stare up at him. "I don't know why you think so badly of yourself, Alan. You seem like a nice guy to me."

Alan is quiet all the way back to the house. It's really odd, but I feel comfortable in his quiet. The morning has just started to come alive and the beach has the pleasant hush and slow stirring of sunrise. I find my UGGs where I left them at the bottom of the stairs, and I pull them on and begin the long climb back up to the house.

I cross the patio and go into the empty kitchen. Alan surprises me. I thought he would head off to the pool house, but he follows me. The clock says 6 a.m. Even Maria isn't awake yet. I stop in the center and look at Alan. I'm not exactly sure how to end this. It has been an unexpected kind of night. I wait for him.

"It's been a pleasure spending the night with you, Christian Parker."

I nod, wide-eyed. "It's been a pleasure spending the night with you, Alan."

I step back from him. His face is washed with seriousness again. I feel the need to say something. Anything. "It's going to be OK. You do know that, don't you?"

His black eyes do a quiet search of my face and he starts to shake his head. "Such a trite thing to say. Only it sounds so real and believable when you say it."

He's waiting for me to leave and I can tell by his expression that he wants this over. I gaze at him. I don't want this to be the end. And I don't want to make a fool of myself.

"Everyone may be angry with you, Alan, but it's morning and I don't hate you. According to you that's improvement. Learn to appreciate the small improvements. Isn't that what they teach in recovery?"

Alan smiles. I've amused him. Good. "If you knew me you wouldn't call that small."

I make a face at him. "There you go again thinking badly of yourself."

He lifts a strand of hair from my face. "There you go again not realizing how beautiful you are."

He takes a half-step back from me. We were standing so close and I didn't even notice it. I want him to kiss me again, but he won't. We are back in my dad's kitchen, and I feel strange, out of place, and really curious to know what it would feel like to have him kiss me a second time.

Alan waits for me to leave first. I can feel him watching as I disappear into the hall.

* * *

"Where have you been all night?"

Rene must have stirred in her sleep. She hates to be alone at night. She's afraid of the dark, but won't admit it.

"On the beach," I say nonchalantly.

She rolls over and pulls the quilt more tightly around her. "Doing what?"

"If I told you, you wouldn't believe me."

Her eyes drift closed. "Tell me later. Don't wake me until it's time to go to the airport."

I stare at my room. The house is quiet. I am too wired to sleep. Wired and weak. I should lie down for an hour before I have to get ready to go to the airport.

I drop before my suitcase and rummage for my journal. I've been keeping it forever. I put the date on a page. I am not going to write about Alan Manzone. It's not that type of journal. It's not that *dear diary* type shit that Eliza and her mob probably have carefully tucked beneath their mattresses. I write about nothing, fragments of dreams, random thoughts, poetry, but mostly just fragments of nothing. Disconnected pieces that aren't meant to make sense or say anything.

I begin to rapidly write. Tonight, though, it is a whole thought and one that is strangely significant to me. So I write quickly before I forget. Rene can be so profound at times. It is why we are friends. We don't think or feel like the other girls. Our dreams are not happy. We feel strange and disconnected from people. The world doesn't make sense to us. We don't make sense to us. And the future, it is there and I can't see it and I don't know why, but it makes me a mess and only more disconnected from the world.

Did I get the words right? I look them over again: "We are the generation of nothing. There is no war. There is no grand social struggle. There is no political wrong to right. There is nothing. We have everything we want and nothing we need. Even the music isn't good. We live in empty houses. We have too much time to think of ourselves. It would be better for there to be a little strife than to be a generation with too much time to think only of ourselves."

I reread the entire quote. I stare at it. Is this why I am the way I am?

Chapter Four

Rene throws her everything bag onto the concrete.

"Crap! What are we supposed to do now?"

Rene is cranky and hung-over.

"We wait," I say calmly. "They said only a short delay because of the fog. Maybe an hour. We'll be on our plane in an hour."

"Yeah, right. They're backed up. We'll take off late. We'll miss our connection in LA, and we won't reach New York until forever." She stares at the airport terminal in frustration. "What are we supposed to do here to amuse ourselves?"

The Santa Barbara Airport terminal is a tiny Spanish style structure with white stucco, red tile roof and tile floor. It isn't really sectioned in any way. The boarding area is merely roped off from the lobby that acts as central location for ticketing, baggage and security check. You can see the interior ticket counter from the front curb. There is only one restaurant and one store within. There is very rarely ever a crowd. Never any excitement. *So Santa Barbara* and the morning has gone badly. Rene is feeling miserable from partying the night before, Maria took us to the airport instead of Jack, and thick morning fog has delayed all the planes.

I sink on the concrete bench. "We could count the cars as they pass."

Rene gives a disgruntled laugh. "There are no cars, Chrissie."

She is fidgety and irritable. I'm selfishly pleased she is so out-of-sorts. By the time she woke, she forgot to ask the details of where I was last night. Another secret I don't want to share with Rene. If I share it, she'll pick it apart minute by minute in her hyper-analytical way until she has pointed out every mistake I made in my encounter with Alan Manzone.

"We can go upstairs to the restaurant," I offer.

"If I eat I'll throw up."

She looks around the terminal again. Her eyes fix on Steve.

"Hey, Stevie, anything fun happen here lately?"

Steve the Valet looks up from his wooden valet stand. It's really bitchy, but that's what we call him: Steve the Valet. We've never asked his last name. And it must be a boring job and he probably makes no tips. How many people could possibly want their bags carried when you can see the drop-off counter from the curb? He's worked here forever even though he is only in his early twenties. Rene likes to pass the minutes annoying poor Steve while we're stuck waiting.

Rene sashays over to him. "Anything interesting in your world of airport curb convenience?"

That was snotty. Steve just shrugs. He's a nice guy. I don't know why Rene is always so mean to him. We ran into him one night downtown in a club. Rene has been rude to him ever since.

Steve looks at me. "John Travolta flew in last week. He's a pretty cool guy. Do you know him, Chrissie?"

I shake my head. Steve thinks that everyone famous knows everyone famous, and it was a subtle put down toward Rene, to look pass her and talk to me.

Steve starts to arrange his baggage tickets. He's trying to ignore Rene. She leans into him at the valet stand. "Hey, how'd you like to go into the luggage sort area and have a little fun, Steve? It's not like you're going to miss a tip."

"There is one hell of a Lear jet parked on the private strip," Steve says only to me. "Been waiting to take off all morning. It must belong to someone who is somebody. If you go upstairs to the restaurant and get a table on the terrace you should be able to see who it is when they arrive."

He wants me to get rid of Rene for him. I smile. "How's school going?"

"Finish this quarter and then I'm out of here. I'm going to grad school at UCLA."

"LAX. Much better airport. You can further you career," Rene says.

A car enters the airport drop-off loop. Rene runs the four steps to the curb and holds out her thumb. God, she is obnoxious this morning. The car drives past. Rene laughs uproariously. She can be so childish at times.

She sinks down beside me on the bench. "Wow, that was fun. Now what, Chrissie?"

I try to focus on my book. I've got an entire carryon full of books I have to read before break is over, since I've procrastinated most of the quarter because I spent most of my hours preoccupied and teary over my break-up with Brad. But I don't really feel like reading and who the hell ever feels like reading Chekhov? Why did I pick Chekhov from the book list? I hate Chekhov. I turn a page.

Rene is walking along the mow-strip like a gymnast on a balance beam. We really are an odd match as friends. I'm sitting beside a cello reading Chekhov, and she finished the entire spring semester reading list in one week, got a perfect score on her SATs, and is now flashing her panties at Steve the Valet, though pretending it's an accident each time she pretends to wobble on her beam.

I hear a car in the drop-off loop. Rene jumps off her beam and is back at the curb again. It's a Town Car with tinted windows, from the local limo service, and now Rene is really amped since it must be Mr. Lear Jet. She has her leg out toward the road this time and is doing a little swish with her hips as she holds out her thumb. The car moves past her and continues on its way to the turn in for the tarmac.

"Maybe I should have flashed a little?" Rene jerks at her shirt. She looks at Steve. "What do you think?"

Steve nods his head toward the road. "I think flashing your panties worked. He's coming back around."

"*HOLY SHIT!*" Rene shouts. She laughs and drops down beside me on the bench. She tries to look innocent. "Oh god, oh god, oh god don't let it be a friend of my parents," she whispers to herself.

A little late to worry about that, Rene. It could very well be a friend of the Thompsons. The limo crowd in Santa Barbara is definitely their set. No one travels by limo here. Such a pretentious thing to do when everything in town is only five minutes away.

The Town Car stops. The door opens before the driver can come around to open it. I focus on my book.

"Holy shit," Rene whispers again.

"Chrissie?"

A low voice, sexy and surprised. *Holy shit* is right. Alan Manzone is above me, staring down at me after Rene just flashed him her panties. *How awful is that?*

I shake my head to gather my wits. "Hello Mr. Whoever You Are."

He laughs. "I thought I'd be Alan after last night."

Rene's mouth drops. I feel my cheeks burn. To distract myself from Rene, who is behind him mouthing the words 'pool house,' I reach down and shove my book back into my bag.

"Why are you sitting on a bench reading while your friend flashes her panties at cars?" he asks, sensual lips curled in amusement. "You left for the airport hours ago. I expected you to be halfway to New York by now."

"Fog delay. You must be the private jet. How nice it must be to have the plane waiting for you and not to have to worry about the pesky delays of commercial travel."

"Yes, non-proletarian travel does have its perks," he acknowledges.

I glance behind him at Rene. She is really irritated with me because I haven't introduced her. Before I can introduce her, he's back at his car barking orders at the driver. Suddenly Alan's luggage is pulled out and he's gesturing for Steve to collect all the bags.

I stand up. "You know you've exited in the wrong place. The private entrance for non-proletarian is down there."

He gives the airport a once-over. "It doesn't look like it makes much of a difference here."

Steve is grabbing all the bags: Rene's, mine, Alan's.

"Wait," I protest. I rush over to Steve. "Leave those. Those are ours."

"You'll travel with me to New York, Chrissie," he says. "I won't leave you sitting on a bench in an airport."

Whoa…. Did Alan Manzone really just invite us to travel to New York with him?

"Really, we can't impose."

Rene is practically having a seizure behind his back from that.

He raises his eyebrows. "Can't or won't? And it's no imposition. I'm going to New York, Chrissie."

Of all the reasons not to accept, the one that claims me isn't the one I expect. Alan hasn't factored in what six hours trapped in a private plane with Rene will be like for him. And I find that I don't want him to find out, and I don't want Rene, who gets every guy she wants, to get him.

"I won't travel with you," I say, ignoring Rene's eyes that are now flashing at me.

He raises an eyebrow. He rubs his chin with a long index finger then runs his hand through his hair. "Did I do something that offended you last night?"

He looks unsure and Rene is listening mouth open.

"No. I enjoyed talking with you last night." It's the truth, but I need to send Alan on his way without us or I will be a mile high with Rene all over him. I know I'm being petty in that petty girl way, protecting my turf that isn't even my turf, and having really unkind thoughts about my best friend. "Listen, you don't have to do one of those 'be nice to Jack's daughter' kind of favors. I was the one who behaved badly last night. I knew who you were the second my eyes opened and I thought it would be fun..."

His finger presses on my mouth to stop me. Oh crap, I'm in nervous chatter mode. Why is he smiling?

"Shush. Will you let me get in a word, Chrissie? You're not confessing anything I don't know. Your entire face lit up when you opened your eyes. It's not a look I'm unfamiliar with. I knew you were playing and I played along. I just wanted to talk to you. Have a reasonable conversation without all the bullshit. I played along. I think it worked out very well."

Oh crap, he saw right through every part of my game last night. I feel as though my knees are about to buckle.

He runs his index finger down my cheek. "This is not a 'be nice to Jack's daughter' gesture. I like you, Chrissie. I consider us friends."

I blink rapidly. "OK."

He nods. "Good. Let's get your things."

I nod, not trusting myself to speak because I can feel that stupid crooked smile on my face, the lopsided one I can't control that I get only when I'm really happy.

Alan turns to face Rene. "I'm Alan Manzone."

"Rene Thompson." She sounds stunned. I've never seen Rene lost for words before.

Those black eyes burn into her before he shifts away with hardly a look. Wow, no one ever looks away from Rene so dismissively. She is beautiful, like stop cars on State Street beautiful. All guys love Rene.

"It's a long flight. I need to sleep," Alan says to Rene over his shoulder. "If you must speak to me call me Manny. You call me Alan I'll have you tossed from the plane even if we're at twenty thousand feet."

I've never seen Rene's eyes so large. Rene cowed by a guy. I never expected to see that.

It is really very bad of me to enjoy her discomfort. I feel myself smiling. "What will you do to me if I call you Alan?"

He grins. "You get tossed from the plane if you call me Manny."

Oh my. There was definitely something in his voice when he said that and I feel my crooked smile growing larger. I bite my lip. "Your own nicely organized system?"

"Yes, my own nicely organized system," he responds, and there is a pleasant, secretive note to that comment.

He leans over for my book bag and hands it to me. He picks up my cello and gestures to Steve. We walk through the airport amid heavy stares, as Steve guides us to the private tarmac exit.

The pilot is outside the plane finishing pre-flight check and the co-pilot is by the stairs. He crosses the tarmac to Alan. "Welcome back, Manny. We're ready to roll whenever you're ready to roll. Tower gave us clearance an hour ago."

It must be his plane. His crew. They are friendly and familiar with each other. Steve is loading our suitcases in the luggage bay. The co-pilot takes my cello and trots up the stairs. The pilot waits for us to board. Alan gestures for me to go ahead of him, but Rene rebounds back into her old self, and runs up the steps before me, and then turns back to the airport terminal, doing a little swish with her hips. "We are independently destitute princesses again. I could get used to this, Manny. Even if you aren't really my type."

God, why does she have to be this way? Why does she have to embarrass me? She disappears into the cabin in a cloud of laughter.

Alan arches a brow. "Independently destitute princess?"

I shrug. "Rich girls without money."

"Oh." He rakes a hand through his hair. I stare as his hair floats down around his face and shoulders. He makes a graceful gesture of his arm. "We should board. After you."

He has such pretty manners. You see none of that in his public persona. Obnoxious. Arrogant. Self-absorbed. Yes, he is right about how the press sees him. But he is sensitive, sophisticated, educated, and elegant. He isn't at all the type of guy I thought he would be.

At the top of the short flight of steps I surreptitiously gaze back at him. I go crimson.

"Are you all right?" Alan is staring at me. I stopped on the steps for no reason. "You really don't like to fly, do you?"

I smile and shake my head and continue on. I stare carefully down at the steps. The light touch of his hand against my back is like an electric shock wave all through my flesh. Every move of his body is graceful and nerve-poppingly quiet, but each touch zapping and potent. *He's like the ocean. He can lure you in quietly and then drown you.*

Desperately struggling for my equilibrium, I focus on the interior of his jet. The interior of the jet is luxurious, with comfy cream-colored leather seats and polished wood tables, with a conservatively dressed flight attendant standing in wait just for him. But it is also a traveling trashcan. There is stuff absolutely everywhere: instruments, stacks of mail on the long bench seat, clothing. I start to laugh. If he were some guy living in a car, *this* is exactly what it would look like. What a strange thing to find. What a strange contradiction.

Rene is sitting before the table, her butt in one seat, and her legs over the armrest in the one beside her. She already has a drink and looks comfy in our temporary digs. *How does she do it?* She looks so comfortable, so at ease with her body and being here with him. I envy her, her soaring confidence and her beautiful female naturalness.

I look around in indecision. There is only one cream-leather seat completely tidy and empty—the one across the table from Rene. The one I'm sure intended for Alan. I don't know where to sit. The seat beside him is stacked high with mail.

"Your plane should be condemned as a hazardous waste site," Rene announces. "Don't you have people who clean up after you?"

"I don't like people touching my things," he says, his voice cold and polite simultaneously. "Try to remember that."

Rene lifts her drink. "It looks like you live here. Are you homeless?"

Eyeing her coolly, Alan shrugs. "If it doesn't meet your standard, please feel free to go back to the United counter and wait for your proletarian travel."

Boy, he really doesn't like Rene and I'm uncharacteristically thrilled by that. I stare after Alan as he pokes his head into the cockpit to say something to the pilots.

The flight attendant gestures me forward. "Please be seated, Miss. We'll shortly be taxiing for take-off."

I step farther into the plane. The steps are pulled up and closed behind me. I'm actually winging my way to New York with Alan Manzone and there is no backing out of it now.

I stare down at the seats just as Alan comes up behind me. His hands touch on my hips. I feel instantly surrounded by him.

"What do you want me to do with all this?" I ask.

"Chuck it on the floor, Chrissie."

Piece by piece I start to move it onto the table into a careful stack.

His hand moves from my hip to my shoulder. His other arm snakes around me. With the swipe of a hand the contents of the seat is scattered onto the floor and I spring back into him and he laughs.

"Sorry, but if we did it your way we'd be on the tarmac another hour."

I drop down onto his seat and scoot over to mine. I concentrate on fastening my seatbelt as the attendant goes through the plane's safety procedure in a calm, clear voice. Alan is relaxed in his seat beside me, long limbs stretched out in front of him, eyes closed. Jeez, he looks good this morning, all tousled hair, simple olive t-shirt, soft faded jeans. Even wearing those crummy worn leather Water Buffalo sandals that I think he took from Jack by mistake, though how could anyone mistake those hideous things as their own shoes is a mystery. But he does look good, even in hideous sandals.

Rene is staring at him over her drink. She looks like the Cheshire cat. Maybe he does intend to sleep through the flight.

The plane surges forward and starts taxiing toward the runaway. I pull down the window shade.

"Why are you afraid of flying?" he whispers.

So he's not asleep.

"Chrissie is afraid of everything. Would you like the list?" Rene answers before I can find my words.

My cheeks burn. *Jeez, Rene how could you say that!* She is just being Rene, but I'm not liking it at all today.

"I don't trust anyone who doesn't have a little fear," he murmurs.

Rene flushes. "Then Chrissie is the girl for you."

She looks out the window, annoyed. I know that look. Icy cold. She's pissed. Rene is pursuing and he's rejecting.

Both of them are silent now. I stare at the stack of mail on the floor. At my feet lies a movie script with a typewritten offer on the letterhead of a well-known studio. I pick it up. This is what he considers just the mail?

"Studios mail you scripts with offers?" I ask. "You don't have to audition? They just offer you roles."

He nods.

"Why?"

"I'm an incredible actor."

"Modest too," Rene scoffs. "What makes you so good that they want you without testing you first?"

His heavy lids lift above his black eyes. "Early childhood training. I was raised in a house of liars."

I hold up the script. "Do you mind if I read this? It looks interesting."

"Be my guest."

Rene motions to the flight attendant for another drink. What is she drinking? Is that why she's being more outrageous than usual? Alan closes his eyes and I open the script.

Once we've leveled off in the air, Rene pops from her seat to go to the bathroom. She is halfway through the cabin when Alan looks at me. His thumb brushes my lower lip and he is staring into my eyes.

"I don't like your friend," he whispers.

Now I'm annoyed. Rene isn't even here and she's dominating the conversation.

I shrug. "She's OK."

"No, Chrissie, she's wired. She's coked up. How long has she had a problem?"

Coked up? I feel instantly protective of Rene. "You're wrong. She's just high-strung. I've known her forever. I would know."

He frowns. "You shouldn't trust her, Chrissie."

"People always get the wrong idea about Rene. It's just how she comes off."

"If you say so." He hasn't taken his fingers from my face and he eases into me until we are very close. "I don't like her. She shouldn't be your friend."

Jeez, who would have thought that Alan Manzone and Father Morris would share the same opinion of Rene? But they are both wrong. Rene is a true friend.

He studies me for a long time and after what feels like an eternity, he inches back from me. Then I see Rene closing in out of the corner of my eye.

He doesn't look at her. "I just got out of Rehab. That story in print is true. I would appreciate it if you don't forget your vial on my plane, and if you go to the bathroom one more time to powder your nose, I'll have them touchdown at the first airport we reach and have you booted from the plane. What the fuck were you thinking, carrying that through airport security? Don't you give a shit about your friend?"

Rene's face is candy red and it betrays the truth. With that, Alan closes his eyes and goes to sleep.

* * *

"Chrissie. We're in New York."

Someone is trying to wake me. I don't want to wake. I'm in a pleasant sleep, curled into something warm. There is sound all around me. I hear voices. His voice. Yes, I'm with Alan. I'd recognize his voice anywhere.

"How bad is it?"

"Bad," says the co-pilot. "I don't know how they knew we were landing in New York today."

"Shut all the window shades. Make sure the car is ready before you lower the steps."

Alan. He is angry. Why is he angry? The snap of the window shade beside my head jerks me out of grogginess. Alan unbuckles my seatbelt and climbs from the seat. I realize that the pleasant pillow beneath my cheek was his shoulder and it's now gone. My eyelids slowly lift and I see Rene alertly watching the fast action around us.

I find Alan standing above me, tense, and his eyes a strange mixture of concern and apology.

He lowers until he's at eye level with me. "Chrissie, we have a problem. About half the New York Press corps is on the tarmac. I need to get you from the plane to the car without anyone noticing you."

I straighten up in my seat. "Why? What does it matter if they see me?"

He stills and his eyes widen. "The worst possible thing I could do to you is let the tabloids see you with me. I should never have let you travel to New York with me."

Oh my…I know why he's worried. For the last year he's existed in nonstop tabloid ink. Just being near him can get you tarred in tabloid ink. *Oh jeez, what will Jack think of that?*

Alan looks determined and grim. It's very sweet that he's so worried about this, but it's not exactly something new to me and I do know how to handle this.

I gaze up at him and smile. "Alan, I know how to be invisible. Trust me. Just let me get off the plane alone and no one will even notice me. This is something I am expert at."

Alan shifts from the flight crew to face me. "If the tabloids realize who you are, Chrissie, it will turn into a shitstorm. I don't ever want you hurt because of me."

I stare at him, stunned. He spoke in an intense way, as though not hurting me really did matter to him, but then how could it matter? We hardly know each other. It makes no sense. As I climb from my seat, I realize there is a lot about Alan that doesn't make sense.

I shrug. "It won't be my first shitstorm, Alan. So don't worry about it. It's going to be all right."

His mouth presses into a hard line, but then, almost reluctantly, he starts to laugh. "I'm sorry, but I've never heard anyone say shit quite the way you do, without the 't' at the end and with lots of 'shhhh.'"

My temper flares. "I'm a Disney character. Remember?" I mutter, in an overly dramatic way to hide the sting I feel from his criticism.

I make an exaggerated face and he rolls his eyes. "You are never going to forget that, are you?" he says in an aggravated way, before he turns to talk with the crew again.

"Here is what you are going to do, Chrissie," he says firmly, but he seems less worried about everything. "You are going to step off this plane without me. If you have sunglasses, put them on. Look at no one. Answer no one. And you will walk, neither fast nor slow, to the car with Natalie. Don't stop. And don't look back. If we're lucky the tabloids won't notice you."

I shrug. "It's what I was going to do anyway." The co-pilot hands me my cello.

"And what am I supposed to do?"

Rene's voice startles me. I'd all but forgotten about her. She is curled on her seat like a cat, irritated at not being the center of attention.

"You will do exactly as I tell you," Alan says, his gaze fixing on Rene. "Exactly as I tell you. And you will be silent."

Alan walks to the cabin door with me, carefully stopping so as not to be seen. "I'm sorry, Chrissie."

I shrug and Alan eases forward to push my sunglasses up from the tip of my nose until they are flush against my face.

"Say nothing." Alan runs his hand through his hair, a nervous gesture I now realize.

I step into the open cabin door and the press below spring into action. I tense like you do when you expect something to hit you, a suspended moment, and then it passes. The cameras don't flash, I notice Natalie the flight attendant at my side, and the voices below are still mute. I touch the metal steps and the press hardly even look at me.

I cross the tarmac toward the car, surrounded by a strange kind of heavy silence. The driver opens the car door and takes my cello as Natalie disappears toward the terminal. I'm about to slip into the seat, when something makes me jump and I look back.

The cameras explode all around. Alan starts to exit the plane, his arm carelessly draped over Rene's shoulder and Rene has that self-satisfied, Cheshire cat smile on her face.

I sink into the backseat to wait. I can hear the shouting voices and every so often I hear Alan's. Why is this taking so long? I try to look through the wall of press, but I can't see anything. Hopefully, Rene is keeping her mouth shut. She never should have let Alan use her that way, and for a brief moment I am angry with him.

Moments later, Rene drops in a heavy bounce in the seat across from me, all bubbly and pretty with excitement. "God, Chrissie! That was incredible," she exclaims, rummaging through the compartments in the car until she finds a bottle of water.

I shake my head in aggravation as she downs a third of the bottle. "You didn't say anything, did you?" I ask.

"What? No. I don't know." Her eyes round. "It all happened so fast. It was all so intense. I don't know. I don't think so."

I lean forward into her. "Rene, think. You didn't tell them your name, did you?"

Irritated, she pushes the hair back from her face. "I don't know. Maybe. I don't know." This time, I can see she is lying.

"Oh, Rene."

She shrugs carelessly. "Someone asked me." She pushes back into the leather seat and gives me that smile, the one I hate, half challenging and half superior. "What's the big deal, Chrissie? God, are you jealous?"

I roll my eyes and clamp my mouth shut, but for a millisecond I am reminded of what it felt like to see them standing together, how right Alan and Rene looked, and how much it bothered me to see her hanging on his arm.

Rene frowns. "You have nothing to be jealous about," she says in that generous way of the truly confident, "and I'm not dumb. Something was going on out there. He didn't want anyone to know you were with him. Which is very strange. Why is he protective of you?"

I ignore the comment, but I do wonder: *protective?* He definitely is an entirely different guy when he deals with Rene, rude and acerbic and not likeable.

Rene raises her eyebrows.

"I think he really likes you, Chrissie. He's a shit, but I think he really likes you. Spill everything. I've been dying since we boarded the plane keeping myself quiet. You spent the night with him last night, didn't you? That's where you were all night."

I look out the window. "Yes. On the beach. We talked."

"Talked? You didn't just talk. I could feel the vibe in the plane."

"No, we just talked," I snap, hoping that will stop the questions. "He acts like we're buddies."

"Buddies?" Rene lets out a harsh, scoffing laugh. "God, you can't be that dense. Did he kiss you last night?"

"Once."

"What was it like?"

"It was nice."

Rene's laughs. "Nice?" She stares at me knowingly. "You like him, don't you?"

I blush. "Yes."

"Do you like him enough to ...?"

I'm suddenly reminded of his touch, the tenderness of his mouth and the feel of the sand.

I continue to stare out the window, but I can feel Rene studying me. "I'm glad you didn't," she says with heavy meaning.

"He's not the kind of guy you want your first time to be with, if you get my…"

Rene's words die and are replaced by a sweetly contrived smile. "Speak of the devil."

Alan drops down heavily into the seat beside me, the car door slams, and in a minute we are speeding from the tarmac.

He leans back against the headrest and closes his eyes. "Fucking Brian and his never ending publicity machine. I'm sorry about that."

In spite of the performance he put on for the press, he's exhausted. It shows in his voice and his posture, and it reminds me of how he'd looked last night: soulful, tired and twenty-six.

I smile at Alan. "It's no big deal. Rene thought it was fun."

Just when it looks like Alan has fallen sleep, he sits up, and everything about his demeanor has changed—he's angry and edgy, energized and focused.

"No, Chrissie. It is a big deal. I nearly fuck up everything my first day back."

Everything? How would the tabloids linking me with him fuck up everything? I've never seen Alan angry before and I find this new facet extremely intimidating and a little bit of a turn-on.

He grabs the mobile phone and angrily punches numbers into it. He lightly kicks the seat beside Rene. "I told you to keep silent. Fuck, you are a useless friend. Get me a water." Alan hits the speaker button and drops the receiver into its rest. "Fuck you, Brian."

A moment of dead air. "Ah, Lazarus has arrived in New York…" I recognize the voice. It is Uncle Brian, Brian Craig, my father's manager and Alan's it seems. "…if you're pissed off and making phones calls again it means they've finally let you out of Rehab. And by the way, fuck you, Manny."

"What the fuck was that scene at the airport about?" Alan growls. "That's the last time you serve me up for publicity without asking."

Alan opens his water bottle and downs half of it.

"Well pardon me for trying to save your fucking career. You needed the publicity. Don't tell me how to manage the business end. Have you any idea what kind of mess you left for me? You wouldn't have a career if not for me. You wouldn't have the band and you sure as hell wouldn't have the cash…"

"I think what Brian means to say is we all need to focus on business or there isn't going to be a business," interrupts another voice, male and less agitated. "About the tapes…"

"What Arnie is telling you is that the execs are going to shelve the tapes, Manny," Brian warns anxiously. "You can't do a solo release. Maybe next round, but not now. The band—they don't have the fucking royalties. Now isn't the time to cut them out…"

"I have creative control. I can read a contract, Brian."

"Listen, Manny, you know me. I would never steer you wrong, and what I'm saying is that the tracks I've heard are genius, but they won't sell. It won't sell, and last year wasn't exactly the best year for you. The label has to shelve it. They've got to stop the bleeding. It won't sell."

Alan sighs heavily.

"You've got to mind the business!" Brian says emphatically. "You've got a lot of overhead. A lot of people depending on you."

"It's my publishing company," Alan snaps. "My production company. Every fucking cent paid comes out of my pocket one way or another. No one is going to tell me what to produce, what to record. I own me."

"No one is saying you don't, but you need a strong dose of reality," says Brian. "The only reason you still have a career is that you're brilliant and you are a genius at self-promotion. But you've pushed it to the limit. You've got to behave for a while. And what I'm telling you is you can't afford to piss off the fans, another year without any cash coming in, and for the critics to vomit up your next album. I'm asking you not to fuck it up again."

"The tracks will be finished next week," Alan says heavily, "and then I'm done. Do you hear me, Brian? I quit."

Silence, dead silence through the phone and all around me. Quitting? Is he really quitting? Is he walking out on his career?

I stare up at him, my eyes round, unable to process any of this.

"You don't mean that, Manny. It's just post recovery emotionalism. I've seen this a hundred times," Brian says sagely.

Alan clicks off the phone.

"Well, I think that went well," Rene says, breaking the tense silence.

I look cautiously up at Alan. "Are you OK?"

He gives me a tired smile. "I wish I was back on the beach with you, Chrissie."

I blush, not knowing what to make of that. He looks different, so strange, and it never occurred to me he would look different, strange, back in his life.

We are at Jack's New York apartment and I wonder how Alan knew where to take us. The car stops and Alan lowers the privacy glass.

"Stay with her all the way to her door," he says to the driver.

"Sure, Manny."

Rene rolls forward in her seat. "Well, it's been real, Manny." She looks at me, and then she climbs from the car.

Now that we're alone, I feel a strange nervousness claim me. I feel the pressure to say something. Anything. "It's going to be all right. You do know that, don't you?"

Alan laughs. "I'd walk you in, but it's better I don't."

The driver has the luggage and is waiting. I stare at Alan, not knowing what to do. Shaking hands goodbye seems stupid. But should I kiss him? And where should I kiss him? A fast peck on the check? The lips? The thought that I probably won't ever see him again enters my mind. I am prospectively depressed.

"Thank you for the lift," I murmur, as I climb out of the car. I lean back in and laugh. "That sounds really lame considering you gave me a lift in a private plane."

"I'd walk you up, but I can't. It's better for you that I don't."

Well, he certainly didn't put anything in that statement to make me hope I'd see him again. I smile. "See ya, Mr. Whoever You Are."

Alan laughs. "See ya. Good luck at your audition, Chrissie."

"My audition." I laugh. I'd forgotten why I came to New York.

I step back from the car and close the door. The doorman pulls open the door for me and I follow Rene into the elevator. I struggle to keep my expression blank as we go floor by floor to the penthouse.

A blast of music pulls me from my thoughts and I notice that the elevator doors are open. Rene is in the apartment, has switched on the sound system and *Blondie* is blasting. Deborah Harry's voice bounces off the wood floors and high ceilings as Rene dances around in the center of the room singing *One way Or Another.*

The driver sets our bags in the foyer.

"Thank you for seeing us to the door."

"You take care, Miss Parker."

I frown. How does the driver know who I am?

He smiles. "You look just like Jack. I thought for sure those assholes in the press would notice and be on his story. They'd know where he's been."

Was that why Alan was afraid they'd see me? They'd be on his story; his months in California, whatever had gone on there with Jack. I realize with a start that I don't even know what that was all about. How Jack was involved. Why Jack brought him home. And I don't know completely what happened to Alan last year.

The driver is watching me. I smile. "I'm sorry, I didn't get your name."

"Colin, Miss Parker."

"Well, Colin, thank you for everything. Take care of him, OK?"

Colin smiles. I shut the door. Rene instantly darts across the room to bounce on her knees on the sofa.

Rene raises her eyebrows. "We should call him. He can get us into all the best parties."

"God, Rene, we just left him. Besides I don't know how to call him."

Rene frowns, then grabs the phone. Who is she calling? I panic and then realize it's the doorman.

"This is Miss Parker. Could you please arrange for a car to pick us up at eleven and that we are on the list tonight at wherever is currently considered the hottest night spot in Manhattan."

Rene smiles. She listens. She nods. "Thank you very much." She hangs up and bursts into laughter. "God, Chrissie, I'd love to be you for just one day."

"I am not going out tonight. I am not partying until after my audition Monday."

"Oh, yes we are, Chrissie. We are alone. It's Saturday night. We are in Manhattan. We are going out."

Chapter Five

Rene sloshes her Cosmopolitan all over my bedroom rug as she finishes the last touches of makeup on me. I'm not sure about wearing her black halter mini dress. I feel like an overdressed Barbie, but Rene is happy so I don't put up a fight.

Rene hands me a tiny silk wallet.

"What's this?"

"It's a bra purse. Mom makes me carry one every time we're out of The States. Put your ID and cash in there so we don't lose it."

I do as instructed and frown. "Do I just take it out right in front of people when I need something?"

Rene laughs. "Yes, Chrissie. It's no big deal. It's not like anyone is going to see anything."

She picks up my drink and hands it to me. "Pound it, Chrissie. You need to loosen up. I want to have fun tonight. I sure as hell don't want to sit around here all night watching you look at the phone every ten seconds waiting for Alan Manzone to call. Face it, Chrissie, he isn't going to call. He's not interested in you. Jeez, he's not even interested in me." She makes a face. "Maybe he's gay."

The intercom buzzes and Rene jumps to her feet. "I have a friend."

I roll my eyes. It's just the doorman informing us that the car is here, but Rene is in a festive mood and is going to be a wild handful to keep up with tonight.

Grabbing my hand, Rene pulls me at a running pace into the elevator and then collapses against the mirrored walls as we chug slowly to the lobby.

Our driver is waiting with Elliot the doorman.

"Miss Parker, this is David. He'll be your driver while in New York."

David gives me a carefully trained smile from an emotionless face.

"It's a pleasure to meet you," I say.

"Miss Parker." He nods.

Somehow David gets to the car before us and is waiting patiently with a door open to the backseat. I turn to stare out the window at the passing lights, as Rene flicks on the sound system, flipping through songs before settling on Paula Abdul.

She rummages through the compartments until she finds the mini-fridge. "Look. A bar."

She pulls out a bottle of champagne, pops the cork, and then lets it fizz all over the carpet before taking a swig from the bottle.

"We're going to have fun tonight, Chrissie," she orders, pushing the bottle on me. "Drink."

I take only a small sip because, for some reason, I hardly touched my dinner and I know this is not a good idea on top of the Cosmos we had in the bedroom.

Rene gives me *the look* and tilts the bottle upward until my mouth is full and I have to take a large swallow.

"We're celebrating our freedom. Just think, in another month no more boarding school...,"she makes a face, "...no more rules. No more Eliza. Freedom, utter and complete freedom."

Trying to match Rene's high spirits, I do a little tip with the bottle. "To our new lives."

Rene beams. "Hopefully, it starts tonight. Face it, Chrissie. Our life in Santa Barbara is so pathetic."

"Which club are we going to?"

Rene shrugs, taking the bottle, and laughs. "I haven't a clue." She rolls down the privacy partition. "David? Where are you taking us?"

David's eyes shift and I can see them in the rearview mirror. "I was told to take you to The Blue Light, Miss."

Rene makes a face at me. "The Blue Light?" she whispers. "Have you ever heard of that club, Chrissie?"

I shake my head.

"It's new, Miss. Very popular. I'm sure you'll have an enjoyable evening," David says, somehow hearing Rene.

Rene chokes on a laugh and eagerly rolls up the partition. "I'm sure we'll have an enjoyable evening," she says with a heavy male voice impression.

I laugh.

Rene takes another long pull on the bottle. "God, David's cute. Like a blond Nordic God. We're going to have to take the car every chance we get."

"Is there anyone you don't enjoy messing with?"

"Nope, pretty much not."

We're suddenly laughing our heads off and we've killed the bottle of champagne by the time the car rolls to a stop. It's impossible to go out with Rene and not have fun. She's got such an *I don't give a crap what anyone thinks,* self-confident manner.

"Are you ready to party?" Rene bellows. The door opens and David offers her his hand. She has a sweetly docile, ladylike smile on her face. I curl over in the seat laughing.

"Elliot assures me you are on the list, Miss," David says formally as he assists Rene from the car.

"Thank you, very much," Rene says slightly aloof, slightly stuffy.

Behind David's back she makes a face at me as I'm assisted from the car. I bite my lip not to laugh.

This must be a popular club. The sidewalk is packed and the line well down the street, and there are plenty of tabloid photographers here. There is a little bit of everything that is New York crowding the concrete waiting to get in: the always hot; the always not; the always freaky; and the artsy.

"I'll be waiting across the street, Miss Parker. When you are ready to leave, don't come to me. I will come to you, Miss."

"Yes, David," I say obediently. *So much for no rules.*

Rene loops her arm through mine as we stroll to the door. "God, Chrissie, you mystify me. I don't know why you don't love your life. If I were you I'd be out having mad fun 24/7. It's like having nothing but E-tickets in the pack. There isn't any place you can't get into. Except perhaps the White House with a Republican President."

I roll my eyes. "Why do you always have to exaggerate? My life isn't like that and you know it."

"It could be like that."

Rene gives my name to security at the door, the bouncer checks the list and we are immediately allowed to enter. Rene makes a face. "E-ticket. I hate it when you downplay thinking I'm jealous that you have the famous dad. It's so annoying, Chrissie."

"It's no big deal," I say fiercely. "I hate that you make such a big deal of it."

"Then let's own it for one night and have some fun, Chrissie. Let's get into some crazy-ass trouble. Let's show Eliza how the real hot girls roll."

She does a loud *whoop!* holding up her arms and makes a sassy swish with her hips. Instead of coming off looking dorky, it draws every set of male eyes to Rene. But that's Rene, everything always works for her.

The three-story club is hot and packed and earsplitting with the sounds of a live band. The walls are black and all the furnishings covered in blue velvet. There are strobe lights and floor steam and two levels for dancing, and Rene drags me behind her as she fights our way through the crush of bodies.

"God, Chrissie, this place is so incredible. Why don't we have something like this in Santa Barbara? Peppers looks so small town lame by comparison."

We finally find two free spots on a sofa near the downstairs dance floor and she plops down with a heavy drop. "We should have gone to the clubs in LA more. We didn't take full advantage of our partying opportunities."

Right now, I'm glad we didn't. I'm feeling a little fuzzy, the champagne from the car finally hit me, and we're just starting our night.

Before our first drink round arrives, Rene has already got a small court of preppy young college guys surrounding our sofa-level table. She does know how to kickstart a party. The college guys from NYU are really only interested in Rene, but by the third round of drinks I'm exhausted from laughing and dancing, and we are crowded around our table playing quarters, since the band is on break and the giant video monitors are blasting.

Rene bounces a quarter, making it into the glass, and she forces a shot on me. She holds the tequila shooter in my face. "Pound it, Chrissie."

I pound it and Rene laughs, but her latest male conquest gives me a sympathetic smile. I can tell he can tell I'm pretty messed up at this point by the way I laugh, how wobbly I am just sitting, and the flush spreading on my cheeks. Rene has forced on me every shooter round she's won, but the guys stopped picking on me three shots ago.

"I think we should take a break from the drinking." Jimmy Stallworth motions for the waitress to bring me a glass of water. "Do you always let your friend get you so messed up?"

I shake my head weakly. "Never. I don't know why she is being so rotten to me tonight. She never forces me to take every shooter."

Rene waves off his concern. "Oh, don't worry about, Chrissie. She's a lightweight, but she never passes out."

I turn my head to find Victor staring at me strangely. "Do you need to go outside for some air?" he asks.

I smile weakly at him, but Rene grabs my arm. "No, no, no! You're not taking her anywhere."

When the water comes, Jimmy Stallworth forces it into my hand and orders me to drink. I'm halfway through the glass when the video on the monitor changes. The moving lights cast strange colors and shadows all around me, I'm in a totally groggy frame of mind, but not too groggy to recognize the gorgeous guy one story tall on the monitor…or is my mind playing tricks on me? Is that what happens after too much alcohol? You just start imagining you see a guy everywhere.

"Is he everywhere?" I try to focus my blurry vision on Jimmy Stallworth. "It's strange…two days ago nothing, and now I see him everywhere. Is he really on the monitor or am I imaging it?"

Rene shakes her head. "You're all right, Chrissie. He's really on the monitor."

I breathe a heavy sigh of relief. "I'm already seeing double. It would be really bad if I were seeing things not there."

Jimmy Stallworth sighs heavily and pushes the glass back up to my lips. "OK, no more drinks for you, and lets have some more water. Do you have a way home? I can get them to call a cab for you. I think you should take your friend home before she passes out. She's really fucked up, Rene."

Rene points to the monitor. "No, she's not wasted. She's talking about the video. We know him."

Victor leans across me to speak to Rene. "You know Alan Manzone?"

Rene shrugs. "We flew to New York with him."

"Bullshit," says Jimmy Stallworth. "California girls are always full of such shit."

I shake my head. "No, we know him."

"Then who is that sitting over there giving Rene the serious *fuck me* stare?"

I turn my head in the direction Jimmy indicates, but I'm seeing double, so this just isn't going to work.

"What? Are we in eighth grade or something?" Rene snaps. She looks. She frowns. "That's Kenny Jones, Blackpoll's drummer."

"Well, if you know Manzone you must know Kenny Jones."

Rene shrugs and springs to her feet.

I just want to sit and Rene is trying to pull me to my feet. I stare up at her. "Are we going home?"

"Come on, Chrissie."

I lean into her and my thoughts fade in and out of my brain and the floor feels like it's coming up to meet me. I am suddenly too hot and I am really glad that Rene is always here for me.

* * *

It hurts just to try to open my eyes. It's not possible to feel as badly as I feel. The light in the room is muted, it must be morning, and I am in bed and every muscle in my body aches.

I struggle to roll onto my side. The spot beside me is empty, but the blankets are pushed down. Rene's everything bag is lying beside me. At least I did manage to bring Rene home with me. On the bedside table there is a glass of orange juice and two Tylenol.

My befuddled brain struggles through fractured snapshots of the night before. I remember going into the club. The drinks. The NYU preppies all hot in their boxers for Rene. The drinking games, but then only bits and pieces. I don't remember how we got home. I'm still wearing my black halter dress and panties, but I don't have my bra on. I find it lying on the floor beside the bed.

I sit up and take the Tylenol and drink the juice. I fall back into the pillows and tug the blankets tightly around my aching flesh.

Rene runs into the bedroom. She is ecstatic. She drops on the bed with a bounce that makes my head swim. "Finally! You're awake. You are not going to believe this. You are never going to believe this."

I pull a pillow tightly over my head.

"I hope you don't feel as bad as you look. I should have stopped forcing shooters on you," Rene says matter-of-factly.

Ya think? And why is she waiving a newspaper?

She collapses beside me on the pillows. Just the motion of her body nearly makes me to throw up. She snaps open the paper.

"I'm on the front page of the *New York Post*, Chrissie."

"What?"

As miserable as I feel, that gets me into a sitting position. She is on the front page. It's a picture of her exiting the plane with Alan. I feel even more sick, but not from the alcohol. There are also pictures of her in the club last night. Did Rene really dance on a table? I don't remember any of this, and even the single photo that has me in it has that surreal feel of not being me because I don't remember any of this.

"Let me read the caption. 'Manzone, the edgy rock superstar lead singer of Blackpoll touches down at JFK with Rene Thompson, daughter of legendary civil rights attorney George Thompson…blah, blah, blah, the couple has no comment on the singer's unexplained six month absence.'"

Rene slaps the newspaper and grins. "The *New York Post*, Chrissie. Eliza is going to die."

I curl in a ball and hug the blankets more tightly around me. Things just seem to work out for Rene without her even trying. Front page of the *New York Post*. Eliza thinking we've taken Manhattan by storm. At the club last night, every man in the room after Rene.

"I have a terrible headache. I want to sleep," I whisper. I hear sounds from the kitchen and lift my aching head. "Rene? Is there someone else in the apartment?"

"Oh, that's just Jimmy Stallworth." Rene does a dismissive shake of her head and then her eyes settle on me and widen. "Oh shit, I knew you were wasted last night, but I didn't think you were so fucked up that you wouldn't remember."

I sit up, alarmed. "What?"

"How much do you remember?"

What's the last thing I remember? What's the last thing? I frown. "I don't know. We were playing some drinking games with some guys…Oh god, was one of them Jimmy Stallworth?"

Rene makes a face. "Yep." And then her eyes sharpen intensely. "Do you remember seeing Manny?"

I don't like how she asks me that. "Oh god. On the monitor?" I ask nervously.

Rene shakes her head.

My eyes round. "Alan was at the club last night?"

Rene nods. "Yep, with Nia," she says with heavy meaning.

Nia? Nia? The latest tall, brunette supermodel du jour. I saw Alan last night. Alan was with Nia. Why don't I remember any of this?

Rene's expression shifts into anger and disgust. "He was such a prick. Pretended he didn't even know us, which is probably good because you were pretty fucked up by the time he strolled in."

My face scrunches up. "I didn't do anything stupid last night, did I?"

"You mean other than getting totally shitfaced?"

"How did Jimmy Stallworth end up here?"

"Well, *that* I'm not surprised you don't remember. By the time we left the club you couldn't even walk, Chrissie. Jimmy had to practically carry you to the car. We put you in the car. David brought you home and put you to bed, and we went to a party and ended up here."

Now I'm alarmed and furious. "You left me and let David put me to bed? How could you do that, Rene?"

Rene shakes her head in aggravation. "Well, you were pretty much done for the night, Chrissie."

"I can't believe you did that."

Rene springs from the bed. "Don't blame me. You were the one who was the downer. I've got to go get rid of Jimmy. He's a total bore."

Rene slams the bedroom door behind her. Between the hangover, Alan, and the paper, I feel completely deflated. My emotions cascade over me in relentless waves, like the nausea that never quite makes me vomit.

According to Rene, Alan ignored me last night. I'm glad I don't remember, it would hurt even more than it already does if I remembered it with clarity. Why do I even care? He's a total asshole sometimes, like how he treats Rene, and last night pretending he doesn't know us. Maybe he's already forgotten about me.

God, I made a fool of myself and the only saving grace is that I don't remember.

I need to forget about Alan Manzone and focus on why I am in New York. I roll over in bed, agitated in my flesh. *You don't really want him, Chrissie. It's not like there could ever be a relationship. With a guy like Alan Manzone it would just be a fuck and a goodbye. Nothing more.*

I close my eyes and begin to drift. Yes, sleep will be good. Very, very good.

* * *

I jerk awake to the sound of the phone ringing. I open my eyes. Crap, its morning. I've slept an entire day away. And how is it possible I still feel lousy? What day is it?

I grab the phone. "Hello?"

"Hey baby girl, I wanted to wish you luck before your audition."

Crap, it's Jack! Crap, it's Monday! I haven't practiced once since arriving in New York. And I have an audition—I check the clock—in an hour.

"Thanks, Daddy."

I remember the *New York Post*. I tense wondering if Jack has seen it.

"So how is it going? You girls keeping busy in the Big Apple without the old man?"

I laugh at the comment "old man." I wonder if he's fishing and what he knows. I can't tell.

"Not too busy. I slept most of yesterday. Jet lag I think."

"Well, I don't want to hold you up. You are going to be magnificent, Chrissie."

He doesn't wait for my response. The phone clicks. I spring from the bed and dart into the kitchen. Rene is sitting at the table with a bowl of cereal.

"Why didn't you wake me?" I exclaim, grabbing a bowl and filling it with Corn Flakes.

"You were dead asleep. I thought it better to let you sleep."

"I have my audition in less than an hour."

Rene frowns. "Is that today?"

I stare and I know. "You went out last night, didn't you? You just left me here and went out."

I think she flushes, but I can't tell for certain.

"I just went to a party with Jimmy Stallworth. It wasn't your kind of scene, Chrissie. I thought it better not to wake you to ask if you wanted to go with us."

I grab a cup of coffee. "Well, don't do it again. I hate it when you ditch me."

My hands are shaking as I try to add cream to the coffee.

"Jeez, Chrissie, we're not in eighth grade. We don't have to do everything together. Next year we'll be at different schools. I've got to get used to not having you around."

I slam down the creamer. I really didn't want to think about that today and I hate that it all seems no big deal for Rene.

Rene sits back in her chair. "Chrissie, are you OK?"

I sink at the table and attack my bowl. "I'm just stressed. You know how I am when I have to perform."

"It's just an audition."

"It's Juilliard."

"So?"

So? So! How could Rene not get this? I hate how self-absorbed she is at times. "The committee will all know Jack. They will all know my mother. Every time I perform I am measured against them. And it's Juilliard, so I don't want to suck."

Rene takes my face in her hands. "No one measures you against them except you, Chrissie." She drops my cheeks and goes back to her cereal. "So stop worrying. You're in. The audition is just a formality."

I laugh in frustration. "God, I hate you at times."

Rene smiles. "I know. That's why we are friends. You better hurry and shower. You smell like booze."

I take a whiff of my arm. Is that what that hideous odor is? Booze seeping from my pores?

I dart into the bathroom and turn on the shower. The warm streams of water feel good. I wish I could just stand here all day. I quickly lather my body with Chanel No.5 body wash. As I wash my face, I remember Alan kissing me on the forehead, a kiss for luck. Such a bit of drama, and yet sweet. He said it wasn't what he intended. What did he intend? He said he wanted to meet me. Why? I still don't know why. And it's driving me crazy.

Stop thinking about Alan Manzone. You need to focus. You'll never see him again. I switch off the shower. I dust my skin with the matching Chanel powder wondering if I still carry the smell of booze on my skin.

Once I'm done brushing my teeth, I stare at my reflection in the mirror. Jeez, I look awful today and that's after twenty hours straight of sleep. Angry at myself, I twist my hair into a tight ponytail and then tuck it into a neat French twist. A little mascara. A touch of lip gloss. Nothing more.

I go back into the kitchen, cello case in hand. "I shouldn't be more than two hours. Don't take off, please. I want you here when I get back."

Rene nods. She crosses her heart. "I'll be right here waiting. You're not wearing that, are you?"

"Why?"

"Too California. Shouldn't you wear something black? Something elegant. Something New York?"

"I feel comfortable in this. I play better when I feel comfortable."

"Suit yourself." She puts the bowl in the sink. "Besides you are already in. It's just a formality."

Why does she do this? Why build me up then shake me down? Then tell me not to worry about it. Why?

"I have to run. Maybe we can go out for lunch when I get back."

"Sure, Chrissie. Whatever you want." She points. "You stay sweet."

I point back. "You stay cute."

"And don't fall on your ass. It's just Juilliard."

I drop the extra elevator key on the entry hall table. "I'm leaving the extra key, but don't go anywhere."

"Yes, Mother!" I hear from the kitchen before the elevator doors close.

I lean against the cool, polished walls, struggling to calm my breathing. I need to stop rushing. Rushing will only make me more nervous. I stare at my reflection in the doors, the distorted shape of my features caused by the reflecting metal and the strange glow from by the dim, orangey light of the elevator. I study my simple blue sundress and flip-flops. Rene is right. This is all wrong. I make a face at myself. *Welcome to Juilliard, Miss Parker.*

I dash out of the elevator and Elliot the doorman takes my cello case. "Do you want me to ring for a car, Miss Parker?"

Damn. A car. I should have arranged for a car yesterday. I always forget the entire world is not Santa Barbara. You don't get from one edge of town to the other in five minutes in New York.

"No, I'm running late. Just hail me a cab, please."

He gives me a dubious look. He steps out to the curb, holds out his hand and blows a whistle. He opens the door for me, and then puts my cello in the trunk.

The driver asks: "Where to?"

"Juilliard."

Reluctantly, I sink into the backseat. The interior of the cab smells. It's dirty. They say you've not had a true New York experience until you've taken a New York cab. I could do without this experience and the Turkish disco music blaring out of the speakers. I block out the sounds of the city and the car stereo blasting. I move my fingers along the neck of an imaginary cello. The last eight bars of the prelude I never do well. I need to play the notes through.

"Are you a musician?"

I open my eyes. What gave it away? The cello case or the imaginary cello I'm playing or that I'm going to Juilliard? God, that was a bitchy thought. Hangovers make people rotten.

I smile. "Hopefully someday. I have an audition at Juilliard."

That is it from my New York cabbie. So much for conversation. I stare out the window. Everything is so close and large and crowded. There is nothing around me familiar. Not a single thing here looks like anything at home. I fiddle nervously with the hem of my dress. Nothing familiar except for my dress.

I give it a harsh glare. What is the matter with me? I couldn't have advertised more that I don't belong here.

That makes me think of Mom and her stark black dresses and knee high boots, the stylish scarves and expensive Italian bags. Lena was always East Coast chic. Mom definitely belonged in Manhattan. She always looked a touch like a fish out of water in Santa Barbara. Or was it the melancholy of her career ending prematurely, was it her illness and the process of dying?

I wish Mom were here with me today. I look up. The cab has stopped. The driver is getting my cello from the trunk. The door is opened and I stare out at the sidewalk.

The driver points. "Juilliard."

Yep, I recognize those fountains in the courtyard leading up to the doors.

"Forty-seven dollars."

How could it be? We only went a few blocks. I look at the meter and the bright red lights do say forty-seven dollars. I rummage through my purse, pay the cabbie. I don't know if I've tipped him well or tipped him badly. He doesn't look as if I've done either. He looks irritated that I am getting too slowly from the cab.

I rush through the fast-moving lanes of people, ignoring the stylishly dressed New Yorkers swirling around me. Inside the building I ask where the auditions are, then flush, because there is a giant sign directing me only few feet away. Everything is just so big, busy and crowded here.

Outside of the audition room, there is a long bench, crowded with waiting applicants. I settle on the edge. Twenty minutes pass before someone comes into the hallway.

A confident, urbane voice inquires, "Are you Christian Parker?"

I nod, feeling instantly lame that, for some reason, I'm cowering on the stark waiting bench. The woman doesn't seem to notice my discomposure, offers her hand, introduces herself, but I am unable to catch her name through the buzz in my head.

The woman makes an almost impossible to see gesture with her hand, ordering me to follow, and walks briskly down the long hallway.

"I should have recognized you at once," she says, in a voice that is neither friendly nor revealing. "I knew your mother very well. Remarkable woman. Such a tragic loss. Is your dad here with you? I haven't seen Jack in ten years. You're the mirror image of him, though I imagine people tell you that all the time."

Breathe, Chrissie, breathe. Smile and pretend you're not on the edge of freaking out right here. Why does this woman have to play *This is Your Life* right before I have to perform?

"Go on in." She smiles. "Good luck."

And then she is off in a puff of perfume and a chorus of clicking heels. Steeling my nerves, I try to empty my mind, try to ignore the chide that it is a mistake to dare an audition at Juilliard. I pull back the heavy wood door and enter.

* * *

Jesus Christ! How long have we been sitting in silence? How long have they been staring at me?

The music director looks up over his clipboard. "I expected you, Miss Parker, to be better prepared. Your mother was the consummate professional."

OK, so the Bach came out a little rough. There is no need to bring my mother into this. I take a deep breath. *Smile, Chrissie. Smile.*

"Do you want me to play my original composition now?"

"That won't be necessary."

"I thought an original composition is required."

The music director stands. "It is. The second piece is unnecessary."

* * *

The elevator doors close behind me and I drop my cello case onto the tile. I find Rene lounging on the bed watching TV in my parents' bedroom.

Rene frowns. "Oh, Chrissie, what happened? It can't be that bad."

I sink down on the bed beside her. "It was so awful, Rene. I sat frozen, unable to play, and then when I finally did, each move was jerky and slow and just awful."

"It's all right, Chrissie. It's all right. It's only Juilliard and fuck them if they were rude to you. It's just a formality. You know you're in."

"But I'm glad I screwed up. I don't really want to get in."

"No?"

I shake my head. "No. I don't want Juilliard."

Rene smiles and throws her arms around me. She sits back. She puts on sunglasses. "Well, Chrissie, looks like University of California Berkeley."

She says it dramatically, like Tom Cruise at the end of *Risky Business*. I laugh.

"How long have you not wanted Juilliard? Why are we here?"

I struggle to answer her, but it's as much a mystery to me as to her. I came here on autopilot and something pushed me here, toward something I don't want.

"I don't know why I auditioned."

"You look better than when you left."

I feel better, sort of like a stay of execution. I would never have expected this failure to feel like such a relief.

"I'm glad you're in a better mood, Chrissie. I've got bad news. Dad wants me down in DC tomorrow. And he asked me to come alone. Something is up. I can't reach Mom."

I sit up. "You're leaving me all alone in New York?"

"I can't help it. I've never heard my dad like this. I'll be back next week."

"You don't think it's because of the papers?"

"No, Chrissie. Something is going on. I can feel it. Something he thinks is going to turn into a shitstorm between us, otherwise he wouldn't care if you were there."

I stare at Rene. I hope she is wrong for her sake. I don't really like Mr. Thompson. He's a narcissistic jerk.

"I don't like you going alone if there is going to be drama," I whisper.

"I'll be fine. I'm used to the shitstorms. I just feel badly about leaving you. Don't do anything I would do, not without me."

Rene explodes into laughter and I force a smile. She reaches over me to grab the joint I didn't notice before on the bedside table. She fires it up, takes a deep inhale before handing it to me.

I stare at the fiery tip. "Where did you get this?"

"Jimmy Stallworth. I snaked it from his apartment."

I take a hit. "What is it about rich, preppy guys always wanting to be called by their first and last name?"

"I don't know, Chrissie. What does it matter?"

The next morning Rene leaves on the 7 a.m. train to DC. The walls of the apartment close in around me and I am anxious in the quiet rooms, anxious and scattered. Now that I've blown my admission to Juilliard it truly feels like there is nothing ahead of me.

I should be reading since I've got about five books to finish before the end of break. It doesn't seem important now. My admission to UC Berkeley is not conditional, unlike Juilliard, which required an audition. I am in. It is where I'm going. Is that good or is that bad? I don't know.

I go into my parents' bedroom and curl on the bed, clicking on the TV to flip through channels. There is nothing to watch. Midday TV sucks. I hug the pillow and try to focus on a game show.

I'm trapped in a void. Not a woman. Not a girl. Going somewhere. Going nowhere. Wanting too much. Wanting nothing. Having everything I want. Having nothing I need. I am completely alone in my life, thinking of a raspy voice whispering *Chrissie* while I fade into sleep.

Chapter Six

I jerk awake, pushing the hair from my face. There is a voice in the room. Low. Raspy. Just enough rough that it brings my senses alive. It's Alan on TV. An afternoon talk show program. Why is he suddenly impossible to escape? I fight not to focus on the interview and find myself doing exactly that. God, he looks different. So different. Harsh. Angry. And I hate the way he's dressed. Leather pants and open shirt. *Definitely, not your type, Chrissie. Not your type at all!*

The phone rings and I fumble for the receiver, my eyes still glued on the TV.

"Chrissie, I'm not interrupting something, am I?" Rene asks, sounding a little miffed.

For a moment, I hesitate. "No, just catching up on my reading. What's happening in DC?"

"Total shitstorm. Dad was right about that. He's bought a house in Georgetown. He is marrying fembot number thirty-seven. It seems Daddy Dearest is about to have a new family. And I can't reach Mom. Apparently Mom went off the deep end. She's probably halfway into a bottle of Cristal consoling herself at Elizabeth Arden. Total shitstorm, Chrissie."

Rene has my full attention now. I mute the TV. It's impossible to concentrate with Alan's sexy voice in the background. "Do you want me to come down to DC?"

"No, it's no big deal, other than Mom and fembot thirty-seven. Really, what did Mother expect? They've been divorced eight years. Dad remarrying was bound to happen eventually."

"I can be in DC by dinner time," I offer.

"Don't bother. I'm OK. Really I am." A pause. "Here's the bad part, Chrissie. The wedding isn't until next week. Thirty-seven wants me to be her maid of honor or some such nonsense. I am going to be trapped here until a week from Sunday."

I freeze. She is leaving me in New York for two more weeks alone. "But we are only here for three weeks. I don't know anyone in Manhattan."

Silence. It is heavy this time. I wonder if Rene's "I'm good rolling with everything" attitude is just a front. I wonder if this is hitting her hard. Is that what I feel through the silence of the phone?

"Do you want to hear something funny?" she asks.

"Sure, Rene."

"Dad saw the picture in the *Post*. Do you know what his only comment was?"

I can't imagine what insensitive, stupid thing Mr. Thompson would say.

"What did he say?"

A harsh laugh. "I should get the number for Manny's press people for him. He's been trying to get legendary civil rights attorney in print forever. Apparently, the headline is very good for business."

Poor Rene. Poor, poor Rene.

"One of these days you should just tell your dad to go screw himself."

"I should have told him that before number thirty-seven. Go get into some trouble for me, will you? I won't have any fun at the wedding. Thirty-seven is forcing me to wear fuchsia. I look terrible in fuchsia."

* * *

124

At 9 p.m. I'm sitting on the couch where I pretty much haven't moved from all day, wearing a pair of old, fuzzy flannel PJ bottoms, my dad's Harvard sweatshirt, and picking Chinese food out of cartons while trying to focus on an HBO movie I've already seen a dozen times.

Maybe I should just fly home. But what would I do in Santa Barbara without Rene? Anyone who is anyone is in Palm Springs. I stab my Chicken Chow Mein.

The phone rings. It's got to be about the tenth time Rene has called today. She is worrying me. Rene is not needy. The blow-by-blow updates from Mr. Thompson's wedding preparations are only an excuse to call.

"How are things with you, Chrissie?"

Oh crap! Jack! In the chaos of everything going on I forgot to call him after my audition.

"I'm great. How are you? Still trapped in your thing?"

Jack laughs.

"I was expecting you to call yesterday. I waited. I didn't want to crowd you. But I got tired of waiting. Liz called. What happened?"

Liz? Who is Liz? Probably that dreadful woman who led me down the hall at Juilliard, the one who made sure I got a healthy dose of *This is Your Life* before my audition.

"Just an off day."

Silence. "It happens. We all have bad performances, Chrissie. You've just got to blow them off."

I laugh. "Well, they didn't boo me. They politely excused me before my second piece."

"It happens. So now what, baby girl?"

Now what? Crap, I must have really blown Juilliard if Juilliard informed Jack before they informed me, and it's real now and it feels really *oh shit!*

"I think I'll go to *Cal* with Rene."

"Oh well, we can't have everything, baby girl. I'll check on you later this week. Don't let your audition get you down. It happens."

I stare at the receiver for a long time before I hang it up. *It happens*. I wanted something from Jack, I don't know what, but not that. Not *It happens*. I mean, this is a pretty big screw up. It deserves some parental response: anger, sympathy, something. Not *It happens*.

I blew Juilliard. That brief uplift of spirit I felt knowing I was off to Cal with Rene is completely gone.

I shut off the TV and go to the sound system. I unwind from the heads the *Blondie* tape and loop another tape into place. I switch it on and crank up the volume. My brother's voice fills the room. God, Sammy was incredible.

I feel tears start to push out and I start to sing as I wander out onto the terrace. An entire city of lights. Eight million people and I am totally alone.

"There's no mercy in death. Death doesn't feel that way," I sing at the top of my voice.

The city swallows my voice. I stare down at the tiny, miniature world below the terrace and exhale a ragged breath. I've been missing Sammy so much lately, more than usual. Why?

The phone rings and I run for it in grateful eagerness. It's probably only Rene with more wedding updates. I gave up my fantasies yesterday —well sort of—of Alan calling, and since the night is totally not promising, I say hello into the receiver in an even less promising way.

"Where's Rene?" says a familiar voice in a harshly imperative way.

I tense and settle on my knees on the couch. "Well, hello to you too, Jimmy Stallworth. She's in DC visiting her dad."

"Listen, I'm not pissed at you."

I roll my eyes. "That's good to know since I really don't care what you think about anything."

"I could call the cops, you know."

I tense. Oh crap, what has Rene done now? "Then why don't you? Why waste my time with this?" I say with a calmness I don't feel.

A long pause. "Listen, I don't want any trouble here. I just want either my weed or my money."

I bite my lip, remembering the joint I shared with Rene in the bedroom. "What? Are you kidding?"

"She copped my weed from my apartment, so no I'm fucking serious here!"

"Call the cops, Jimmy," I say, fiercely defensive. "Let's see how far that gets you. I'd really like to see you do it."

"Well, you don't have to be a bitch about it. I just want to know where Rene is and to get my money. Listen, there are guys I've got to pay."

"Not my problem."

"If I tell them about Rene it is your problem."

Oh shit!

"I just want my stash back or the money. Get it? No reason to make a big scene out of it. I like Rene, but this isn't cool. I don't have the cash to cover the weed she took, so you've got to help me here."

I feel sort of sorry for Jimmy Stallworth. Still, I say, "Your weed isn't my problem. I don't know who stole your weed, but someone lifted some cash from my apartment. When are you going to give me back *my* money?"

I don't know how I manage to pull off this ruse with such a believable, accusatory tone, since I know Rene did snake the weed and lift my cash. I also know that my cash will mysteriously reappear without me ever saying anything because it's only a temporary lapse for her to steal from me. Jimmy Stallworth is pretty much out of luck where his weed is concerned.

"We were talking about my weed," Jimmy reminds in heavy frustration.

"And I was talking about my cash."

"Are you accusing me of stealing?" Jimmy yells heatedly. "You fucking rich girls never give a shit about who you shit on. It's your fucked up friend who light fingers everything she sees. Don't think I didn't see her lift the glasses at the club."

"Sorry. I can't help you."

"When will Rene be back? Listen, I'm in a tough spot here."

"I don't know when she'll be back."

"Shit."

Silence. I wait for Jimmy Stallworth to slam down the phone. But nothing. Silence. Frowning, I listen to him breathe into the receiver.

"So what are you doing tonight?"

I stare at the receiver, mystified. "Talking to you. Then forgetting about you. Then going to sleep."

"Listen, I'm not pissed at you. I'm just in a tough spot here." More silence. "I'm heading down to CBGBs with Richard and Victor. You remember them from The Blue Light, don't you?"

Why is he telling me this? "I remember."

"Hit us up there if you want to."

OK, that was a strange turn in the conversation and my internal turn was even stranger. Why am I considering it? Rene would be pissed if I took off with Jimmy Stallworth without her, and he did just threaten me and accuse Rene of stealing.

"I really like Rene," he breathes into the phone.

I roll my eyes. Not this again. What is it about Rene that she can totally shit on a guy and still have them on the hook?

Jimmy lets out a ragged sigh. "It was there and then not, and she was the only person in my room. Fuck, I don't know what to think now. You should meet up with us if you want to."

It is truly amazing how desperate having no one to hang with can make you. Am I really considering going to CBGBs to try to console Jimmy Stallworth over Rene? *Crud...*

"What time do you guys think you'll hit the door?" I ask.

"Richard and Victor are already in line. I just took off to call Rene. I really like her. Why does she have to be such a bitch?"

I hang up the phone without committing to anything. I start to compile in my head a list of things that would be smarter to do than going to CBGBs with Jimmy Stallworth. I'm up to ten and I sit on the floor in front of Rene's clothes to see what she left to lighten her suitcase for DC. I settle on a backless, black, glittery halter top and Italian leather spike heel shoes.

In the car to CBGBs I stop questioning myself about why I decided to go. As pathetic as it is, I don't want to be alone in the apartment; I don't have anyone to call; I don't have anywhere to go; and I don't have anyone to be with.

It's nearly midnight and it's packed even on a Tuesday night. There is a long line down the street waiting to get in, and I scan the crowd trying to see if I can see Jimmy and his friends.

My car pulls over at the front door on Bowery, and David springs out and around the car to open my door.

"Are you meeting someone inside, Miss Parker? I can give their name at the door."

I shake my head. I spot Jimmy Stallworth about thirty bodies deep in the line. "It's OK, David. I see my friends."

My blond Nordic protector doesn't look at all confident about leaving me here. He steps back. "I'll be waiting there, Miss Parker." He points at a spot across the street as if I need a visual aid. "I'll pull up to the door when I see you. Don't come to me."

To keep my hands warm, I shove them deeply into the pockets of Jack's scarred leather bomber jacket as Victor calls out to me, though I make a point of not smiling, and fix my eyes on Jimmy.

He's leaning casually against the concrete wall, smoking, and I can see why Rene is attracted to him even though he's a total loser. His smile of perfect white teeth accentuates a face that's a little James Dean edgy and lost. Dark haired, dark eyed. I suppose there are some girls who'd find the black t-shirt, jeans and biker boots tough-guy look appealing, even if the slogan on his shirt does say *Fuck the Free World*.

Richard and Victor, on the other hand, I am certain are complete dorks. That crappy clothes, *I don't care about trends* sort of grunge thing only works if you've had a hard life or are interesting. But these are uptown NYU boys, posers for the evening, wanting to keep up with Jimmy Stallworth, and have neither a hard life nor are interesting. Total dorks. I didn't see that at The Blue Light, but then again I was pretty drunk.

Jimmy takes a long drag of his cigarette and watches me over the plume of smoke. "You showed up. I wasn't expecting you to."

I shrug. "Why are you waiting in line? It's freezing out here."

"It's packed. Supposed to be on the list, but someone screwed up," Victor informs me.

Jimmy looks me over carefully piece by piece. "You get us into the club tonight, I'll call it even on the weed Rene stole."

Oh shit... "What?"

Victor shrugs. "How did you get into The Blue light? You know, they don't just let anyone in. You have to be on the list or you stand in a fucking line going nowhere."

How could I have been so stupid as to come here? "The only reason you asked me down here was to get you into the club," I hurl in disbelief.

Jimmy shrugs. "I've got someone in there I've got to see. Tonight. I've got to make some cash to make up for Rene fucking me over. You owe me."

"I don't owe you anything."

I turn to walk back to the door so that David can spot me and bring the car around.

Jimmy catches up to me, grabbing my arm, and I don't quite know what to make of his facial expression. "Listen, I could use your help. It's nothing to you. It's everything to me. I'm just asking you to get me into the club, then we'll call it even and I'll be on my way."

I stare at him. Damn Rene and her messes. And damn Jimmy Stallworth.

"I'll forgive everything she owes me," he adds. "The weed. The six large for the coke and the pills."

Jeez, in under a week Rene ran up quite a tab in New York. I would have paid off Jimmy Stallworth right then and there, and told him never to come around Rene again, if Rene hadn't stolen my cash. I exhale a harsh breath. "Everything?"

"Everything."

"And you'll stay away while we're in New York. I mean, you won't sell to her ever again."

Jimmy stares at me, insultingly amused. "Your friend does a lot of drugs. Getting rid of me won't help her, and I don't think it's necessary to point out again that she stole from me. But you can consider me gone after tonight if you do me this solid."

I work my way past the line of agitated, waiting New Yorkers, face averted downward, with Jimmy Stallworth following. I'm hardly able to believe I'm about to crash the door at a New York rocker club so a New York drug dealer can finish a deal, all because Rene ripped off the wrong guy and I was desperate enough to come here.

"Wait here or I won't do it," I tell Jimmy a few feet from the door.

"Don't even think to try to ditch me out here," Jimmy warns.

I roll my eyes. The tough guy routine is really getting old. He may be a thug, but I don't think he's dangerous, and David my blond Nordic driver could kick the shit out of him without breaking a sweat if I called for him.

There is a pretty brunette in a sequined mini dress haranguing the bouncer with the list, and there's altogether too much jostling near the entrance. Pushing through the crowd is an effort, getting the bouncer's attention more effort, and the way he looks at me not worth the effort of acknowledging.

"Talk to me," is all he says.

"I'm on the list."

"Name," he snaps.

I bite my lower lip and curse Rene in my mind. "I'm not on that list. I'm on the other list."

Burly man looks up from the clipboard as if he wants to punch someone. "There is no other list."

"Parker," I whisper. "My dad is Jackson Parker."

Oh crap, I don't think this is going to work. As I turn away, a hand harshly grabs my arm and the bouncer gives me a hard stare. He jerks me behind him and I call out for Jimmy

Stallworth, as the crowd in front of the door pushes me through it.

The walls and floors vibrate from the music of an edgy alternative rock song, and I feel like I'm suffocating in the packed, dimly lit room, trapped against the far wall beside Jimmy Stallworth and breathing in heavy waves of secondhand smoke.

Jimmy gives me a curious stare. "OK, what just happened?"

I shake my head. "I got you in. That's what you wanted. Now leave me alone."

He's combing my face intently. "You're not some Congressman's daughter or something like that?"

I ignore the question and try to push through the bodies. A fat person in leather barges into me and knocks me into the wall, and Jimmy Stallworth pushes the fat guy away to give me room to walk.

We stand against the wall not talking. The band breaks, runs off stage, and the bodies in front of us become less compressed.

"I'm going to find a table," I say.

"Good luck with that," counters Jimmy sarcastically, lighting another cigarette. "Do you want to dance?"

Did Jimmy Stallworth really just ask me if I wanted to dance? I roll my eyes. "There's no band on stage."

"Later. When the next band is up."

"I thought you had to meet someone here?"

"Later."

"What about Victor and Richard? You should probably figure out how to get your friends in."

Jimmy crushes out his cigarette on the floor. "Fuck them. Rich college punks. They're the ones who screwed up getting me on the list."

I start to walk away.

"Where are you going?" Jimmy scolds me. "I expect you to come back."

You do, do you? "I'm going to the ladies' room. Don't follow."

Of course, there's a line, but at least in the quiet and cool corridor I'm away from Jimmy Stallworth. I hate that I'm waiting alone. No respectable girl goes to the bathroom alone, and I hate that I can't seem to shake Jimmy or form a better plan about how I should pass the rest of my evening.

I lean against the wall, staring at the line that seems never to move. I give up. I didn't really have to pee, but the time was well spent because Jimmy Stallworth is no longer lounging against the wall where I left him. *Free at last. Fuck the world of Jimmy Stallworth!*

Over the noise of too many voices starts another deafening assault of music that turns the crowd totally haywire, into a churning, bouncing swarm that I can't completely avoid even flattened against the wall. Trying to stay out of their way, I slowly inch to the door. A stocky punked-out Italian stops me.

"Miss Parker? Who the hell left you standing in the doorway?"

I am face to face with a man who has more than his share of tattoos and piercings and an authoritative air about him. He takes my arm and eases me away from the cold concrete.

"I'm Kevin, the manager. Anything you need, anything at all, you ask me. Jack and I go way back. How is Jack? I haven't seen your Pop in over a year..."

I go from being completely ignored in the club, to getting a healthy share of stares as I am directed to a table roped off with a reserved sign. *How Rene would love this!* I sink into the chair held for me, frantically scanning the crowd, hoping that Jimmy Stallworth doesn't see me here.

I look up, realizing Kevin has already asked me twice if I'd like something to drink. "I'm sorry. That band is good. I've never heard them before." What was the vodka drink Rene ordered for us? "Bring me a Kamikaze."

Kevin crouches down at my table. He smiles. "That's Rip the Cord. That's Vince Carroll on the drums."

I sit back, stunned, and stare. "Vince? Vince Carroll?"

Vince; Sammy's best friend his entire life. I haven't seen Vince since Sammy's funeral. The drummer from Sammy's band. I fight to see through the crowd the musicians on stage. Shirtless, dripping with sweat, long wavy chestnut hair, yes that is Vince wielding the sticks.

Kevin's eyes soften with emotion. "That's Cory Jensen on bass. That's JR on lead guitar."

Oh god, it's all of them, all the members of Sammy's band except Sammy. New name, new lead singer, and still a band. I didn't know that they were still a group. Everyone from my brother's world just seemed to disappear after his death.

Jimmy Stallworth cuts across the floor, turns a chair backward against the table and sinks down.

"Good. You got a table," he says, rummaging into his pocket for another cigarette to light.

I frown. "What are you? A curse? Why don't you bother some other girl?"

He ignores me, orders a drink when the waitress arrives, and stares fixed at the stage. I sip my Kamikaze and watch Johnny Ramone arriving, telling me it's way past midnight. Jimmy Stallworth rises from my table. The relief I feel hoping that he's leaving is overpowering.

"You owe me a dance," Jimmy says staring down at me.

"I don't owe you anything."

He has me by the hand, dragging me to the floor before I can stop him. On the dance floor he returns to fixed-stare mode, and I realize it's the band he's dogging with his eyes. He tries to get us near the stage, but navigating the crowd is like trying to swim in the ocean; two strokes and then a wave pushing you back.

Jimmy leans into me. "Do that pretty girl thing where you dance up next to the stage."

Without warning, Jimmy creates a diversion, body slamming into people near us, so much so that security comes, leaving enough territory unclaimed that I rather easily sashay to the edge of the stage. Like the bad penny he is, Jimmy Stallworth somehow reappears, dancing in front of me.

He's dogging the band again with his eyes and I can't help but to wonder if Vince and the guys recognize me.

Jimmy stops dancing and grabs my hand. He pulls me back to the table. I stare at him. "What was that all about?" I ask.

"I needed to get someone's attention."

I make a face. "Since we've danced, can I assume our date is over?"

Jimmy laughs. "You can leave if you want to. I've still got business here."

"But it's my table."

"Not if you leave." And Jimmy turns away to order another drink.

"I could call security."

Jimmy shrugs. "But you won't. I'm carrying enough that they could bust us both for possession."

Jeez, how could I have forgotten that he was a drug dealer? I rise from my chair without paying. "You can take care of the tab. I should get something out of this."

I start to leave when a voice stops me. "Chrissie? Chrissie Parker?"

I'm surrounded by Vince and the band. And shit, Vince is telling Jimmy Stallworth more than any smart girl would want him to know about her. I grow agitated as the guys sink down at my table, flooding it with beer bottles, and nervously I listen as Vince talks about Sammy, telling Jimmy Stallworth things I usually prefer to keep private.

Vince smiles at me. "I never expected to see you here with Jimmy," he says. "How do you two know each other?"

"I don't know her," Jimmy replies quickly. "She cleared a debt by getting me into the club tonight."

It's a moot point, but I'm really pissed that Jimmy didn't specify that it wasn't my debt, but if Vince thought anything of that, it doesn't show on his face.

"About that thing…" Vince says to Jimmy.

Jimmy's dark eyes harden coldly. "That thing."

Vince rises. "It's all good. Why don't we step into my office? Clear everything up now. It's cool." Vince smiles at me. "Why don't you hang out with the guys until I get back? I don't want you wandering off tonight. What's that you're drinking? A Kamikaze?"

I nod, even though I have every intention of slipping away the second I can. I watch Jimmy Stallworth and Vince disappear.

The conversation resumes and there is an irritated heaviness within Vince's band that tells me they know about Jimmy Stallworth, and are not at all pleased with Vince's association with him. Studying my glass, I try to follow the fast moving conversation, but I feel that edgy feeling you get when something is nagging at your memory.

I look up to see one of the guys watching and waiting expectantly for some kind of answer. What was the question?

Oh, yes… "I'm just in New York just for a few days. No, Jack isn't here. I had an audition at Juilliard."

The conversation flows rapidly past me, and I stare at my glass, lost in my thoughts, feeling strange and not knowing why. I look up as Vince and Jimmy return. I can tell by Jimmy's satisfied smirk that he just got paid by Vince whatever he needed to make up from Rene's stealing. Vince's glassy eyes reveal that some things never change. I feel a knot strangling my throat and try to escape the vividly rising pictures in my mind of Sammy and Vince in the old days. Only Sammy is dead and Vince is here, exactly the same.

Vince lifts my near empty glass from the table and sets a fresh drink before me. Their laughter and talking swirls around, not penetrating whatever this strangeness is that's overtaken me.

Vince points at me. "You've got to sing one song with us, Chrissie."

"No. I don't sing. I'm a cellist."

My words are slightly slurred. Did they notice? It's hard to tell. Vince looks the same, but Jimmy Stallworth is staring at me in a way I find worrisome. I sway in my chair and Jimmy darts out a hand to steady me.

Jimmy leans into me. "You OK?"

"I want to go home," I whisper, though why I implore Jimmy Stallworth for help makes no sense at all.

"She has the best set of female pipes I've ever heard and that was at eight," I hear Vince say. "Come on, Chrissie. One song."

"No, Vince. I really can't."

The action around me suddenly seems very fast, it moves in and out like a movie shock wave, and my befuddled brain registers that Vince has called Kevin the manager over.

Through my foggy senses I feel panic. "No, Vince. I can't. I really can't..."

"Sing one for Sammy tonight," Vince says, rising.

Sing one for Sammy, and I would because I loved Sammy and it would make him smile.

Vince has me by the hand, pulling me through the crowd. I'm staggering slightly and I don't remember answering him. Did I answer him? *Oh shit,* he's taking me on stage. Vince pulls off my jacket and the cool air touches my sweaty flesh.

I have to grab his arm to hold steady center stage. I don't know if it's my vodka-based fire drink or the welling panic inside me that is making it nearly impossible to stay balanced. It feels like I'm about to hyperventilate as he explains who I am. Jeez, now they know who I am, and I'm about to sing in front of Johnny Ramone and whoever that is from the Beastie Boys. And this is a New York crowd. A tough sell. I'll be lucky if they don't throw things and boo me tonight.

I shake my head and body to loosen up. The guys are waiting for a song. "Death by Degrees," I say into the microphone.

Sammy's one and only hit before he overdosed. It was the first song up on the tape in the apartment. I already sang it once to the city from our terrace. The words are fresh in my mind. Just pretend you're on the terrace, Chrissie, and be prepared to run for the door.

Stay on the beat, Chrissie. Listen. Listen. Hit the beat. I never perform. I never sing for anyone. But I just know how to do this. How to sing. How to move. How to use a stage and an audience. I always have.

Shit, one of my lockboxes has opened and I'm remembering things I don't want to. Sammy used to say music was in our blood. We had no choice—it was who we are. The only place he felt alive was center stage. He was going to die on stage. *But you didn't, Sammy, you died in your bedroom. And I'm the one who found you. Damn you, Sammy, I'm the one who found you!*

I lean against the mike stand, breathing heavily, fighting the emotion, relieved that it's done, and trying to figure out all the other stuff going on inside of me.

"One more, Chrissie. One more," says Vince from the drum stand.

I am shakier and whatever is inside me is running loose, even more wildly than before I left the table. I should never have sung Death by Degrees. Why did I pick that song?

Across the room by the entrance there is a stir, a sudden gathering of people. I wonder who has arrived. It must be someone. The entire chemistry of the club has changed. An electric current shoots up my flesh. Black eyes lock on me. Alan. And I can tell by how he is staring that he heard every part of that wretched performance.

Oh god, I want to die. That's all there is to it. I rush across the stage. I'm beginning to feel nauseated, but not from the alcohol, though the Kamikazes are making my head spin. It's seeing Alan with Nia, and knowing he just saw me make a fool of myself.

I hit the cooler air in the dirty, dark walkway leading from the club to the back alley and realize how messed up I am. I'm not seeing double, but I did let myself get pretty messed up. And to make matters worse, I am cowering in a back alley, afraid to go back into the club because I just made a fool of myself on stage in front of Alan Manzone, who couldn't care less, because he is with Nia, and I haven't a clue how to get from the alley to Bowery to find my blond Nordic driver.

Oh shit! Oh Shit! Oh Shit! I lean back into the chilled wall and want it to swallow me whole.

"Chrissie?" Vince has joined me. "You OK?"

I fan my burning checks with a hand. "I'm OK. Just feeling a little overwhelmed."

"I get that. I miss Sam too."

He steps closer, putting his arm around me. I look up at him. "Is there a way to get to Bowery from this alley? My car is out front and I don't want to go back into the club."

If he thought my request strange, it doesn't show in his expression. Instead, he looks very *no big deal* about the whole thing.

"I can get you through the club without taking you through the club."

"Thanks. I'm sorry to be such a pain."

"You're Sammy's sister. I wouldn't leave you hanging in an alley."

I smile weakly at him and relax into the comforting coolness of the wall. I won't look completely alone and pathetic if Alan should see me leave the club. Not that Alan would notice. Not that he'd care. I feel my emotions start to churn again.

"Chrissie, it's amazing that we just bumped into each other," Vince murmurs, and I look up to find his eyes regarding me intently. "I'm glad you're in New York." He steps closer, putting his arms on either side of me, and I now feel trapped against the supporting wall.

I fumble for words. "I won't be in New York. I've decided to stay in California."

"But you're here tonight," Vince says, and now I'm in his arms being pulled into him.

Panic. The feel of him sends me into instant panic. "Vince, please!" I try to squirm out of his hold. *He's going to kiss me and if he does I think I'm going to be sick.* I twist and he quiets me with his hands.

"You know I've always liked you, Chrissie."

That small child voice in my head screams: *No you didn't. You were always mean to me.* His hand is on the base of my spine moving me into him and his face is lowering. His mouth flattens against mine and the feeling is suffocating.

"Please stop, Vince," I plead, as his lips move to my jaw.

I slip my hands between us, up against his chest, but my arms are like putty and I can't force him off of me. His breath smells of beer and pot, his mouth is cruelly hard against me, and his hand is moving upward under my shirt.

"Miss Parker? You have a phone call," says a voice in the darkness. Vince jerks off of me and I see Kevin in the shadows.

"I do?"

I clumsily pull my clothes into place as my disjointed thoughts function enough to warn me to hold it together, Kevin is rescuing me. I take his outstretched hand and nearly stumble as I walk to keep pace with him.

A few more steps, Chrissie. A few more and then you'll be in the safety of your Blond Nordic Driver and it won't matter that Vince is following and you can't seem to shake him any better than you could shake Jimmy Stallworth.

Kevin stops at an open office door and reaches in, then shoves the receiver at me. I stare at the phone, my brain snapping. I couldn't possibly have a call here. My shaking hand holds the receiver against my head.

"Hello?"

If there is a person on the other end talking, I can't hear them. There is too much blaring noise and background music. "Hello? Is there anyone there?" I shout.

Quiet. It's almost as though whoever is on the other end stepped out of a noisy room. I can hear street sounds now.

"It's Mr. Whoever You Are. I thought I would see how you were doing," says a low, raspy voice.

Whoa. My head spins. Is Alan really calling me while on a date with Nia or am I so messed up I'm imagining things?

"Really. How remarkable. Where are you?"

"In front of the club."

My head buzzes and I lean tiredly against the wall. "How New York chic of you. Do you always slip out of clubs to escape your supermodel dates to call other girls in the club?"

Alan laughs. Vince is watching me like a hawk. I don't understand why Alan is calling me. I don't understand anything at present or why I feel like I'm about to faint.

"So, what are you doing on the street talking to me?" I ask my tongue heavy with my words.

"You disappeared so quickly from stage it seemed the logical next move. I heard about your audition, by the way. What happened?"

How does he know about my audition? Jack probably, and again I feel that strange sense of curious disbelief knowing that they talk about me.

"Your kiss didn't work. I could hardly play."

"That bad?"

"That bad. Didn't permit me my second piece. Excused me after one."

"Maybe they didn't need to hear more."

"Oh no," I counter, my words very breathy now, "that's Juilliard's version of booing you from the stage. They don't throw things at Juilliard. They just say *enough*."

"I should have kissed you better."

I think of his mouth on mine. "I hate New York. I can't wait to get home. I don't want to live here."

"Do you need a shoulder to cry on?"

"I just want to go home, Alan."

"OK, Chrissie, we'll do that, but you have to hold it together. Exit the club and climb into the car waiting."

"Sorry, Alan. I don't do threesomes. Not even in limos."

Oh god, what made me say that? I feel Vince's eyes dig into me.

"I'm alone," Alan says, and this time there is a raspy caress to his voice.

It feels as though the floor beneath me has given away. Did Alan Manzone just dump Nia to pick me up in a club? No, Chrissie, no. I don't know what's happening here, but that would be entirely too crazy.

"What did you do with Nia? Send her shopping?"

"No. I told her I had to go. I left her my car. I'm in yours."

Mine? How did he know that the car out front with the blond Nordic driver was mine? I inhale deeply, willing myself calm. "How gentlemanly of you."

"No. Actually very ungentlemanly. How much have you had to drink, Chrissie? Is Vince Carroll still with you?"

How does he know that Vince was with me in the alley?

"I'm a little buzzed. Two..." *Why is my head swimming again?* "...maybe three drinks. Nothing more. Just a little buzzed."

"Put Vince on the phone."

I hand Vince the phone. Vince is nodding and saying aha, aha, aha, then hands the receiver into the office.

I don't like the way Vince is looking at me.

"What the fuck is going on, Chrissie? Are you involved with Manny?"

Manny? It takes a moment for my fuzzy brain to realize he's referring to Alan. "Why?"

"Because Alan Manzone just told me to get your ass out front now and if I touch you he's going to kick the shit out of me."

The whole situation is beyond the abilities of my befuddled mental state: Vince and his prowling hands; Alan and the phone call; and how messed up I feel after only three drinks.

Vince is pulling me through the club and I can't get my thoughts to keep up with the rapidly shifting scene as he drags me out onto the front sidewalk. My car is parked by the door, my blond Nordic driver is waiting, there is a crowd, and the tabloid photographers are no longer relaxing against the brick of the building. They are rapidly clicking away. Flash, flash, flash.

The popping flashes make me sway a little on my feet and Vince reaches out to me. I panic, nearly tumbling to escape his repulsive touch and I'm suddenly swallowed by an angry swarm, taking pictures, shouting questions, so many questions, and I can't get out of the swarm and I can't breathe.

"Keep the fuck away from her," someone shouts behind me, and then the swarm evaporates and there are people everywhere, the cameras are flashing like a meteor storm, and Alan and Vince Carroll are fighting. Everything is moving slow, like I feel inside: Vince on the ground; Alan kicking him in the gut over and over again; Vince trying to crawl away; the hard snap of Vince's arms; the girls screaming.

"Oh my god!"

Frozen in panic, I stare at the ensuing chaos. Shit, did Alan Manzone just kill Vince Carroll right in front of me? I feel frantic screams rising inside of me, but I can't get the air from my lungs to push them out. Then Vince groans, and I'm relieved and I don't know why, but it's probably because Alan is shouting to put me in the car and I have David's kind steadying hands helping me there.

I'm pushed down onto the seat, the door slams behind me, and I am trapped inside. Strange flashes mar the tinted windows, and there is shouting, so much shouting and my head hurts. Nightmarish images flash in and out of my head and I struggle to try to lift myself from the seat. I need to call David to get me away from here.

I'm pushed back into the leather and Alan drops heavily into the seat beside me. The car door slams. I can feel the pressure of the car moving forward with rapid speed.

The only sound within is Alan's heavy breathing and I warn myself to hold steady, but his eyes are blazing and I don't understand what is happening. Why would Alan Manzone show up out of nowhere and beat up Vince Carroll on the sidewalk in front of CBGBs?

I can feel Alan all around me and I know without looking at him that he is very angry. Why is he angry? Why doesn't he say something?

"What the fuck are you doing at CBGBs with a known drug dealer and Vince Carroll?" he growls through gritted teeth.

"You know Jimmy Stallworth?" I ask, though why that seems a reasonable question I don't know.

His eyes are blazing as they lock on me. "Everyone in the industry knows Jimmy Stallworth. Fuck!" He lets out a long and primal exhale of anger. "What the hell are you doing making the rounds of the New York club scene alone? Do you have any idea what could have happened to you? Fucked up? Alone? With guys like Vince Carroll and Jimmy Stallworth? Where the hell is that useless friend of yours?"

"Rene," I supply contritely, though I don't know why I am contrite.

"Whatever," he counters, sharply dismissive.

I've never heard *whatever* with a British accent and I can feel myself being swept away by laughter. The laughter feels strange, a disobedient force, but I can't seem to stop laughing and am vaguely aware that there is nothing funny happening here.

Alan's eyes lock on me, blazing. "Stop laughing. This isn't the least bit funny. It would have been better for us both if you hadn't done this."

My head buzzes. Nothing I do has anything to do with him. He has no right to stomp about like a caveman and then yell at me. I want to tell him to go to hell. I've obsessed over him for five days, and now he has the nerve to pop up out of nowhere, create that horrifying scene, then behave as though I've behaved badly. What I do is none of his business.

"I really wish you'd stop telling me what would be better for *me*," I exclaim in frustration. "How would you know what's better for me? I don't even know."

He arches a brow. "Exactly. If you did, you wouldn't be stupid enough to be out partying with Vince Carroll and Jimmy Stallworth."

I hear it in his voice, concern, something I understand. My combativeness fades. My limbs relax all on their own and it's as if I'm melting, my flesh is melting, until I am deep in the leather seat, against him, my cheek resting on his shoulder. It feels so wonderful to be touching him, to be close. I tilt my face. I stop when he fills my eyes.

"Why are you angry with me?" I ask and those captivating black eyes flash at me.

"The Blue Light was awful enough, you stumbling and drunk and making a fool of yourself. But I didn't expect to see you tonight wired on stage singing with Vince Carroll."

The interior of the limo has calmed, less full of angry Alan. I take in more details of him. He definitely looks rock star New York chic tonight: Leather pants, open shirt and all. The same clothes from his television interview earlier today.

"I hate how you're dressed," I whisper.

"I don't particularly care for your attire. That top must belong to Rene."

I crinkle my nose. "Attire? My we are British again. I guess this does make me look a little slutty. And you are right. It is Rene's."

Those black eyes lock on me. I begin to burn. "No, Chrissie. You don't look slutty. You look like a girl out looking for trouble. That's how you look tonight. Incredibly hot and looking for trouble."

His thumb runs along my jaw line. I can feel a jolt shoot down, all throughout my body. He turns my chin until I'm looking straight at him.

"You are a very beautiful girl." He kisses the underside of my chin. My organs tighten. I pull in a sharp breath. "And unfortunately," he whispers, "you are very, very fucked up."

He sets me back against my seat. My body screams. I can't tell if he's mocking me, toying with me or angry with me. "Behave yourself," he commands.

I jerk away from him and sink into my side of the seat. "And I was about to take my top off because you are right—I would never buy this for me."

"You can take your top off if you want. I don't fuck fucked up little girls and I'm sure the tabloid photographers would enjoy it."

OK, he's mocking me, and through my deadened senses I feel my anger surge. "Yeah right, Alan. I'm yellow carding you. That's bullshit. Do you mean to sit there and tell me you don't go to bed with drunk women? You'd be the first rock star in history…"

Those black eyes swivel. I shiver. "No, what I'm saying is you are too much shit to deal with for a fuck. I fuck drunk women all the time. I don't do bullshit, Chrissie. If you ask me a question, I will tell you the truth. You need to decide how far and in what direction you want to go before you start something."

OK, this is a little frightening and a little bit of a turn-on. And damn, if he doesn't know it. I stare out the window.

"Where are you taking me?" I ask quietly.

"Back to your apartment. Where did you think I was taking you?"

"Shopping with Nia. You said you didn't like my top."

The car rolls to a slow stop. He did take me home. I don't understand anything that's happened tonight. And I definitely don't know what to do now. Do I invite him up, Mr. I don't fuck fucked up little girls? Do I thank him for seeing me home? Do I kiss him goodnight? Christ, why is this all so hard to figure out? It's just goodnight. What's wrong with me that I can't figure this out?

The car door opens. A blast of cool air rushes in and it makes me feel not at all good. I begin to feel faint and I am definitely aware of my dizziness as I climb awkwardly from the car with the assistance of my blond Nordic driver.

My shifting vision fixes on Alan. God, why does he have to look so good? No, don't think about that. You've got to send him away. Tell Alan goodnight and send him on his way.

"I'd invite you up but you don't want to fuck."

Oh shit, those weren't the words in my head. The world shifts. Alan grabs me before I fall, and some moments later the world refocuses, I'm in his arms, tucked against his chest, being held close against him. He is firing off rapid words to the driver and I can't catch any of them. Maybe I could figure out what was happening if the building would stop spinning. Why is he yelling at David?

The doorman pulls back the door, proceeds to the elevator, but Alan waves him off before he enters with us.

"What did you do with your elevator key?" he asks me.

"Key? Oh, it's in my pocket. Back. Left cheek."

The metal doors of the elevator slam shut behind us. I can feel every motion in the elevator, the long ride up floor by floor, the feeling of his pulse beneath my cheek, the slow, deep breathing. I curl more closely into him. I can feel the heat of his body as I tuck my cheek against his shoulder and watch the pulse move in his neck. I want to kiss that spot.

"Don't start anything," he castigates me.

My face burns. I am kissing him on the neck. I stop and his features are very tense. We are in the apartment foyer. "Are you staying the night?"

"Of course." He says it stiffly. "I don't want you vomiting in your sleep. You can die that way."

I squirm in his arms, wanting now to be put down, but he ignores me and goes into the hallway.

"Where is your bedroom?"

"I'm not letting you to take me to bed."

"I thought we covered this. I'm not taking you to bed. I'm putting you in it."

"Oh." I shrug. I point at a door at the end of the hallway.

His arms fall away and I'm sitting on my bed. I am as close to going to bed with a guy as I have ever been. And I want to. I really, really want to. Being near him is like some voodoo aphrodisiac. My blood is on fire. There is a wild pulse in me. I never feel this way, not ever. It is such a delicious feeling. The agitation in my flesh, the pulsing, the want, the anticipation.

"Where are your t-shirts?" he murmurs as he carefully unties my halter top.

Oh my…Alan Manzone is undressing me. Fantasies do come true. Cold air touches my skin and I am quaking like a leaf. I am topless. The first guy ever to see my unclothed breasts is Alan Manzone. How freaking unbelievable is that? He is so beautiful.

"Where are your shirts," he repeats quickly.

This is it. I'm finally going to do it. I can't find my words. I can't take my eyes off him. My body is raging and he's unbuttoning my jeans.

He slips them off. He goes to a chest of drawers and removes a white tank top. He pulls it over my head. *No, no, no. This is wrong.*

He jerks back the blankets and points at the pillow. He eases me into the bed until I feel the coolness of the sheets behind me. I want him to cover me with his body. He moves back from me, pulling the blankets up around me.

He grabs my hip and turns me onto my side. "Don't sleep on your back," he says softly and he switches off the light.

Fully dressed, he lies on the bed behind me, curled into my back. His arm casually snakes over my body. His long fingers rest carelessly against my stomach. I can hear him breathing. I can feel the warmth of him. How am I supposed to sleep with him behind me?

I roll over until I'm on my other side, my face a breath from his on the pillow. The tease of my shirt and the blankets make my breasts ache for his touch. I'm claimed by raging desire, and sleep just isn't going to happen.

"I can't sleep. I'm too restless," I whisper. "Don't you want to…?" I can't finish the thought.

He gently strokes my hair, and those worldly black eyes harshly fix on my face. "It's being fucked up and the aftereffects of being on stage. The combination makes it an adrenaline rush.

You get off stage and the first thing you want to do is fuck someone. It's just the adrenaline rush. It goes away. Go to sleep."

"I'm too wired. I feel like I could crawl out of my skin."

His features look strained. "Chrissie, go to sleep."

I stare up at him. "But I want to. I really, really want to with you."

I move into him, my lips on his neck and my hands clumsily fumble for the fastening of his pants. His breathing grows deep and ragged. He stops my hands.

"Behave, Chrissie."

He is gently stroking my flesh. My breathing won't calm. My body is ruthlessly demanding more and he thinks I'm going to sleep. My fingers search for the buttons on his shirt. My lips find the warm flesh of his jaw. My pelvis lifts upward into him. The taste of him runs wildly through my veins. I want him and there is no power on earth that could make me stop this…I want him…I want him…

Chapter Seven

I come awake slowly and open my eyes to streams of parallel ribbons of sunshine peeking through the half-open slats of the shutters. I am comfortable and warm in bed, wrapped in a cocoon of blankets.

I shift my head and my hair falls across my face. Unfocused moments slip by. It is my room, I know that. It is bright and airy and the walls are covered with that hideous pink and white striped wallpaper with the flowered border that I picked out when I was seven.

There is an arm carelessly flung over my hip, gentle yet holding. There is a dark tattoo on the forearm. The fingers are long.

All at once, like a door flying open, my sluggish brain jerks into overdrive and I know two things: I am nude beneath the covers, and that arm and warm body behind me belongs to Alan Manzone.

Oh god, what the hell did I do last night? There are memories, but they are foggy. Was I drunk? I must have been, but I don't feel hung over. I don't feel wretched like I did after clubbing with Rene. How much of what I remember is real? Did I really go to CBGB's? Did I really run into Vince Carroll? Did I sing on stage? Did Alan really dump Nia and beat up Vince Carroll?

Snippets of the night come to me in greater clarity. I couldn't possibly have said the things I remember saying to him last night! I couldn't possibly have all but attacked him sexually!

I cautiously lift the blanket just to confirm that I'm really nude. No, no, no. I don't know what's wrong with my memory. But *that* could not have possibly happened. It was a dream. A drunken dream. Only I don't feel like I've been drunk. I feel funny. Spacey.

I cringe. More disjointed minutes come to me. There is a flash in my memory of Alan's face as he undressed me: angry and worried. Why was he angry? Why was he worried? The last thing I remember is being naked in bed and then nothing. I blush. Did we make love? I don't think we did. I don't feel like we did. Wouldn't I feel it? I frantically look at him. He's still dressed. My memory stirs. He didn't want to make love to me. He said no. I offered and he said no.

I want to die! I would climb from the bed, but I can't. Even if I could slip free of his arm, I'm naked and there doesn't look to be any clothes handy. In slow, careful movements so as not to disturb him, I gently turn beneath his bicep so I can see him. I'm surprised he's still in bed with me, though technically not, just lying atop it.

Why is he still here? Shouldn't he have slipped out the door long before this? Isn't that what most guys do? Sneak out before morning? At least that's what Rene says, and she would know. It would have been better for me if he'd made an escape, because I really don't know how I'm going to keep from making a fool of myself when he wakes up. How do you face a guy in the morning after he didn't want to have sex with you?

I need to talk to Rene. I wish I could get out of the bed. I wish he'd just screwed me last night while I was crazy, so I could just be done with my virginity. It wouldn't make this morning any more nerve-rackingly awful.

The phone rings and I tense. I peek back over my shoulder to find Alan awake. He looks at me, and it's almost as though he's studying my face, looking for something, and then feels relieved he doesn't find it. His eyes become soft, his expression gentle.

"Aren't you going to answer that?" he asks.

I shake my head.

"It could be Jack." He says it nonchalantly.

Does he really expect me to take a call from my father while lying nude in bed with him? OK, technically not *in* bed with him, but my frazzled nerves don't seem to draw a distinction.

The phone stops ringing. Thank god.

"How do you feel? Any dizziness? Are you sick?"

What kind of questions are those? Say something, Chrissie. You can't just stare at him. "I'm OK."

He looks relieved and smiles. Why does he look relieved?

He brushes back his tousled waves. "Are you hungry?"

What are we playing? Twenty questions? Why do I feel like the questions are more than just questions? Like I'm at the doctor's office or something...*how are you feeling, Chrissie? Any shortness of breath? Or just a fever today*...Jeez, enough with the third degree. Am I hungry? I'm starving, which is strange since the last time I spent a night getting myself trashed on booze the thought of food made me want to wretch. But, I'm hungry this morning.

I nod.

He pulls away and sits on the edge of the bed. "Would you like me to cook you something or would you rather go out?"

I try desperately not to look flustered. "You don't need to cook me anything. I usually just have cereal in the morning."

"Cereal. Sounds charming. No, Chrissie. I'm going to cook you something. You need something substantial in your stomach today."

My eyes round. There is something strange in all this, but I don't have a clue what it is. Twenty questions and now meal planning. What difference does it make what I eat?

In a moment, he is rising from the bed and pulling off his shirt. "I expect you to decide what you want by the time I'm done showering."

With a casual smile, he tosses his shirt onto my chair. I can hardly take in air. Every inch of him has been kissed with perfection. His back and chest are sensual planes of firm, defined, and tanned muscles. Regrettably, there is also quite a bit of ink there, though on him the ink is a turn-on. His tattoos playfully move with his muscles.

My eyes follow him as he moves into the adjacent bathroom. I hear the shower turn on and then the sound of him peeing. He hasn't closed the door. Clearly, waking up with a strange girl in bed isn't something uncomfortable for Alan.

The shower door opens and closes. I dart from the bed, pull on the white t-shirt I find on the floor, and frantically grab from the back of the chair my pair of flannel PJ bottoms. Now what do I do? Do I stay in the bedroom or do I make a run for the kitchen?

I curl in the chair where he tossed his shirt and stare at the open bathroom door. There is nothing to panic over. He is being very nice today and definitely as if none of this is any big deal. Deep down I know it isn't a big deal. It's perfectly normal, millions of girls are probably just like me, waking up somewhere with a guy they don't know.

My inner voice taunts me—*But Alan Manzone didn't want to have sex with you. You are the only girl in America waking up in this circumstance still a virgin.*

I shake my head, trying to ignore that thought.

Hugging my legs, I curl into a ball, laying my cheek on my knees. He must like me a little. He's still here. I pull his shirt from beneath me and toss it away. I don't know what's going on, but face it, Chrissie, the guy isn't interested in you.

I look up and Alan is standing in the open bathroom doorway, hair wet, and a towel hanging loosely from his hips. My heartbeat picks up and I am suddenly very hot everywhere. He frowns.

"Are you sure you feel OK, Chrissie? You'd tell me if you weren't, wouldn't you?"

He's giving me *that* look, that one I really have grown to hate, the one guys give a girl when they are unsure if something is wrong with them. God, I'm behaving stupidly.

"Of course. I don't know you well enough to lie," I say in what I hope is a nonchalant tone.

Alan laughs. I feel each muscle in my body relax in slow increments.

"Do you think Jack would mind if I borrowed something from his wardrobe? I'm not going to have time this morning to swing by my place to change."

I shake my head, though the thought of seeing Alan dressed in Jack's clothes is just a touch creepy for me. He leaves my bedroom and I stay curled in my chair.

Minutes pass.

"Where is Rene?"

Alan's rich timbre fills the apartment effortlessly. I rise from the chair and go into the hallway outside my parents' bedroom.

"In DC with her dad."

"For how long?"

"Until a week from Sunday. Her dad is getting married."

"That can't be fun for you. Are you going to DC or are you flying home early?"

Alan reappears in the hall, tucking his shirttail into his pants. He's wearing a pink button down cotton shirt, a pair of worn jeans, and loafers. Somehow he makes Jack's clothes look casually chic.

He lifts a brow. "Are you flying back to Santa Barbara early?"

I shrug. "I haven't decided. Everything just changed yesterday."

He smiles. "Have you decided what you want for breakfast?"

He doesn't wait for an answer. He's moving down the hallway to the kitchen. It's almost as if he's hurrying. Is this Alan's version of the guy escape? Cook a girl breakfast, feed her, and run.

In the kitchen I find him going through the refrigerator, removing things and stacking them on the counter. It's fully stocked. I hadn't noticed. Jack must have seen to that before we left Santa Barbara. I never once thought about where the food came from. But the kitchen is fully stocked, and has been since we arrived.

"Would you like an omelet? Vegetable or meat? You have broccoli, you have peppers, and you have sausage, ham, bacon, a variety of cheese. Basically, everything for any kind of omelet you want."

How does he know this? I don't even know what goes in or how to make an omelet. Maria does our cooking. I don't even know how to boil an egg. Alan looks right at home.

"I don't care. Whatever is easier or whatever you'd prefer."

"I like everything."

"Then everything."

I settle at the breakfast bar and watch him. I've never had a guy cook me breakfast before, and I feel a touch useless just sitting here. I watch him fill one skillet with bacon, and then bend to watch as he precisely turns up the heat. He moves to the coffeemaker and sets a pot to brew. He pours me a glass of orange juice and sets it on the mat in front of me.

"Don't wait for me. Drink," he orders. I lift the glass. I take a sip. I start to put it down. "All of it."

He goes back to the stove. He turns the bacon. "Who brought you drinks other than the waitress last night?"

What an odd question. Why would he want to know that? "Vince."

"Just Vince? Or did Jimmy bring you drinks too?"

I don't like the way he's asking me that.

"I'm not sure. I don't remember. Why do you want to know?"

He looks over at me. He smiles. It's totally disarming. It bothers me for some reason and it shouldn't because it's just a friendly, no big deal kind of expression. I frown.

I watch him whisk eggs in a bowl before he pours the mixture into the heated skillet of melted butter. Damn, if he isn't good at this. Where did he learn to cook?

"I have a thing in about a half an hour," he says, carefully swirling the omelet in the pan. "A pretty full day." He folds the omelet and slides it onto a plate. "I'll swing by later to look in on you."

Look in? What does that mean? What an odd thing to say.

He sets the plate in front of me. "Now, eat."

I stare as he starts cleaning up his mess. "This looks good. Aren't you going to make yourself one? Aren't you going to eat?"

"My first thing is a breakfast thing."

What is it about "thing"? Why does every male in my life take off for *thing?* I stab the eggs with my fork. Hmm... it is good, very good. He sets a cup of coffee in front of me.

I look up to find him smiling. "I've got to go, Chrissie. You should probably just stay in today. Take it easy."

He doesn't even wait for my answer. He disappears down the hall and I hear the elevator doors close.

* * *

My mood shifts immediately once Alan is gone. The rooms feel empty again. I set the candles in the living room ablaze and sit there and stare at them. I wish Rene were here. I can fight the mess inside me when Rene is near, since her mess is so much more naked and real and absorbing. What am I going to do for two weeks without her?

By two in the afternoon, that spacey feeling has left me and I'm sick of reliving minute by minute my latest encounter with Alan. I am crawling the walls of the apartment. For some reason, Rene hasn't called today. I hope everything is all right in DC. Jack hasn't called. A good thing, because after all that's gone on the past few days, behaving normally in our completely abnormal father-daughter fashion just isn't in me today. And as I suspected, hoping Alan would come back was a very foolish thing.

A familiar anxiety, impulse and sadness whispers through me. I stare out through the terrace doors at the April day. *Get out of the apartment, Chrissie.* I pull on a sundress and a pair of white Keds, grab my book of Chekhov and shove it into my woven rope tote with the small snack I packed in the kitchen. From the back of a chair, I grab the throw. It's a beautiful day. I'm only a few steps away from Central Park. *Get out of the apartment now!*

Outdoors is not a good ally to Chekhov. I discover this after twenty minutes sitting in the sun and finding myself still on the page I started. The good weather seems to have brought out all New Yorkers. The park is busy and crowded, with couples, children, dogs, bikes, and a group of young college age guys playing hacky sack. There are other people here alone, and yet New Yorkers seem to do the alone thing so much better than I do. They don't look alone when they are alone.

Chomping on an apple, I watch the playful dance of hacky sack. It's better than watching the couples when you are a single. As I set down my book, I catch from the corner of my eye one of the guys giving me a fast once-over. He's cute, with dark wavy hair. Sort of looks like Alan, though no one looks like Alan. I lean back on one arm and watch him. I tilt my face toward the sun, closing my eyes. I look back at him.

He smiles. I smile. His friend punts the sack farther over, nearer to me, and then he begins to bounce it from ankle to ankle, inching closer to me. After thirty minutes of watching them, one of them has finally noticed me with interest. Rene would have had all ten of them sitting on the blanket with us in half a minute. But Rene is not here, so I have to make do with my less than stellar skills if I don't want to spend the next two weeks in total silence.

The sudden enthusiasm of his movements tells me he's trying to impress me. He loses the hacky sack and tumbles onto my blanket at my feet. He pushes up on an elbow and smiles. "Hi."

"Hi."

OK, so he's not much of conversationalist. The way he says "hi" tells me he's probably not the sharpest guy in the world, but this is weird. I've never lost the interest of a guy so quickly. One minute all smiles and stare, dropping at my feet, and now no smile..and his staring eyes shift ever so slightly.

My less-than-interested new friend looks up. "Aren't you…"

"No, he died last year."

I suddenly realize the shadow now covering my body is Alan standing over me. He came back like he said he would. I ignore the riot of my blood and my rapidly increasing heartbeat.

I make a face at Alan to cover my ridiculous pleasure at seeing him. "That's not funny at all. You shouldn't say things like that. Not even if you're joking."

Alan settles on the blanket beside me. Mr. Hacky Sack is still with us. My afternoon doldrums have instantly vanished, because I'm really glad Alan did look in on me and that he's saving me from Mr. Hacky Sack who was a disappointment from word one.

I frown at him. "I thought you said you never do bullshit. That fib is a yellow card."

Something in how he looks at me makes me shiver. "So you do remember parts of last night. This morning I wasn't sure if you did."

My face burns and my mind whirls. Why would Alan think I didn't remember what happened last night? I wasn't passed out drunk. Just sort of spacey and weird and not myself.

I bite my lip hard to stop my thoughts. I look at Alan. "Should we invite my new friend to stay for lunch?"

"Only if you think you have enough to go around."

The heat rises in my cheeks like a burn. I wasn't expecting that naughty comment.

Mr. Hacky Sack looks uncomfortable. He springs to his feet and makes a fast excuse.

Once we're alone, Alan gives me a harsh, rebuking stare. "I thought I told you not to leave the apartment, and after Jimmy

Stallworth I would have thought you'd figure out that you just don't pick up any guy you meet in New York."

I give him a frustrated glare. "What? Girls don't date in New York? Where am I supposed to meet someone? Barney's or Saks Fifth Avenue?"

He rolls his eyes and reclines back on his elbows next to me. "I think it's safer for you to wait until you're back in Santa Barbara to try to hook up with someone. You just don't have that New York girl savvy and instinct."

"How would you know? You don't know anything about me."

Smug, burning black eyes. "Jimmy Stallworth and Vince Carroll. A savvy girl would have run from both of them."

I drop my gaze first because he made that point insultingly well. I still get nauseated when I think of Vince touching and kissing me. And I still haven't processed that I was actually stupid enough to meet a New York drug dealer and help him crash a club to close a drug deal.

"I really hated leaving you today," Alan says heavily.

I look up and my heart accelerates.

"I couldn't stop thinking about you all day." Those penetrating black eyes lock on me. "I couldn't stop worrying. How do you feel?"

I frown, more than a little irritated. "Why do you keep asking me that? It's really getting on my nerves."

He ignores the question.

I bite my lower lip and brace myself. "Why did you beat up Vince Carroll last night?"

If Alan has any reaction to that question I can't see it. "Because he was stupid enough to let the tabloids get hold of you. He was supposed to quietly get you into the car."

I frown. "That's a severe response to a mistake, don't you think?"

He starts to rummage in my bag. "Do you have aspirin in here? I have a terrible headache. I could really use two aspirin and about an hour's sleep …Cheez-Its, Oreo cookies, Diet Coke…"

"Here, give me that!"

I grab my bag from him.

"Oreo cookies and Diet Coke. Really? I'll never understand the logic of a girl."

I hold out the bottle of aspirin and a Diet Coke. "I'll have you know that Oreo cookies and Diet Coke are one of my favorite things."

He downs about four tablets. "Why? It sounds repulsive."

"I'll have to show you. This is something you can only get by doing it."

I take a cookie and hold it up to his mouth. He looks suspicious.

"The whole cookie. It only works if you do the whole cookie, and don't break it and don't swallow."

That prompts a look that makes every cell in my body burn while I put the cookie in his mouth. My fingers touch his lips and that draws my eyes to his. This is so childish. Why am I doing this lame stunt with him?

"Now fill your mouth with Diet Coke."

In a half second, it's fizzing and I can hear it. I start to laugh.

He swallows, makes a face and I laugh harder. "God, you are amused by the strangest things."

I ignore the jab. "Rene taught me that at ten."

He rolls his eyes. "Yes, Rene would definitely be amused by things that swell and fizz in your mouth."

"Be nice." I give him a napkin to wipe his mouth. "Why don't you like Rene?"

"I've known lots of girls like Rene. The world is full of girls like Rene. You get sick of them after a while. I can't figure out why you like her."

He settles back down on the blanket and puts his head in my lap. The unexpected closeness hits me like a freight train. Such an intimate thing to do, violating personal space, and he does it so naturally.

"So what have you been doing all day?" I ask, trying not to sound completely flustered.

He closes his eyes. "An appointment with my lawyers. Lunch with Lillian, misery in every way. Seven interviews."

Lillian? There is something in the way he says that name that tells me this person is important to him. "Who is Lillian?"

"My mother. Terrible mother. Marvelous agent."

I feel absurd relief over learning that Lillian is just his mother.

Those black eyes focus on me. "Why are you laughing?"

I blush. "You sound more British than when you left this morning and I was wondering if that's the aftereffect of having lunch with your mother."

He rolls his eyes. "Have you decided what you are going to do, love? Are you staying in New York?"

"I think I'm staying. I want to be close if Rene needs me."

"That's a stupid reason for spending your vacation alone. Personally, I don't think she's worth it."

A dozen sharp, defensive retorts about Rene fill my head, but for some reason I don't say any of them. Perhaps, it's because he sounds tired, halfway to sleep. I watch the slow softening of his features and stare at his lustrous, dark hair. I really want to touch that hair. I grab my book instead.

Ten minutes pass with me pretending to read before I realize that it's just not going to happen. Chekhov in the sun was difficult enough. With Alan it's impossible. Instead, I peek over my book and just watch him. Is he asleep? I can't tell. He's still. His breathing is quiet.

My hand refuses to obey my command. My fingers find his hair. The black strands are soft and they flutter through my fingers. I like the way his hair feels. What is it about a guy's hair? It's always softer. Probably because they don't do so much to it.

A woman walking on the sidewalk smiles at us. A random smile from a New Yorker. Miracles never cease. I look at Alan. Two miracles in a single day. He did look in on me. I never expected that. And a woman smiling at me as though I were part of a couple instead of the dreaded single that I always seem to be. I wonder how we look together?

"If you don't turn a page eventually, you will never finish that book."

I still. His eyes are closed. How did he know I was reading? How did he know I haven't turned the page?

"I can't focus on this book. I hate it."

His eyes shoot open. "Is that a recent problem?"

I frown. Jeez, another of those questions that seem like more than a question-question. I roll my eyes in frustration.

"I've been trying to read this book for three months. I will never finish it, only I have to before I return to Santa Barbara."

"Why do you hate the book?"

I crinkle my nose. "It's Chekhov. Everyone hates Chekhov. I picked it because it was short, which is completely stupid logic because long and enjoyable is better than short and yuck."

Did I really just say that? Yep, I can tell by the shimmers in Alan's eyes that I did. My cheeks burn.

Alan laughs in a lazy, loose way. "Yes, I can see how long and enjoyable would be preferable to a girl."

I have no choice. I hit him with the book. "You are so obnoxious. Do you know that?"

He makes a contrite face and turns to look at the book cover. Those black eyes lock on me intensely. "Do you want me to help you with your short and yuck?"

Now the color has moved down my cheeks, across my neck to the swell of my breasts. Exactly what is he suggesting here?

"Can't you ever just be nice?"

"I am being nice."

His fingers snake through my hair. In the blink of an eye, everything about him, the way he looks at me, the way he touches can switch into a total turn-on.

"Do you want me to help you, Chrissie?"

I nod.

He looks at the page I'm on. He leans into me. "*I suppose I am dreadfully guilty, but my thoughts are muddled, my soul is in the grip of a kind of apathy, and I am no longer able to understand myself. I don't understand myself or other people...I should like to tell you everything from the beginning, but it's a long story, and such a complicated one that if I talked till morning I couldn't finish it...*"

I let out a ragged breath. All that just to quote to me Chekhov. His theatrics are really starting to wear on me and I can tell he knows how effective they are. I'm certain it's just a game he plays with girls, though I don't know why he's playing it with me. He could have had me last night, no effort, if he had wanted another notch for his bed.

I push him out of my lap. "Ha, ha, ha. And you got it wrong. You skipped a bunch."

He sits up, with an adorable half-smile on his face. "I can quote it line by line. And I skipped for theatrical affect."

"I'm yellow carding you. You can't quote Chekhov line by line."

"Pick another page."

I do. And he begins to quote that damn book line by line, word for word, in that exquisite voice that could draw me into bed with him if he ever used it to do so.

I make a face when he's done. "No, that was wrong. You missed a whole bunch of words."

He holds out a hand. "I did not. I can quote line by line an eclectic collection of classic literature. It is what we did as a family instead of having conversation."

For a moment, I stop to wonder if that's true. I know nothing about his upbringing, where he is from beyond what his accent tells me. Strange, but there is never anything in print about Alan from before he was famous, his family or his history.

I shake my head. "You did it wrong."

In a second, he's wrestling me for the book and I'm doing a darn good job of keeping it away. What is this? A point of pride for him? And then, very quickly, without the slightest idea how it has happened, I'm lying beneath him on the blanket, and we are laughing.

It all happens so fast—one minute we're laughing, and the next he is kissing me, from only mildly aware of me into completely into me. His lips are knowing and slow, the sweet gentleness so potent that it's painful, and I feel my muscles inside clench violently. I moan into his mouth and he takes full advantage of the slight parting of my lips. The tongue that touches mine is dancing and erotic, all about sensation and drawing me into him.

Without breaking the kiss, he turns until he's lying back on the blanket with me on top of him. His fingers move in a feather-like touch, up my neck, my jaw, my chin. I don't care that we are in Central Park. I don't care if people are watching. He's pulling me into him and I am desperate to go there.

It all stops. He pushes away from me in the blink of an eye, leaving me hanging with my heart rate through the roof. Other than the aggravated hand he jerks through his black shoulder length hair, he looks calm, disinterested, and suddenly focused on something other than me.

He stands up and holds out his hand for me. "I'm tired of the park, Chrissie. We're leaving."

We are, are we? I sit up and hug my legs with my arms. "I'm not going anywhere with you," I say, shaking my head in absolute frustration. I pick up my book and I struggle to keep my eyes from him.

"We're not staying here," he says and oddly his voice sounds mildly urgent. I glance up at him. Those burning back eyes lock on me and he lowers until we're at eye level. "Let's go to bed and be good to each other."

My eyes flutter wide as I look at him, wondering if this is more theatrics, and hating that it doesn't feel like a game in my flesh. Is he serious? I thought it would be different the first time a guy asked me to bed. Something clear, something in focus, something I knew what to do with.

I don't even know if he's really asking me to bed, yet there is an alarming sense that that is exactly what he's intending.

He holds out his hand.

"Nope, as tempting as you make it sound, I think my answer is no," I say petulantly to cover my confusion. "I don't want to go to bed with you. You're too much of a weirdo. "

"Yes, you do. It's why you can't stop thinking about me," he says softly. His voice is hypnotic.

It's the truth, and worse, I can see in his eyes that he knows it's the truth. *Crap!* I have no idea what to do. Right or left. I haven't the faintest clue how to deal with him, but the prospect of returning back to Jack's apartment alone with my internal mess growing only more insistent is not a wise thing.

I shove my stuff jerkily into my bag and take his hand. Alan doesn't say anything and I'm glad he doesn't. He is impossible to read and I don't need even one more ounce of confusion.

I'm filled with trepidation as we walk back toward the apartment. Does leaving with him mean I've said yes? And a part of me is a little disappointed in how this is unfolding. I always thought it would happen the first time in one of those heated, *From Here to Eternity* type moments, or in the least with me drunk so I could stay out of my own way until it was over.

Butterflies fill my stomach. Maybe we are just leaving the park, nothing more. It might have all been drama. His actions are impossible to process logically.

I slant a look at him and some of my anxiousness wanes. He doesn't seem the slightest bit aware of me. Even walking side by side, anyone who looked at us would probably think we're not even together.

The doorman has the lobby doors open and Alan's hand stops me.

"No, not here. I want to go to my apartment."

His apartment? I flush.

"I want you to spend the night with me at my place." His gaze is intense.

"Oh." The world has ceased to be beneath my feet. That was direct enough. We aren't just leaving the park. Alan is taking me to bed.

Once in the car, I realize there is no turning back. I remind myself that I've been obsessing about him for days. I don't know why this is so difficult.

It is a short drive to Alan's apartment. In only a few minutes we're slowing down. Jeez, why did it have to be so short, so quick? I need time to think. Time to calm myself.

His residence is in Central Park West. As the car rolls to a stop, I realize that I am only a few blocks from Jack's apartment, and I can make a run for home should anything happen that I don't feel completely comfortable with. That last thought makes me even more frustrated with myself.

Once through the building doors there is an impeccably dressed attendant waiting to serve him. Inside the elevator, Alan leans back against the polished, mirrored wall and studies me, while the attendant remains carefully invisible.

"Are you hungry? Would you like to go out to dinner or would you prefer I cook for you? Or are you full on Cheez-Its, Oreos and Diet Coke?"

He gives me that friendly sort of nothing smile, but its effect is the opposite. I am quaking like a leaf now. How does the attendant manage to look like he doesn't hear us? And why is it embarrassing to me that he's listening to us discussing dinner? Really, Chrissie, that is too lame. We are talking about dinner.

I shake my head.

Alan frowns. "Is that shake: I'm not hungry or I don't want to go out or I don't want you to cook for me?"

The shake is *I don't want to talk about food.* I am here. I can do this. Dammit, can't we just get it done and out of the way so I can feel comfortable again?

I stare up at him. "Whatever you want so long as it's not Chinese takeout delivered would be fine with me."

He laughs. "I think I can do better than that."

Oh my. He's put just enough in his laughter to make me tremble. I look at the attendant. Is he smirking? It's hard to tell in the split mirror tiles.

The doors open. "Come." He has my hand again. It is warm inside, dimly lit, a giant open space with glass on the far wall, overlooking a terrace and the New York skyline.

I can feel my eyes widening and I don't want them to. Music's most self-destructive bad-boy has an apartment that is elegant and one of the most magnificent homes I've ever seen, with its tastefully decorated rooms before a stunning expanse of the city. Alan knows art and Alan has style. I wander into the open space living room, with its lustrous hardwood floors, where there is a remarkable collection of pre-Columbian pottery that I only recognized because I'd studied some similar pieces in an art book last semester. On a far wall, an eclectic collection of art: A Picasso, a Warhol, a Monet and a Salvador Dali, all original, somehow arranged with a collection of Americana that pulls the pieces together and gives them a sense of cohesion.

The furnishings are plush and graceful, every surface spotless to the point that it looks as if no one lives here. I think of his plane, the traveling trashcan. So many contradictions. Most definitely not what I expected. Not this symmetry. This precision. This tasteful luxury that screams of old money.

I turn to find him still in the foyer, standing beside a polished table with a crystal vase filled with the stems of white tulips.

I tense. "Do you have a phone?"

Alan laughs. What a stupid question, Chrissie. You couldn't have phrased it more stupidly.

He steps into the living room and sinks on a sofa. The room is so perfect I'm afraid to step into it. "Unfortunately, in every room," Alan says. "I hate the telephone. I don't know why I have one in every room."

"Really? Why do you hate the phone?"

"I never want to talk to who's on the other end. Usually the press, even though it seems like they change my number every week or so."

"Really? What a pain. I've had the same number since I was five." I make a little face. "May I use one of your too many phones?"

"Why?"

"I haven't checked my messages today."

He gestures with an arm toward a stunning mahogany table. I can feel him watching as I dial the number to the answering service. Shit, there are ten messages from Rene. All day I waited for her to call, and once I left for the park she called ten times. Good one, Rene. Where were you when I really needed you?

I click down the receiver without calling her back.

"Everything OK?" Alan asks.

I nod. "Rene. Ten calls. She doesn't want to wear fuchsia to her dad's wedding, but number thirty-seven insists."

"Thirty-seven?"

"That's what Rene calls her soon-to-be stepmother. Thirty-seven. She counts her father's girlfriends. This one is number thirty-seven. So that's what we call her."

Jeez, why did I tell him such a childish thing? Please laugh, Alan. I'm nervous as hell.

I move to the far corner of the room and the full-size shiny grand piano. I lift the lid. I touch the keys lightly with my finger so they don't make sound.

"How many girls have you been with? I bet it is more than thirty-seven."

I turn from the piano to find his eyes on me, his expression enigmatic. I can hear the sharp sound of my own breathing in the intense quiet of the room.

It seems like neither of us talk, neither of us move, forever. I can't tell if he's angry, insulted or amused by the question.

"I don't keep count," he says finally.

"Ah, probably not. Did you care about any of them?"

Those black eyes burn into me. "No," he says, slowly, softly. "It doesn't mean that I haven't kept some of them around for a while. But did I care about any of them? No, Chrissie. I didn't. Is that the answer you were looking for?"

Heck, no. I wish I'd never asked it. "If you didn't care for them, why did you keep them around?"

"I meet lots of girls. Some of them later become friends. Some of them are just sex. Lots of girls, Chrissie."

"So what kind of girl am I?"

"I thought we were already friends." He gives me a smile that makes me suck in air.

"Why am I here?"

"I want you here."

"That's not what I mean."

"I know."

He rises. He crosses the room to me. He leans into me and kisses my nose, the gesture silly and unthreatening, deliberately so, I think. He doesn't kiss my mouth, but I am tense from head to toe and my heartbeat is soaring anyway.

Alan smiles. His eyes are stunningly bright. "I want you to stay with me here while you're in New York. Do what you want. As much or as little as you want. Let's keep this simple. Stay here and do what you want."

Simple? Nothing could be further from simple. I don't know how to do any of this.

I need time. Time to process this new, more confusing wrinkle. He just asked me to stay with him the rest of my spring break. It's crazy. Why would he ask me such a thing?

I move from the piano into a small sitting area with a full wall entertainment system. On a table is a neatly stacked tower of tapes, and as I sort through them I realize that they are all first run movies currently in theaters or soon to be released. Some of them have handwritten notes on them from studios, directors, or actors.

He notices my preoccupation with the tapes. "Do you want to watch a movie?"

A movie. Yes. A little bit of normal. Perhaps that will take the tension and premeditation out of this.

I pick up one. "This looks interesting. It has John Candy in it."

I turn it over. *Uncle Buck*. The promotional cover makes me laugh.

"There are two dramas in there that are supposed to be good. One with Robin Williams and another with Daniel Day-Lewis. Have you seen them?"

"First run movies not released? Of course not. That would violate Jack's commitment to proletarian normalcy. I go to the theater when they are released like everyone else. I'd like to watch a movie. Do you want to watch this? Even though I'm sure it's lame, I bet it's funny. John Candy can be so funny."

He takes the movie and reads the jacket. "Americans have no taste in cinema."

I laugh. "Cinema? My, we are so British proper when we are in our fancy penthouse where the world can't see."

It was meant to be a silly joke, but those black eyes sharpen on me.

"Yes, I'm so proper I'm standing here imagining what it would be like to boff during the opening credits."

I blink twice and stare at him. There was an angry edge to his voice that I didn't expect, certainly didn't like, and definitely didn't want. That pissed him off and I haven't the first clue why.

I shrug and search for something funny to say. "Then let's fast forward through the opening credits. I haven't at all decided what I want to do just yet."

The oh-so-British sitting room has a a full screen for movie viewing. I settle on a comfy couch and clutch a throw pillow. I laugh. Striped pillows with small flowers. Who would have taken Alan for a stripes with small flowers kind of guy?

I look up to see him watching me quizzically. "You laugh during the credits?" he asks.

I blush, remembering the boff comment. "No, it's your pillows. So dainty and proper."

He shakes his head and the expression on his face relaxes as he stretches out on the sofa, back against the armrest. I try to focus on the movie and I can't, which is a disappointment because I can tell from the little I absorb that it is funny. He is watching me and not the movie. I don't know why he's doing that or what's up with this strange sort of play date we're having. And that's what it feels like. As odd as that sounds, it feels like those silly dates I used to have in eighth grade when I let a guy come over to watch a movie at Jack's.

It wasn't what I expected when Alan brought me here. I chance a look at him out of the corner of my eye. "You don't like the movie?"

"Not particularly."

I lean back into my armrest until I'm facing him. "So is this what you do in your down time? Invite strange girls home and then watch them watch movies you don't particularly like?"

Alan's smile is potent and sexy. "No, this is a new experience for me. I've not been alone with a girl who's selected the movie option."

I lift my chin and smile and sidestep the last part of that comment. "Really?"

"I've not really done the date thing before." His tone is one of wry amusement. "How do you think its going?"

"Date?" My voice hitches up from mezzo-soprano to soprano. "Is that what we're doing? I thought we were watching a movie so I could pretend you didn't bring me here to boff."

Alan rolls forward on the couch until he is very, very close to me. "Only if that's what you want to do," he whispers, and then kisses me lightly.

I smile. "I can never tell if you're being serious or making fun of me."

His eyes are earnest. "I would never make fun of you."

He reaches for a cigarette and lights it. After a puff, he holds it up. "Do you mind?"

I shrug. "Of course not. It's your house. Jack used to smoke until he thought it was ruining his voice."

With my eyes, I trace up one wall across the ceiling and then down another. "Are you all alone here, all the time, in this horrible quiet?"

"No. Not usually. I have people who work for me. They come in and out. I don't know their schedule. Most of them I don't know what they do. I prefer the quiet. It's hardly ever quiet. And I'm not alone. I'm with you."

I look at the priceless collection of art on the wall. "Are you as rich as they say you are?"

"Is that the latest criticism of me? That I'm rich? Usually it's that I'm too commercial. But it depends."

"On what?"

That intense black stare meets mine directly. "If you are the kind of girl who gets turned on by money."

"Nope, I'm the kind of girl who gets turned on by really bad American cinema."

Alan arches a brow. "You find John Candy sexy?"

I do a little lift with my brows. "Extremely. There is nothing sexier than a guy who can make you laugh."

He takes another drag of his cigarette. "Not even a guy who sings?"

I roll my eyes, toss the pillow and rise from the couch. I wander out onto the terrace. The patio is lovely, like a tiny English garden encased in cement. Everything tasteful. Everything correct. I sink down on a cushioned, double seat chaise lounge. His view of the city is spectacular.

After a minute or two, Alan follows. He relaxes casually against the concrete wall, smoking and watching me. "You don't want to watch the end of your movie?"

"Nope. You don't find it funny and you're just indulging me."

"Do you want to stay here to see the sunset?"

"No. I hate sunsets. I only like to watch the sunrise."

I feel the sudden heavy pressure of his eyes.

"What's going on inside that head of yours, Chrissie?"

I look at him and tense. His eyes are smoky and a potent caress, but hidden within their shadowy depths I see curiosity, caution, and something I've never had a guy look at me with before...pity.

I struggle to maintain my composure. "I'm just trying to figure out what I want to do since you really don't do the date thing well." Then sarcastically, "What's going on inside that head of yours, Alan?"

"I'm trying to figure out why you are here. You're a very confusing girl to read."

I frown. "That's the second time you've said that. I'm not confusing at all. Why do you say that?"

He takes a long drag of his cigarette and stares at me through the smoke. "There are usually four types of girls who end up with me: addicts, fame-whores, gold-diggers and rich little girls with daddy issues."

Oh god, he stole my line and is using it cruelly. "Very organized. A nice system," I say with a calm I don't feel. "Which kind of girl am I?"

"I don't think you fit in my A through D list."

Forcing an air of amusement, "No?"

"No." There isn't even the slightest hint of lightness in that. He puts out his cigarette. "I'm not sure what it is I see in you, but whatever it is, it worries me, Chrissie. And I never expected that and I really don't like it."

Oh shit. My body grows cold as the entirety of my body heat concentrate in my cheeks. I rise to my feet.

He crosses the terrace to me. "You don't have to leave."

I look at him and find those black eyes watching me, assessing every change in my expression.

Afraid and flashing with internal anger, I head toward the door. "Sorry, Alan, I'm out of here. Go play your games on another girl. You are just too weird for me."

He smiles, unruffled, and lightly brushes my hot cheek with an index finger. "No, I don't think so. I'm not too weird for *you*. I think I'm exactly what you look for."

I slap his hand away. "What the hell does that mean?"

"You think I'm a fucked up asshole who's going to fuck you, fuck you without ever getting to know you, and then toss you aside. And that's what you want. That makes me safe for you. That's the reason you're here with me."

He walks away, not waiting for an answer. He disappears through the terrace doors and leaves me alone in my anger, knee deep in verbal shit and emotional mess. Wanting to scream, I shake my hands to contain my reaction, and then I realize I'm containing tears. Is that really what Alan thinks of me? It shouldn't matter, but my insides grow icy as I realize he pities me.

He pities me! Numb with humiliation, I flee the orangey sunset glow on the terrace into the dim corridors of the apartment.

I'm almost to the door before I turn back. Oh no, Alan Manzone, I am not going to sulk off like a wounded child without answering that. Who the fuck does he think he is? He's the one with the life that's a train wreck.

Livid, I storm into the kitchen. There are two place settings set up on the butcher block island, two empty wine glasses and something sizzling in a pan on the stove. Alan is focused on gently moving the contents of the skillet with a spatula.

I struggle to organize my thoughts and find a way to launch my tirade.

"I offered you dinner so why don't you stay," he says quietly.

I exhale a long, ragged breath. "Why should I stay? You don't even like me."

He looks over his shoulder and the expression on his face is puzzling, yet strangely unthreatening. "I never said that I didn't like you, Chrissie. I said that you worried me."

I sit on the high bar chair and let out an angry breath. "How can I worry you? You don't even know me."

Alan ignores that question and concentrates instead on transferring the contents of the pan onto the plates. "There isn't much here to cook," he says, smiling in an apologetic way. "The kitchen hasn't been stocked yet, but I promise it's edible. I make a very good Un Croque-Monsieur."

I stare at the plate as he opens the wine. "I hate to ruin your fancy dinner party, but it's a grilled cheese."

He arches a brow and starts to fill the glasses. "In Paris it is Un Croque-Monsieur."

"In California it is a grilled cheese. Only you did it wrong. The cheese is supposed to be on the inside."

I don't know why I'm being so combative and petty about this. It's just a freaking sandwich, but I don't want to relax my guard and I'm not exactly certain why I am here eating with him.

He takes a bite and studies me with curiosity. "Haven't you ever been to Paris?"

I pick at the layers of my sandwich, trying to figure out what's different. "I've hardly been out of California."

"You don't travel with Jack?"

"Jack hardly talks to me. Why would he have me travel with him?"

I regret that comment the second it's out because it makes me sound pouty and little girlish. His eyes fix on me like a laser. I take a bite of my sandwich, and then a sip of the wine.

"It's the Gruyère cheese," he explains, smiling over his wine glass before taking a sip. "That's what's different."

I watch as he downs two thirds of his wine. "So much for recovery. Why are you drinking?"

He sets his wineglass before him. "I stayed sober in Rehab to get out of Rehab. I stayed sober at Jack's to stay out of jail, but I don't buy into that total sobriety bullshit and I never will. You should know that up front."

His mouth sets in a grim line. He looks angry and it feels like he's assessing my reaction. I frown and return to my food. "How did you end up at our house in Santa Barbara? Maria said you were there four months. And what did you do to fuck up so completely?"

His lips quirk up in a half-smile. "Ah, you've opted not to playact. There are consonants with your expletives. It's a boring story. Not worth repeating."

We eat for a while in silence

"Addiction isn't like it is in the movies, Chrissie," he starts, his voice raspy and tired and strangely sounding far away. "It's more insidious, more fun, and less obvious. Unfortunately, it always ends the same way. I just got absorbed in the pain of living. I tried to escape it. But you can't no matter what you do. So I pushed the limits a little more. And then a little more. And then I'm dragging down my best friend with me, and Len is trying to hold me together, and all I can think of is that I want to stop fucking thinking for a moment."

I don't want to be enthralled by this and find that I am. *Stop fucking thinking for a moment*...yes, I understand that. It is the first thing about Alan I understand.

"One day we were in Chicago. I don't know exactly where and I don't know exactly how. I was pretty fucked up by then. I'd been clean for eight years and I was quickly all back in it, doing more and more, and more not being ever enough. I don't recall who gave it to me. But I sort of thought, fuck it. Why not today? It was a speedball. Do you know what that is?"

I nod. Of course. Stupid question. My brother was Sammy.

"It was good shit. Really pure. Enough for a nice size party. And I lined it up and I snorted it all and I said, fuck it, maybe I'll just stop thinking today."

The naked honesty in his voice is mesmerizing. He is a private and guarded guy. Why is he telling me this?

"The days after that are a blur. I don't remember anything except waking in a hospital room somewhere, and Jack is there. He took me to detox. I bolted. Then there are some days in Chicago that I really don't remember clearly. Then I'm in Rehab in California. And then I'm released and Jack is waiting on the steps to take me home with him. And then I wake up in the pool house and Jack is barbequing like everything is fucking normal. Except nothing is fucking normal. I don't care who you are. You don't expect to wake up to find Jackson Parker tossing a burger on the grill for you. And then slowly *Jack's everything normal* takes over the fucking world and he's got me straight and sober and recording again. And I'm still fucking thinking, but I'm off the smack, so something good came from it, I guess."

He shakes his head, but the phrase *'Jack's everything normal'* tears me up inside. Jack's everything normal helped Alan. It has never done a fucking thing for me. I feel the tears behind my lids.

"So, that's it, Chrissie. End of story about me. But that's not really why you asked that question, is it? You don't give a shit what happened to me. You are trying to understand yourself."

Startled, I look up. Oh god…how effortlessly he can turn my world into a shaky, shadowy mess. I can't feel my arms, I can't feel my legs and the words I want to scream are trapped inside my head.

"Do you want to know what I thought the first time I met you?"

Instinctive fear rises through my center and the small child in me screams: *No, I don't want to know! Go away, Alan. I don't want you or anyone stumbling around in my lockboxes!*

"I thought, what a beautiful girl. How is it possible she's so sweet and charming and innocent in this fucked up world? So emotionally fragile that she playacts to hide how afraid she is. Sweet and charming and totally forgettable."

I feel as though I am shrinking, diminishing.

Alan arches a brow. "Then I met Rene and I thought, how interesting. What's wrong with Chrissie that she would have a friend like that? Maybe there is something beneath the surface of the girl she doesn't let people see."

The child in me screams: *There is nothing. There is nothing. Go away!*

"And now three days in New York," he continues with a voice like velvet and words that burn, "I'm wondering how Jack fucked this up so completely. You're a pretty fucked up girl. You hide it well by being charming. For what it's worth, I think you should work at being less charming and more real."

Scrambling in an emotional avalanche, I snap, "I am not fucked up and Jack didn't fuck up a goddamn thing."

His calm in the face of my welling panic is wholly defeating. It is the truth. No one ever sees it. No one ever speaks it. No one ever sees my truth. I don't know what to do with this or what to do with him.

Alan rises, grabs the dishes off the counter and deposits them in the sink. "I don't do bullshit, Chrissie. That's why you are here. There are seven bedrooms. Pick the room you want." And without looking back, Alan walks from the kitchen.

I sit in the quiet, in the kitchen that somehow got clean as though no one was ever here, and I want to run, but I don't know why I'm not running or why I am still here.

I've been angry for so long, with all the things trapped in my lockboxes, and then finally there is truth in the room. I thought this moment would feel better. It doesn't. It feels only different; a different kind of weirdness. The weirdness of letting truth in the room.

I suddenly know why I am so obsessed with Alan, and what is pushing me toward him. Alan Manzone can see right through me. It should make me run, it should terrify me; instead, it draws me toward him.

Alan sees *me* and has done so from the first night we met. I push off the counter and I am trembling and afraid.

Chapter Eight

The room is so quiet it is deafening.

I find Alan on his bed, casually reclined against a stack of pillows, dressed only in flannel pajama bottoms, and reading—of all things—the *Wall Street Journal.* There is a fire lit, the silver candlesticks flicker with flame, the bedcovers invitingly turned down as if in preparation for some sort of romantic scene. But he is focused on the *Journal.*

He doesn't look at me and I feel stupid hovering by his door, so I start to wander around the bedroom, trying to still my frantic pulse. It's a good thing that it's an interesting room, otherwise my deliberate study would seem silly.

Even Alan's bedroom is something I find weird and demands a certain amount of mental analysis. It looks like something from a nineteenth century English manor, elegant to the point of being almost a touch prissy. There's an antique mahogany king-sized bed facing the fireplace; floral wingback chairs with pillows positioned before the hearth; and high-tech conveniences camouflaged in antique furniture. There's a Monet on the wall; tall, polished sterling silver candlesticks; crystal; and fine, leather-bound, first edition books of classic literature. I sink down before a small, mahogany table where I find a stack of newspaper: *Barons;* the *New York Times;* the *Washington Post;* and the *Daily Telegraph.*

The warmth of the fire surrounds me like a caress, but I am quaking like a leaf. I wasn't sure what Alan expected after he walked out of the kitchen. It would have been logical to assume that I would leave. But he knew I'd follow him. I don't know why he's ignoring me now. I look at the lit candlesticks—he wanted me to follow him.

I bite my lower lip and stare at my knotted fingers. I stayed alone in the kitchen for what seemed like ages, and now that I've done exactly what he expected me to do, *nothing.*

I struggle for something to say to break the silence. "You do have seven bedrooms. I counted them twice. But there are seven only if I include yours."

He folds the *Journal*, tosses it on the table and fixes those penetrating, mesmerizing eyes on me. "Is this the room you want?" he asks, his voice gentle. "I meant it when I said you could have any room. It doesn't have to be my room for you to stay."

Does he not want me in his room? A ragged breath forces its way from deep in my lungs. "Do you want me to go?" I murmur.

"Of course not. I want you here." His voice is husky and his eyes are wandering in a leisurely hold that is tender and oddly comforting. "But I'm not going to fuck you, Chrissie. I want so very much to make love to you."

His gaze is intense, and the effect of his words travels through me. His precise tone, his odd phrasing; it should have made me laugh from nothing else but the weirdness of it. Instead, I want to cry because that statement reveals a lot of what he sees inside of me.

"Can we turn the lights out?" I whisper.

He crosses the room and stands in front of me, staring down into my eyes. "If you want, but I undressed you last night. I've seen you nude. I saw every part of you. Everything."

I flush...*everything?*... what is he trying to tell me? Then the lights flip off and there is only the sweetly forgiving glow of firelight, and Alan is lifting me from the floor.

He is surprisingly strong, and he carries me with so little effort that it makes me feel fragile and beautiful and weightless. Tentatively, I touch my lips to the warm flesh of his neck, the taste of him running through my veins like fire, my blood pumping all through my body. But I get only a fast taste of him before he eases me down on the bed. I think he's going to cover me with his body, but he doesn't; he settles on his hip in a relaxed arrangement of long body parts beside me.

Every move he makes is with such exquisite, slow grace, but his eyes are smoky with eager desire. I take the initiative and curl into his chest to kiss him, wanting him to feel my own urgency, but he changes the flow of the current so subtly, it takes a moment for me to realize he is slowing me, calming me with his mouth, moving me where he wants. I want to melt into him, into the play of his fingers, the feel of his lips, but he holds the space between us.

His mouth leaves mine in a slow disconnect, and agony shoots up my center. He opens his eyes. The corners of his mouth lift in a diffused, sort of blurred smile.

"What do you like, Chrissie?" he whispers and leans down to kiss the inside of my thigh, hidden by my dress.

He hovers over me, watching my shifting emotions as I squirm with need. *What do I like? I don't know. I've never done this before.* He is so seductive I realize that there isn't anything I wouldn't want to do with him.

"Everything," I breathe and he answers me with a soft, raspy laugh.

Then one of my legs is in his hands. He's slipping off my shoe, a kiss on the ankle, a gentle return of my flesh to the mattress, and then the other leg, surrounded by his touch, air hitting toes, lips touching ankle.

"You have no idea how beautiful you are," he says softly. His hands are on my sundress. "Why can't you see it? Why are you so unaware of your own beauty?"

Cold air surrounds my flesh. My dress is gone. My breath hitches, excitement and fear, knotted-bands running through my senses. I can't look away from him. He is staring at me naked beneath him, seeing every inch of my flesh, and all I can do is watch him look at me.

His fingers are fluttering along my thigh, tracing and touching everywhere, and his other hand is on my breasts, and he is kissing me: my mouth, my neck, the rise of my breasts, the swell, the nipple, my belly, my navel. My skin is burning. Every move is patient, deliberate and potent.

Oh...it is getting stronger. It is getting wonderfully worse. I want to touch him. He begins to move slowly up my body with his kisses, and my nipples harden beneath the play of his mouth and fingers. I can feel his breathing, ragged and hard, and yet I'm bathed in that exquisite slowness of his moves. He is drawing me into him.

I want to melt into this slowness, hover in this deliciously wet and aching anticipation.

"How do you want to come?" His fingers gently tease me and then he cups my sex. "My hand or my mouth?"

I've never done any of this. I don't know what I want. I want to hover in this as long as I can, and yet my body is demanding completion. His hand or his mouth?

Through the dim, flickering light I hear more laughter.

"I'm going to take your silence as my choice."

He eases back and gently opens my legs. His fingers float up the inside of my legs, my thighs. He hovers. I squirm with need. A kiss on my ankle. A touch behind my knee. I am going to climb out of my skin and climax before his mouth ever touches me. He kisses the inside of my thigh. Lightly. A light breath. My fingers curl around the sheets. Another kiss higher. A light breath. A kiss on the top of my pelvis. I tense and he kisses lower, lighter, feather-light.

My head moves on the pillow. My hips begin to move. He steadies them with his fingers. And then his mouth is there, in a knowing rhythm of tongue and fingers and kisses and touch. And I am quaking and moaning, being seduced to the edge, and then pulled back, over and over again. It is not me controlling my body. It is not me stopping the delicious pleasure that is repeatedly stirred. It is him. He is coaxing me there and pulling it away, deliberately.

"Oh… please," I beg. I want him to finish me. The building is painful and demanding and I want it. I want it now. What is he doing to me?

"Don't fight, Chrissie. Stop fighting your body and come alive," he murmurs, before the work of his mouth and fingers devour me, this time guiding me straight on the path, knowing exactly where he is taking me. My legs stiffen. My back arches. I don't even recognize the panting groans in the room. Every part of me releases into his touch and mouth. A complete, slow event all on its own.

His mouth closes over mine, swallowing my breaths as he covers my body. I'm still quaking as I feel the head of his erection at the entrance of my femaleness. He is moving slowly, touching me ever so slightly in there, teasing me to drive me mad. But the pounding urge to feel him inside is overpowering. I arch up, pushing him deep inside of me, then a rip and a burn that makes me cry out.

Alan stills, his eyes blazing, bright with question and something else I can't identify. At the moment of penetration, Alan has stopped.

"Jesus Christ, Chrissie." His voice is breathy. Ragged. Intense.

His mouth is open slightly, his breathing is harsh and I can tell he is struggling to stay still. He doesn't move. The way he's looking at me, his intense stare and frozen posture, makes me collapse inside. It wasn't that bad. Why doesn't he just finish it? No guy stops. You hurt, they finish and then it's done with.

I taste the salt and realize I am crying. The tears come harsher, thicker, in a steady stream. It's almost as if by acknowledging the tears I've broken a pipe.

He closes his eyes. "Please, Chrissie, don't cry."

The kiss he drops on my lips is sweetly tender. My eyes round and I stare up at him.

"I'm going to start this very slowly," he whispers, his voice quiet but urgent. I feel his thumb, gentle, lightly brushing my cheek. The effect is calming and arousing.

I close my eyes, trying to keep my breathing and flesh under control, wanting to absorb the tenderness of his touch, his kisses, that drown the memory of the pain and make me acutely aware of his body filling me.

He eases in and then out with careful slowness. A gentle kiss. A quiet move of his flesh. A touch. The glide of his flesh out. His mouth, here and there, every part of me kissed, stirred and made chaotic. His fingers gentle in tending, knowing and cautious. My fingers, moved to touch him. His, erotic in my mouth. And the feel of him, *there,* even when he is not there.

We move in a fluid rhythm and there is no pain. Every touch bringing me to the point where I could match his was patient, tender and arousing. Every kiss pulled me deeper into him. My body meets his in unforced perfection as my hands roam his flesh in wayward sureness. Ours bodies are soaring in a single glide and it is beautiful. It is giving. It is tender. It is Alan.

* * *

An ember crackles from the fireplace, jolts me from deep sleep, and I open my eyes. The nearly pitch black room is warm, the flesh beside me is warm, but I am cold and shaky. Alan is sound asleep and he is facing me. And I haven't made up my mind if I should stay and face him.

As wonderful as last night was, there hovers in the room all that was deliberately left unspoken. Slipping from the bed, I find the shirt Alan was wearing yesterday laying over the back of a chair and I shrug into it.

As cozy and elegant as his bedroom is, his bathroom is the opposite. It is pristine, glaringly colorless, cold and filled with unforgiving light. Spartan and spotless, it is dominated by a giant mirror filling the wall above the double sinks. There is a tub, a shower, a commode and a bidet.

I sink on the icy marble floor, hugging my legs with my arms, facing that gigantic and grotesque mirror. What did Alan see when he looked at me last night? I can't remember the last time I looked at myself nude in front of a mirror. And I have never let anyone else, not even Rene, see me completely undressed.

I change in the bathroom of our dorm even though Rene ruthlessly taunts my little girl behaviors, and at the beach I'm never without my one-piece suit and wraparound sarong. Rene makes fun of that, as well.

Alan has seen all of me. What did he see? I stand up, biting my lower lip, and cautiously ease his shirt from my trembling flesh. It shouldn't surprise me, but I still suffer a harsh punch of emotion when I look at myself, which is why I never look at myself. If I don't see it, it's not real, it's not me, and I don't have to deal with it. I anxiously cover myself and sink to the floor.

Last night Alan saw all of me and, more, he kissed each offended spot on my flesh. I don't understand why he'd do that, why a guy I hardly know would be more gentle and loving to myself than I am.

A light trickle of tears spill down my cheeks, and I brush them furiously aside. I should never have stayed and it hurts, it hurts so badly now that it's shared and real. I just want to curl up someplace safe, curl up and pretend this night never happened.

What was I thinking? Why did I let him see? Why did it seem safe to share with Alan the dark in me?

I wrap his shirt tightly around me, curl up and really let the tears go. I want to cry until every part of me is drained and without feeling.

I hear the door click open and I lift my face to find Alan staring down at me.

"Chrissie, why are you hiding in the bathroom crying?" he says after a long while.

I brush at my dripping nose and order the tears to stop. Jeez, how stupid I must look to him, curled on the floor like a little girl, sobbing.

His eyes are black and guarded as he closes the space between us and sinks beside me on the tile.

"Everything just got a little too close and real," I whisper.

He lifts a wayward hair from my face and looks at me puzzled. "Did I hurt you?"

I shrug. "Not in the way you think." I swallow. "It's just, I've never done that before." Tears swim in my eyes again. "It's a lot to process."

His eyes soften. "Never?" The way he says that tells me he knows I'm not talking about my virginity, that I'm talking about the more significant part of me I shared with him last night. But he's not pushing, and quietly trying to assess how to deal with me.

We sit together like this, neither of us saying anything. Alan uses quiet better than most people use words. An interesting contradiction, since his gift is creating sound. But Alan's quiet is never empty. It is filled with him. I relax and stop crying, and the quiet filled with him is a comforting thing.

I brush the hair back from my face, and the wide platinum bracelet that I never remove slips down on my arm far enough that now *it* is here in the room.

"How did that happen?" His voice is without emotion, deliberately so I think.

I stare at the top of my wrist. How ugly it looks in the spotless brightness of Alan's bathroom. "It's old. I did it when I was thirteen. I spilled candle wax. It's no big deal. It's old."

"Has Jack seen it?"

Jack saw it and didn't comment. Jack hardly looks at me. Instead of speaking the words in my head, I shake my head no.

"How about Rene? Surely she's seen it."

Rene saw it, but she's totally messed up, and too completely absorbed in her own mess to spare much thought about my little weakness. I nod.

"What a fucking useless friend," he whispers, his voice raw.

Shame and panic turn me protective. "It's not what you think. It's no big deal. It was just an accident."

The lie sounds foolish even to me and I know better than to expect Alan to swallow it or to let it go. In a flash, he has my arm in his hand and that ugly scar held beneath his penetrating eyes. "Don't try bullshit with me, Chrissie. There are not just addicts in Rehab. There was a girl there who cuts herself and another who burns. The burner had a scar that looks just like this. She said it took years burning over and over again the healing flesh until it puckered and protruded from the rest of her flesh. That's not a fucking accident, and I won't pretend with you that it is."

My scalp prickles as every cell in my body turns to ice.

"When was the last time you burned yourself?" he asks.

I shrug. I really don't know. It is something that exists inside of me with merciful fogginess. I burn when I cannot stop myself, and I don't feel it afterward. And by not feeling it, it isn't real. It comes in waves and it goes. It isn't real.

He shakes his head, and I can tell he's growing frustrated with me. "Why do you hurt yourself?"

The world falls away from me, leaving in clear view that tormenting abyss I never look in on.

"Why do you hurt yourself?" he repeats acidly.

"I don't anymore, so just drop it."

His hand not holding my arm turns my bracelet until the infinity clasp is staring up at us. With painful and harsh movements, he takes the bracelet from my wrist.

"Hiding it won't change a goddamn thing," he says, and then to my horror he lifts my shirt. "Especially since you've got little burns all over your thigh and abdomen made with the infinity clasp of a Tiffany bracelet. Is that supposed to make you proletarian normal or something? Burning your flesh with the clasp of a Tiffany bracelet? What the fuck is wrong with you?"

He tosses the bracelet into my lap. I look at Alan, then I see the barely contained fury in his eyes. "I don't want to talk about this," I implore.

Alan runs a frustrated hand through his hair. "You wouldn't be here if you didn't."

I lift my bracelet and quickly return it to my wrist. "Maybe, but that doesn't mean that I want to talk about it with you," I say weakly.

"You're going to have to talk about it someday."

Alan leans away from me and opens a vanity door. From a polished, black lacquer box, he lifts out an already rolled joint, lights it and then takes a puff.

You've got your own share of issues, Alan. When is it fair game to talk about those? My vision focuses on the cherry flame and I watch the smoke curl from his lips.

He holds the joint out to me. I shake my head. "It will make you feel calmer. It's been a rough night for you."

"I don't do drugs."

He laughs, shaking his head. "Oh no, Chrissie, you're an addict. Your preferred drug is something you don't ingest, but don't try to bullshit a bullshitter. You're an addict. I thought you decided to stop playacting."

When I don't take it from his hand, he fills his mouth with smoke and then his lips are pushing wide my lips and he's filling me with smoke before I can stop him. Struggling and coughing, I push him away.

"Fuck you! I said I didn't want that."

He stands up. "Too bad. There are better ways of numbing yourself than mutilating your body. I just didn't want to smell burning flesh."

I stare up at him, furious, not knowing what to say or how to deal with him. *That was mean, Alan. So mean. Why do you have to be so mean sometimes.*

He leans over me and turns the knobs on the bathtub. He pushes in the stopper, and in between hits of weed, lights the candles along the white tile ledge.

The room has a light film of smoke in it and the tub is half full before he tosses the joint into the open commode and sinks down in front of me. He begins to unbutton my shirt without asking.

"What are you doing? I don't want you to undress me," I exclaim.

The shirt is jerked from my flesh and I am lifted from the ground and set into the tub. He forces me to lie back against the tile.

"Fuck, Chrissie, will you stop being such a pain. I've already seen you nude. It's not like there anything new to see in the last five minutes."

He looks both angry and amused. I still, flush, and give in to defeat. I need time alone, away from him, to think, and maybe he'll just leave if I take the freaking bath.

Alan sinks down to sit beside the tub, waits until the water is high, and turns the knobs off.

"Close your eyes." This time his voice is a raspy, seductive whisper.

I close my eyes. I really don't know why I do it, except that he asked me to. I feel his arm move over me and then I hear his other hand in the water. I tense, thinking he's going to touch me, and he does, but not in the way I think.

His hand moves slowly down my arm, foaming the lather as he washes gently. The inner tension I didn't even know I had slowly leaves my tired limbs, as his hand crosses my breasts. He is only washing me, and there is care in the way he touches my flesh, so gentle in his tending that I melt into the sensations. He doesn't linger long in any one place, but his rough-tipped fingers glide everywhere.

He leans into me, a hand on my shoulder and a hand washing between my thighs. His lips touch my neck, my breathing increases, my head tilts back as my heart accelerates.

"Your body is beautiful, Chrissie," Alan whispers in my ear. "You were afraid to let anyone see you nude. That's why you're beautiful and eighteen and still a virgin. That's why you playact to keep the world away. You think your body is repulsive and you'd rather hide and playact than let anyone see your pain. But I'm not repulsed, and I find you so beautiful, Chrissie."

He pulls away and I open my eyes. My breath catches in my throat. He is standing above me, at ease in his maleness, his eyes a burning black seduction.

He lifts me from the water, doesn't dry me, and carries me to the bed. The room is mercifully dark, though the darkness between us now is really an unnecessary thing. Without a word, he is in me hard and quick. He kisses me hard, pushing his tongue into me with the same powerful thrusts.

He cradles my head and holds me with his body in a tight cocoon beneath him, relentless in his taking, harsh and fast and consuming. My heated blood moves through my body and I begin to groan, fighting awkwardly the restraints of his flesh. But this time he doesn't slow, he isn't gentle, and a part of me glories in this brutal take. I writhe. I release the air from my lungs into him, and then I am lost and there is nothing but Alan. The world dips and disappears from view, and it is rightly so.

* * *

When I open my eyes, I'm trapped in a room filled with cruel morning light. I can feel Alan beside me and I feel drained. I must have fallen asleep.

I hear a funny sound. The sound of a Polaroid? My eyes fly open and I try to jerk up the sheets.

Alan laughs. "Too late."

He is balanced on an elbow, staring down at me, with a camera in the other hand. How long has he been awake? How long has he been watching me sleep? Why is he taking a picture of me?

"Give me that."

I try to get the square of film from him as he waves it in the air. He turns on his back, holding it above his head and I'm on top of him and I can't reach it.

"No. I want to preserve how you look at this moment," he whispers, and his voice is so damn seductive and the feel of him is all around me, and the flesh beneath me feels happy. I don't know if I've ever felt Happy Alan before. He feels happy.

I stop fighting him for the picture. I sink down on his chest. I peek up at him. "Why? Why do you want that?"

He takes another picture. It's of both of us. He drops it on the bed. He turns me in his arms until I'm curled beside him, my head and arm on his chest.

"When we are old," he whispers, and I know the voice now, the silky ribbons of theatrics, "and you don't want to forgive me, I will show you these pictures, so you will remember us now and perhaps forgive me later. I don't need a picture. I will remember you always at this moment."

I feel his words in my center, but my calm inside suddenly vanishes and I am messy again. Will I know him when we are old, or is this all there is? A brief fling that only I will remember always? This has been so much more for me than it could ever be for him, and I hate the suspicion that his theatrics mean he is only toying with me.

I kiss his chest and turn in his arms. I link my fingers through his, lifting them up above, studying our differences.

"Are you like this with all your girls?" I ask. "Do you have a drawer somewhere full of Polaroids with moments to remember?"

The body beside me tenses, and I shift my gaze from our fingers to his face. Jeez, he looks pissed. My mouth goes dry.

"They're over there in that cabinet. Why don't you burn them?" he snaps harshly.

I pull away from him, taking the sheets with me

"And burn the sheets while you're at it," he continues. "Who knows what I will do with the sheets since you're the first virgin I've ever popped."

Popped? Really, Alan? I drop my gaze from his and see my blood there on the sheets. I flush, embarrassed.

I take in a steadying breath. "Well, there's a first for everything. Perhaps I should go." I pick up the camera. "Let me get a picture of asshole Alan to remind me not to come back here."

"Fuck, I hate it when you playact," he growls.

"Fuck, I hate it when you're theatrical. You do it deliberately to keep me off-balance so you can mess with me."

I am almost out of the bed and his hand stops me. "There are no other pictures, Chrissie. There are no other moments I want to remember always. You're the only girl I've ever made love to."

I make an exaggerated face. "Really? What do you do with all the others if you didn't make love to them? Play scrabble?"

He shakes his head, frustrated with me. In a flash I'm hauled up against him, back in his arms, back in the bed. "Even though you are playacting to pretend that the answer doesn't matter to you, I will tell you the truth. I fucked them. That's what we did. We fucked. There is a difference between fucking and what we did. The others I only fucked. Nothing more. You, Chrissie, matter to me."

He is kissing my neck. I don't want to argue. I don't want to ask this, and yet I can't stop myself. "Why do I matter?"

"Because you are you."

I roll my eyes. "Can you be more specific than that? What does 'because you are you' mean?"

He is fingering my breasts, his thumb brushing my nipple. His starts to lightly tracing at the apex between my thighs. "Are you sore?"

I lift my face from his chest. "Of course, I'm sore. The second time you were not at all gentle."

Alan's eyes glow wickedly. "Are you too sore if I'm really gentle?"

I shake my head to prevent Alan kissing me. I turn my cheek on his chest to keep my mouth away from him. I study his arm, debating with myself. I sink my teeth into my lower lip. I take in a deep breath.

"Should I be worried?"

He frowns. "Worried?"

I can't keep the color from rising on my face. How do people manage this conversation comfortably? Shit, how do I say it without saying it?

Alan lifts my face from his chest. Those black eyes drill into me. I wait. God, this is awful. It takes him a moment to comprehend.

"Oh. They check everything when you go into a hospitalized recovery center. I may behave stupidly most of the time, but I am always paranoid and careful. And since the hospital, I haven't been with anyone until you."

Paranoid and careful. I don't like that at all. I don't like being reminded that us like this is nothing new to him, and I definitely don't like being reminded that he's a heroin addict.

I lie beneath his touch as he starts to sweep hairs from my face. He leans in to kiss me, stops, and then stares at me. "Paranoid except with you. Should I be worried?"

I roll my eyes. "Ha ha ha! Worried? Be nice. Don't make fun of me."

He doesn't laugh. His eyes grow more intense. "Have you taken all your pills?"

This moment has just gotten extremely awkward. Oh shit, my pills. I am very poor at keeping track of them. Say something fast, Chrissie. Something funny.

I pretend to slowly comprehend. "Oh, worried. Yes, I've had all my pills. Birth control is a constitutional right fought for by women."

Alan laughs. He relaxes. "That sounds like Jack."

I smile. "Of course, because it is. I've been patriotically taking the darn things for two years and lying to the Priest each week in confession to exercise my constitutional right to spit in the eye of the Pope."

Alan rolls his eyes. "Do you talk this way with other people?"

"No! It wouldn't work with anyone else. You're the first weirdo I've ever been friends with."

He laughs. With a finger, I begin to trace the lines of the tattoo on his stomach. The ink is growing on me. It gives me a reason to touch without being so obvious that I want to touch. God, I want to touch him always. He's like a drug. He is at times too intense, at times too aggravating, at times too mean, and at times too glorious. Like a drug. I can't get enough, and I am slipping so quickly into the hold of him.

What was I thinking? I'm not ready for him. Being with Alan is like being trapped on a runaway train, and his reminding me of the pills I need to count is a monumental wake-up call. In twenty four hours, he's delved farther into me than anyone I've ever known. He's no good for me. Maybe he's right. Maybe I am an addict. I want him even though I know he's going to hurt me.

I suddenly feel frazzled and disoriented. I climb from the bed. "I need to go back to my apartment."

I can feel him watching me. "I'll go with you." He starts to move.

"No."

I continue to gather my clothes. After what seems like a monumental amount of time, he sits on the edge of the bed near me.

"What's changed?" he asks after a long while.

"Nothing. I just need to go."

Those black eyes grow even darker. "Why are you running, Chrissie?"

How does he know that I've decided to leave, to get away from him? I stare at my feet. I take in a deep breath. "I need to go home and count my pills. I don't have them with me. I'm glad you reminded me."

His eyes widen and his expression changes. He runs a hand through his messy waves. "Is that all? Why didn't you just tell me? Why is it so hard for you to talk about normal things that people talk about?"

I make an exaggerated comical face. "Probably the Pope."

He shakes his head at me and starts pulling on his jeans. "Would you like to go out after we stop by Jack's to collect your things?" Now he's reaching for a shirt.

Oh god. How did we get from me leaving to us going to collect my things?

I stare. He is nearly dressed. "I expect you to decide what you want by the time we're done at Jack's."

My head is swimming. He really does expect me to stay here with him and I don't think that's a good idea.

I find my panties at the foot of the bed, pull them up and then look about for my shoes. *Nowhere.* I sink to look under the bed and out of the corner of my eye I see Alan lift a drink from the bedside table and down it in a single gulp.

God, when did he pour that? I can tell by the golden brown color and the cocktail glass that it's alcohol. I stretch underneath the bed to grab my shoe and am just easing into a sitting position when I find him gazing down at me, his expression hard.

"Whatever you're thinking, Chrissie. Don't say it. Rule one: You are not going to change me."

How dare he order me when there seems to be no topic about me off limits for discussion, in his opinion?

I jerk my laces into order and tie a bow. "I don't like drunks," I murmur.

Alan runs a hand through his hair, exasperated.

"Then I won't be drunk while you're here, but you are staying the rest of your vacation," he commands softly. "Get used to the idea."

I frown, trying to process his words, and then resolve to make a face. "I can't even get used to the idea of you."

He smiles, though there was nothing about either my words or tone that should make him smile. God, he's a frustrating guy and impossible to deal with.

I am silent as we take the elevator down to the lobby. If he's irritated with me, it doesn't show. He is just sort of there beside me and not really with me at all. This deliberate distance he seems to hold between us at times is a strange feeling, now that I've been to bed with him.

On the sidewalk we find Colin beside Alan's car, waiting for us.

"Do you mind if we walk?" I ask, noting the warmth of the sun and the pleasantness of the day.

He shrugs and tells Colin to follow. The streets are crowded, but it comes as a welcome relief to my overtaxed emotions, having a little bit of space and time to focus on something other than Alan.

There is an odor to New York City that you don't smell anywhere else. A stench that crawls up from the concrete, through the grates, on steam and air that is an absolutely repulsive smell. I don't know why I always prefer to walk in the city. The stench is so hard to bear and I like ocean air and quiet streets.

I've gone four blocks without a word from Alan. "I hate the way New York smells. It smells like rotting death."

He glances quickly at me. "That's an interesting way of looking at it. I'm surprised you wanted to walk."

I shrug. "I always want to walk here. Morning. Night. It doesn't matter. Sometimes I spend hours just walking these stinky streets."

He is watching me again in that way he has, as if I baffle him. Jeez, we're just making chitchat about walking. Why is that so confusing?

Inside the elevator, I can feel him watching me, but he doesn't say anything. I struggle to keep my face carefully averted and only look at him when he precedes me into the apartment.

Alan stays in the great room while I gather my things. The first thing I do is check those damn pills. Why do they package them in a way that they are so hard to keep track of? I study them. OK, I think I've taken the right number. I pop out today's and go into the bathroom for water to take it with.

I catch a glance of myself in the mirror. I stare. I look different, more aware of myself, more like a woman, less like a girl. Everything changes. It changes quickly. This is what I look like when I am with Alan. Will I still look like this when I am back in Santa Barbara, same old Chrissie? Same old life?

I go back into the bedroom, pull on a fresh change of clothes, and shove my things into my duffel. I stare at my wallpaper with the horrid stripes and the floral border. I never feel comfortable in the New York apartment. I feel really out of place right now. I head toward the great room, lugging my duffel.

My heart stops. Alan is on the phone. I heard it ring. I ignored it. I heard it stop. I thought the service had grabbed it, but Alan answered it. He is reclined comfortably in a chair. His feet are bare, he has a bottle of Jack Daniels in hand and he's talking into the speaker.

"No, Chrissie is fine," Alan says, making me cringe.

"What are you doing at my place?" Jack asks and I tense. The question is so bizarre on its very surface and yet somehow Jack's voice is perfectly normal.

"Just checking on Chrissie. She doesn't know anyone in New York. I thought I should check in on her. "

Silence.

"I would have thought that Brian was keeping you too busy for social calls. Everything going all right, then?"

"I'm good. Working. Almost done. A few problems here and there, but most things settled."

I walk over and curl on the arm of Alan's chair.

"I heard an interesting rumor the other day," Jacks says casually. "I heard you got into a fight with Vince Carroll on the sidewalk in front of CBGBs and broke his arm."

"Since it's made press coast to coast, I think we can safely assume it's not rumor, Jack."

"Does Chrissie have anything to do with it?"

"No. That was between me and Vince. I just gave her a ride home when it was over."

A long pause. "You're not drinking again, are you?"

"Fuck, Jack. I've been clean six months. I don't need the sponsor bullshit."

"It's a fine line between drinking and shoving a needle in your arm."

"I'm not fucking up all over again, so you can save the lecture I'm sure you're itching to give."

Jack lets out a long, aggravated breath. Silence through the phone. "Put Chrissie on the line."

I tense, lifting the phone from the rest and take a steadying breath. "Hi, Daddy."

"Hi." Long pause—the kind he makes when he's not pleased with me, but won't say it. "Why didn't you tell me that Rene took off on you?"

"I didn't want to worry you."

"I want you to fly home. We can spend some time together."

"I don't want to leave Rene. She's really out of it over all this. I want to stay in New York in case she needs me. How did you know she left?"

"George called with his news."

"Oh."

More silence.

I change the subject. "You staying busy?"

"You know me, baby girl."

"Well, try not to work too hard."

"Talk to you soon, Chrissie."

I feel my stomach knot and grow cold. Tears well behind my lids. "Talk to you soon, Daddy."

Click. I hang up the phone. Alan is staring at me and there is something in his eyes that nearly makes the tears give way.

* * *

The candle flames flicker and dance all on their own. I am quiet. Alan is quiet. The mood is quiet, a comfortable quiet. He's wrapped all around me. Neither of us seem ready to sleep. It's after midnight. He is awake and still and being quiet for me.

We've had a day of strange quiet that felt oddly comforting and necessary. We walked in the park and Alan took me to dinner in a small, tacky eatery. We barely talked, and since returning to the apartment we made love only once and then just hovered in the quiet of the bedroom.

The sex was long and it was slow and it was tender. I cried all through it and I really don't know why. Alan seemed not to need to ask why.

Alan has spent the rest of the night just holding me. It is good. Very good. This comfortable quiet. I feel better inside of Alan's quiet, much better than I do alone inside of my own quiet.

I turn onto my side and Alan turns with me. He doesn't release me. He is warm against my back, still holding on. Why is he with me? I feel his face in my hair as he inhales deeply. Why does he hold onto me this way?

"Go to sleep, Chrissie," he whispers. "I want you to sleep. You'll feel better in the morning."

Chapter Nine

Something moves behind me and there is a whispering voice in the darkness.

"You talk in your sleep. Do you know that?"

I ease away from Alan and gaze up at him, blinking. There is enough light in the room that I can see the perfect lines of his face, and I frantically search his eyes, desperately trying to read them. But they are hooded and probing.

How long has he been watching me? It's the middle of the night, his posture in bed tells me he's been sitting up for quite a while, and he's been drinking.

I scoot away from him, dragging the sheets to cover me. "Why are you sitting in the dark getting loaded?"

He takes a long drag of his cigarette. "You've been crying and mumbling for hours. It was the crying that woke me up."

I push the hair from my face. "I'm sorry."

"Why do you have nightmares? You have them almost every time you sleep," he says, and his eyes are suddenly scrutinizing mine.

"Alan...I...I just have nightmares. It's no big deal. OK?"

"The things you mumble in your sleep. Is that why you burn yourself?" he breathes, his eyes widening.

How did we get to talking about this again? I struggle to collect the right words to get out of this.

"I don't do it anymore. I told you that. I don't want to talk about it."

He ignores my words in that completely Alan way. "What's up between you and your old man? There is definitely a strange vibe between the two of you."

"There is nothing. What does it matter? It's two a.m."

"It's so strange how you talk to each other." He shakes his head. "I've been sitting here trying to figure that one out. It's like you're both afraid to speak, which is completely strange since I find it usually impossible to shut Jack up."

"God, do you have any idea how irritating you can be? Why do you want to dig around in my shit? Don't you have more than enough of your own shit to deal with?"

Alan shrugs. "Yours is more fun."

I sigh. "Really. Is that why I'm here—so you can amuse yourself psychoanalyzing me?"

"You're here because I have three weeks to kill before I go back on the road. I'm between girls. You didn't seem to have anything better to do. And I thought you'd do what I tell you and not be too much of a pain in the ass."

He says it succinctly, like he's reading a grocery list. I hit him, but Alan only laughs and rakes the tumbling hair from his face. "I was wrong about the pain in the ass part," he teases, his eyes dancing with humor.

I stare at him, trapped in a storm of warring emotions, and then I burst out laughing.

Alan smiles. "I like you. That's why you're here."

I roll my eyes. "I haven't made up my mind about you just yet."

His eyes soften. "Oh yes you have, Chrissie. You never know what you want, but you always know how you feel."

From light spirited to all-knowing asshole again. "Now that we've got that settled, can I go back to sleep?"

He shakes his head and his eyes glow wickedly. "I'm glad you're awake. I never sleep through the night."

And before I can focus, he grabs my hips and pulls me back against him, angling my body until I'm tucked into the bend of his groin.

I try to wiggle away. "Stop it. I'm not having sex with you. I don't like you right now."

"That's fine. You can just lie there and let me have you," he whispers, the rasp of his voice stirring me deep inside even though I don't want him to. He is kissing my back and I can feel him adjusting my body into his erection.

He eases into me slowly, exquisitely, filling me. My fingers curl around the sheets and I am pulsing in anticipation.

He kisses my shoulder lightly. He doesn't move. "Do you want me to stop?" he breathes, his words a warm tickle against my flesh. He flexes his hips, forward, once, slowly and then stops.

I groan, closing my eyes and I revel in the feel of him. *Want him to stop?...how could he ask me that?* I try to move and he stills me.

"You have to say it, Chrissie," he orders. "You have to say it or I won't move."

"I want you."

He moves deeper in me and stops. *No! Jesus what does he want?* His hands and his lips are moving across me and my flesh is all sensation and his touch is all consuming. I try to move again and he won't let me. Peeking over my shoulder, I find him watching me. He looks so serious, his breathing is ragged and his perfect white teeth parted. I don't know why he's looking at me that way. I don't know what he wants.

He moves and I moan into the pillow, feeling my body melt away into the feel of him. He starts to move faster and faster, holding my hips, and it's so unexpected, so wonderfully filling to be taken like this. I am close. I am starting to understand the delicious signals of my body.

Oh god, I am completely absorbed with Alan: with his body; his meanness; his tenderness; his mess; his unpredictability.

"You are here, Chrissie," he breathes, "because I'm in love with you," and I have a startled moment of reaction before his arms tighten around my middle as he releases himself into me.

I curl on the edge of the bed, facing away from Alan, naked, awake and not talking.

"There are clubs open. Do you want to go out?" Alan asks. I ignore the question. He refills his cocktail glass, lights a cigarette and waits. "Do you want to sleep?"

Into my silence he just stares, beautiful, enigmatic, and frustrating.

"Nope. I'm not tired." My voiced is clipped. "I want to talk."

"OK. About what?"

I turn in bed to face him. "You being an asshole."

He grins. "Not my favorite topic, but nothing new."

"You're an asshole."

He watches me, unruffled. "Are we finished?"

"Not exactly."

"There's more?"

"I was referring to you saying that you love me. Don't mess with my head, Alan. Like you said, I'm already a pretty fucked up girl. Don't say things you don't mean."

Those black eyes swivel and fix on me. "Don't ever tell me how I feel."

"You can't love me. You don't even know me."

He closes his eyes and starts to laugh. "Oh, Chrissie. I know you. I know you better than you know yourself." He reaches up and gently wipes away a tear with his thumb that I didn't know had fallen. "We are so alike it's scary."

I push his hand away. "I'm not like you at all."

He runs a hand through his hair in frustration. "Fuck, I'm playing the honesty card first. I'm not messing with your head, Chrissie. Cut me some slack if I haven't done it well. I've never done it before. It seems necessary with you."

"It is totally unnecessary. I don't want anything from you other than what we're doing."

Now his eyes are burning. "And what exactly is that, Chrissie?"

The words clog in my throat, my thoughts jumble in my head, and I can feel her, the little girl inside of me who can spout meanness on a moment's notice.

"Fucking until I go home."

He closes his eyes and exhales. Then in a flash I am wrapped in a sheet and scooped from the bed. He is carrying me toward the door, but he keeps his eyes on me, unblinking. I can feel the tension in his body, and while nothing is showing on the surface, the anger is jolting through him.

Jesus Christ, we're in the hallway. "What are you doing?" I scream in panic.

"I don't think you're worth the effort," he whispers calmly.

"Then I'll go, but if you put me in the elevator naked in a sheet I swear to god..." I grab hold of the doorway and try to stop him. "Put me down."

"What the fuck do you want, Chrissie?" he growls.

Oh no. There is something in his face that warns me that I could blow this very easily. Fuck—truth or dare? Would he really dump me on the streets of New York undressed?

"I don't want to go," I whisper haltingly.

"I don't want you to go either," he counters, his voice raw. "Tell me why I should let you stay. You're a fucking pain in the ass most of the time."

And now I know. I know why he's angry. I know why I am here. "Because I'm a messed up girl and you care about me."

We stand together like this by the door for ages. He just holds me and very gradually relaxes, and I relax.

He lets out a shuddering breath. "You can trust me, you know. I saw it on your face. The uncertainty. I would never have put you out naked in a sheet."

I nod. "I know."

He kisses my forehead. "You don't trust anyone, Chrissie, and that's not a good thing. I want you to trust me. Not for me, Chrissie. For yourself. I think you really need to start trusting someone very soon."

Everything in my body goes cold and numb. The way he said that, the look in his eyes. I've never had anyone stare at me with such knowing worry in their eyes. Not Rene. Not Jack. Not anyone.

* * *

I am alone in Alan's bed when I wake. I roll over to check the clock. Holy crap, it's two in the afternoon.

I settle back against my pillow and lift his pillow to my face. The smell of him is there. The smell of us. And the smell of sex. How funny that I can smell that now. The smell of sex.

I turn onto my side and stare at the closed door. Alan never closes the door when he leaves the room. He also never leaves me when I'm asleep. He is always here watching me when I wake.

I go into his bathroom to pee. I finger his things on the counter. It is all so neat and organized. My bathroom doesn't look anything like this. My bathroom is a wreck, but there is a precision to everything in his world.

Alan is not your typical musician, not by a long shot.

Strange, but I haven't heard any music since I've been here. I see the instruments. They are all throughout the apartment. He never picks them up. One of the world's greatest guitarists and he never touches an instrument. I have never seen him play.

Weirdly, he is pathologically tidy. It isn't just the apartment that is in perfect order. Alan is a creature of perfect order. If he cooks, he cleans. If we toss our clothes on the floor, he later takes them to the hamper. If he pulls something from a drawer or a shelf, he returns it to its exact place.

Unexpectedly, he is like a symphony in bed: at times quiet and slow; then passionate and building; then haunting and intense; then gentle and peaceful, but totally, all consuming. Every emotion can be unfurled in a single event.

I didn't expect that. Not with his reputation. I expected a hard fuck and a harder goodbye. And I definitely never expected him to say he loves me. I'm still blown away by that and unable to get my head around it. If it is nothing more than typical Alan theatrics, I definitely don't want to find out. I already have enough emotional overload without trying to navigate that one.

After about ten minutes of staring at the bedroom door, I make a face and then open it. I can hear people. I peek into the kitchen. Thank god it's empty. I pad across the room, grab a cup and make a beeline for the coffeemaker.

"Can I help you, Miss?"

I whirl and the coffee sloshes from the pot and cup all over the floor. *Shit!* I anxiously put both on the counter and bend to wipe up my mess.

The woman crosses the room. "I'll do that, Miss. Was there something you needed? Breakfast perhaps?"

I stop my stupid movements with the towel and drop the soaked cloth into her outstretched hand. Her expression is neither kind nor critical, she is not surprised to find me, and for a domestic she is far too young and beautiful.

"Would you care for breakfast?" she asks, rising slowly until she is towering above me.

I shake my head. "Where's Alan?"

She raises a brow above an intense stare. She walks over to the counter, and in aggravation flips open a day planner. She skims the pages with a long, red manicured nail. "Manny has been gone since seven. He has fourteen interviews, a photo shoot and a meeting at the label."

I take a sip of coffee. He left without a goodbye and he'll be gone all day. I look up to see the girl staring expectantly.

"Breakfast, or would you like me just to ring for a car?"

Ring for a car? Why did she ask me that? Has everything changed without me knowing it?

I flush. "I'll just take the coffee."

The cup is only half full because half went onto the tile, but I don't refill it, I don't add the cream and sugar, and I quickly leave the kitchen. I go back to the bedroom and shut the door. I sink on the floor. Would Alan really sick that dreadful girl on me to get rid of me without bothering with a goodbye? I stare at the phone.

I haven't spoken to Rene in days and she would know the right move here.

I pull from my bag Mr. Thompson's DC number and punch it into the phone.

I hardly get a word in before Rene says, "Chrissie, what the hell is going on? I've been calling you for four days. You haven't called back. I've been worried sick. Where the fuck are you?"

That does it. The tears start. I've been fighting the tears since the kitchen, Alan is intense, and Rene is yelling and I never handle that well.

A long pause. A frustrated groan from Rene. "Why are you crying, Chrissie?"

"Would you please stop yelling at me?"

"Oh, shit. I'm sorry. You worried me. OK. What's going on? Are you OK?"

I run the back of my hand up my dripping nose. "What question do you want me to answer first?"

"Where are you?"

I take a gulp of air. "I've been in Alan's apartment for three days."

"Oh my god. You finally did it. And you are telling me your first time was with Alan Manzone and its lasted three days."

She starts to laugh.

"I'm glad you find this funny," I say quietly.

Her laughter stops at once. "Why are you crying, Chrissie? Was it awful?"

"I don't have anything to compare it with, but it wasn't awful." My lower lip quivers. "He's just really intense and I'm feeling a little overwhelmed, so if you could be a good friend it would be a good thing."

"Why overwhelmed?"

For some reason, that question unleashes a blow by blow news update of everything that has happened in the past four days, from CBGBs to being offered a car to leave in by that dreadful woman in the kitchen. Now that I've finally told someone, I feel calmer inside, less frantic, and it is all less scary.

"Oh shit! I forgot about Jimmy Stallworth," Rene says cavalierly. "Completely forgot about him. Is he still pissed about the weed?"

217

"God, Rene. Who cares?"

"Jeez, you don't have to be a bitch."

"I need you to help me figure out what I should do. Do I leave? Do you think that's how he gets rid of the girls when he's tired of them?"

"Fuck no. You don't leave. If he is going to be a bastard you make him be a bastard to your face."

I point my feet until my big toes touch. "OK, I won't leave."

"Did you come?"

"Why do you have to be so personally invasive?" I can't hide my exasperation. She's just being Rene, but it's irritating me today. "How are things in DC?"

Rene sighs in exasperation. "Less exciting than with you in New York. Who would have thought that?"

That gibe pricks me. "Definitely not you," I say a touch more prickly than I want to.

"Chrissie, what did he say when he saw your body?" she continues. "What did he say when he saw the burns?"

I tense head to toe, now hugging my legs until I'm in a tight ball. I never let her see me nude and we've never talked about my burns. Until now I've never been really sure she knew.

"He kissed every scar," I say quietly, trying to keep the emotion from my voice.

"Do you think he knew what they were? Guys are stupid. They don't always get everything."

"Yes." My voice hitches up several octaves. "He knew. Besides I told him the truth."

"You did?" Rene sounds astonished. "I'm glad you lost it to a guy who was kind. I would have never expected that to be Alan Manzone. When are you going back to the apartment?"

"I'm not. He wants me to stay with him while I'm in New York."

"Do you think that's a good idea?"

I feel the tears and I fight them.

"Chrissie? What is it?"

"I feel different. There is something going on with me."

"It's the sex, Chrissie. It fucks up all your emotions. It passes. It's just the sex."

"No. It's something else."

"I can be in New York in two hours. Fuck the wedding, Chrissie. Do you need me there?"

The offer stuns me. It's not like Rene to be generous and willing to drop everything for me.

"No. Don't bother. I'm OK."

"You sure?"

It's strange, but I don't want Rene. Whatever this is with Alan and me, I need to see it through on my own. "I'll call you in a couple days," I say quickly and hang up.

I climb into Alan's bed and curl around his pillow. I stare at the door. A day alone. I don't want to be alone, but at least in Alan's apartment the air still feels of him. But the time alone is a very good thing. A few moments to be calm and think.

By 11 p.m. I am angry and climbing the walls of Alan's bedroom. The noise from the apartment hasn't ceased, and I am trapped here without even a phone call to tell me what's up. Wouldn't a phone call be a reasonable expectation? He left without a word, but at least he could let me know if he plans to return anytime soon.

I flick on the TV. There's never anything worth watching, even though Alan has everything from BBC to some really awful porn stations. I stare at the cabinet where Alan said there were

Polaroids of other girls if I want to burn them. I don't know why I remember that, except it reminds me how little I really know about him.

The cabinet is a magnificent eighteenth or maybe nineteenth century armoire, deep, with a mirrored front, and graceful lines. It's full of highly personal stuff and this is just plain wrong. Messed up.

There are letters from Linda, whoever Linda is, and family photos from when he was young. Such a cute little boy, but why does he look so sad? So very sad, even as a child. And older. Like a harsh, stressed forty-year-old and he can't be more than ten.

Jeez, this must be a photo of Lillian, the terrible mother and magnificent agent. OK, not such a mystery why he's sad. She intimidates the shit out of me pressed only on photo paper. Severe. No other word for her. Severe.

I rummage through the type of keepsakes that everyone keeps, little bits of this and that which only have significance to the person who retains them.

I pick up a small ceramic bowl that looks handmade by a child. It is lopsided and the colors don't match and it makes me smile. What do they do to children? Teach them deliberately how to make awful pottery? I gave Jack a small bowl that looks almost exactly like this. I turn it over. *Molly*. I wonder who Molly is. Maybe Alan has a sister.

What I don't find is a treasure trove of Polaroids. There are pictures, but none seem of a particular girl, and the collection has the feel of a friendship stack like Rene and I keep.

I'm lifting the pictures one by one, when suddenly I freeze. Why would Alan have a picture of me? God, and when was it taken? Maybe last year? I don't remember the picture, I definitely don't know how he got it, and I sure don't know why he would have it.

I sink to the floor on my knees and turn the photo over. It's a note from me to Jack. My freshman year photo, the one I gave to Jack to carry with him. But why would Alan have it?

Frowning, I tuck it back in its resting place on the shelf and then notice the cello case. Why would Alan have a cello? Does he play the cello? There is a note taped on it, and I open the note:

"Dear Chrissie, Please accept my apologies for ruining your Christmas Holiday. Regards, Alan Manzone."

I set the cello case on the floor, open it, and my mouth drops. *Oh my god.* I've never seen one except in a book, and I can't even imagine what it cost. This is Alan's idea of an apology gift for ruining Christmas for a girl he doesn't even know?

It is a Domenico Montagnana, from the seventeen hundreds. Yo-Yo Ma has one. They are extremely sought-after by collectors and musicians, but no one can afford them and you don't ever see one unless it's being played by a virtuoso or in a museum.

I lightly finger the wood and then quickly pull back my hand. I shut the case and carefully return it to its resting place. I tuck the note back in the envelope, and then slip it beneath the tape.

Why would Alan buy me a Domenico Montagnana cello before he even knew me? I haven't called Jack in days. I've been avoiding the emotional confusion of that experience, the weirdness of calling my dad from the apartment of a guy I'm sleeping with.

I crawl onto Alan's bed and reach for the phone. What time is it in California? I check the clock. Eleven here means eight California time, right? Good, Jack should be home.

Ring. Ring. Ring. Dammit, Maria, answer the phone. Don't send me to the service. A call back number would be a crummy thing at present.

"Hello?"

Finally, Jack.

"Hi, Daddy."

"Baby girl, I was just getting ready to call you…"

I tense.

"…I wanted to see how you were getting along without Rene and if you changed your mind about flying back early."

I relax. "I'm doing well. Catching up on my reading. Seeing the sights."

"So long as you are doing well."

"I'm doing well." A pause. We've run out of chitchat. You are not going to learn anything unless you ask, so here goes nothing. "Can I ask you something, Daddy?"

Jack laughs. "Sure, baby girl. You can ask me anything. No boundaries. No limits. You know that."

He always says that, but I've never felt that, so this is going to be one of those trial-balloon moments.

"It's just…" I run my tongue along my lips to wet them and take a deep breath. "Why would Alan Manzone give me a Domenico Montagnana cello as an apology for ruining my Christmas?"

Silence. "Oh, shit." More silence. "Chrissie, did you accept it?"

"No. It's a Domenico Montagnana."

Another pause. "Don't accept it. I've already told Manny I won't allow him to give it to you. Manny is in a rough place right now. He needs to learn new habits. The only way he will ever learn to deal with his issues is if the people around him don't let him buy his way out of them."

"I don't understand."

"I know, Chrissie. Just don't accept the cello."

"But…but, Daddy, why does he think he owes me an apology?"

A heavy sigh. "He's the reason I flew off at Christmas. The reason you were left alone. The reason I haven't been around as much as I should for you lately."

"Oh."

"Hey, I'm glad you called," Jack says. "I'm glad you felt you could discuss this with me. You don't tell me enough about what's going on with you and you *can* tell me anything."

I am plunged into that familiar anxiousness and whispering sadness. I can't tell what my father knows, and if he knows everything, why won't he just talk about it?

"Listen, Chrissie. Another thing. I would prefer you stayed clear of Manny."

Now I'm cold and shaky. Jack being parental. "Why?"

"Manny's got issues. He's complicated, and he's not ready for even a friendship thing with you."

"I know about the drugs. About Rehab."

Another pause. "Baby girl, drugs are a problem, a symptom, they are never the issue. And he's got big issues."

What could be bigger than drugs?

"He seems very nice," I say.

More silence. It feels through the phone line almost like Jack is debating with himself how much to divulge.

"I can't tell you the details. And this is in confidence, Chrissie. You tell no one. Somehow we've managed to keep it from the press. He wasn't in Rehab. He went from detox to a lock-down mental hospital. He's not ready to be in New York. He's not ready for the circus. Manny tried to kill himself last year."

*Oh god…*Alan's voice whispers through my head: *I lined it up and I snorted it all and I said, fuck it, maybe I'll just stop thinking today.* Oh god, I didn't even realize what it was he told me.

I manage to hold it together through the remainder of the call, but long before I drop the receiver back into the rest I am shaking, and everything is running wildly loose through my body.

Oh god, what is wrong with me? Is that what I feel in him? Why I am drawn to him? I've touched a dead person before. My brother. It changes you. Death lingers in your flesh. It is not something you can shake off; it is metaphysically altering. Am I even more fucked up than in the ways I already know?

Oh shit, oh shit, of shit! There is more going on inside of me than ever before at any time, like a fast free-fall instead of a wave, fragments in my brain running and colliding, emotions accelerating. What is that pounding on the edge of my consciousness, fighting to get in? I am feeling it again, like I did at CBGBs seeing Vince Carroll, this horrible picture fuzzy and fighting to become clear.

I want it to stop. Oh, please make it stop. I realize I am sitting on my knees on the cold marble bathroom floor, in front of the vanity cabinet, unaware of how I got here. I jerk the heavy black lacquer box out and dump the contents on the floor: pills, so many pills, weed, pipes, coke vials, balloons, a tie off, needles…

I pick up the needles in my shaking hands, the world falls away beneath me and I sink to the floor. Oh god, please no! And the messy inside of me is no longer mess. It is dark and ugly, in focus and real.

Chapter Ten

My name is being called and it sounds far away, as if in a tunnel. I stay motionless, curled on the bathroom floor.

Then the cold and lifeless air around me is supercharged with the feel of Alan's presence.

He drops to his knees beside me. "Fuck, Chrissie! What did you do?" I feel limp like a rag doll, as he pulls me from the ground and drags me into his lap. "What did you do, Chrissie? Baby, what did you take?"

He is rummaging through the mess of his stash box splashed across the floor. He slaps my face. "Baby, you've got to tell me what you took." He slaps me more. I can't feel his touch, I can't feel my lips, and I can't find the words in my head.

Panicked and terrified, Alan starts to drag me across the floor. "Oh fuck! Damn it, Chrissie. What did you take?" He is pushing me over the toilet and his fingers are pushing in on my mouth.

Part of my brain focuses. *No, no, no. This is wrong. I don't need to throw up.* I plant my hands on the porcelain and struggle to break free. "I don't do drugs. I didn't take anything," I say, my voice breathy and toneless.

Alan releases me and sinks on the floor. He is shaking. "What the hell is wrong with you? I thought you OD'd. Jesus Christ, I thought you'd OD'd."

His breath is rapid, hard and ragged, as if he's just run himself to exhaustion. When I finally look at him, he is sitting elbows on knees, face in hands.

His eyes, burning and angry, lift to fix on me. "What the fuck is that doing scattered all over the floor? What game are you playing here? Are you fucking out of your mind, pulling a stunt like that?"

I curl into a ball and stare. Alan starts picking up the mess from the floor, tossing it back into the lacquer box before slamming the lid shut and putting it back beneath the vanity.

He stands above me, rigid and enraged. "Goddammit, speak to me. Is this some fucked up little girl tantrum because I had to leave today? I don't do bullshit, Chrissie, and I don't play little girl games."

When I don't answer, he reaches out and grabs me from the floor. He is hauling me from the bathroom, his fingers tightening and tightening with each step. They press too hard into my side and I wince.

He jerks up my shirt and the color drains from his face. "Oh fuck, Chrissie. Why did you do that today? Baby, just tell me. I don't know how to help you."

I curl on my unburned side and wrap myself around his pillow. I start to sob, quietly at first, and then harder and harder because the numbness is fading and the distraught look on Alan's face made it all come tumbling back.

The things I now know for certain to be real. The things I remember. The things I want to forget. The things about Alan that terrify me. The things about myself that I hate. My thoughts are echoing and bouncing inside my head, and he wants me to tell him how to help me. He can't help himself. We are two fucked up people. Jack had it half right. Neither of us are circus ready.

I feel his fingers in my hair. "Hush, baby," he breathes, and gently he pulls my paralyzed body into his arms, burying his lips into my hair. "Can you tell me what happened?"

His voice is so achingly anguished. I force myself to shake my head no. He exhales what sounds like a sigh of relief that I'm responsive and continues to kiss gently all through my hair.

"Did something happen to you, Chrissie? Did someone hurt you?"

I shake my head. He exhales again.

"Are you upset that I left?" He runs a shaking hand through his hair. "I should have called. I would have called. I didn't have a chance to."

I shake my head. His hands, soothing and tender, move to my arms, gently rubbing up and down. "Shit, you're freezing cold. How long have you been laying there?"

I shrug. He scoops me up and carries me back into the bathroom. He is worried and almost despondent. "I don't know what I did. You have to promise not to do this again. Just get angry. Just yell. Why can't you talk instead of doing this?"

I watch him from my perch on the toilet while he fills the tub. After shutting off the knobs, he comes back, eases off my shirt, examines the infinity burn on my lower left abdomen, and then transports me into the warm water of the tub.

Alan collapses into a sitting position beside the tub, long limbs exhausted, and I curl in a ball in the center of the tub hugging my knees silently.

We sit together like this, neither of us moving or talking for ages.

"Does the water make it hurt?" he asks after a long while.

I turn very slowly until my cheek is against my knees so I can face him. "A little. Not bad. I like the pain."

His eyes flash. "Well then you are one fucked up little girl, because I can't even stand the sight of you in pain."

I don't know why that does it, but it makes me cry, a more normal and emotional cry.

"I'm sorry. I didn't mean to put you through that." I use the towel on the ledge to wipe my nose.

"I've never had anyone scare me more in my life," he whispers, eyes widening, the fearful expression returning.

"It's no big deal. It's just what I do when everything gets too close and too real."

"I understand the too close and too real." His eyes close again and I watch myriad emotions cross his face. "But please, for me, don't do that again. I've seen a lot of shit, but that was the fucking worst. You looked dead. Why did you do it? Goddammit, talk to me!"

I don't answer him.

He opens his eyes and looks at me. "OK. But soon, baby. Please make it soon."

He lifts me from the tub and sets me onto the waiting towel. He pats me dry, sets me on the bed and goes to my duffel for fresh clothes. He covers me in a long sleeve t-shirt, pulls on my panties and then a pair of sweatpants.

"Do you want to go to sleep?" he asks.

I shake my head no and then notice the exhausted lines on his face. He's been at it since 7 a.m., he's still dressed in the types of clothes he wears for interviews, it is 4 a.m., and he came back to the apartment having to deal with me. I feel my heart clench anew, but for kinder reasons.

Fucked up he is, but Alan is a good guy, more than he believes.

"Are you hungry?"

I shake my head no.

"Have you eaten today?"

"No. Too many people in the apartment and a hideous girl in the kitchen."

That makes Alan laugh in a tired way. "Hideous girl would be Jeanette. My secretary."

I struggle to make a comical face. "See, you do know what someone does here, who works for you."

He pulls the blanket from the foot of the bed and wraps me in it. I'm transported down the hall to the kitchen, where he sets me on the butcher block island before going to rummage in the refrigerator.

He starts pulling out cartons and setting them on the counter. "Kitchen finally stocked. An entire buffet of readymade here. What do you like? Does it matter? I just need something to kill the pain."

I shrug and watch. I haven't the energy for behaving as if I'm OK. Not just yet, but I'm nearer.

He dumps the cartons and a fork on the counter, settles in a bar high chair, and then scoots me around until I'm facing him, my legs dangling at his side.

He fills a fork and holds it up for me. "I'm not sure what this is. Eat."

I take a bite. A reluctant laugh whispers out of me. "It's potato salad."

He takes a bite. "Not bad. Let's see what we have here."

Fork to my lips. Another bite. "Macaroni salad."

He takes a bite and sets it aside. "This I know. Meatloaf. Do you want me to heat it? I like it cold."

"Then I'll eat it cold."

We pick at the meatloaf until we've both had our fill. At some point between forks full, he poured himself a very tall glass of whiskey. A part of me really wishes he wouldn't, and a part of me taunts *Who are you to be critical of his weaknesses? We are both messed up. Equal. The same.*

As he cleans up the mess, he asks, "Are you tired? Are you ready for bed yet?"

I stare at my toes. "No, I don't want to sleep. I don't want to go back to the bedroom. I was trapped in there all day."

Alan laughs, tired. "You didn't have to stay in the bedroom. I told you to do what you want to do here."

I shrug. "That's what I wanted to do." I stare out the wall of glass. "Can we sit out on the patio for a while? It's nearly dawn. I want to watch the sunrise."

He settles us on a double chaise lounge and it is not long after we've curled into each other that Alan is asleep. As I tighten my arms around him, strangely finding comfort in holding him, the taut bands of emotion inside me finally finish unraveling. And in this moment—this moment of quiet with Alan—I am completely overcome by my feelings for him. I don't know if he loves me. I don't even know if I love him. But for the first time, I am offered a glimmer of understanding of what it should feel like to love.

The sunrise comes and spreads across the sky. Just having Alan near has made me calm faster inside than ever before. Last night in the bathroom was the worst of the worse, lockboxes fully opened, fragments of memories joining into clarity. I expected the horror of finally understanding all the tormenting, unrelenting images to drag me down for weeks, but I am calm today, strangely calm, more than it is logical for me to be.

It is well into morning when I hear sounds from the apartment, the terrace door open and then clicking heels on tile. I lift my cheek from Alan's head, and open my eyes to find Jeanette hovering in front of me, setting a breakfast tray on the foot of the chaise. One plate. One setting. One cup of coffee. Message received, as if I couldn't read the look she's giving: Jeanette hates me.

Susan Ward

"He needs to wake," she says, imperatively. "He needs to eat, shower, dress and leave here by ten. Do you think yourself capable of communicating that to him?"

"Yes, I think I can manage that."

She doesn't offer me breakfast. I watch her leave and I don't give her the satisfaction of seeing me wake him. The perfect lines of Alan's face look so peaceful when he sleeps, his breathing is so shallow as if he still needs sleep, and I hate the thought of waking him.

I touch my lips to his forehead. "Alan, you need to wake up."

He straightens up, from dead asleep to wide awake in a blink, those penetrating black eyes fixed on me. "Are you OK?"

I nod. "It's just your breakfast is here and I have a message to communicate, and I wish to communicate before I forget it and make a mistake: You need to eat, shower, dress and leave here by ten."

Alan laughs, stabbing his omelet with a fork. "Ah, you don't like Jeanette. She's supposed to be a slave driver, Chrissie. She keeps me organized and on track with where I need to be and what I need to do. She is very good at it."

I take a sip of his coffee. *She is also very beautiful.* I smile. "I'm sure she is."

We eat, taking alternating bites, until his plate is completely clean.

"Are you really OK, Chrissie? You wouldn't lie to me would you?"

"Yes, I'm fine today."

I change the subject. "How did you guys come up with the name Blackpoll?"

Alan laughs, a lazy, sort of quiet laugh. "I can tell by how you say that, that you are one of the three Americans under thirty who know what a Blackpoll is."

I make a face at him.

"Len has a thing about birds," he explains, smiling. "Blackpoll is what you get when you don't have a name for a band and Len answers the phone drunk, holding an Audubon book. There is symmetry to it, so I kept it."

"A small songbird surrounded by needles and cones?"

Alan laughs. "I didn't say good symmetry."

I hug my legs with my arms, pressing my cheek against knees, following him with my eyes as he returns to the kitchen for more coffee.

When he settles beside me, I decide to ask the question I've turned in my head since we settled on the terrace last night.

"Why do you keep the box in the bathroom?"

"I told you, I don't believe in that total sobriety bullshit. It's no big deal, Chrissie."

"But the smack, Alan. Why keep the heroin if it's a good thing you've kicked it?"

He hands me the cup of coffee. "Tossing it won't change a thing if I decide to use again. It would be a meaningless gesture. Christ, I'm surrounded by it all the time. Tossing it would be as pointless as me taking your bracelet away."

I stare at my toes and I can feel him watching me.

"Jeanette, bring me my book!" Alan bellows.

Clicking heels on the tile close in on us. To Alan, she smiles and sets the book in front of him before taking away the breakfast tray. Alan rummages through the pages.

"There isn't anything here I can't cancel if you want me to stay today."

He gives me a smile and what's in my center is nearly a happy sensation.

I shake my head. "No, you don't have to stay. I'm all right. Really, I am."

"Only if you're sure."

The tone of his voice tells me he means it, and it still amazes me that out of nowhere there is this guy who worries about me. "I'm sure."

His lips touch mine in such a sweetly gentle kiss that I instantly regret that I am sending him on his way. The tender kisses and touches are always the most potent, they light a fuse that makes me desperate for the rest of him.

I don't know if my impulses are normal, they are too new and fresh, but right now it feels as if it would be desperately right to make love with him.

"My day isn't long. I'll be back late afternoon. Jeanette knows how to reach me." His eyes fix on me sternly. "Call, Chrissie. If you need me, if you need anything, call me. You have to promise me or I won't go. If something happens again, baby, you will call me first."

I nod and watch Alan disappear through the doors.

After Alan leaves, I put on my one-piece and sit on the terrace, letting the sunshine soothe me and put me nearly to sleep.

I hear sound from the apartment and I jump.

"Shut the fuck up, Jeanette!" I hear from the great room. "Go back into your coffin or something. I'm not leaving and you are not keeping us away any longer."

The voice is loud, female, and edgy.

"You really need to leave, Linda," says Jeanette.

Linda? The girl from the letters in the cabinet? I'm wide awake now, I haven't a clue who Linda is, but by how she handles Jeanette I know she is someone to worry about.

"And you really need to get your fucking face out of my face before I toss you over the patio railing. Len! Get your ass in here and dispose of Cruella."

She comes through the terrace doors like a hurricane. Linda's severely beautiful face turns toward me, locking me in an absolutely diminishing stare.

"Aha," she says. She sinks on the chaise beside me. "So that's it. Manny has a new house cat. Who the fuck are you?"

I don't have a chance to answer.

"Len, get the fuck out here!" she screams. "We've been worrying about nothing. He is fine. The band is not breaking up. He is ignoring everyone because he has a new house cat."

Her eyes shift back to me. "Well, pretty little kitty, I'm Linda Rowan. Who are you?"

"I'm nobody." Oh crap, why did I blurt out the first thing that came into my head?

Linda laughs. "Is that your name or your vocation? One can never tell with Manny's girls." She grabs a cigarette and lights it. She studies me over the smoke. "You're a smart girl, aren't you? You keep your mouth shut. That's good. Don't trust anyone, that's my motto."

She fixes her intense stare at the terrace doors. Even sitting silently, it feels as if the entire terrace is electrically charged from her.

I would have considered Linda Rowan a flawless beauty like Rene, if not for the ring through her nose, the ring through her eyebrow, and the ring through her lower lip. The stud in her tongue is something particularly irritating since it clicks against the back of her teeth whenever she speaks. It's hard to tell how old she is. Anywhere between twenty and thirty. The eyes look a lot older, but her face is fresh and young.

I focus on the large pansy tattooed on her wrist, as she reaches to pour herself a hefty glass of whiskey.

"Well, fuck! Don't just sit there staring at me. Say something."

"I have nothing to say to you."

Linda laughs a husky laugh that tells me she laughs often. "I like you, little house cat. I'm never wrong about these things. And I like you."

I'm really getting irritated at being called the "little house cat" and I'm about to say something when Len Rowan decides to join us. I'd recognize Alan's bass player anywhere. He is not good looking, but he has an interesting face.

"Len, meet the house cat," Linda announces. "I can't give you her name because she won't tell me. This one is a clam. House kitty, this in my husband, Len Rowan."

Len sinks too close to me on the chaise after grabbing a full bottle of Jack Daniels. He's reclined on one side of me, Linda in front, so I feel surrounded.

"You're a pretty little thing, aren't you? All fresh and cute like he plucked you from an Iowa corn field. Where do you imagine he picked up this one, Linda?"

Linda sighs and shakes her head. "She's too good for him. I can tell that at a glance. And I like her, so stop messing with her Len and stop staring at her tits."

Len leans over to kiss his wife. "I only have eyes for you, love. And so long as you like her, that's all that matters."

"So, where is Manny?"

"I don't know," I say cautiously.

The Rowans laugh.

"We're all family here," Linda says.

"You're not exactly catching us at our best," says Len humorously.

"Ya think, Len?" Linda shakes her head. She leans forward into me, chin in hands, eyes sharply on me. "Cruella has a way of bringing out the worst in me. I've been trying to call Manny since he touched down in New York. Cruella has been running interference and we worry about him. OK?"

"Haven't had sight or sound from him in nearly six months," Len explains. "The only things we hear are from Arnie Arnowitz. How's a guy supposed to react to finding out his best friend is breaking up the act via a phone call from the accountant? Not even the fucking manager. The fucking accountant. After all that's gone on, it was time to find out what the hell is going on directly from the source."

"We got tired of being shut out, so we barged in," explains Linda, reaching for another cigarette. "Len and Manny are like this." She crosses her fingers. "Like brothers, and who the fuck tells their brother to kiss off via the accountant."

I try to keep any reaction from surfacing. The phone call in the car from the airport: I knew before they knew that Alan was quitting.

Linda smiles. "So how long have you been with Manny?"

"I'm only visiting New York."

That brings a sparkle to Linda's eyes. "Interesting. We've had no contact with him since December so we'd very much appreciate a no bullshit, no carefully spun answer. We're not the fucking press. We're family. How is he?"

That question is far from simple, multifaceted, and serious. Linda is worried. Very, very worried. I can feel it underneath everything else.

"I don't know. I don't know Alan well enough to know for sure."

Len spits out a full mouth of JD across the chaise. "You call him Alan?"

"Jesus Christ, Len, it's nothing to split a gut about. It's probably part of that Rehab getting to the true, honest self shit. You know how they love to fuck with your mind in Rehab. Pull it together, who gives a fuck what the little house cat calls him. It's probably therapy."

I'm ready to be done with this. I stand up and quickly secure my sarong.

"Don't run off, little kitty," Linda says mockingly. "We're not done with you."

Every muscle in my body tenses and I wonder where the flash of anger so unlike me came from. "Well, I'm done with *you*," I say pointedly.

Linda rolls her eyes. "Not a smart move, little kitty. Not if you plan to stick around. I'm the last person you should make an enemy of."

I meet her stare for stare. "No, Linda. *I'm* the last person you should make an enemy of. So back off."

Girl stare. Serious girl stare.

Len spits out his drink again and then falls laughing on the chaise.

"Oh lighten up, lighten up, love. She got you good there, Linda. We don't need a cat fight. Not today."

Linda relents. "You don't have to run off."

I lift my chin. "I'm not running."

"Then sit down dammit. It's going to be explosive enough when Manny returns without you being pissed off at us."

What the heck does that mean? Is she warning me that things are going to get worse from here? It's already awful.

Linda takes a steadying breath. "I'm sorry, and I'd be more than happy to call you something other than little house cat, but *you're* the one who won't tell us your name."

Good point. I sit back down. "Chrissie," I say stiffly.

Linda smiles, and when she really smiles it's quite spectacular. "There now, we are friends. I want you to stay here with me. Keep me from doing something stupid. This is not going to go at all well."

Holy crap, what does that mean?

"So, where are you from, Chrissie? Where did Manny find you?"

I look at Len. "California."

Linda crinkles her nose. "You didn't meet in Rehab did you? You don't look the type."

"No."

"I didn't think so." Linda shakes her head in exasperation. "You know, you don't have to be so cautious about everything. We're just making idle chitchat until it's time for the fireworks to go off."

"So, what do you do in California," Len asks.

"I go to school and I play the cello."

The minute I say it I realize how lame that sounds. When do you outgrow these moments of embarrassing conversational awkwardness?

Len starts to rummage around the remains of my buffet table Jeannette unexpectedly set up for me while I was inside putting on my swim-suit.

"Aha." Linda takes a plate of fruit from Len. "She's a smart one, Len. All college posh and cello. Maybe the Rehab shit is good. Maybe this one will keep him straight. I like her."

I know she means it as a compliment, but for some reason each time Linda announces *I like her* it's like nails on a chalkboard. It is incredibly irritating, the self-importance she gives her own opinions.

Len Rowan's eyes sharpen on me. "So, you're the reason he bought the cello."

How do they know about the cello?

Linda and Len lock stares.

"That means they've been together since January," Linda announces with an air of discovery.

"I just met him last week," I say emphatically, though I don't know why I feel an urgent need to clarify that.

"Oh, don't play coy with us," Linda chides shrewdly. "Quite a retirement fund. Better than the jewelry. I knew you were a smart one. Jewelry always loses its value. But the cello. That was smart. And we know exactly when he bought the cello. Like I could ever forget that day. Remember, Len?"

Len gives her a sympathetic, heavy nod.

"I cried into my magazines for nearly a week," Linda continues gravely. "It is a sad day when the only confirmation you get that your dearest friend is alive and well, since no one will tell you whether he is or where he is, is when he buys a cello for 1.7 million at auction at Christie's. The *Times* in January. That was the first time we knew for sure he was OK."

Linda starts to cry. I don't know what to do. She is crying and Len is staring off into space. I inch across the chaise lounge to tentatively put an arm around her. Linda feels so fragile when I touch her. The hurricane is scary on the surface, but fragile within.

"I can see you care about him," I whisper.

She is suddenly buried against me.

"It's just been really, really hard. The three of us—Len, Manny and me—that's all there's been for eight years. The three of us. From London here. Then one day it falls apart. You don't see it. You don't prepare. And you are writing letters to your best friend, the guy who's like your brother, because they won't let you do anything else. You can't call. You can't visit. And he's not writing back. I've been so afraid. Really, really afraid."

She's wrapped around me as if she's holding on for dear life, and I'm uncomfortable and I can't figure out why she's wrapped around me instead of her husband.

"He has your letters. They're in a cabinet in his bedroom," I inform her gently.

Linda's face snaps up. "Really? Then why the fuck didn't he write back?" Linda sits back on her heels. "OK, you've seen it. I'm running on my last nerve here."

I start to move away. She grabs my arm. "No, stay with me. This is going to get awful. *They* have history together that even I don't understand. It's going to get awful and you need to keep me out of it."

Len is reclined on his lounge chair asleep, and Linda and I are laying side by side as though we are the best of friends, waiting, though I don't know for what. The fireworks?

"Do you know where I'm from?" Linda asks.

I shake my head.

"The Valley. Encino. I'm a Valley Girl. I miss Southern California. I miss the sun."

I laugh.

Linda turns on her side. "How did two California college girls end up with this strange herd of Brits? They only want to marry us for the citizenship and the tax advantage. Take my advice. Finish school. Don't run off with the first Brit who wants to marry you for a green card."

Linda falls asleep. I sit beside her, watching the sun move across the sky, dip in the horizon, and then the expanding swirl of sunset. The hours are punctuated only by the sound of

Jeanette's clicking heels and Len's snoring. Clearly, the Rowans are not leaving until Alan returns. It's evening. *Good one, Alan, you could have returned when you promised to!*

A sound makes me jump, and the movement of my body jolts Linda awake. There is noise in the foyer. Is Alan back? I start to rise, but Linda latches onto me like a barnacle. "No, stay. This is going to get ugly. Stay with me."

Len goes from asleep to turbo-charged in a blink of an eye. He's through the terrace doors. And then there is shouting, lots of shouting, but it is mostly Len, and shouting and breaking glass.

After what seems like a monumental amount of time, I shake Linda off and run toward the great room. Inside I find Alan and Len tangled on the floor, and the room is a mess. I start to move to break it up, but Linda stops me.

"I am not going to fight you, Len," Alan snaps, trying to break free.

"I'm the one who fucking found you!" It rings through the room with acid potency. "So, is that what you're pissed about? You're pissed I didn't let you screw things up permanently? I happen to love you. And you let my wife cry. You don't take her calls. You don't answer her letters. You just disappear, and then come back to New York, smug as you please all secretive and shit. And then you slap us in the face with Arnie Arnowitz."

"I fucking deserve a little time after eight years," Alan says, shoving Len back and then sitting up.

"Fine. You can have time. What you can't do is leave us all hanging around with our cocks in our hand, not knowing what we're doing, not knowing if you're all right, and not knowing if there's a band. Some of us need the fucking work. We don't have the royalties. Some of us ain't rich as the Federal Reserve."

"So is that where we are? It's about the money?"

"No. It's about you not telling us you're in trouble. I thought you kicked that shit. Next thing I know, I'm finding you dead on smack, and they're bringing you back to life. Fuck you! You were dead, you witless bastard."

Len pushes back against a sofa, sitting on the floor sprawled and weak, and he is crying.

I'm frozen at the terrace doors, but Linda is suddenly across the room, with Len in her arms, and he's crying against her.

After several minutes, Linda looks at Alan. "How could you think that it was ever about the money, Manny? Not us. Never us. That's unfair. Len's just letting all the garbage out. It's been rough. But don't ever accuse us of having it be about the money."

Alan rakes a hand through his hair. "I never thought it was, Linda."

Linda brushes at the tears on her face. "You scared the hell out of us, Manny. You've really got to stop this shit."

"I'm working on it." Alan's eyes find me and his expression changes into something that looks like apprehension. "Why are you staring at me like that, Chrissie?"

I break free of my thoughts. Alan is still breathing heavy, still trying to calm himself. Before the Rowans, somehow everything managed to remain in my lockboxes. But they are all open again and the mess is here in the room with me, his truth, my truth. I don't know how I was looking at him and I don't know what he can see.

I drop to my knees beside him and Alan pulls me fiercely against him. The room is so heavy with grimness, and my thoughts and emotions are in free fall again.

Say something quickly, Chrissie. Something funny. It doesn't matter if Alan hates the playacting. Right now it is all there is to get me through this. I kiss his cheek. I make an exaggerated face. "It's the bowl, Alan. The Columbian pottery. I wish Len had broken that horrid little piece over there on your head, but the one he broke was exquisite."

It's Linda who laughs, and her laughter, when it flows, is infectious. "I like her. I really do."

In a minute, they are all laughing, but what I hear in the room is despair.

* * *

I slip quietly from the great room into Alan's bedroom. The Rowans are hovering in the apartment and somehow I hold it together until I'm alone.

I shut the door and the tears instantly begin to flow. I lie down on the bed, my emotion-drained limbs almost without sensation, and I curl into a tight ball around Alan's pillow. What do I do? Do I stay? I'm so afraid of what being with Alan is doing to me.

I hear Alan open the door. I don't move. He crosses to the bed, pulling me into his arms, all warm and compassionate.

"I'm sorry," he breathes.

I want to pull away from Alan. I want to melt into him. I want not to be afraid. I want to know for sure that we are both not totally fucked up. I want him to be all right. I want me to be all right.

"Don't hate me, Chrissie. Please. I can stand anything else, but not you hating me."

What does he feel inside of me that he would ask me not to hate him? And what is he apologizing for? I don't understand him.

Gently, he pulls me full length against him, his face in my hair, and he is kissing my neck. He is sad. Achingly sad. My heart clenches and I cry harder. He kisses me softly across my face, and he doesn't pull away.

We lie quietly together, and I feel myself slowly calming, slowly coming back into comfortable order, slowly melting back into him, into this consuming connection I have felt from the start.

I turn in his arms to put space between us. His eyes are midnight black and guarded, and he is afraid too.

"Did you really try to kill yourself?" I whisper.

He closes his eyes and exhales.

"Alan, is it true?"

I need to know this. Know this for sure. So I can figure out later how it fits into me. It is a selfish thing, but I need to know. This is part of who I am, too, in a weird French movie subplot kind of way.

He opens his eyes.

"Yes, it is true."

"Are you OK now?" I ask cautiously.

I know the answer. I can see it so clearly now. All the things that he hides behind his male beauty and his charm and his brilliant extremes. Or did I just miss it, being too absorbed in my own shit? He hasn't come back together yet. Not completely. Jack is right. He shouldn't be in New York. Not yet.

"I'm working on it, Chrissie." His voice is anguished. He exhales a shuddering breath.

"What can I do for you? I don't know what you need me to do."

His eyes widen and he blinks. He reaches up and wipes away the tears from my cheek with his finger, those callused fingers that can touch with such velvet care.

"Just stay and be good to me."

I bury my lips in his hair. I wrap my arms around him. I let him sink into my breasts. Alan is crying, real tears, real sounds, and it feels like it is something he has really needed to do for a really long time.

Chapter Eleven

I wake alone in the bed. It is still dark and it feels like the middle of the night. I don't know if I should stir and let Alan see that I'm awake. He is playing very quietly and it is the first time he's even picked up an instrument. The music is beautiful, quiet, and unlike anything I've ever heard out of him. It is haunting and it is sad and full of pain.

What hurt him so much that his life would disintegrate into the train wreck of last year? Something hurt him. Jack is right, the everything else of last year is only a symptom, and the real issue, whatever I am hearing now fighting its way out of him, is something dark and very real.

The Rowans stayed late. It was almost as if Linda was afraid to leave, almost as if she could see inside of Alan. There is something special, emotionally entangled between them, and I can see it and Len can see it. Alan is connected to Linda in a way I don't understand.

We had sex after the Rowans left. I didn't want Alan to touch me. I was still rattled inside, emotionally messy from all that happened. He knew, he sensed it, and it hurt him.

It was just touching at first. Those gentle touches he does with such care. And I could not stop myself from touching him. And that was it, it started as it always does once I reach out to him.

I wouldn't call what we did making love. And yes, now I completely understand the difference between making love and fucking. No, this was fucking—hard, intense, erotic, violent fucking. It was draining in a strange way. Oddly necessary. Life affirming. Yes, that was what it was. Intensely violent fucking to affirm we are both alive.

Afterward, we lay sprawled on the bed, naked and sweaty, and we didn't touch. There were no tender touches and kisses from Alan. We just lay. Disconnected. Limp. And yet, really connected in a way unlike any other way I've known with him. Connected in the disconnect. I don't know how to explain that.

We stayed where we had finished until I could crawl on the bed to my pillow, and I went to sleep without him holding me and for some reason, it was OK. The distance. The quiet neither of us seemed to want to disturb.

And now there is music in the room, and there is some undefined emotion in it, something I've not heard before, something complex and beyond me. And here I lie, pretending sleep, because I do not know what he is revealing to me.

The bedroom door closes. I sit up in bed, hugging my knees with my arms, and turn to check the clock. It's only one in the morning. I thought it would be much later. The Rowans left at eleven. Then there was the fucking. Then I dozed. It all happened in only two hours. So much and it was only two hours.

Every human emotion in two hours has flowed through my flesh and veins. I have touched death. I have touched life. I have fucked. I have felt love. I have lain in the quiet. Alone. Lost in someone. Connected. Untouched. Disconnected. There is sadness. There is hope. There is the past, haunting us both it seems. And there is no future. I can't see it. Is that why I am lost inside myself? Is that why Alan is lost as well?

I lie back against the pillows. I wonder where he went. How long will he be gone? I don't want to fall back asleep to open my eyes and not see Alan watching me. There is a smile in his eyes he has only at that moment; the moment I wake when he is watching me.

I need that smile right now. It is life affirming, as well, and it is hopeful.

I let an hour pass before I pull on my panties and Alan's t-shirt. I love wearing his shirts, the scent of him brushing my senses, feeling surrounded by him by just being tucked into his clothes. There are so many new emotions, richer and fuller, now that I've shared myself with Alan.

Everything changes. It changes quickly. Even the feel of my body is different. I move differently. I have a different level of awareness of myself. I touch myself differently, even if I'm only brushing back my hair. I want richness of feeling in everything I do, awareness, and a sense of being female. It is such a mind blowing change, to have been so not aware of myself seven days ago, and now completely aware of myself, to feel my own femaleness in me, awake and dominant.

I can feel it as I walk down the hall trying to figure out where Alan disappeared to. In the great room, I find Jeanette curled on a sofa reading. Linda warned me that Jeanette lives here. I didn't see her the first three days I was here, and now I can't seem to avoid her. She was hovering in the background the entire time the Rowans were here.

I ignore Jeanette as I look out onto the terrace. I can feel her watching me. Why does she dislike me so much? I search the patio furniture. No Alan. I turn around and go back down the hall.

I turn down an artery I have not explored before. Alan's apartment consumes the entire top floor of the building and there is a maze of interior construction, encompassing the space. The elegance and the scale had seemed strange to me, and I couldn't understand why Alan would want to live in a place that's practically a museum. It is so formal and unwelcoming.

Linda explained that it was Lillian's apartment, purchased with some sort of trust fund Alan had from his childhood—one-hundred million pounds, she'd whispered confidentially with raised eyebrows. Alan was a child genius and musical prodigy with a highbrow, British clan of theatrical people, but the posh tea and biscuit image only works after a musician is famous, so *pouf*, there was Manny. Manny hides most parts of himself from everyone except his inner circle. Alan is not good for the brand.

A year ago, he booted Lillian out and took possession of the place. As for their most recent feud, sometime early last year, Linda knew none of the details. She avoids Lillian like the plague. And Alan was starting to unravel at that time. Linda didn't know what happened, only that he walked away from them all, and then began to crash and burn: A total downward spiral, Len chasing after his heels, Len trying to keep him sane, Alan unmanageable, and then that one, great, terrible awful that Len won't talk about, where Alan was whisked away, *"for six fucking months."*

That part of the story is the only part of the story I know. He was with Jack.

I peek into rooms, guest rooms and sitting rooms, each stunningly arranged, unique, the stylish décor of old money. Whatever can be said about Lillian, she is a woman of exceptional taste.

At the end of the hall, there is a heavier door and I know what it is before I enter it. A recording studio, tucked away in the English Country Manor. Alan's only alteration to Lillian's showplace. His space to work.

There are two guys sitting at the sound board talking quietly. So, Alan slipped off in the night to work, probably to finish the tracks that are going to be shelved by the label according to Arnie Arnowitz.

I shut the door. The room is heavy with the smell of weed, there is booze all over the console, and ashtrays overflowing with cigarettes.

The chair swivels around to face me and I am held in a stare that makes me breathless. Oh my, Ian Kennedy—golden blond hair, deep California tan, twinkling caramel eyes from a face thirty-five and youthfully roguish, and wearing crumpled clothes as if he's just rolled from bed.

"It's Chrissie Parker!"

He's on his feet and I grin up at him. "It's Ian Kennedy!"

He laughs, pulling me into a bear bug. "Jesus, girl, what are you doing here all grown up and everything? Would you look at you. I knew you were going to be a stunner once you got those braces off."

I blush furiously. When I was fifteen, I had an absolutely, humiliatingly obvious crush on Ian Kennedy, music producer extraordinaire. He was such a good guy about it and I wonder if he remembers.

Arm draped loosely around my shoulders, he turns to his mix engineer. "Ryan, do you know who this chick's old man is? This is Jackson Parker's girl."

We shake hands and Ryan returns to his work. Ian sinks back into his chair, holding my hands as I settle on the couch.

Those lovely caramel eyes smile at me. "We've got to do dinner while you're here. We've got to catch up. Is your old man here?"

"No, just me in New York." I look through the glass and I don't see Alan. "I never expected to run into you here."

He tosses me a wink. "I never expected to run into you *here*."

I change the subject quickly. "Is it going well?"

Ian laughs and lights a cigarette. "He's almost human tonight. Amazing, since every exec at the label has their head up his ass over this."

I study the whiteboard chart. An X and Y schedule with each track labeled, the various tracks that go into the track, color coded, filled in as completed. Fourteen tracks. Instrument tracks completed for all, but only five tracks completely finished. He's got nine vocal tracks left to go.

I search the studio with my gaze. "Where's Alan?"

"Five minute lyric break," Ian explains. He points to the ground, and I ease up to find Alan huddled on the studio floor, staring down at a yellow notepad.

"He writes lyrics in five minutes?"

Ian laughs and props his feet on the console, leaning slightly back in his chair. "You've never seen him work? He's like Mozart. A fucking musical genius. Every track written in his head before he enters the studio."

Ian rolls across the room and grabs a tape. "I don't know who he worked with on the instrument tracks. The execs didn't know he was working while on...sabbatical." Ian grins and winks. "They just flew in last week. Every track. Every instrument. Him. No band."

I smile and refrain from comment.

Ian studies me. "So, did your old man send you east to keep Manny on a leash until this is finished?" Ian shakes his head. "I don't think me finding you in the middle of the night in Manny's t-shirt is quite what your old man had in mind."

Oh shit, I blush and try to stutter out a reasonable diversion.

Ian throws his head back, laughs, and plants his feet loudly on the floor. "Jeez girl! I'm just messing with you. Your secret is safe with me. Jack would kill Manny if he knew about this, especially since it's obvious who Manny's been working with. I recognized the mix day one, and there are quite a few riffs that are a giveaway."

Ian is queuing up the tape. "Do you want to hear? It is unbelievable work."

Ian grabs the cans and rolls away from the viewing glass. He pulls me down on his thigh, and I laugh, since three years ago this would have been a dream come true, but today it is nothing. Then I realize that the headset can only stretch so far, and he's trying to keep Alan from seeing us.

"I'm not supposed to do this," Ian says. "For some reason, no one hears this until it's finished. Don't tell him I did this. I don't want to manage a pissed off Manny."

Ian motions for Ryan to roll the tracks, and I'm consumed by the music practically from note one. I've never heard anything like it. It starts quietly, acoustic quiet, precise and haunting and then building waves, angry, sad, powerful, intensely quiet, and unlike anything I've ever heard in contemporary music. It's definitely not music like anything Alan's ever released. His raspy voice and gifted fingers flood my senses with waves of intensity, penetrating, a blending of darkness and light.

I look at the white board and I know which track it is. It is *All I want* and it is a five minute reveal of all that is Alan. I blush... it exemplifies what it feels like to go to bed with him, to be consumed by him, to exist inside of him. This is the music of his touch and his lovemaking and his pain and his regrets. Extremes and contradictions, every emotion unfurled, hauntingly him.

I pull off the cans, and for a moment I am breathless and can't speak.

"The only music he didn't record on these tracks are moments of background symphony."

I shake my head, searching for words to describe it, realizing that the label is right. This will never sell to his fan base.

"It's acoustic," I say in disbelief, "and yet the sound is so powerful."

"I don't know how to describe it, either. It is brilliant and it will never be released. It is a masterpiece. It's not commercial. The label will shelve it. They have to avoid another year of loss. Manny is the only one who doesn't believe that."

I fix my eyes on Ian. "I want to hear another track."

Ian laughs. "You've got it bad, girl. I've seen that look before. But don't worry. Being on the merry-go-round with Manny is the antitoxin."

I feel my cheeks burn scarlet. Ian tells Ryan that it's OK to queue up another track.

Alan's five-minute lyric break stretches into forty-five minutes and four more tracks in my ears. Each track individually a complete event. It makes me think of us in bed. Each kiss. Each touch. A complete event. The tracks all connected, a different complete event. I want to hear it all, but there are only five tracks complete. In the music there is much about Alan to be learned, much I don't think he will ever share with anyone any other way.

I don't know what's on my face as I listen, but when I pull the headset off, I realize that Ian has watched me, fascinated, through it all.

He takes the headset, tosses it on the console and holds me in a sloppy bear hug, giving me a little shake. "I shouldn't have done that. You're already under his spell, but after watching you listen to that I don't think I'll ever be able to steal you away from him."

I roll my eyes. "As if you'd try."

Ian laughs giving me a big sloppy wet one on my cheek. "Keep walking around dressed only in his t-shirt and I won't be able to stop myself."

I relax back against him as we laugh, and it is funny how we've slipped into this comfortable friendship-like flirtation, when there had once been a time when I'd have given anything for Ian to notice me.

I am breathless and smiling. "How long do you think he'll work tonight?"

"I don't know. Five minutes. Five hours. Five days. You know the drill, Chrissie. You can never tell what it's going to be until it's over."

I do know the drill. Sometimes Jack would go into the studio and I wouldn't see him for days. I debate with myself whether to go back to bed, but I'm wide awake now and sleep just isn't going to happen.

I move from Ian's lap and settle on the couch. Alan is still absorbed in his five-minute lyric break, and Ian grabs a bottle, settling on the couch beside me. We are slouched into each other, taking alternate drinks from the bottle, reminiscing about the old days and all the California shit.

Laughing, I cover my face, curling into Ian because some of his memories embarrass me. So, he did notice my awkward crush on him.

I peek from behind fingers covering my reddened face. "You are a jerk to let me know you remember any of that," I exclaim.

I part my fingers and find Ian smiling at me.

"Oh, Chrissie. It was flattering. You were like my own little groupie. So cute and shy."

I'm giving him little nudges with my leg when the studio door flies open. Ian Kennedy is suddenly shoved up against the wall.

"You don't look at her," Alan growls. "You don't talk to her. You don't touch her. Or I will put you through this fucking wall so that you'll remember."

I jump from the couch, but Ryan has already flown across the room.

Ian is struggling and trying to push Alan away, but Alan is an unrelenting force.

"Shit, Manny, get your hands off me!" Ian shouts, panting and furious. "Chrissie and I are old friends. Get the fuck off of me."

Ryan pulls them apart, and Ian slides down the wall to the floor.

"What is wrong with you, Alan? We were just talking," I whisper, stunned.

Alan doesn't look at me, and his anger is very extreme. It was like it was at CBGBs, out of nowhere, illogical.

"Take it easy. We're all on edge, and nothing happened, so let it go, Manny." Ryan says intensely. There is a uniquely soothing quality to Ryan's voice.

I can see the tension shuddering through Alan's flesh. He looks at me. "Fuck, Chrissie! First Jimmy Stallworth, then Vince Carroll and now Ian Kennedy. It's like you're a magnet for fuck-you-over guys."

I flush scarlet. That was insulting, and worse, it has a hurtful ring of truth because it could be said about me being with him, the recovering heroin addict, train wreck, blasting extreme emotions without warning.

"So what are you going to do, break his arm like you did Vince Carroll for not getting me out of CBGB's quietly?" I snap, smarting and indignant.

"I broke Vince Carroll's arm for drugging you," Alan growls at my departing back, clipping each word harshly.

My hand freezes on the knob. *Oh shit,* and suddenly everything about that night makes sense. I sink away from him onto the couch, feeling small and stupid and struggling not to cry.

The studio is nerve-rackingly tense. I can't even look at him now. "Still, you shouldn't have broken his arm," I whisper. "He's a drummer, Alan."

I'm held in the raging burn of his gaze. I look at him and the tears rise behind my lids. On top of all the other things I'm feeling, I'm scared because I have never done a hard drug in my life, am terrified that I'd become an addict like my brother.

"What did he drug me with?" I ask on a trembling voice.

Alan drops to sit on his knees in front of my curled legs. "Just ludes. I'm pretty sure it was just ludes by the way you were acting." I nod, and he starts to brush the hairs from my face. "It was only ludes, baby. If I thought it was something worse, I would have broken his other arm the next day."

A soggy laugh bursts out of me after Alan's weird reassurance.

I blink at him rapidly. "Can we pretend I never came to the studio?"

Alan kisses my cheek. "No. Besides, I was about to go get you. I need you here."

I roll my eyes. "Me? I seriously doubt that."

"I want you to record a song with me."

It feels like someone has just punched the air out of my lungs, and it is absolutely impossible to assimilate this turn.

"Alan, I don't sing. I'm a cellist."

"Wrong. You have that backwards. You are a singer, not a cellist."

I frown at him. "What is that supposed to mean?"

He meets my eyes directly. There is something in those penetrating black orbs that makes me tense.

"You were never going to get into Juilliard. You are a competent cellist, technically proficient, but when you play it's like a beautiful meal with no taste. You hide behind the cello and put nothing of yourself in the music. I don't even get a sense that you enjoy it. As a cellist, you will never be more than third chair in a third rate orchestra."

My entire face burns from the humiliation of truth. I know he speaks the truth, and it is something I've always known, that no one would say to me. But it really does hurt the first time you have it confirmed by someone else.

"You told me I was flawless. Perfect."

"Technically flawless. No taste."

My brain and my emotions are not working cooperatively. "So why did you lie to me? Were you trying to hit on me?" I fling.

"Yes, I lied because I was hitting on you. But spending time with you made it something I just couldn't do. Not that night. Not that way."

I am caught completely off guard because I've forgotten Alan's warning that he doesn't do bullshit and to be careful what direction I go.

This conversation has deteriorated in ways I never imagined possible. I am breathing heavily, hurt, acutely aware that Alan let loose some really ugly truth in a room where we are not alone and he expects me stay to record with him.

"God, you're an asshole." I can't hide the pain from my voice.

"Why? Because I prefer to be honest with you?"

My wounded eyes fix on him. "It's not about honesty, Alan. Its meanness. You can be so mean sometimes."

"I confirmed that you are not a cellist. That should be a relief to you. I asked you to record a song with me. That should be a compliment. I told you that I wanted to fuck you. That should be obvious by now."

"Conceited and an asshole." I rise. "I don't sing."

"Bullshit. You were willing to sing for Vince Carroll."

I stare at him, shocked.

He leans against the closed studio door, crossing his arms, blocking my exit. "I changed my mind about how I wanted to complete this, the moment I heard you sing. I knew when I heard you. I knew what I wanted. Why are you being so stubborn about this?"

"Because I don't want to record a song with you," I counter in growing frustration.

He runs a hand through his hair. "You asked what you could do for me, Chrissie. Do this."

It feels like the earth has fallen away again. *Oh that was unfair, Alan. That was unfair.* His quiet, raspy plea makes all the junk inside me stir up again.

Aggravated, I run my hand through my hair. "You are such an asshole."

"I need you to do this," he orders.

"You don't need me for anything," I say, feeling my resolve weaken.

He grabs my chin and kisses me roughly. Against my mouth, he breathes, "You are everything I need for everything I do."

More theatrics. I let out a shuddering breath. "I'm not a singer."

Alan touches my cheek with his callused thumb. "You are not an artist when you play the cello, but, baby, you are an artist when you sing. Perfect pitch. Beautiful tone. Believable. You don't playact when you sing. You are magnificent."

I brush at my face and realize I am crying. That was why Alan brushed me gently with his thumb, touching the tears I didn't even feel because I am completely emotionally drained.

"Fine," I agree, not all graciously.

Getting his way has made Alan shift in the blink of an eye, now energized and focused as if none of the prior thirty minutes happened. He's talking with Ian like *their thing* was normal. He's holding me against his chest like *our thing* was normal. And he's about to record a song with me as if *that is normal.*

"Hit track seven, Ian."

Alan is pulling me into the studio and he is all work again. I can feel Ian staring at me through the glass. Watching. The lyric sheet is forced into my hand. And then there is music in the studio. The melody is so beautiful. It's a ballad.

I scan the lyric sheet. His words are so moving and yet nakedly revealing. I feel a sick suspicion that this incredible ballad is about us. Allusions to the beach and other things. How the heck does he expect me to record with him a song about us? And jeez, why did he title it *Long and Hard.* It's a beautiful ballad and he gave it the title of a porn movie.

Alan sinks on the floor in the middle of the room, guitar in hand, and he is looking at me, but I don't look at him. He is waiting for the music to end.

"Come, sit. Watch my hands while I play. Just sing it, Chrissie. Don't worry about being perfect. Don't worry about even hitting the right notes. We'll just sing through it until you're comfortable."

The first-run through is halting, off-key and just plain awful. I glance around. How long have we been here? Ian and Ryan are still at the console and the expression on Ian's face says it all.

Alan reaches for a CF Martin acoustic guitar and lays it in my lap. "Again. This time you play, Chrissie."

I stare at the instrument and I don't pick it up. How does Alan know I play?

Those penetrating black eyes are watching me, amused. "Six instruments by the age of nine. Flute, guitar, piano, cello, violin, piccolo. It wasn't bullshit, Chrissie. You are all that Jack talks about."

I let out a shuddering breath and can't stop myself from thinking: *if that's true, Alan, then why doesn't he talk to me? Why does he ignore me? Do you have that nifty answer conveniently located in your head?*

"Don't roll the track again," Alan shouts into the intercom. "We're just going to play until Chrissie is comfortable."

I feel on the verge of tears. "I don't want to do this, Alan."

"Play!"

I do as I am told and, for some reason, now that we are playing together, this is effortless. Like when we laugh or when we argue or when we have sex. We gel without trying. Whatever we do together is easy, and it feels right and I feel completely absorbed into him.

When we've run through it about fifteen times, Alan springs to his feet. He takes away the guitar, then grabs my hand and pulls me to my feet. He puts the headset on me.

"This will be one take, Ian, if you don't fuck it up," he says into the intercom. "And then we can call it quits for the day."

His long fingers gently message my shoulders. He smiles. "It will be perfect, Chrissie."

There is so much on his face, in his voice as we do this. For some reason, it flows through me, and my voice flows from me deep, throaty and powerful. He looks so beautiful when he lets the emotion run freely on his face.

When we are done it is quiet.

"Give me a minute and I'll play it back." Ryan's voice echoes from the intercom.

Nervously I wait, but Alan is reclined beside me, long limbs relaxed. I don't know how I sounded. I couldn't hear myself, as absorbed I was with his haunting rasp and the feel of him. I pray that it wasn't awful, and I'm more worried than I let on, since I've never heard myself on tape. I've never permitted Jack to record me, not even for shits and giggles. And I know the natural voice, the recorded voice, and the voice in your head are all different voices.

I have some natural talent, no training and, cords I rarely exercise, and for the life of me I can't understand what Alan hears when he listens to me sing that would make him want to record with me. Then the playback starts and the tight curl of my body grows anxiously tighter. It is my voice with Alan, but it is not a voice I've ever heard. I sound like a female version of my brother, throaty and pure and wispy, woven with emotion.

Halfway through the playback Alan touches my cheek. "Perfect," he murmurs. He stands up, pulling me with him. "And no, baby. That's not your brother you think you hear. It's a little bit of Jack and all the things you don't ever let show that are Chrissie."

In the bedroom, I curl on my side, on the bed, while Alan draws a bath for me. I am a touch panicky about what I just did, since now that it's done I can't take it back.

I recorded a song with Alan Manzone. Our voices will be linked forever on vinyl. Even if no one ever hears the song, it will always be a piece of me forever connected with a piece of Alan.

My limbs feel like putty and I am weak. I am not used to letting so much emotion to the surface.

Alan takes me to the bath and he undresses me. It is the first time I notice that neither of us has spoken since we left the studio. He puts me in the tub. Why are we both silent? What is this I feel?

Alan starts undressing and my eyes round. He climbs into the water and eases me back against his chest. I relax and close my eyes. I feel my head move with the rhythm of his breath. My hair is all around us. The steam and dampness makes it puff out and cling. Those long fingers are gently washing me. Up and down my arms very slowly, and then everywhere. And by the time he is done, I am languid and aroused and I can feel his erection.

I want him. I want him now.

"Close your eyes."

"Why?"

"Just do it."

I close my eyes.

"Don't open your eyes until I tell you."

I feel him touch me between my legs. My hair is lifted from my shoulders and his lips are on my neck. He turns me in his arms until I'm straddling him and he is devouring me with his mouth, the kisses are deep, greedy, ragged with unspent adrenaline, and I want him in me, but he keeps us separate.

There is something different in me. I can feel something different in Alan. My fingers curl in his hair as his mouth moves to my breasts. I am impatient inside in feral way, and I don't know where this urgency comes from. It is as if I can't get close enough to him, that nothing I do, not even sharing my body, will get me close enough to him.

Alan lifts me from the tub and carries me back to the bed. He spreads me on my stomach. He lies down beside me and we are both damp. He starts touching and kissing me. The back of my body, up from my feet, down my back. When his tongue touches at the base of my spine, I feel his fingers between my legs and then in me. As he cups my sex with his fingers expertly teasing me, his tongue and kisses are in a different orifice of my body, since I am on my stomach, and I am mildly disgusted and incredibly hot. He is kissing me there. Around it. Near it. In there. All the while, his hands are cupping my sex and filling me with his fingers. As intense as my muscles have clenched during sex, they have never clenched in anticipation this way.

Why am I letting him do this? It's disgusting and wrong and I don't know why he wants this. He knows he is driving me crazy, and I can feel his excitement as he makes me more and more frantic.

He turns me on the bed and I can feel his damp, naked body surrounding me. I am breathing hard. And I am pulsing there. My eyes are still closed because Alan has not said I can open them, and for some reason I am raging in this in a way unlike any other time before.

Alan is all around me, totally consuming my body. His lips are against my ear. "The opposite of death is not life, Chrissie," he roughly breathes into my swirling senses. "The opposite of death is you. You are my opposite of death."

Oh god…and I am afraid. I am desperately aroused. I want him and Alan is in me.

Chapter Twelve

I am exhausted. I want to sleep. I don't know how Alan manages the pace. Every hour he gets more energetic. Every hour I just want more to hide beneath the covers and sleep. The last forty-eight hours have been grueling. Hours in the studio. Sex. Sleep. Then the cycle all over again.

I don't even know what day it is. Time has lost the feel of realness. I have lost the feel of realness. We have only been together for seven days and so much about me has changed. I think of the lying to Jack, ignoring Rene's mountain of messages, the singing, the sex, and that I am all but living with a guy. I am lost in Alan and I have no feel of realness without him.

Alan made me sing three more tracks with him. I don't know how he got me to do it. Maybe I just did it not to fight with him. He asked. I did. Maybe it is as simple as that. Alan asked me. Maybe that's all there is to it.

The sex is only getting more intense and more frequent. I thought it would calm with time. I thought I would calm with time. I want him more. I am willing to do more.

The adrenaline-fueled intensity while he works is frightening and a turn-on. I feel something new, something different in him. I haven't figured out what to label it in my head yet.

I curl into the blankets. I need sleep. Tomorrow I will think about how to slow this down.

* * *

When I wake, it is mid-morning and I am surprised to find Alan in bed with me. He worked the entire night and I slept, really slept, for the first time in days, until he woke me up in the early morning to make love to my drowsy, hot body. Once we were done I went immediately back to sleep.

He is sitting beside me reading. Panicking, I realize what it is he is reading. I grab for my black journal that I must have forgotten to put back into my duffel.

"Give me that."

Alan looks up. "Why? It's very good. I didn't know you write song lyrics."

Song lyrics? I make a face at him. "I don't write song lyrics. That's just a journal. Fragments of nothing. Thoughts. Dreams. Sort of streams of consciousness, James Joyce type shit. And it is my personal shit. Do you always just invade people's privacy and read their personal thoughts?"

He ignores me and continues to read.

I push my hair back from my face and sit up, tugging the blankets with me to cover my nudity. I hold out my hand. "Please, give it back."

He continues to read. Hyper-focused Alan. He turns a page. He looks at me. "Chrissie, these are song lyrics. Look at how you've put them together. You even have chord notations on some of the margins."

I roll my eyes. "Can I have my journal back, please?"

He glances down at me, grinning. "I haven't finished it. I'm still looking for the parts about me."

I stare at him. "There aren't any."

"No?"

"No."

He looks hurt, but I know he's just pretending. He's in a good mood. He's suddenly all around me, kissing me. He starts kissing my armpit and I squirm, frowning at him, knowing he's just doing this to irritate me, because he knows I am overly ticklish and he knows I hate it.

God, he is in a wicked good mood. What the heck is up with him today? Happy Alan on turbo-drive. Happy Alan is never on turbo-drive.

I wiggle beneath him, and I see my journal on the bed beside him. I cautiously move my arm. He stops me. He plants his body spread eagle atop me.

"You can't have the journal back until you make love to me," he says, grinning.

I twist and squirm beneath him so he can't kiss me. "Oh, go away. Don't you have Ian waiting in the studio or an interview or something else to do? I'm irritated with you right now."

He laughs. "Nope. Nothing but you to do, Chrissie."

I still. "You mean you are done? As in done, done?"

He rolls off me to lie beside me, stretching on his pillow, and rakes his hand through his hair. "Yes. Done. Ian took the tracks this morning."

"Ian took the masters? Did he leave a copy?"

Alan nods. I start to jump from the bed, but he stops me with a hand. "I have something I need you to sign."

He rummages on the floor beside the bed, through papers and whatever else got stacked there while I slept.

I sink back on the bed. "Sign? I don't understand."

"Just bullshit legal paperwork. No big deal." He is scanning the documents, frowning as if trying to find the right one.

He hands it to me. I scan the papers. I only half understand what I'm reading. "What is this?"

Alan yawns and relaxes back against his pillow, turned attractively on his side, facing me. "Just your standard release, Chrissie. It's nothing. Just sign."

I make a face. "Maybe I don't want to. Is it for the label?"

He hands me a pen. "No, me. Just something my management company makes me get. It's no big deal." He raises an eyebrow at me. "Unless you count that paragraph on page four that says I own you for the next ten years."

I make a face at him. "What happens if I don't sign? Am I free of you at last?"

He gives me a sexy half smile and his eyes glow wickedly. "I dump you right out the front door in a sheet for wasting my time. You either trust me or you don't, Chrissie. Sign the damn thing."

God, why is everything a test of wills with him? I'm having that feeling I sometimes get when he's mocking me, that inside of the mockery he is really being serious. Fine, Alan, Fine. You win.

I take a pen and, angry and heavy, I scrawl my name on the signature line. I'm about to toss it back in his face, when he takes the contract, and starts pointing here and here for my initials.

I stare down at it, studying the papers in my lap. "There. Happy now?"

"Ecstatic." He stretches back on the bed and closes his eyes.

I focus on the signature next to mine. "Who is Alan Wells?"

"Me," he whispers through another yawn. "My real name. The lawyers require it."

I frown and curl into him. "I didn't know that Alan Manzone wasn't your real name. It's kind of creepy to have to have a lawyer tell you who you've been sleeping with."

He ignores that comment and tosses the papers on the floor. He starts to rummage through the junk again and pulls out a board, sitting cross-legged beside me on the bed.

He holds it up in front me. "What do you think of this?"

I shrug. "What is it?"

"The artwork for the album. I like it."

I give it a thorough study, since it is flattering and unexpected that he wants my opinion on this. The imagery is dark, swirling shades of gray and black, grim with a simple title in bold black lettering: *Long and Hard*.

I crinkle my nose. "You should change the title. Your fans are going to think it's a self-titled album about your dick."

He laughs and drops a kiss on my nose. "Well, that's better than you thinking it's short and yuck. Besides, it's not a phallic reference." Smiling into my face, he starts to brush the hairs away from my brow. "Long and hard is the way out of darkness that leads to light."

I turn the art board in my hands. "It's you, they are going to think phallic. No one is going to think Alan Manzone is referencing an obscure literary passage by Dante."

Alan laughs. "Probably not. They are also not going to think Milton and *Paradise Lost*. Fuck, don't they teach literature in California?"

My cheeks burn, I ignore the jab, and toss the art onto the floor. "I still think your fans are going to think pornographic."

"My fans won't buy the fucking thing," he says exasperated.

Anxiety floods my stomach. I curl into him and lie with my head on his chest. What will happen to Alan if this is as big of failure as the label warns? He's coming off a rough year and artists have fragile egos and Alan, ego exempt, is right now more fragile inside than he admits to himself or me. Why is he determined to push forward with a project everyone believes should be shelved? Is this all part of Alan's self-destructive personality?

I wish I knew how to help him. How to make him OK. I kiss the warm flesh of his neck. "Do you want to play with your long and hard or are you too tired?"

He turns until I'm in his arms, we are face to face, curled into each other. "I'm never too tired for you."

He leans down and gently kisses me, and I can't help myself, I kiss him back hard, pushing myself into him. He pulls back, his eyes hooded and probing, while his hands knead the soft flesh of my buttocks.

"You don't have to give me a pity fuck just because you're worried about me," he mutters, and I can't tell if he's angry.

My entire face burns scarlet.

"That doesn't mean I won't take a pity fuck when it's offered," he breathes, a salacious smile flashing from his perfect face, as he shoves himself into me without warning.

I groan as his body fills me, curling my leg around his hip, holding him to me.

"Fucking you is all I will ever need, baby," he whispers in veneration. "You are the light beyond the darkness…"

His raspy theatrics fade with the sudden thrusting of his body. I close my eyes, feeling the buildup inside of him that came so quickly, so hungrily. I revel in his possession; in his flesh that swings from carnal to tender; in his moods from light to dark; and in how when he touches me I want to feel everything, and he makes it so.

I cry out, my nails digging into his back. "I want it harder. I want it to hurt," I gasp.

Alan's body freezes even though I can feel him climaxing, and that is usually when he is his most passionate. He doesn't move, his breathing is ragged with sound withheld, his body shudders but doesn't thrust, and I am panting and breathless. I want to feel that building climb and he won't let me.

I open my eyes and he pulls his body from me. His expression is disconcerted, alarmed, and even sad.

He grabs my chin, his eyes smoldering. "If all you want is a guy to make you hurt, get the fuck out of here!"

What? Why did he say that? Jeez, he says nastier things than that to me in our most tender moments. "Alan...I..."

He rolls over from me and covers his face with an arm.

I sit up in bed. "I'm going to shower."

"Since you're in the mood for pain, why don't you take this with you?"

He tosses something at me. I stare down at the shiny silver lighter on the floor. I hold back the tears until I'm in the bathroom.

* * *

When I return to the bedroom wrapped in a towel, Alan is on the bed reading my journal. The room is smoky, as if he's chained smoked the entire time I was gone, and there is an open bottle on the night table. Not even one of his elegant crystal cocktail glasses.

So, he's still pissed off. The quiet room is pulsing.

I lie down beside him, but he doesn't touch me. "Are you going to be pissed off at me the rest of the day," I whisper. "I didn't mean it the way you took it."

He sets aside the journal and takes a long drag of the cigarette before he stomps it out. "No? I think you meant it exactly how I took it. Don't turn me into a substitute for your fucked up addiction."

"You are so mean at times," I mutter, completely confused by him. "I don't know how to deal with you."

I roll away, sighing in frustration. Emotionally, I'm rattled by his suspicions and internally more than a little panicked that there is truth in what he said.

"Why is it so hard for you to believe I care about you?" he asks unexpectedly.

Now, on top of everything, I feel like I'm going to cry. "I don't know. Because you are you."

"Don't give me bullshit, Chrissie." He lifts my chin, forcing me to look at him. "I love you," he whispers. "Don't ask me to hurt you. Not ever. I won't be a part of that."

I nod. I understand. "I'm sorry."

"Why do you get all uptight whenever I say I love you?"

Oh god! I blink at him. How did we get back to psychoanalyzing me again? I've been contrite. I've apologized.

"It's just not something I'm comfortable with. Please, can we not do this today?" I whisper.

"I'm just trying to understand you. You are a very confusing girl."

Frustrated, I jerk into a sitting position, letting my towel drop. "How confusing can I be? You've seen my burns, you are in my head and I do pretty much anything you ask without a fight. I'm not confusing to you. Sometimes it feels like you know me better than I know myself."

"Not exactly," he murmurs, a trace of irritation still in his voice. "I don't know why you hurt yourself. I don't want to be just an extension of that."

"You're not. So let it go."

"So, then what am I to you?"

I let out a shuddering breath. "I don't know what you are to me. I don't know why I'm here or why you want me here or what we're doing. I don't know. How's that for an answer?"

He leans into me to kiss me very gently on the lips. His eyes are soft and glowing as he pulls back. "I don't like it, but it's a truthful answer."

He takes me with him as he sinks into the sheets, his body molding into me, his arms holding me closely. "Sleep, Chrissie. I need to sleep now."

And shamefully, I'm reminded he's been awake thirty hours. I'm not tired, but I lie in the tuck of his body, listening to his breathing change. I stare at the album artwork on the floor. In the center of the swirling darkness there are shapes. I didn't notice that before. *Long and Hard.* They look almost like eyes. They look almost like me.

* * *

"Don't laugh."

Jeez, why did he say that? Of course, I'm going to laugh now. I fight it but I can feel my body shimmy against him.

"You're laughing," he chides.

"If you tell me not to laugh I will laugh."

He is smiling down at me fondly. After twenty hours straight of sleep, he woke no longer pissed off at me. He is playful Alan since we've finished having the sex he always wants when he wakes. Sex, quiet time, and then hopefully food. And maybe if I'm lucky, getting out of the bedroom today.

"Don't move," he orders.

"Why?"

"I don't want to leave you, and if you laugh or move you will force me out."

"How long do you plan to stay?"

"Until I am forced to go."

"Why do you always want to hang after?"

He grins against my skin and I can see he's fighting his own laughter. Oops, I didn't phrase that well. I bite my lower lip, but it's Alan who laughs and his body slips out of me.

He rolls onto his side beside me, still laughing, and runs a hand through his hair. "You make horrible puns. I can't figure out if you do them deliberately or by accident."

I crinkle my nose. "Unintentionally."

"So, what do you want to do today?"

I pretend to give it serious thought. "How about a date-date?"

Alan laughs. "What's a date-date?"

"An evening that doesn't include an entire evening in the bedroom."

His eyes sharpen. *Shit, what have I said now?* It seems to take him a long time to decide how to answer. "You are not getting bored with me, are you?"

I look at him, puzzled. "Why do you have to be so touchy? I'd just like to get out of the apartment today."

"Do you want Colin to take you shopping?"

Shopping? I make a face. "I didn't say I wanted to go out without you."

A knock on the bedroom door saves me from what I can feel is going to be a quickly escalating argument.

"Fuck, Jeanette," Alan growls. "Stop pounding! What do you want?"

I enjoy his flash anger directed at someone other than me, right up to the point where Alan jerks open the door butt naked in front of his secretary.

They talk in quiet tones I can't hear. Then Alan rakes an aggravated hand through his hair. "Shit! Is that today?"

"You can't put this off, Manny," Jeanette says sternly.

"Fuck." He closes the door and jerks on a pair of jeans and nothing else.

"Get dressed," he orders.

I don't like the way he sounds. "Why?"

"Just do it."

I roll my eyes and pull on a long sleeve T-shirt, shorts and my UGG boots. I'm still struggling to pull one up as his hand practically drags me down the hall to the terrace. It's packed with chattering bodies, balancing food and drinks from a long buffet. My insides go numb as I recognize the well-known faces of his band, and what must surely be assorted wives and girlfriends.

There is no time for Alan to explain what this little unexpected interruption is about, or even why he wants me here for this. We are quickly swallowed up by fast quips and greetings, the unrelenting flow between him and the people competing for his attention. There is too much going on all at once to catch any of it in clarity, and it is a particularly haunting pathos to be trapped against him in the drape of his arms while they all fight to get near him.

Everyone seems to just bounce off Alan with hardly any notice, except Linda. She cuts her way through the circle, ruffles his hair, kisses his cheek.

"Poor Manny," she teases with a pout. "Thought you could hide out here with the little kitty forever, didn't you?"

The entire cluster sinks in unison, almost like a moving football huddle, onto the large cushioned chaise lounges. I'm still against his chest, and they're like a firing squad in front of us.

"Listen. We're just going to clear the air," Len Rowan says, silencing the disjointed chatter of the mob. "No pressure, mind you. But we just all need a no bullshit, straight answer about what's up."

Kenny Jones, Alan's drummer, is not quite as pleasant in his manner. "I'm tired of being fucking jerked around by you. We hear things, OK. We leave on the road in three weeks and we need to know: are you going to be there?"

Alan takes a long sip of his whiskey and smiles at me. "Yes. We will be there." He says it clipped, succinctly, but I tense in every muscle. We? What does he mean by we?

"But it's not enough just to show," Len says intensely. "You've got to really be there. No barricading yourself away for days in your room. No jumping tour and disappearing. You've got to be on the road for the show to be any good."

Alan nods. "I get it. You don't have to lecture me, Len."

"We need to get back into the space. Rehearse," Kenny adds.

"Soon. I have things to take care of in the city, and then we'll go to the rehearsal space," Alan says tonelessly.

"You are OK, aren't you?" Pat Despensa asks.

"I'm OK," Alan states flatly.

From there the conversation diverges into shoptalk, the upcoming tour, and everything Alan's missed in the last six months. Silent, I listen and watch this totally bizarre dynamic, where the limit of their concern over Alan and all that has gone on the past year was to ask him once, evasively, if he was OK. It makes me hate each and every one of them, and it reminds me of Alan's comment about real people and the *everyone else* in his life.

I stare at my toes, trying to ignore the group. No wonder he wants me here with him. I may be a fucked up girl, but on my worst day I'm better than them. I feel Linda watching, and I lift my chin to look at her. Except perhaps Linda. She is totally weird, but under the weirdness I think she really does care about both her husband and Alan.

I feel the steady pressure of eyes on me and shift my gaze to find Kenny Jones studying me. "I know you," he says, almost as an accusation.

"No, you don't, Kenny," Alan says flatly. I don't know what was in that *no you don't* but Kenny backs off and changes the subject.

I realize we've been on the terrace quite awhile and Alan hasn't introduced me to any of them, and I wonder why. I can feel that they are all curious about me, the yet-to-be-determined significance of my presence.

The talk shifts into that strange guy-world mode, half talking and half laughing. Guys talk about nothing, and yet they give the air that everything they say has a deeper, important meaning. Stories I know nothing about. Places. Things they've done, girls from the road...I feel myself get a little queasy. Music, parties, concerts and nothing. Guys talk about anything. All shit. Except the real shit. There is no real shit in guy-world.

All the girls except Linda have vanished, and I would have vanished too, except Alan hasn't relaxed his grip on me.

"I am bored, Len." Linda breaks through the talking with her voice, which can be so earsplitting at times.

"Why can't you be a good house cat like the little kitty, love? She just sits there looking beautiful and smiles. The perfect girl."

Len winks at me.

Linda pushes up from the cushion. She downs her margarita and then sets the glass on the table. She makes a face at Len. "You're right, Len. I am not the perfect girl. I'm the expensive wife." She springs to her feet. "Come on, Chrissie, let's get out of here. They are almost to resurrecting Hamburg. If I have to hear the Hamburg shit one more time this little kitty will go ballistic."

The thought of escaping instantly lifts my mood, I'm halfway off the chaise before the impulse is in me is to look to Alan for permission, and I feel relief that he nods. Would I have stayed if he hadn't? God, I don't even want to try to figure that one out.

As I walk into the apartment, Linda follows behind me all the way to the bedroom. My duffel was beside the chair when I left, my things still inside, but now it's gone.

She plops on the bed. "God, that was awful!"

I'm really glad she said it first. "Are they always like that?"

She nods. "We're a dysfunctional family. I never thought they'd last after the first year."

"Is Alan always like that with them? Tense and withdrawn and sort of just tired of them all?"

She starts randomly rummaging through a drawer in the bedside table. "Just for the past two, maybe three years. It's hard to be the star. Everyone pulling on you, depending on you. Using you. It's made him cynical, and I don't think he'd be here at all if he wasn't loyal. Alan is the most loyal guy I know."

Loyal? Interesting. I hadn't really thought of Alan in that way.

I return to my search for my things. It's then I notice that the bed is made. Alan and I were in it right up to point when the band arrived. I frown. Bed made. The room no longer smells like sex and everything is back in perfect order. Sheets changed? Who cleaned the bedroom? Jeanette? I cringe. Too creepy of a thought for today.

Linda grabs the phone. "Colin, its Linda Rowan. Can you bring the car around? Now, please."

She hangs up the phone. Her eyes lock on me. "What's the matter, Chrissie?"

"I can't find anything. I want to change and I don't know where my clothes are."

Linda shrugs. "Why are you changing? You look cute in the little shorts and fuzzy boot thing."

"Who do you think cleans the bedroom? Do you think it's Jeanette?"

Linda makes a face. "God, I hope not. I'd rather have a bullet in my head than that bitch touching my things."

"What's up with that, Linda?"

Linda lifts her brows. "We used to be best friends. She was my roommate at USC. We did our year abroad together in England and that's when we met Alan and Len. We've been enemies ever since. I'll leave it at that."

And then I know, I just know. Linda had a thing for Alan and Jeanette was her best friend. And only one thing can turn that into a feud that never ends. Alan had a thing with Jeanette. Yuck, she's his ex-girlfriend and now works as his secretary. God, no wonder she hates me.

I can see exactly when Linda realizes I put together the pieces. She crinkles her nose. "I wish he'd fire her. It's been over like forever. Manny hates her."

"Then why does she live here?"

Linda shakes her head in aggravation. "Showed up on his door maybe a year ago. That's when everything first started to get weird. Manny all secretive and shit. Cruella in the background. And then all the shit started. That's all I know, Chrissie. And I shouldn't have told you that. Manny is going to be pissed at me."

I am suddenly very uncomfortable and feeling very territorial. "I don't give a shit who she is. I don't want her touching my things."

Angry, I stomp into the bathroom to see if my clothes are there.

"Chrissie? Let's go," Linda calls from the bedroom. "You don't have to change. I'm not changing. Fuck the New York foo-foo bullshit on Park Avenue. We can do what we want. Let's roll."

* * *

Lunch and four hours later, we're still shopping. I can't even count the number of stores we've been to. Linda is right. She is the expensive wife, but I wonder if this marathon of shopping isn't really her ploy to keep me away from Alan for the afternoon.

So far, I've bought only one thing: sunglasses from Versace. As I rummage on a rack, I admit I've sort of enjoyed the afternoon. Linda is fun, like a hurricane version of Rene, and it's been nice having a small break from Alan. He's just so intense, and it's like you don't realize that you need time for your emotions to quiet, because he is all-consuming.

I look up from the dress I'm studying to find Linda watching me. "You OK, Chrissie?"

I smile. "I'm fine." I hold up the dress. "What do you think of this?"

Linda nods. "I love Prada. Drew Barrymore wore a dress almost exactly like that to the Oscars."

I bite my lip and stare. It is completely impractical for Santa Barbara. There is no place at home to wear this. Even at the most posh restaurants, I never wear anything fancier than a sundress and flip flops. This would be too much even for the clubs.

I start to put the dress back and Linda frowns. "You are taking care of yourself, aren't you?"

I flush scarlet. *Are we really about to have a sex talk here in the middle of a New York boutique?* Oh my god…Linda is beyond weird.

I smile. I nod. I pull out another dress and pretend to focus on it.

She comes around the display rack. "You need to take care of yourself, always. You can get home, can't you? I mean, you do have people waiting for you should you need to go home?"

Oh. Is that was this is about? She thinks I'm some girl Alan just snatched from the road and brought home with him.

"Don't worry, Linda. I can get home. I have a return ticket in my bag."

"You do?" Linda sounds surprised and relieved. "I just … I just wanted you to know that if you ever needed anything that you can depend on me. You know they don't think of us girls. Not really. Not ever. And with Manny, you are everything until you are not, and then before you even know what's hit you, it's like he doesn't know your name."

I know Linda means well, but that warning helped me not in the least. It's hard enough to try to figure out what this is with Alan without someone telling you its most likely nothing. I'm starting to feel a little sick and very unfocused.

I search through the rack for the Prada.

"You going to try that on?" Linda asks. "I think you're going to look sensational in it."

"Um, maybe." I hand the dress to our shopping associate.

I just want to get away from Linda right now, but unfortunately she follows me to the dressing room. The salesgirl stays, as well. It didn't occur to me that the salesgirl would stay or that Linda would follow, and, Jeez, I just want a moment alone.

Linda is lying on the couch sipping champagne. Every store. Champagne. She looks at me, since I've been here several minutes doing nothing but staring at the dress.

"What's wrong, Chrissie? You haven't gone cold on the dress, have you?"

"Can you find me some shoes, Linda? Size seven. I want to see it with shoes."

Linda springs to her feet and smiles as if thrilled to be of assistance. "I'll find you just the perfect ones."

Thankfully, the sales associate leaves with her. I shed my clothes and pull on the dress quickly. Linda gapes when she returns with several pairs of black spike-heeled shoes.

"I love that, Chrissie. You should get that dress."

The sales girl gushes that it looks like it was made for me, but then that is her job. I look in the mirror. I do look kind of sexy. It is short, it is black, and it is tight, with a straight cut low neck and small sleeves at the bicep. A little red flower design on each sleeve. And the Tiffany bracelet I never take off is just the right jewelry for it.

Prada. I've never purchased anything Prada before. Rene will positively die when she sees it. I do like the dress. I do like the shoes.

I smile at Linda. "Fine. The dress. The shoes. Can we go home now, Linda?"

Linda laughs. "Sure, Chrissie. One afternoon and you're already hot to get back. Not good, Chrissie. Not good. It doesn't pay to let them know you want them."

I flush, but Linda is already out of the room to call Colin, and I quickly pull on my clothes and then hand the dress and shoes to the sales associate.

We meet up again at the sales counter. I stare off in horror when I'm told the total. *Four thousand dollars? How could it be more than four thousand dollars? Some panties, some bras, one dress, one pair of shoes! Four thousand dollars!*

I've never spent four thousand dollars in a single day. Everyone around me looks like it's no big deal. I frown. I don't have that much cash. I'll have to charge it. Jeez, what will Jack think when he sees this?

Linda laughs. "Are you OK, Chrissie? You have the funniest look on your face."

"I wasn't expecting it to be so much."

"It's Prada. Just give her one of Manny's credit cards. It's not like he can't afford it."

I stare at her. "I have my own credit cards. Why would you think I would have Alan's?"

Linda studies my face, confused. "You're living together. I just assumed."

I can feel the color drain from my face. Is that what Linda thinks? Is that what they all think?

"We're not living together, Linda," I say emphatically. "Why would you think we are living together?"

Linda's eyes round. "Because you are. He moved you in. You go to sleep there. You wake up there. Your things are there. He moved you in, Chrissie. He doesn't do that just for fun and kicks. It's not his thing."

Is it possible that I've moved in with Alan without knowing it? Not just in a stay-for-a-while-then-go-home thing, but in a we're living together type way? No, no, no. Alan is unpredictable and confusing, but he was very clear about my staying in his apartment only while I was in New York. Linda misunderstood.

"I've not moved in. I'm not living with him."

Oh, shit. Why did that have to sound so irrational and why did it have to be so loud? The salesgirl is staring. Linda is staring. Burning color is moving down my cheeks.

Linda shakes her head and reaches for her bag. "Fine. You're not living with him. It's nothing to get all pissed off about, Chrissie."

"I want to go home."

"Fine. Except you are not living together so I don't know where to take you."

In the car on the way back to the apartment, Linda is sulking.

"I'm sorry," I whisper. "I'm not usually so...snappy."

She shakes her head. "I get it. I shouldn't have been rude." She unbends and smiles sympathetically. "I'm just really glad he has you. I just want us to be friends and for you to know you won't get any garbage from me."

I'm not certain what that assurance means, but I smile.

"It's hard for him, you know," she adds sadly. "Out on the road, never anyone like him. You're like him, I think."

Like him? What does that mean? Alan and I are complete opposites, in all ways, except the one way I still am not comfortable admitting to myself.

"I think I might be in love with him," I confess, shocking the hell out of myself. I don't have a clue why I am telling Linda this.

Linda laughs. "It's obvious that you're in love with him."

"It's almost impossible to get a feel that you really know what's going on with Alan. And the living together thing. Definitely not something I expected having someone say to me. I'm still trying to figure out what it is we're doing. He's good for me. And he's bad for me. And I don't know what to do."

Linda grins. "Yeah, well, welcome to guys. He's used to having things his own way. And all the other shit, the stuff in the papers, well that's just what it is, Chrissie, just shit. You know everyone has it wrong about him. The only place he's ever real is on stage. Off stage is the show. That's where he doesn't trust anyone enough to be himself."

I expel a long, shuddering breath. "I feel that way sometimes when we're together. Like he's sometimes putting on an act."

"No," Linda counters, "he's totally himself with you. I've known him a long time. I saw it at once. He's never been that way with a girl, just totally himself from the start, but then what is there usually for him to meet? It's nearly impossible for him to meet someone worth caring about, and the guy is a giver to the core."

There is acid in Linda's voice when she says that last part, as if she's thinking of someone particular in Alan's past. Was it a girl that hurt him so badly? I debate with myself whether to ask her.

I smile weakly. "So, that's where I am. I don't know what I'm doing."

Linda laughs and leans in to hug me. "I've been married five years and I don't know what I'm doing. Keeps life interesting, though. Doesn't it?"

We're laughing as we take our bags from Colin and step into the garage elevator. I lean back into the mirrored walls, smiling and feeling OK. It was good to get out with Linda, to just let all the emotions rest for a while. There is no law that says I have to figure out everything today.

Linda is chattering on, probing what I would like to do tonight, when the elevator doors open. My face falls and my heart stills.

The music is blasting and there are hundreds of people in the apartment. It's packed, packed with famous faces: the currently hot; the always freaky; the artsy; a hodgepodge of everything that is the music industry. There are bars set up everywhere and I wonder where the set-up bars and serving help came from. There is food, lots of food, floating around the room on pretty trays: sushi, dim sum, caviar, and a lot of food I can't even identify. And the air is suffocating with laughter, talk, and smoke.

Linda studies my face. "Fuck! This is what you get when you leave them alone for more than an hour. The party is on speed dial."

"Really! How convenient."

We have to fight just to get through the entryway. I spot Alan on the terrace, exactly where I left him, only now he is New York Rock Star chic. He is laughing, barefooted, cross-legged on a cushioned chaise in a black flowing shirt and leather pants with tousled long hair and twinkling black eyes.

Exactly where I left him, except he's surrounded by girls, being pulled at, claimed, kissed, fawned on and wooed. It is a surprisingly unsettling thing to see him like this, restless with adrenalin, surrounded by swarming admirers. He doesn't even look like the same guy I left at four.

At four he was tense, aloof, almost as if he were uncomfortable with people near him, but now he is the magnet in the center of the universe, making all things twirl, holding everyone captive of him, and completely engaged and alive and dominant.

Len is reclined on a chaise across from Alan, and they are laughing and drinking as if they hadn't nearly killed each other earlier this week. Beautiful women are all around, pressed up against them. My heart goes out to Linda. *Poor, Linda. Poor, poor Linda.*

"Are you OK, Chrissie?"

I can feel Linda staring at me.

"I'm just going to put my things away. Do you want me to take yours?"

I slip quickly down the hall into the bedroom and close the door. That familiar anxiety and sadness whispers through me. I've never liked parties. Why did Alan do this? Shouldn't he have at least asked me if I wanted a party? I'm starting to feel chaotic inside, off balance and disoriented, and I wish I could just go out there and make everyone go away.

There is a push on the bedroom door, and I slam it shut and lock it. I sink on the bed, running my hands through my hair. That party has nothing to do with me, so there is no point in being a pissed off mess about it.

I go into the bathroom, wash my face and brush my hair. As an afterthought, I grab the phone and call the service for messages. Seven from Rene. One from Jack. The call from Jack surprises me and I wonder what's up with that.

I cringe. Has the gossip from New York reached Santa Barbara? Santa Barbara only just feels like the edge of the earth. It isn't really. It's a phone call away and I was stupid not to consider that, after working a week in a studio with him, that Ian Kennedy might mention it in passing to Jack. They're good friends.

Ring, ring, ring.

"Hello?"

I exhale. "Hi, Daddy."

"Chrissie! I was just thinking about you."

I try to pick out clues in Jack's voice to figure out where this conversation might take me. Jack sounds happy. He doesn't sound like a father who has just learned that his daughter is having a relationship with a recovering heroin addict.

I curl the phone cord around my arm until it pinches hard. "So, what's up? You called yesterday. Sorry I didn't call you earlier. I just got the message from the service. Everything going OK?"

"Everything is fine. I was just checking on you. It's allowed. I am your dad."

My cheeks burn. Even though he's laughing, there is something in Jack's voice I can't read.

"Daddy, I need to tell you something."

Silence. "OK. Why so serious?"

I'm having an affair with Alan Manzone! "It's just…I spent four thousand dollars shopping today."

I roll my eyes at myself. A long pause. God, that came out so lame.

"Are you worried that I'm going to be angry that you spent four grand shopping? Is that why you sound so strange?" Jack laughs almost in relief. I stare at the receiver. *Do I sound strange?* "It's relative. You're shopping in New York. I wouldn't want you to get in the habit of it, but it's no big deal, Chrissie."

Jack laughs harder. I almost start to cry. He says, "Shit, you had me really worried for a while. I don't know. Something in your voice. I thought you were going to tell me something I don't want to hear."

I brush at my tears. "I went shopping today with a girlfriend. I know it's a lot of money. I just sort of got carried away and before I could stop myself it was done."

I'm talking about shopping, but not really, not inside of me. Tears fill up my air way.

"Whoa, Chrissie. Slow down. Why are you crying? Why are you upset?"

Oh god, why did I start this? Why did I call Jack today?

"Are you OK?" he presses more insistently into the phone. "Did something happen?"

"Nothing happened, Daddy."

"Then why are you crying?"

"I'm just emotional today, I guess."

"Is that all there is, Chrissie? I sense something more. You can tell me anything. What's wrong?"

I bite my lip. *I'm in love. That's what's wrong.*

"Is there anything you need to talk to me about, Chrissie?"

What does he know? Why does it always feel like he knows everything, but won't ever tip his hand about anything?

"There's nothing, Daddy."

I expect to hear the click. Instead, "Tell me about New York, baby girl."

I curl around the phone, and for the first time in a very long time I just talk to Jack. I can't remember the last time we talked this way and I'm not exactly sure why we are doing it today. But it feels good. Really, really good.

* * *

I've just finished my call when there is a soft tap on the bedroom, and instinctively I know its Linda. I open the door to find her holding two glasses. She sinks beside me with a look of heavy dread and pushes what I think is a daiquiri into my hand.

"You OK?" she asks.

I nod. "I'm OK."

"I want us to be great friends."

I remind myself that Linda is a fragile girl. I take a sip of the daiquiri. I smile. "It's good."

Linda downs her daiquiri in a single gulp. "I really, really hate this shit."

I nod. We both know she's not talking about the drink.

Linda sighs. "I should have brought the whole pitcher!"

Chapter Thirteen

When we return to the party, Alan is slow dancing with Nia, and it really bothers me that he looks completely into her. His body presses against her flesh in a way that tells me they've been intimate before.

The sharp, burning knives cutting my insides take me completely by surprise. I never expected to feel flash jealousy over Alan, and I realize that is exactly what I'm feeling, standing here like an idiot watching him dance with another girl.

"Alan and Nia are old news, Chrissie. They've been over forever," Linda informs, reading me without effort.

I shrug. "It's no big deal. We are not exclusive or anything. He can do what he wants. I think I'm going to get another drink before I go out there."

I decide not to follow Linda to one of the bars set up in the great room. There are people crowded several bodies deep around all of them, and I don't have Linda's nerve. She just pushes through, telling people to get the fuck out of her way, and they do.

I go instead into the kitchen and find it empty, when in California the kitchen is often the party room.

I rummage through the refrigerator until I find a Diet Coke.

"Hi. You hiding from that mess out there, too? An hour ago there were only about fifty of them. I ducked out at somewhere around one hundred. How many are in there now?"

I whirl around to realize that "hi" is intended for me. There's a guy sitting alone on the counter, nursing a beer. Very attractive, blond hair, hazel eyes, light tan, good body. Why is he hiding in the kitchen?

"Nope, I'm not hiding. Just didn't want to have to fight for a drink. It didn't seem right to fight for a Coke. I'm shocked to find practically no one else in the kitchen. New Yorkers, very strange people. Who knew?"

He laughs. "You must be from California. I thought my brother and I were the only ones here. Sandy is a promoter. He's the idiot who dragged me here. But I can tell you are from California."

Now I'm intrigued and I smile. "OK, how can you tell?"

He smiles. He points at my shoes. "Beyond the nice tan and the shorts? The UGG boots. Definitely a California thing."

"How very observant of you."

"I'm a writer. That's my thing. Crowds, not so much. But people watching definitely my thing."

He says it in a silly, self-depreciating way that is kind of charming. I can tell he's quiet and a little shy like me.

"Have you written anything I might know?"

"Maybe. I'm a reporter for the *Los Angeles Times*."

I tense and have a sudden urge to flee the kitchen. He notices. "I am off the record tonight, so relax. I'm just a guest here like you."

He extends his hand. "Jesse Harris."

"Chrissie."

"Good, now I've officially met one person and I can go home. That was the deal I had with my brother."

I laugh and pop open the top. I don't bother to get a glass and take a sip from the can. I ease up on the butcher block table in the center of the room, to sit on the edge with my legs dangling.

"So, who are you here with?" he asks.

"Sort of a guy."

God, that came out stupid.

Jesse laughs.

"Just my luck. The cute ones are always with sort of a guy. So, why are you in the kitchen instead of with your sort of a guy?"

I usually hate it when people make fun of me, but there is something just plain nice about Jesse Harris. He seems too nice to be a reporter.

I shrug. "He's dancing with an ex-girlfriend. I'm not sure what I should do."

He takes a sip of his beer. "I'm a writer. Give me your options. I'll give you expert advice on the right option."

"You're a reporter not a novelist. You're the wrong kind of writer."

"I'm a reporter to pay for being a novelist. So give me a shot. Let's see if I'm going to be a good novelist."

I laugh, and I am suddenly aware of some of the nicer changes in me since Alan. I am more confident. More comfortable in my skin.

"Well, I was debating just going out there planting a big wet one on him and locking myself to his side like a Siamese twin."

"I can tell you right now that that one is definitely wrong."

"How do you know?"

"Because he'll like that, and he was a jerk to leave you all alone ending up in the kitchen with me."

"Why do you say that? Is there something wrong with you that I should be worried about?"

Those gorgeous hazel eyes lock on me. "I find you incredibly cute and I'd take you out of here in a heartbeat if I thought I had half a chance."

Whoa, where did that come from? Shy and yet direct. Interesting.

I shake my head and push away that thought.

He smiles. "What's the other option you were thinking to do?"

Boy, he is really good looking when he smiles. Why isn't he out there enjoying the party?

I take another sip of my Coke and say, "Just going out there, forgetting all about him, and having a good time at the party."

He holds up a hand, palm down and gives me the iffy wobble. "Better than option one, but not good."

I cross my legs at my ankles and make them swing a little more. "OK, since you're the writer, what would be better?"

Hazel eyes lock on me like a laser. "Leave with me."

Oh my, not what I expected. I've gone as far in this as I should. It was fun, for some reason Jesse hitting on me was fun, even though he's right. He doesn't have a chance. Three weeks ago, he would have. But not today.

I pretend to give it serious thought. "Sorry, I don't think I can do option three."

"Why not? I sort of had the feeling I was doing this better than I usually do. Why shoot me down now?"

I start to laugh. "Because the guy I'm sort of with is Alan Manzone."

He gives me the oh-shit-good-one face. I push off the counter and go to the freezer. "Are you hungry? They have all this fancy food out there, but you know what I'd really like is some ice cream."

I rummage through the cartons and pull one out. "Häagen-Dazs, Swiss Vanilla Almond."

I grab a spoon and ease up on the counter next to Jesse. I pull off the lid, take a bite, and offer him the spoon.

"Why are you really hiding in the kitchen?" I ask.

Jesse takes a spoonful and then laughs. "I'm not hiding. I'm exhausted. I flew in from Afghanistan wanting only a hot shower and sleep, but Sandy dragged me here. I've been covering the aftereffects of the Soviet withdrawal."

I haven't a clue what he's talking about. "Sounds interesting," I say, filling my mouth with ice cream.

Jesse laughs. "No, it doesn't. Most Americans don't even know where Afghanistan is or what the hell the Russians did there."

My cheeks warm, their color betrays me. "I'm not political. My father, extreme '60s radical. It's made me not political, but I'm sure lots of people find your work interesting."

"Thanks for the encouragement." Jesse laughs. "So, what are you then? A model?"

I kick him with a leg. "No, a cellist." I frown, shake my head, and take another bite. "Well, sort of, or maybe I should say, used to be. I'm kind of confused about that part of myself right now."

Those divine eyes lock on me. "So, tell me one thing about yourself that you are not confused about."

"That she already has a date for the evening."

The voice I hear is not the one in my head.

I look up, startled, to find Alan in the kitchen doorway. He crosses the kitchen, planting his hands on either side of me, and gives me a kiss that would have embarrassed me if we'd been alone in the bedroom: wide open mouth, full tongue, hard, fast and sexual.

I force my body not to respond and when he finally pulls back, his black eyes are burning and probing. "You've been back for two hours. Where have you been?"

So, he does know when I got back. Why didn't he look for me? And why is he angry with me?

I shrug. "I called Jack. Had daiquiris in the bedroom with Linda. And I've opted to eat ice cream with my new friend, who wants to take me home with him."

Shit, what made me say that last part? *Not smart, Chrissie. Not smart to say something that might set Alan off.* Ian and Vince rise as vivid warnings in my head, and on top of that, it was a really shitty thing to do to Jesse.

I shift my gaze to find Jesse watching uncomfortably from his perch beside me.

Those black eyes burn into me. "I hope you said no."

"Nope, I said maybe. He thinks you're a jerk for leaving me alone at a party."

I wait.

Alan tosses a terse smile at Jesse. "Hi," he says in a tight, clipped way. Jesse doesn't bother to respond, he just sits there watching, and then I realize he's trapped just like me, with Alan's body between the counter and the door.

"You're pissed," Alan accuses.

I look away from him. "I'm not pissed."

He runs a hand through his hair in a jerky, irritated way. "I'm sorry about the party. Will you leave the kitchen with me now?"

"No. I hate parties. I never go to parties. You didn't even ask me if I wanted to go to a party tonight. I come back and *pouf* there's two hundred people here."

"This has been on the calendar for weeks. I forgot about it," he explains in heavy frustration. "This is work. Part of what

I do. Everyone important is here, giving me the once-over, making sure I'm worth the investment. It's part of the business. Seeing if I'm sound before they put up the money."

I lift a brow. "I understand the business. You don't have to lecture me on that. I just don't like parties, OK?"

"Not even with me?" He gives me that smile with the slightly downturned corners of his lips; not happy, not sad, just in-between and endearing.

My eyes round. "No. *Especially* not with you."

He nods and is a little more friendly when he looks at Jesse. "You're right. I am a jerk. I'm lucky she stayed."

"Very lucky!" Jesse says in that affable way he has.

That annoys Alan. "Very lucky," he amends.

Alan takes my spoon and scoops out a generous bite of ice cream. "So, how is Jack?"

"I don't want to talk about Jack."

"OK." Alan takes another scoop. "Are you going to stay in the kitchen all night?"

"No. At some point I'll probably go to bed."

Alan frowns. "You are not going to bed. There are people out there you really should meet."

I ignore trying to figure out why he would say that. "There are too many people out there I already know," I exclaim with heavy meaning.

His jaw clenches. "Fuck, is that it? Ian was here, Chrissie. Half of New York knows by now we're sleeping together. There is no way to keep it private. You are going to have to deal with it. Learn to deal with the bullshit."

My entire body burns deep red. I really hate this habit of Alan's, of letting loose any thought in his head whether we're alone or not. "God, you are an asshole sometimes."

Alan rolls his eyes. "So how do we fix this?"

"I think you were right about not being able to change you. You are pretty much stuck being an asshole."

Alan laughs. "Maybe, but I am not spending my entire night going to the kitchen if I want to see you."

He lifts my chin, lightly brushing my cheeks with his thumbs and gazes down at me, his expression unfathomable. "Why don't you marry me? We'll get married tomorrow. Then it won't matter what anyone writes, what anyone thinks, what Jack thinks, and we'll both know exactly what the hell we're doing."

I shove him away. "Very funny. God, you're obnoxious tonight. Are you loaded?"

He lifts the glass he carried in off the counter behind him and holds it beneath my nose. In surprise, I realize it's only soda in the cocktail glass. He leans in to kiss me softly, and when he pulls back his eyes are shimmering.

"Marry me, Chrissie," he whispers.

I let out an aggravated growl. "If I thought you were serious, my answer would be no. Since you're not serious, my answer is: I should have warned you that Jesse is a reporter with the *Los Angeles Times*."

Jesse holds up a hand in a continental gesture. "Off the record tonight. I didn't hear a thing and I'm a foreign correspondent. Our gossip columnist is the redhead out there with my brother."

As frustrating and awful as this has been, I start to laugh. My cute new friend is a dork, Alan is weird, and I am...oh golly, I don't know if I want to try to put a label on myself right now.

I smile up at Alan. "Will you go away? This is how I do parties. Will you just let me do what I do?"

Alan brushes my lower lip with his thumb. Everything inside me shivers. "Come out to the party, Chrissie. Something terrible might happen. You might have fun."

I shake my head.

"No?" He kisses my nose. "Do what you want to do, but I'll miss you. Maybe you can leave the kitchen occasionally and pretend you're not with me, so at least I can see you."

I give him a small, reluctant smile. "Maybe."

"That'll have to do. Give us a kiss, love. I've got to get back. I've not completely charmed everyone yet."

He eases into me, and with the lightest touch presses his lips to mine. I melt into him on contact, dissolving into his warmth and wishing he'd take me in his arms.

I watch Alan disappear through the door and I feel stupid for not having gone with him. I slap the lid on the Häagen-Dazs, grab the spoon, and slip from the counter.

I put the carton back into the freezer.

"He was serious, you know," Jesse says quietly.

I shut the door and turn. "Excuse me?"

Jesse's eyes bore into me gravely. "He was serious when he asked you to marry him, and you shot him down like it was a joke."

All my nerve endings tingle from my quickly rising embarrassment. "It was a joke. That's just Alan. He's theatrical and it's the way he talks to me."

Jesse shakes his head and takes a sip of his beer.

I give a small, frustrated laugh that makes my shoulders lift. "Really. You are completely wrong about this."

Jesse smiles. "Do you want some advice? Go out there and apologize to him. You did a really crummy thing a few minutes ago. Why are you in the kitchen with me?"

The color on my face is no longer a pleasant feeling flush, but the burn of humiliation. I look up at him, ready to be defensive, but his expression stops me.

"Do you want to go dance with me?" I ask. "Just kind of ease me into the party so I can go apologize."

Jesse's eyes widen.

"I don't think that's a good idea. You probably missed it, but the entire time in the kitchen he looked like he wanted to put a fist through my face."

"Please," I urge. "That part about me not liking parties is true. But it's worse than that. I do parties really badly. And even though you're wrong, he wasn't serious, I was pretty rotten to him."

He searches my face, then exhales heavily, and takes my hand.

The great room is a smothering cluster of people, and I try to spot Alan as we make our way through the throng to the dance floor. Beyond the glass, I see that he's returned to the terrace and he's got quite a circle around him of the who's who of music. Those black eyes touch on me, empty and fleeting, and I can tell by how he tosses down his drink that there is alcohol in the cocktail glass now.

A slow song starts and I step into Jesse's arms, silent, my hand a tense curl on his shoulder.

We dance in silence for what seems like ages. "Are you OK?" Jesse asks me quietly.

I look up at him and nod.

He shakes his head. "Why don't you go over there? Act like everything is normal. Guys hate conflict. He'll act like everything is normal too."

I don't go out onto the terrace. Instead, I curl into Jesse and continue to dance. The dance is almost over. Somehow Alan has moved without me seeing. He is standing beside me, staring down with only partially leashed anger. I can feel heavy stares from every direction in the room, the kind that warns that you're in the midst of what will soon be a scene.

Jesse steps back from me.

"I can't believe you fucking did that," he says in a tight, clipped way. "It was a joke. A fucking joke. And you've reduced me to a fucking joke."

Oh shit, he is pissed. Why is he pissed?

He regards me coolly for what seems like a century.

"We might as well dance since we've been seen together," he says, almost inflectionless.

Alan fills the space between Jesse and me, and he drags me up against him. There is scorching anger in his body and he molds me so intimately against him that I can feel every detail of him through his clothing. His fingers are a never-ending run on my back, making every inch of my flesh grow hot. He fills his palms with me, softly kneading, then he strokes, erotic and slow, until the pattern of my heart is an uneasy, altering flow between arousal and fear.

I try to ease back from him, enough to see his face, but his hands flatten on my back and hold me in place.

"Let me go, Alan. I don't like this," I whisper, cautious and unsure, but my voice is thick, feverish.

"It's working very well for me, love," he says softly, biting my shoulder instead of kissing it. "What part isn't working for you? I'll change it."

My breath quickens. "All of it. If you keep this up, they're going to start tossing room keys at us."

I pull back and have a vague awareness that he is letting me. I raise my eyes slowly to his face and wish I hadn't. His eyes harden and some marginal parameter of my brain warns that I have fucked up big time here.

My heart turns into a confused, frantic pulse as he grabs my arm, steering me through the crowded apartment, mindless of the sharply fixed stares that follow his rapid trek. He pulls me into the bedroom, slams the door, and releases me.

"It was a joke, Chrissie," he yells harshly clipping each word.

He leans against the door, running a hand through his hair, his eyes cuttingly black.

"If you don't like my out of bedroom manner," he starts up again through gritted teeth, "or my public manner or my work manner, deal with it. The world isn't only about Chrissie! Fucking learn to deal with something for a change. But don't playact with me and don't you ever pretend I am nothing to you again. Are we clear? Do you understand?"

I stare up at him. There is no point in trying to understand him, he is just too angry, but I really don't know what nerve I struck in him and I really never expected to be on the receiving end of anger like this. Oh no, not like this, never like this.

I cross my arms and stare at the floor. "Maybe."

"Then get the fuck out."

My face snaps up. I feel shaky inside. My heart stops. How did we get here, a near break-up moment, from this strange, disconnected, angry sort of night we've had? Is he breaking up with me and tossing me out in the middle of a party?

I don't know how to deal with this. I don't know what to say. "Do you know where my things are? Someone put them away." It's the only thing I can think to say.

"So, is that it? You want to leave?"

God, why are we doing this? How did we get here?

And before I know if this is it, if we're over, my shorts are on the floor and I am propped against the wall, and we are having sex. Really, really rough sex, standing up with me pinned against the door. I wrap myself around him, eagerly meeting the violent thrusts of his body, the aggressive joining of his flesh.

Each thrust against the wall is painful, and I am drowning in the consuming fire of his anger. It is stormy, but it subsides quickly with a ragged climax and the abrupt retreat of his flesh from mine.

My back against wall, I slip to the floor. I sit there breathing hard and staring up at him. And then I realize, when he doesn't look at me as he jerks his pants in place and smooths his hair with an angry swipe of his hand, that he intends for this to hurt and humiliate me. What did I do to make him angry enough to hurt me?

"You just screwed me like a whore in the middle of a party!" I hiss, wounded and accusing.

His expression doesn't change. "If you are going to behave like a whore, guys will treat you like a whore."

"Get out!" I scream.

His clothes are all put back together on him. He is staring down at me. "Your things are in the closet off the bathroom."

I nod, and just like that Alan leaves. I manage to hold back the tears until I've counted to twenty in my head, just to be sure he's not coming back and won't see me cry.

My body feels heavy as I pull myself up onto my feet. Shaking, I go into the bathroom, but I feel spacey, disoriented, and uncoordinated. My trembling flesh sinks onto the ledge of the bathtub.

What am I supposed to do now? I can't just pack up my things and lug them out in the middle of a party where everyone will see me. Raw, bitter, humiliating emotion runs like ice through my veins. What did I do that was so awful that he would screw me at a party then dump me? Scalding tears pour down my cheeks. Frantically, I replay the minutes in my head, but for the love of Jesus there is nothing to explain this—his lashing out at me and ending us.

I curl into a tight ball, rocking, trying to stop my tears. What did I expect? You have only to open a newspaper to get a pretty clear idea of what kind of guy he is. I knew—but I thought he cared about me. Really cared. How could he do this to me? How could he turn in a flash into an asshole that screwed me at a party and tossed me aside?

My gaze darts around the bathroom trying to figure out what to do. I can't leave. I can't go back into the party. And I don't want to stay here, trapped in a bathroom, humiliated and alone.

I hear sounds from the bedroom and my anxious heart betrays me, wishing that it might be Alan returning to apologize to me. Maybe it was just a fight? A big wicked nothing.

I peek through the open bathroom door. The wives and girlfriends, all but Linda, are huddled around the table where the newspapers magically appear each morning, and it's covered with white powder, and one of them is using a credit card to line it.

Shit, now I'm trapped in a bathroom while the wives snort coke.

I hear my name mixed in the chatter of the room.

"Who does she think she is that she doesn't think she needs to talk to us?"

"Talk to us? She doesn't think she needs to talk to Manny. She ignored him the entire night."

"Who is she? I've never seen her before, not anywhere, and out of nowhere she's just here."

"Where do you think he found her?"

"She reminds me of that girl. Remember that girl he dragged around with him on tour in '86? The one who took it all too seriously and didn't know Manny was just messing with her. All sweet and small town cute."

They all laugh.

"I think she is cute. In an understated way. Her clothes are awful and she really needs to do something about those eyebrows. But she's cute."

The bedroom door opens. Linda enters the room and sinks down among the circle.

"OK, Linda. What gives? Is the little princess living with him? And where the hell has Manny been for six months?"

Linda snorts a line. Then I hear the snort sound of fingers to nostril to clear the powder from the nasal passage. She wets her fingers, snorts it in again, and then dabs her finger and rubs it on her gums.

"I like her." That's all Linda says.

"Well, I don't. Such a bitch. Where does she get off thinking she is so superior?"

Linda stares at them all. "Don't mess with her. This girl matters."

This girl? I shake my hands to shake the icky feeling away. *This girl.* That's what I am. *This girl.* Just another girl, just the girl of the moment, and not even the girl of the moment any longer because Alan dumped me.

"Christ, Linda. He makes them all feel like they matter."

Linda arches a brow. "No, I didn't say he makes her feel like she matters. I'm saying she does matter. And we've got enough fucking drama and enough problems without you messing with her. Leave her alone."

"I don't know. Everything feels so bizarre. Stranger than usual since Manny came back with her, which is strange enough."

"Does anyone know what happened?"

Linda says nothing. Not one piece of what she knows falls on the table. "He's just went into Rehab. Why do you all make such a drama about everything?"

"Rehab certainly hasn't helped with his anger issue. Did anyone else hear that he broke Vince Carroll's arm for drugging her?"

Linda rolls her eyes. "If you are going to get your gossip from the tabloids, no one will ever take you seriously, Bianca."

Bianca looks up at Linda. "Ryan told me Manny almost put Ian through a wall just for talking to her and then admitted he broke Vince's arm for drugging her. I don't think the Rehab shit helped much with his anger issues."

Linda is now like a laser-guided missile. "Manny has been with Ryan and Ian?"

"You didn't know?" Bianca asks. "He's recording a solo album with the little princess. Manny didn't tell you? Len doesn't know?"

Linda says nothing. She stares. She shrugs. I can feel how upset she is, but she is loyal. Always loyal.

Linda stares them all down. "Shut the fuck up! I mean it. No more gossip. No more chatter. Nothing. And if you fuck with her you are fucking with me."

The door slams behind Linda. The girls stare at each other.

"God, what's up with her these days?" Bianca asks.

"These days? It's every day. Len fucks everything that moves and she goes ballistic on us."

Another line snorted. The door opens and the wives all look up at once, as Kenny Jones saunters in.

"What's up with the hen house? You all look guilty. What are you cackling about now?"

Kenny sinks to the floor and pulls his girlfriend back against him. He takes the rolled hundred, does a quick line, and then cleans his airways.

Bianca says, "The little princess. Ian says Manny is recording a solo album with her. That he's quitting the band."

Kenny leans back against the bed, laughing so hard that his face reddens and tears sparkle in his eyes. "Where the fuck do you get this shit? The girl is nothing. Just something to do. She's just some bird he picked up at The Blue Light. Her friend was a crazy ass bitch. He fucked her in the bathroom at the club. You know how Manny is. Fuck 'em and on to the next one."

Bianca fixes intense eyes on Kenny. "How do you know for sure Ian is wrong?"

Kenny does another line and stands up. "Because he fucked her and dumped her thirty minutes ago."

Chapter Fourteen

I grab from the closet a black cardigan of Alan's. Someone can deliver my things to Jack's tomorrow. I leave the bedroom with only my purse, and spot Jesse Harris still at the party.

I cross the room to him, unable to look up as I speak. "Can you walk me home? I would really appreciate it if you'd walk me home. It's not far and I want to leave here."

He stops me with a hand on my arm. "Are you OK?"

"I'm OK. But it would be really, really cool if you just walked me home and didn't ask any questions."

He nods. He is a nice guy. I wasn't wrong about that. At least I wasn't wrong about one thing. Don't cry, Chrissie. Don't cry. Not yet.

"Stay right here," he says in an urgent and soothing sort of way. "I should tell my brother I'm leaving. I'll be right back. Don't leave without me."

I start to shake, realizing I must look more of a mess than I thought. I fight not to look from the entry hall into the party. In a moment, Jesse returns.

The streets are as close to empty as New York ever gets. We walk without talking and I focus on the stench in the air. It is only six blocks to Jack's apartment. A fast walk. It feels long. Very long, and I'm tired by the time we get there.

The doorman opens the door the minute he sees me.

"Home?" Jesse smiles. "Nice digs."

I stare at him. "Would you like to come up?" I am on the verge of meltdown and grab his arm. "Please, come up. I don't

307

want to be alone just yet. Please, I don't know anyone in New York and I could really use a friend."

He follows me into the elevator and I take the key and insert it in the panel.

"Penthouse, huh? Nice digs."

Small talk. Jesse's just making small talk. Trying to insert normal here, when there is absolutely nothing normal about any of this.

I smile. "It's my dad's apartment. I live in California. Remember?"

Jesse gives me a kind smile. "UGG boots. How could I forget?"

Why does it feel like it takes forever to get to the top floor? Chug, chug, chug. Metal can move so slowly sometimes. I don't want to cry until I'm through the front door.

Too late. Tears. And my body curls into Jesse's chest. "I hope you are an ethical reporter. I would die. Absolutely die. If any of that makes print. Ever. Please. Never, ever, ever."

His fingers lift my chin. He has such kind eyes. "Never, ever, ever. I'm a lousy reporter because I'm ethical. My family lights candles in church every week, praying my novel sells. Otherwise, I'm not going to have much of a future as a writer."

I give a soggy laugh, though it isn't much of a joke.

Jesse looks disconcerted now. He's studying me almost as if he's debating with himself. "But, Chrissie, you need to know. I'm off the record tonight, but I wasn't the only reporter there."

Oh shit! What have I done?

Jesse folds me into a comfortable, protective type hug. "Don't break on me now. It doesn't matter. Who cares if it does make print? It will all go away in about thirty seconds. My professional opinion. You can bank on it. This will all go away and be nothing."

I can't will my legs to carry me out of the foyer, and I stand surrounded by my mother's priceless collection of glass encased violins. But that's not all that's there is in the cabinets. There are family photos. Lots of family photos in between the spruce and ebony, and Jesse is staring at them as if the mysteries of the universe have just been revealed to him.

"Now I know why you look familiar," Jesse says, his voice quiet and a trifle grim. "You're Jackson Parker's daughter. I'm sorry, Chrissie. This is going to be a long night."

* * *

I curl on a couch, wrapped in a blanket, sipping a cup of tea that Jesse made for me and the phone just won't stop ringing.

Ring. Ring. Ring. I'm afraid to answer it. We let it go to service most of the time. Jesse suggested unplugging it. I don't know why I won't let him do that. Why do I want to know Alan is ringing? Why do I need to know it? He humiliated me, he hurt me, he dumped me and he is the cause of this horrid, horrid night that never seems to end.

The sound of the ringing hurts me. It makes me more shaky. It makes me cry. I need to hear the ring, even though every ring isn't Alan.

If Jesse answers, sometimes it's Linda, but it is most frequently the press. And I won't talk to anyone, and Jesse is very good at getting rid of people. He is a born crisis manager.

Jesse answers a call, makes an abrupt response, and hangs it up quickly.

"It's part of being a nice guy," he jokes. "Knowing how to deal with a girl's relationship problems. And I'm a reporter. I definitely know how to handle the press."

I laugh. I don't feel like laughing. I don't want him to go. How long will he stay?

Shit. It's 6 a.m. and this hideous night feels like a slow moving century. It feels like it's never going to end, time isn't making me feel better, and the phone won't shut up. I miss Alan and I don't want to.

I stare into my cup of tea. Only a stupid girl would miss Alan after what he did to me. I grab another tissue.

Jesse is staring at me. "It's going to be OK."

"Don't you have somewhere you have to be? How long do you think this will last?"

He shrugs. "I don't know. It will blow over. It always does." He's trying to be calming, nonchalant. "I can stay as long as you want me to."

I wipe my cheeks and blow my nose. "There is food in the kitchen. I'd cook you breakfast except I don't know how."

He laughs. He puts a pillow on his lap and instructs me to lie down. I curl into a ball and he tugs the blanket around me. His fingers start to gently stroke my hair.

"You look exhausted, Chrissie. Go to sleep. I'll stay right here."

He takes the receiver and lifts it off the rest. My eyes round. "Don't worry. I'm not going anywhere, just giving us both a break. If you want, I can stay until it's time for your plane and I can take you to the airport."

I nod, too overwhelmed by his kindness to answer him. I close my eyes. I need to try to sleep. I will never make it from New York to California if I don't sleep.

I hear the elevator and then the door open. Jesse tenses and nudges me. "Didn't you tell the doorman not to let anyone up?"

My eyes round as I stare up at him. "No, because they don't. Not ever. Not without permission."

"Oh shit," he says, staring at the entry.

I look toward the foyer.

Alan.

* * *

Alan stares and I remain curled on the couch next to Jesse. I focus on wrapping my fingers around my lukewarm teacup, though internally, even as hurt as I am, I am pathetically thrilled that he came after me, even if it took him three hours to go six blocks.

"If you've got something to say, say it. And then please go," I snap and every line of his face hardens.

"May I sit down?"

I point at a chair a good distance from me.

"I did not expect you to leave," he says in a rough desperate sort of way.

"You told me to go."

"It was bullshit at a party, Chrissie," he says, his voice ragged and low. "I didn't want you to go. I was angry. I never thought you would leave."

I still haven't looked at him. I stare hard into space in a part of the room away from him. In my peripheral vision, I see Alan fix his burning stare on Jesse.

"Would you mind leaving us alone," he demands tersely.

"I'm not leaving unless she asks me to," Jesse replies firmly. He tilts up my chin to look at him. "Do you want me to leave, Chrissie?"

I shake my head, biting my lower lip because I can feel myself weakening. If Jesse leaves, I will fall to pieces and Alan will mold me any way he wishes.

"Are you going to make me do this in front of the press, Chrissie," Alan says.

"Whose fault is that?" I snap, in spite of my resolve to stay emotionless. I look around. "Did you bring my things, Alan?

Can you have someone bring them over today? I'm catching a plane to Santa Barbara this afternoon."

"No," he breathes, his eyes wide with panic. "You are not going anywhere, Chrissie. Not like this. Not over this, please."

"This? You call it *this*?" I look at him directly then. I can't stop myself. "You humiliated me, dragged me out of a party, and then told me to get out. And while I was packing my things I was trapped in a bathroom being humiliated all over again by your friends. Do not call it *this*."

"You're the only person in my life who matters to me," Alan says quietly.

"Well, you've got a strange way of showing it," I scream and my voice cracks.

"I don't know what you heard, but whatever it is, I apologize for it. It won't happen again, Chrissie. I swear."

"Please go."

"NO. And I am not going to tiptoe around what I want to say any longer." Alan is on his feet, angry and full of restless energy. "I am tired of this, Chrissie. Send him on his way so we can really talk."

"I don't want to talk to you," I say, and I hate that my tone sounds pouty and little girlish.

His penetrating black eyes burn into me. "If we don't talk this through today, we will never speak to each other again."

I blink at him. What does that mean? That easily he can send my chaotic emotions into full free-fall. I am angry. I am hurt. And I am the injured party here, but that doesn't mean I'm ready to never see him again, and I don't know for certain that that isn't what he is warning.

It is probably stupid, but right now it feels like if he walks out the door I won't make it through the day.

I wipe my nose with another tissue and sit back a little away from Jesse. "Can you go, please?"

Those kind hazel eyes search my face. "Are you sure?"

I nod.

Jesse pulls something from his wallet and scribbles on the back of it. He holds out a business card. "I've put Sandy's number on the back," he explains. I don't take the card. He puts it on the table. "If you need me, if you need anything, call me."

I feel on the verge of tears again and I don't trust my voice. I can't push out my words. I nod.

I will call to thank him, when Alan is gone. He was such a nice guy to me and I hate that I can't be gracious because right now it feels like a machete is hacking at my insides.

Once the elevator doors close, Alan sinks back into his chair. "Thank you."

"I didn't do it for you. I did it for me. You, I owe nothing."

That hurt him. I can see it in his eyes. He moves toward me until he is sitting on his knees in front of the couch beneath me. "I love you, baby," he breathes. "It was a bad night. I had a lot going on and I could have really used you being there for me."

I shake my head. I feel my heart accelerate. I feel my limbs go weak, and I just want to bury myself against him and cry.

"You were horrible to me. There are times I don't feel like I know you at all." I don't know why this is the place I want to start. I rally my strength. "Did you screw Rene?"

His eyes flare and widen. "I'm repulsed by her. Why would you ask me that?"

"Someone told me you did. She's my best friend, Alan. How could you do that and think it wouldn't matter later to me?"

He sits back and runs a hand through his hair, confused and angry. "Is that what that bitch told you? No. Never. I did not fuck Rene."

"It wasn't Rene who told me. Apparently everyone knows you did it in the bathroom at The Blue Light. It's funny how everyone always seems to know everything you do."

"Well then it's news to me because it didn't happen," he growls, his gaze so intense, his expression so open I nearly believe him.

"Are you saying that you didn't take her into the bathroom for a fast screw?"

"I'm saying I didn't fuck her in the bathroom at the club," he grounds out. "You were loaded and she was too absorbed in herself to give a damn if something happened to you. I took her to a bathroom and I got in her face and made her take you home. And that's the end of what happened, and if she tells you otherwise she's a liar."

I can barely breathe because I know he's telling me the truth. I can also feel the power he wields over me, how my traitorous emotions pitch and chase after him.

He starts to pace the room, and I can feel his body pulsing with anger. "The bullshit always fucks everything up, Chrissie. I can't stop the bullshit and you're going to have to learn not to listen to it. I have always told you the truth. I will always tell you the truth."

"How many girls have you been with?"

God, why did I bring that up again?

"I don't know. Does it matter?" He takes a sharp breath, running a hand through his hair. "Fuck, I'll list the ones I can remember. Will that satisfy you? Christ, Chrissie, why does any of this matter?"

I look around the room.

"Don't bother," I whisper. "Better question. Why did you screw me in a bedroom and dump me last night? You wanted to humiliate me last night. Why did you want to hurt me?"

His eyes widen with pain and almost tortured reluctance. "I didn't like that you wanted to be with him instead of with me," he admits after a long while.

"I didn't want to be with him. I just didn't want to be at the party. Your reaction was completely irrational. I didn't do anything to deserve any of that. What did I do that was so awful that you would want to deliberately hurt me?"

He's frustrated again. I can tell he doesn't want to answer, and he doesn't like the direction I'm taking this.

"Lillian was a very popular actress in her day and the biggest whore in London, Chrissie," he says through gritted teeth. "I didn't even know who my father was until I was eighteen and he died. Lillian gifted me with the truth and a trust fund, as if everything would be fine. I knew him my entire life and never once did he acknowledge me. I didn't have a clue he was my dad."

He turns away from me and I can see something powerful coursing through him. "My father was Vittorio Manzone."

My eyes round in surprise. "The Italian tenor?"

He nods.

He stares down at me. "You hit a nerve, Chrissie, not wanting to be seen with me, and I fucked up. I'm still working through some things. You have to be patient with me. I'm doing my best here."

"I don't think your best works for me, Alan," I whisper with more injury in my voice than I want to show.

"I'm doing my best," he repeats, raking a hand through his hair. "I'm being honest with you, I've told you things I've never told anyone, and if you were anyone else I wouldn't be here or trust being honest."

I change course. "I'm not staying in New York any longer. I have to go home."

He takes a deep breath and doesn't move.

"You are not leaving, Chrissie."

He leans in to kiss me and I inch back instinctively. If he touches me I will crumble. I pull farther back.

"You need to go." I'm proud of how my voice sounds this time. Calm. In control. Firm.

"What? No." He eases back from me, blinking. "No, I'm not leaving until we've worked this out."

"There is nothing to work out."

"Don't say that."

"You're not good for me."

"How can you say that? We are good for each other," he says in desperation. "I am completely lost in you and that's a good place to be, Chrissie. A very good place to be."

I look away from him again. *I am lost in you too, Alan, and I'm not sure if that is a good place to be.* I feel the tears. I grab a tissue. I hate that I'm crying, that I couldn't hold it back until he was gone.

I stare about the room. I'm so tired. I don't want to do this. I don't want Alan to leave. I want to curl up in bed, cry, and then fall asleep next to him. But I can't forgive him. Not after last night. I need to send him away.

"When will you send my things over?"

"Never. You're not going."

He sinks down on the sofa beside me. I can suddenly see how tired he is. It feels so very right to have him close to me. "I love you. I don't want to fight. Please, don't leave."

"You hurt me."

He swallows. "I love you."

He inhales sharply, lies his head back against the cushion and closes his eyes. He looks so despondent, so weary, and so young. It's so unfair that he can shift effortlessly into someone who melts my heart. It makes me want to curl into him, hold him, even after the horrible things he's done.

"I'm so tired, Chrissie. Tired of the bullshit. Tired of everything. I just want one thing in my life not drowning in shit. I just want to be with you and be happy, be with you and let all the other fucking shit go."

His lids lift just enough so he can look at me. Gently, he tugs my hand from beneath me, where I'd buried it so he couldn't take it. He places a feather-light kiss in my palm.

"Can we just go to sleep and finish this later, Chrissie?" He sets my teacup on the table. "Never argue when you're tired. It's not good. And I won't be able to sleep unless you are next to me."

I hesitate. Alan picks me up and carries me to my bedroom.

* * *

Reluctantly, I open my eyes. I don't want to wake. I don't want round two of the fighting. I don't want to end us. And I don't think I should go any farther with Alan. I'm at a point where I can exit. Only I don't want to exit, though I know deep down I should.

I check the clock. It is 10 p.m. We've slept fifteen hours straight, and I have not moved from the tight ball on the edge of the bed where I deposited myself after Alan released me. I didn't argue with him about postponing our fight or lying down with him to sleep, but I wasn't about to lay down with him as if everything were normal. I don't know where we are, but we are not in normal. Not that we are ever in normal, not really, not in the way I used to think normal would be. Alan and I together are a lot of things. Normal just isn't one of them.

I carefully turn to look at him. I want to get up, but I don't want to wake him. He is wrapped around me in that warm, surrounding way that feels as though he is holding onto me, even in sleep. His flesh is warm. His breathing is quiet.

How do I get out of here without waking him? I need a little distance so I can think through what I should do.

Suddenly, my panties are gone and I am pressed into Alan in a perfect, side-by-side fit, and he is in me without foreplay or stirring touch or kisses. He's just in me and this is different. It feels dark and angry as he slams into me, filling me, even more so than it did being pounded against the bedroom door.

His groans are different. His touch is different. His fingers on my breasts are different, the way those callused tips roll my nipples, tugging and pinching. He is something beyond angry, I can feel it, and I close my eyes, absorbing him, part afraid, a greater part hungrily savoring. The sensations through my flesh push me higher, too quickly, so right.

He grasps my hip firmly, eases out of me slowly, and then again, harder this time, slams into me.

"Don't ever leave me."

I lie panting beneath his touch, feeling his intense anger, knowing he's going to get rougher. My femaleness courses through my veins. It is messed up, but my insides quicken, excited by my femaleness and his temper.

I'm about to surrender to the heat of my own flesh. A ragged whisper penetrates my near exploding senses.

"Did you fuck him?"

What? No! My senses halt in their march toward climax.

"Did you fuck him?" he repeats fiercely.

He stays still.

"No," I hiss furiously, the shock of him asking me that leaving me breathless and flashing with anger. "No."

He closes his eyes, there is a ragged shudder through his limbs, and the feel of him is different, frenzied and possessive. He starts again, a brutal, divine rhythm. I hear his groan, a guttural thing, desperation, relief, sadness. He moans low in his throat and I can feel the tension change, as his adrenaline runs through his veins, a different type of current.

"I've been out of my mind since you walked out the door with him," he breathes, his face buried in my hair. "Don't do that again. Don't walk away from me. Don't make me feel like I don't matter to you. I can stand anything, Chrissie, except not mattering to you."

And then the words are lost. Alan is letting go, calling my name, and I surrender and explode with him. I sink to the bed. I sleep.

* * *

Alan gazes at me, assessing my expression as I stare up at him.

It's morning and I don't have a clue where we go from here. Last night was different. I don't know what is happening beneath his surface, but there is something and I can feel it. I should be furious that in the cease-fire between the rounds of our fight, he decided to have an extremely rough "did you fuck him" fuck.

His anger issues. I've seen them, but last night I felt it in his body, in the way he had sex with me. Did I fuck him? God, Alan, how could you ask me that?

I try to rally my anger, fortification for today's round of fighting, but I'm slightly disappointed in myself. I realize that I am less angry with him because I really got off on the angry "did you fuck him" fuck. It was weird, consuming, and a turn-on.

His anger is dark, complex and layered, just like mine. But unlike me, he lets it surface, in his music, in his impulses, and in his body when he fucks instead of making love. Maybe that was why it was a turn on? I fight my anger, I struggle to keep it contained, but last night my anger ran with his through my flesh and it was a sensory right sort of thing.

I stare at him. So what's up today, Alan? Are we going to continue talking? Are we going to continue having angry fucks? Or are you just going to lie there staring at me as though everything is fine, perfectly normal in this alternate universe of not normal.

"Do you want to go on a date-date today?" Alan asks.

Oh crap, how did he remember that? Date-date. How lame.

He starts to move my hair from my face. "I owe you a date-date."

So, it's going to be door number three: act like everything is fine. What do I do? Do I roll with it? What did Jesse say? *Guys hate conflict. Act normal and so will he.* But is that what I want? To act normal and just leave it all alone?

I don't answer.

He climbs from the bed, naked, and completely comfortable in whatever we're doing now.

I sit up in bed against the pillows.

Alan is sorting through his clothes on the floor. "Are you hungry?"

Normal conversation in not normal context. I take a deep breath, willing myself calm.

"I'm starving. We didn't eat yesterday."

He gives me a look that makes me quicken all through my flesh.

"Do you have any clothes here other than the shorts and UGGs? Maybe jeans, a long sleeve shirt, and some kind of closed toe shoe?"

Why is he asking me this? "I don't know. I'll have to look. Rene left a lot of junk."

He makes a face and continues to rummage through his things.

I frown. "How did you get into the apartment yesterday?"

"I have a key."

You do, do you? I stare.

"You left the extra key on the entry table." He is distracted and looking for something. "Not smart, Chrissie. Anyone could have just come in here, a delivery person, taken it, and then where would you be?"

It's not worth pointing out, but just anyone did take it and look at where I am. With you, Alan, sore after a night of angry fucking.

I watch Alan disappear into the bathroom. I hear the shower turn on. He doesn't ask, he takes my hand and pulls me into the shower with him.

As I stand beneath the warm streams, his damp body pressed against my back, his gentle hands wash me from behind. "Did you ever finish *Ivanoff*?"

Oh, Alan, why are you so weird? I shake my head. "You could always give me the Cliff Notes really fast."

He smiles. His chin rests on my shoulder and he continues washing me, and his voice, so sexy, makes it arousing to do this, even listening to a brief synopsis of Chekhov.

By the time we're toweling off, I'm kind of wishing he'd just take me back to bed. Sexy Alan was a turn-on, even reciting Chekhov, but it's probably not a good idea. I'm sorer than I thought and I could feel it when he touched me *there*, even lightly while washing me.

I make a face at him, since he used my toothbrush without asking, and I pat my face dry with a towel.

He is already fully dressed when I join him in the bedroom.

I'm pulling on my panties and bra. "You know, you can only be useful in my study of literature if you tell me how the play ends."

Alan is sitting on the bed waiting for me, as I rummage through Rene's clothing. I look at him, and for some reason the complete lack of emotion on his face turns me cold.

"*Ivanoff* runs off stage and shoots himself in the head."

Oh Alan, what's going on with you? Why did you bring up *Ivanoff* today?

* * *

After Alan makes me breakfast, I set off to try and accommodate his clothing specifications. No matter how I try, I can't make any of Rene's clothes work. She is a lot taller than I am and has a leaner, less curvy build. We can share tops, an occasional skirt, but that's about it. Jeans, never an option. And shoes, not even worth trying, since Rene definitely doesn't have any that are closed toe.

I go down the hallway to Jack's bedroom and into my parents' closet. Lena's things are still hanging here, in perfect order, where they have been since that day she left New York for California permanently. A lump swells in my throat as I stare at her neatly arranged wardrobe. Twelve years and Jack hasn't cleaned out her things. I never gave a thought to it, but it is all still here.

Alan comes into sharp focus in my mind, as I rummage through the cedar-lined drawers. I am lost in him. I have become lost in him so quickly, so quickly that he could end us in a humiliatingly public way and then I would spend the night in angry fucking wanting to please him.

I shake my head to push away my thoughts. Jeans. Closed toe shoes. I have only a few options with my mother's clothing. Lena was not the casual type, and what she has left behind in the casual department was New York chic in 1977. The only positive is that we are nearly the same size, though Mom was taller.

I settle on a cute pair of dark, denim overalls that I can make work by rolling the cuffs. The long sleeve shirt is a baggy beach-type thermal of Jack's. The shoes are bucks-up buckskin ankle high hiking boots that never saw a trail or dirt. They are spotless twelve years later and I wonder why Lena even has them.

A camping trip? A hike? Something planned to please Jack, but never done. Yes, that was my mother. She definitely knew how to please him without ever doing anything she didn't want to do. Mom was highly competent at being female and in loving Jack.

I stare at myself in the mirror. Today, I look like an incompetent girl. All I need is braids. How lame is this outfit?

Crossing into my bedroom, I hold my arms wide. "Well, what do you think? Have I managed the wardrobe specifications? And what's up with that, anyway? Who cares what I wear?"

Alan smiles. He kisses me. "You will."

"I will, will I?" I notice he is carrying Jack's old leather bomber jacket atop his own leather jacket that I didn't even notice him wearing yesterday when he arrived.

"Tie back your hair," he orders, waits, and then tosses a bandana at me. "And put this on. It will help."

"Help what?"

"Hurry up, Chrissie. We need to roll."

323

* * *

In the parking garage, I freeze and just stare at him. It took Alan three hours to go six blocks and he did it on motorcycle? These clothes now make sense.

"I am not getting on that thing," I protest, pulling my hand free from his.

Alan ignores me. He zips up Jack's bomber jacket, tugs my collar high and pulls up the bandana until my nostrils and mouth are tucked in.

"I am not riding on that. Where are we going?"

He swings his leg over, turns the ignition and primes the engine with gas. He points. "Get up behind me. Put your feet there. Whatever you do, don't let go of my body."

I hate motorcycles. I'm more afraid of them than airplanes, and jeez, he's got me sitting on the back of one.

Alan laughs. "Don't worry. Neither of us is twenty-seven."

I raise my eyebrows. An obscure literary reference they don't teach in California, most probably, but I don't get the joke.

"The great ones die at twenty-seven," he explains glibly. "Hendrix. Joplin. If we are both around after we're twenty-seven, we'll both know what we are."

I could have done without it being cryptic. *Don't mock death, Alan, it's not funny.* I snuggle into him closer. I press my cheek against his back and hold him tight.

"Good girl."

"But why the motorcycle, Alan? Where's Colin. Can't you do something normal like drive a car?"

At the top of the garage exit, he stops, setting his feet on the ground while the metal door rolls up. He turns to look at me. "We went public, Chrissie, in a very ugly public way. I would have preferred not to do that. Ignore everything on the street. We'll be out of the city in a couple hours."

Everything on the street? Oh shit, and then I see it. How is it possible that there are so many of them? There are tabloid photographers blocking the exit. They are blocking the road. They are running from the front of the building, all while shouting and rapidly taking pictures.

He pushes through them, he doesn't answer, and he speeds off really fast. It would scare the hell out of me if I wasn't relieved to be out of there.

* * *

The traffic is thick and slow, as New York traffic is, but Alan drives like a maniac and I wonder if he really thinks he can't die because he isn't twenty-seven.

My rational self, trying to keep me from freaking out about all this, points out that he is only doing it because the tabloids have tried to follow. But cutting through cars at high speeds has given us an advantage that Colin and the car would not have.

I hold on and let him whisk me away. Still, I'd sort of like to know where we are going.

We lose the last of them by the Garden State Parkway, and he immediately eases off the speed when we enter the New York State Thruway. We are going north and away from the city.

With each mile, the tension ease out of Alan, and the feeling of soaring up roads, in the open air, is strangely liberating and soothing. I feel calmer inside and less frantic holding him. We feel good again, so connected, and so very right.

I feel a slight letdown as he turns off the highway and onto an off-ramp, gradually slowing. I lift my cheek and study the little village by the lake in front of us. I guess this is where we are going, but really Alan, couldn't you have asked if I wanted to leave Manhattan.

He can be so highhanded at times. I add it to the rapidly growing list of adjectives about him: highhanded, brilliant, gentle, kind, sensitive, sophisticated, angry, elegant, obnoxious, and harsh. What else have I forgotten? I know that's not the entire list.

We stop at an intersection. We haven't spoken for hours. "Where are we?" I ask.

"Lake George. I think you'll like it. Rural New York is very different than the city. Too many people go to New York and never leave the city. Totally different world. A good place to stay until things quiet down again."

My gaze locks on a hokey little place with white cabins. "Well, they certainly have lodging here. I vote for the Seven Dwarfs Motel and Cabins."

He gives me a smile that tugs at my heart. "Are you still angry?"

What's in his voice floods my heart. "No. I should be, but I'm not." I make one of my little playacting faces. "And heck, why fight. I'm about to be bounced in a room named after a Disney movie. How great is that?"

He laughs. "Are you hungry?"

I nod. I could eat. I point to the Papa bear statue wearing a plaid beret. "How about there?"

Alan laughs. "Really?"

I shrug. "Why not? I like A&W. I never get fast food. There doesn't seem to be much choice here."

He rolls us into the parking lot and turns off the bike. As I study the menu, I look at Alan and I laugh. I wonder when the last time it was he did something like this. Probably never. Somehow I don't think many girls drag him to fast food.

I listen to him order, then take the plastic number stand and find a table. I settle in an outdoor plastic booth, but he pulls me up from the seat, until he's eased back against the wall, slightly turned with me between his legs and sitting against him.

His chin is resting on my shoulder and he is holding me. He is quiet, troubled beneath the surface. Something is bothering him. I can feel it.

"Is this your first date-date at fast food? Something tells me you don't go to this type of place very often."

He pretends to give it thought. "Actually, yes."

The food service girl comes to our table, delivering our tray. She gives Alan that look, the *I know who you are look*, but when I glare she takes off without saying anything. Back at the order window, she is rapidly talking to the others in the fast food box. I can feel their stares.

"It's a good thing there are no tabloids here," I say, prepping my food to eat it. "People would really start to wonder what's happened to you if they could see this."

He doesn't even give me a slight laugh for the effort. He just picks at his food. My Alan radar is not askew. Something is bothering him.

I squeeze some ketchup and ranch dressing into neat swirls on my plate. "So, where are we staying? How long are we here?"

"I own a farm, not far from here. It's on the lake. We use it as rehearsal space. It's a good place to chill and other things. I want to stay on The Farm a few days."

I stare at him. A few days? I don't have anything with me except my purse, which he tucked into his pack, and my birth control pills. God, Alan, I'm a girl! I don't have anything with me.

"Why are you frowning?" he asks.

"Because you just did this. You didn't ask and the only things I have are my darn pills and my wallet."

He smiles, a touch wicked. "Then you have everything you need, Chrissie."

"Very funny."

I stare at my food. I take a handful of french fries and onion rings and angrily dip them into the ranch dressing, then the ketchup.

"Why do you mix your food like that?"

Really? He wants to talk about that? *That* seems important to him.

"When you eat the onion rings with the fries it makes them both taste better."

He studies my face. I can tell he knows I'm angry. And then, because he's decided to be irritating it seems, he starts to sing one of my favorite Dylan songs but has changed the verse to "she eats just like a little girl."

"That was terrible. And it is sacrilege to change the words to a Dylan song."

He pouts. "I had to. I couldn't sing that you break. You don't break, Chrissie. You don't know that, but you are not the kind of girl that's ever going to break."

I stare at him. So, I don't break? Oh Alan, as much as you understand me, sometimes you don't get me at all.

* * *

We roll to a stop on the gravel drive. The Farm. It looks like something from a Norman Rockwell painting. Whitewashed wood, with pretty little porches and picket rail fronts. Apple trees. A barn. An old, open framed jeep that is little more than a rust bucket.

I can hear sounds from the two story farmhouse and that's when I notice that there are cars in the driveway. Lots of fancy cars. Who is here at Alan's farm?

The front door opens. Linda rushes out in shorts and a tight tank top. She is carrying a margarita glass.

She waves. She smiles. She laughs.

She pounds Alan's chest with a finger. "You bring everyone up here, and then you don't show. You were supposed to be here yesterday. Not smart, Manny. Not a good way to start."

She fixes her laser-focused stare on me. "I'm glad you made up. I'm glad you're here, Chrissie. I could use a friend."

The Farm.

The larger dysfunctional family.

This isn't a date.

I remember the adjective I forgot: mean. Yes, Alan can be mean and this is very mean.

He tricked me. He deliberately dragged me here with him, knowing very well I would never want to see any of them ever again. I watch him ease off the bike, unzip his jacket, and toss it across the seat.

Oh Alan, you make it so easy to hate you at times. Only it's not. It is not easy to hate Alan.

Chapter Fifteen

We follow Linda into the house to find the entire dysfunctional family downstairs. The room is spacious, comfortably understated in shabby chic country furnishings coordinated in yellow and blue. From the dark wood floors to the open beamed ceilings, it is vintage Americana, windows of colored stained glass, blue check curtains on black iron rods, and heavy wood everywhere. The farmhouse is charming.

It would probably be a wonderful place to stay if the aged wood walls didn't feel like they were about to burst from the pressure of containing the earsplitting cacophony of a tight knit cult. God they are loud, and they feel like so much more than ten people. I really hate that Alan brought me here.

"At last the band is together again," Len Rowan announces, and Alan instantly becomes the focal point of the room among a dazzling display of exuberant hugs and vacant pleasantries.

Alan stays at my side, his hand tightening its hold on me, and no one really looks at me except to give a fast greeting or smile in a move-on-quickly sort of way. It's unnerving. Something has changed. My standing with these people has changed and it has made them less openly rude and more standoffish. Interesting.

I glance at Linda, and she winks as if in reassurance, her eyes bright and wide. Before I can say anything to her, Alan steps deeper into the center of the room, pulling me with him. The rapid voices swirl all around him as I step out of his hold to remove my jacket, and it's then that I notice he has that expression again, dominant and aloof and tired of them all.

The strange undercurrent in the room isn't just about me, part of it is about Alan. I get an internal warning that this little adventure could go either way, peacefully or a total shitstorm. What the heck is happening here?

"Oh my god, Chrissie, where did you get those?" Linda says, her piercing voice punching through the loudness of the room. "They are vintage and I absolutely love them."

I flush. I'd forgotten about the out-of-style 1970s overalls underneath the jacket, and I am in a room of girls dressed in expensive, provocative chic. *Good one, Linda. Now all the wives are looking at me.*

When I turn to hand Linda my jacket, I realize she is sincere and she really does like the darn thing. She grabs me by the hand and pulls me toward the kitchen. "Do you want a glass of wine or something? Dinner is almost ready. Don't believe that nonsense about Jewish women not being able to cook. I'm an excellent cook."

As she pushes through the swinging door, I note that whatever is cooking in the kitchen does smell delicious.

Once the door swings closed behind us the chatter stops, she turns to stare at me, and her lively eyes are alertly searching. "Are you OK?"

The way she says that tells me it's not a casual question and that she's been worried about me.

I nod. "I'm fine. We talked. It's good."

Linda slams open the oven door and shakes her head. "I've never seen Manny like he was when he realized you'd left. At first I thought it was just ego. Girls just don't walk out on Manny…" Linda lifts her brows with heavy meaning. "…And then I realized it was something more. He was frantic, he was going to bail right then in the middle of the party to go after you until Len stopped him. That's when I knew he must have done something pretty fucked up with that temper of his."

Frantic? Alan is many things, but he is never frantic. Surely, Linda is exaggerating.

She straightens up and leans back against the counter. "And then when the last of the party cleared out, the fireworks. Oh, Chrissie, you missed one hell of an explosion. Kenny made some stupid comment—nothing new for him, by the way—and then *boom*. I've never seen the five of them fight so badly. I thought, this is it. They are over."

She starts to lift lids from pots to give each an aggressive stir—something that looks like rice and chorizo and cheese, Mexican style refried beans, some kind of spicy red sauce, and if I'm not mistaken, those are enchiladas I smell in the oven. I never expected to find traditional California Mexican cuisine cooking in the kitchen, and then I remember Linda is from LA.

She pushes a glass of wine into my hand. "Then the shitstorm of press started. That's when things got really interesting." She turns to pour herself another margarita. "I don't have to tell you that this is a pretty paranoid group of guys. Every one of them just waiting for the day Manny walks out on the band. You wouldn't believe some of the shit I've heard out of them since he landed in New York with you."

She shakes her head and takes a hefty sip of her Margarita. "Manny's drama, exhausting, and then all the strangeness suddenly makes sense. Why he was so secretive and shit after he returned to New York. And so careful about keeping everyone away. You're Jackson Parker's daughter and Manny was delusional enough to think he could keep you out of the eye of the tabloid hurricane. Mr. Fucked Up British Superstar with the daughter of an American Icon. Yeah, right? Like that was ever going to happen."

Oh shit. I've somehow managed not to think about this the last twenty-four hours. Do I have hours, days or weeks before I have my own shitstorm to face with Jack?

"How much print has there been? Is it awful?" I ask in dread.

"Nothing much yet, but its coming. There is no way to stop it. And it's going to be a lot and it's going to be ugly. Manny's made a fortune kicking up black tar ink. The tabloids live for this shit. So now the paranoid lot out there in the living room doesn't know what to be paranoid about, and the tabloids are picking out your wedding dress."

Linda starts pulling out blue-edged plates from a glass front whitewashed cabinet.

"So was Manny really just in California with you the entire five months after Rehab?" she asks with a hint of irritation.

I sputter into my wine. Oh shit, he is lying to them and I don't know what that means or what I should do here.

"Well?" she demands.

"He was in California the entire five months," I reply with awkward, truthful diversion.

Her eyes narrow on me. "Why didn't you tell me you were Jack's girl, and all this drama was just to keep the two of you hush-hush? It really hurts that you guys didn't trust me."

I sigh and stare off into space, that last question not even worth making an effort to construct a lie in response. I've got my own problems here and Linda, succinctly, with the speed of a machine gun, made sure I'm reminded of each one: a tabloid bloodletting en route to me; a pissed off Jack eventually en route to me; Alan's confusing never-ending drama...*oh, and the album, Chrissie, don't forget the album*...and all the things in me that I have to work through when I get home, within my perfectly fucked up life that I just fucked up even more.

Linda points to a drawer. "Can you start pulling the silverware out for me?"

I start to slam knives and forks on the wood block counter.

It's funny how delusional you can be when you want to do something you know you shouldn't. How could I have ever thought that Alan would be someone who just quietly passed through my life privately? There isn't a single thing Alan does that is ever private. I'm delusional. How the heck did I get so deep into a hole so quickly?

"You don't have to murder the flatware, Chrissie, just because everything is fucked. That's pretty much SOP."

Humor has returned to Linda's voice. I wish I had her emotional dexterity, but then Linda has existed for a very long time in Alan's epic universe.

Linda slams open the wood shutters above the splash counter and begins to lay out heat mats for the pans.

I stare out into the living room at Alan. He is relaxed in a chair, laughing, long limbs in front of him, disheveled dark hair, shimmering black eyes, an unrelenting centerpiece in any setting, almost too perfect to be real. I jumped into the hole willingly. I wanted to, and I want him.

But wanting him doesn't mean that it wouldn't be nice if having him didn't involve all the rest of the complicated shit, if it were something even slightly approaching normal and familiar. A month ago I didn't even have a boyfriend. How quickly I've been swallowed up by Alan and his world. Why does it feel like I've jumped a track in my life, that I am speeding on a road where I can't see where I'm going? Alan and I are just a temporary thing. Why doesn't it feel temporary?

God, why did he bring me to The Farm? I stare at the wives, and something about how they cluster and cling to the circle makes me shudder inside.

"So, what do the girls do at The Farm?" I ask.

"We get fucked…" Linda lifts her glass. "…and we get fucked up. This is guy world, Chrissie. That's all there is. Fucking and getting fucked up. There aren't even phones here. Alan thinks it interferes with their focus. No phones. Not even TV. They have music, their bullshit stories, getting fucked and fucked up. But all we've got is getting fucked, fucked up and kitchen duty. Thank god there's a cleaning girl who comes twice a week or we'd be mopping floors, Chrissie. The ERA hasn't reached here yet."

That comment makes me laugh even though it's repulsive. Linda is funny, even when she is being coarse and vulgar.

"Dinner!" Linda shouts, in a voice the shakes the rafters.

By the time I've filled my plate and left the kitchen to join everyone sprawled in the living room eating, there isn't an inch of empty space near Alan. I don't really want to be near any of them, I don't fit in and probably never will, and my anxious glance searches the room for somewhere to sit apart safely.

"Come here, little kitty. Come sit with me."

My startled gaze shifts to find Len Rowan patting a floor cushion beside him and studying me in a very peculiar way. Oh yuck, I don't really want to sit all cozy on the floor with him, but I can't just ignore him and walk away.

I smile and let Len take the plate to set it on the low table in front of him. He puts his hand on my arm to guide me down beside him. I almost pull away, but I forcibly stop myself.

It's just a friendly touch. Nothing more. Don't be an idiot tonight, Chrissie. I grab my fork and start to cut into an enchilada.

"You OK?" Len whispers.

I look to find Len quietly probing with his gaze, as if trying to figure out something I must have let show on my face.

"I'm great." I fill my mouth with a forkful of Mexican. He's still staring, expectant. Shit, why is he doing that? "Linda is a great cook."

Len smiles. "Linda's a great girl. You need anything, you go to her. Linda won't ever steer you wrong. The rest of them..." He doesn't finish and reaches for his beer. "So, what is Jack thinking about all this?"

Oh god, from totally ignored girl to let's have heart-to-heart girl. And what does he mean by all this? I flush and I look at Alan. Thankfully, he's absorbed in Linda's overly animated chatter.

"Nothing to think," I say quietly, evasively.

Len laughs. "OK. I get it. Mind my own business."

He nods, smiles, and places a light kiss on my cheek, to my great surprise. I realize he wasn't being invasive; he was being concerned. I peek at him as I eat my dinner. By the time I've finished my meal, I know I read Len Rowan all wrong.

Len may be an ass on the surface, but there is a shrewd sensitivity to him that I think most people miss. It suddenly makes sense that he's with Linda. They are the balance in this strange cluster of personalities: Linda with the girls and Len with the band. They're the glue that somehow keeps everyone together.

After dinner, everyone just lounges around talking and laughing. The minutes turn into hours and it's starting to feel like this evening is never going to end. I've spent the better part of four hours listening to an endless stream of industry talk and gossip, there is nothing of the substantive world here. There's meaningless dialogue occasionally spiced with a quick anecdote about Jack, which feels weirdly inserted into the conversation as a polite attempt to include me. Nothing could be less polite. Every time Jack's name comes up in passing, I tense. I can't even imagine what the fallout for this will be when I go home.

Never before have I done anything that would test the boundaries of Jack's tolerance or his approval. In all moments, I work desperately hard to remain as close to perfect—or at least if not perfect, then privately a mess—so as not to tip the strange balance of our totally careful father-daughter relationship. I've always been so afraid to tip the balance.

I stare down into my wine. Well, Chrissie, you better come to terms with the fact that you have tipped the balance. For some reason as I analyze this, it's anger I feel flooding my tissues instead of my familiar apprehension and worry. *I've fucked up your image of me big time and this time in a public way, Jack. Are you going to ignore this?*

I study the strange herd of dysfunctional people I've fallen in with. It's like a public service announcement. Even Jack couldn't move past this with his '60s axioms and nonparenting for parents bullshit.

By the time the group starts to break up, there is breathing into life inside of me, a carefree sense of not giving a shit what anyone thinks about anything—not Jack, not them, not anyone. I fell in love. I let a guy love me. What's fucked up about that?

I tilt my head to find Alan crouched down beside me. It's strange, but we passed the entire evening not even together. Those mesmerizing, penetrating black eyes are slowly absorbing the details of my expression, and then he takes my face in his hands, his fingers spreading across my cheeks.

I'm just starting to lean in for a kiss when he stops me. "Are you OK?"

I laugh, frustrated. "God. You're like the tenth person to ask me that tonight. What's up with that?"

Alan laughs and shakes his head. "Just checking to see if you're angry with me again. I'm tired, Chrissie. Take me to bed and be good to me."

I make a face, lips turning downward in simulated pouting. "Don't count on it," I tease.

He shakes his head just enough for the dark waves to dance. "No?"

Beneath his unreadable surface I feel just a smidge of silly Alan in there.

"Nope."

He takes my hand and pulls me to my feet. The staircase is old, the wood creaks while we walk, and there is something in the creaking sound that is strangely comforting to me. I can see the moon through the round windows, high on the wall, and there is the lovely sensation again that we are alone even though I know perfectly well there are people in every upstairs bedroom. The staircase is narrow and dark we're in a magical transition away from them to only Chrissie and Alan again.

Alan pauses at the door and flips on a switch before he pulls me in behind him. The room is simple and dominated by a charming, antique brass bed invitingly arranged with hand sewn quilts and country check pillows. The furniture is heavy and old and spotless, and the windows are dual-paned and framed with patches of swirling blue stained glass.

With easy grace, Alan reclines on the bed and stares up at me. Those black eyes are alive with tenderness and lust. It's a disarming mix. I swallow and lean back into the door. It would be so easy to forget all the questions in my head when he stares at me like this.

"I thought you said you weren't angry with me," he murmurs softly.

There's a sweet kind of smile on his face now, cajoling and affectionate. I feel my body respond.

"Depends on why you brought me here."

He pretends to be confused. "To The Farm? Or the bedroom?"

I sink on the bed beside him, settling my chin in the upturned palm of my hand. "What's going on here, Alan?"

He leans into me, long fingers closing on the fastenings of my overalls. He gives me a full mouth kiss that I feel all the way down to my toenails. It leaves me breathless and just a touch angry. *So Alan, you don't want to answer my questions.*

I stare up at him, completely committed to being resistant. "You're lying to them and I want to know why, since you've made me a part of it."

He lies back on the pillow, irritated.

"I'm quitting," he says, just when it was looking like he wasn't going to answer me. "You know that. But I'm not a solo act, Chrissie. I can't walk out in one day. For a lot of reasons, most of them legal and involving lawsuit settlements, I'm doing the tour, I'm doing one more album with the band, and then I'm through. Will you kiss me now?"

"But why lie to them about me?" I stare at the quilt, fingering the design, trying to make sense of this. "You made them think we've had this long, hot, and heavy affair going on for months. Why? Why don't you want anyone to know you were with Jack?"

His eyes widen with a mix of disbelief and irritation. "Fuck, you don't know anything about Jack, do you?"

I feel my face flood with a burn, and uncontained hurt unfurls within me. "Why don't you enlighten me?"

I can tell he can see he fucked up with that comment. He runs a hand through his hair and his expression softens.

"Your father is an extraordinary man. He's the guy people call for you when you've fucked up big and you want off the road you're on. He helps you clean up your shit, get your head straight, and get you on a different road. I've got fifteen more months, Chrissie. I just want it all to end. If they know I've been with Jack, they'll know I'm leaving."

I don't know where to begin to process my emotions. I didn't know any of this about Jack, and that's not the Dad I've had, not by a long shot. It makes everything inside of me somehow hurt even more. And even though it's trivial and secondary, it reminds me of that day at the airport, Alan's concern over the tabloids spotting me and how sweet I thought his worry was. It was never about me. It was about him, and for some reason I wonder: how much about us is only about him? There is that sense there is something going on between us that I don't fully understand yet.

I focus on the wood slats of the ceiling, trying to calm my inner turmoil.

"What's wrong, Chrissie?"

I look to see Alan studying me, trying to assess my reaction to this. I muster an overly bright smile. "I just want to go to sleep."

I curl on my side, feeling as if I've grown smaller, filled with childish resentment about how little Jack was there for me, and a petty type of jealousy that Jack was there for Alan. It's so bizarre how the random pieces of your life can suddenly join into something so heartbreaking. I'm a little unsteady, a little dazed.

He plants a feather-light kiss on my lips and then moves to the door to lock it. He starts shedding his clothes. When he gets to the bed, his eyes have that smoky quality to them.

He is trying to undo my overalls. I stop his hand and he frowns. "What's changed? Why are you upset, Chrissie?"

I fumble for a fast excuse for my sudden change of mood. "I'm not doing it. Not in a house full of them."

Alan starts to laugh and visibly relaxes. "It's going to be a very long week if you don't, love. Miserably long for me."

"Then long week. Learn to live with it. Suck it up."

He eases me back on the bed, and then starts to work free the fastenings of my overalls. I can see it in his eyes. My mood has changed his mood, as well.

I don't resist as he undresses me and I lie atop the bed as he gazes down at me. The cool air of the room touches my flesh, and the warmth of his fingers pushes the chill away.

A kiss on my arm. "I'm sorry."

A touch on my shoulder. "I love you."

He covers my entire body with a kiss, a touch, an "I'm sorry" or an "I love you." And I know he isn't talking about just highjacking me to The Farm. Or his obnoxious behavior at the party. Or being stuck here with the dysfunctional. Or even all the complicated shit. He can see inside of me even when I fight not to let him, and he is apologizing for my pain.

I relax into his touch and his words and his lips, and the things I am feeling seem to melt. Soon, all I am feeling is him.

He kisses the inside of my thigh and then he stops, his face lifting. "I love you. That's why you are here with me."

I don't know why, what it was in his voice that time, but it washes away any doubt that he loves me or that I love him. It is all there in his voice, his touch, and his eyes when he looks at me, in the ease with which I give myself to him, and the ease in which he takes, and how very right it is.

Suddenly, I am out of my mind with the feel of him. I begin to move, more demanding, more greedily into the play of his hands and lips. He puts a finger in my mouth, scented of me, and I take it. He moves faster, harder, and I am whimpering and he is flooding my mouth with fingers, overfilling me as I greedily melt into him.

He pounds me in a frantic rhythm much faster than what I am used to with him. He doesn't hold back. He pumps his body directly there and lets go into my climax.

As we lie before sleep, I don't want to talk. I just want to sleep with him, to feel him all around me, in the perfection that is sleeping with Alan.

We are fitted like puzzle pieces, his bicep beneath my head, and I am playing with the dark hairs on his arm.

"I'm sorry about the fingers," he whispers into my neck.

I frown. "Fingers? You've lost me."

"I would have preferred not to have to put almost my entire hand in your mouth, but I did it for you. Me, it's all good. Your high pitched whimpers and screeches are such a turn-on. But I knew you would prefer the fingers." He kisses my cheek. He settles against me with a wickedly teasing grin. "You, love, are very noisy."

The laughter takes me by surprise, but it is welcomed and needed. There are times when Alan completely gets me.

* * *

OK, what do I do now? While I slept Alan deserted me. I haven't any clothes. I haven't any things.

There is warm, orange light pouring through the windows. Late morning. The room is surprisingly hot and the air in the room is still. I should open the windows. It's too hot in here to stay comfortable, but I can't hide in here forever, naked and in bed without Alan.

I look around the room, realizing there is no adjoining bathroom. Shit, that's all I need.

The bedroom door slowly creaks open. Linda's face appears. She smiles and enters quickly, closing the door fast behind her.

She plops on the bed beside me. "I'm glad you made up."

I try not to sound too relieved that we did. "Me too."

She lies on the bed on Alan's pillow, as though she doesn't realize I'm naked beneath the sheets.

I turn on my side, keeping myself carefully covered by the blankets. "Do you want to go with me into the village? I need to buy some things."

Linda shrugs and smiles. "Don't worry, Chrissie, whatever you need I'm sure I have. I always pack too much, but I am a world class packer."

"I need everything, Linda."

She frowns. "What?"

"Alan didn't tell me he was bringing me to The Farm. I don't have anything."

Linda shakes her head and rolls her eyes. "Oh shit, Chrissie. What is it about guys? Come with me. Linda can fix anything."

Linda jumps from the bed as if she expects me to climb from the sheets butt naked and follow her. Carefully tucked behind the bedding, I pull on my panties and the long sleeve thermal of Jack's I wore yesterday. It reaches halfway down my thighs, and though I cursed it yesterday, trying to tuck it into the overalls, I am grateful for that today.

By the time I catch up to Linda, she is already sitting on the floor in her room, busily rummaging through her suitcase. The

Rowans' room looks like a storm hit it and I have to pick my way across the clutter on the floor to get next to her.

Linda smiles. "It's a good thing we look like we're about the same size."

She starts tossing things into a stack. Linda does have everything, everything in buckets. Unfortunately, she doesn't have anything I like, anything I would feel comfortable wearing, and since we're nearly the exact same size I can't politely beg off of the loan of her things with a "they don't fit."

I am suddenly knee deep in eight outfits: a two-piece black, baby doll nightie set; panties; bras (if you can call them that because they are absolutely useless); a brand new hairbrush and toothbrush; toothpaste, hairspray and four changes of shoes.

"Something for every kind of outing, Chrissie," Linda announces, shoving things into my arms. "The guys like to tear up the village at night. There is no telling where we'll end up when we stay at The Farm."

Tear up the village. So there is more than getting fucked and fucked up. There is tearing up the village.

After thanking Linda, I go back to my room and toss everything on the bed. I make a face and start to search through my new wardrobe. I'm relieved to find a little yellow sundress almost exactly like something I would buy, and a pair of panties not too stripper awful. I settle on a pair of high-top tennis shoes to finish off my outfit.

The guys are not downstairs when I go into the kitchen to find Linda. There are only the wives in the living room, lounging and laughing on the cushy furnishings there. I hear music, muffled and distant, and I wonder where it's coming from.

"Where are the guys?" I ask Linda. I so don't want to spend a day indoors with the girls.

"Rehearsing in the barn."

"So, what are we supposed to do?"

"You're watching it, girlfriend." Linda tilts her head as if it helps her to hear the guys in the barn. "From the sounds of it, it sounds like they're trying to behave nicely together. I expected fireworks, since they haven't played together in six months. We're lucky we're not hearing the barn being torn down around us. I really thought the shit was going to hit the fan in five minutes."

I pour a glass of orange juice and grab the toast Linda was kind enough to make for me. I look out into the living room with dread and reluctance.

Linda looks at me. "Come on, Chrissie. Let's get out of here for the day. The guys are going to be tied up all day. Let's go to the village."

We take the Rowans' shiny red Ferrari to the village, top down, and there should be a law passed against Linda driving anywhere. It's not just the speed that's getting to me, but her complete lack of focus on the road. She doesn't stop talking, not ever, and when I talk she fixes on me, hanging on every word as if unaware she's going nearly eighty on a narrow country road.

She cuts into a parking spot in the center of town, and as we walk down the street it soon becomes clear that Linda Rowan is nothing new in the village. The locals watch us as we walk and stare at Linda, not in an *oh, they are famous* sort of way, but rather an *on my god the weirdo has returned* type way. For what it's worth, Linda behaves nicely in Lake George. Please, thank you, and other pleasantries.

Unexpectedly, she pulls me into a thrift store. "If you need any more clothes this is the best place to find it in the village. You wouldn't believe the shit they have here."

She starts searching busily through tables and racks. We try on silly hats, rummage through purses, and Linda falls in love with an incredible sixties style mini dress that somehow managed to end up on a Goodwill table. She looks beautiful in it, Linda looks beautiful in everything, and I smile as she pays for the dress. This the little dress from the thrift store makes her happy in a way I haven't seen before. Is Linda happy underneath it all? It's hard to tell. It is hard to tell what any of the dysfunctional feel.

Linda tucks her wallet into her purse. "Why didn't you buy anything? Are you a snob or something?"

I laugh because I know she's just messing with me. "You got the best dress there."

She smiles and drags me from the store. "I used to love thrift shopping when I was in college. No money, just trying to find treasures. Do you girls do that in Santa Barbara?"

"Not so much."

Linda's face lights up. "I love this place. I need to grab some books. It's going to be a long week without any new ones."

We next stop at a used bookstore, because Linda likes used and not new. We are very similar in some ways. I toy with the idea of stopping in at the little boutique on the corner to buy some new clothes, so I can return Linda's things to her, but I haven't worked out in my head how to return them without hurting her feelings. She was happy to be able to lend them to me. I don't have the heart to tell her I hate them.

As the day wears on, I start to feel a little emotional. Linda's manner is almost parental, and I wonder if shopping with Mom would have felt like this if she had lived. I never got to do any of these girl things with my mother, not like this.

As we buy ice cream, I get the courage to ask. "How old are you, Linda?"

Linda's laughs. "I'm thirty, and yes I know I come across as a mother hen. Just part of always having to be the one who keeps everyone from killing each other."

We take our ice cream to a bench by the lake and sit there, staring out at the water.

Linda closes her eyes, exhales slowly, smiles, and then opens her eyes again. "I love sitting and just watching people."

"Me too."

"It's good that you're getting a little quiet time for yourself. This can't be an easy adjustment. I remember what it felt like for me when I was you."

"You?"

Linda laughs. "New girl in the pack. Fortunately, only Kenny and Bianca were together back then. The guys hated me. Len gave me such shit."

Oh no. Something in her voice makes it nakedly clear why she and Alan are so close. They had a thing together, probably before Jeanette. At some time in Alan's complicated history they had a *thing*.

I look at Linda and I feel sick. Why does everything about Alan contain some sort of hidden bomb, unexpected and emotionally unsettling. I toss my cone into the trash.

"Can we go back now?"

She rummages through her purse for her keys. "Sure. It's almost dark anyway, and I hate to drive those roads in the dark. No street lights."

Linda takes a fast lick of her cone, tosses it, and springs up from the bench, totally unaware that she's just killed the enjoyment of the day for me.

She plops down into the driver's seat and waits for me. "I think you have dinner duty tonight. Bianca turns into a total bitch if we ignore her schedule. Like she'll have to wash one extra dish once in her life. So obsessed with the equality thing."

"Then we have a problem. I don't know how to cook."

I turn to stare out the window. She jams the car in gear and pulls from the curb.

I can feel her eyes studying me. "That's OK. I can help you."

"No, Alan can fucking do the cooking for me since he's the reason I'm trapped here."

"OK."

Linda backs off. We drive in silence, Linda alternately staring at me and the road.

I start to cry halfway back to the farm. Linda is trying to drive and is anxiously studying me.

"Please, Chrissie, stop crying!"

I stare out the window and ignore her.

Linda slaps her mouth with her hand. "Me and my big mouth. I'm sorry, Chrissie. I would never do anything to hurt you. It wasn't deliberate. I don't think sometimes. I just really like you. I feel comfortable talking to you, and I just don't think." I can feel her stare on me. "Shit! Me and my big mouth."

"It's no big deal. I'm fine." My voice is quiet, hollow, like a pouty child and I hate that.

"Bullshit, you are not fine and I can see it."

The Ferrari screeches as she turns off to park on the side of the road.

Her probing stare is locked on me again. "Chrissie, if it's no big deal, why are you crying?"

"I'm just a fucked up girl. Can't we just leave it at that," I snap, still not looking at her.

"No," Linda says, in a long and heavy way. "You brought me into it, so no I'm not leaving it alone. And by the way, everyone is fucked up. That doesn't make you special around here."

Her weird reassurance pushes a soggy laugh out of me. I look at her now. "OK, this is stupid. I know it is stupid. It's just people...they're not easy for me. I never feel like I'm close to anyone. Like I get them. Not my dad. Not you. Not Alan. And not my brother. And I'm just so tired of always being surprised and hurt by everyone."

Linda sits quietly for awhile, waiting for me to calm. "People have shit, Chrissie," she says intensely. "It has nothing to do with you. We've just all got our own shit that we've got to deal with."

"I hate my shit, Linda. I wish it would all go away."

"What the fuck are you talking about?" she says in sudden alarm. "Chrissie, you're scaring me. I don't like the way you sound."

I take off my Tiffany bracelet and I show her. For the love of Jesus, I don't know why I'm doing it, why I want to share this with Linda.

She stares at my scar, shaking her head in a way that tells me I don't need to explain. "Why the fuck would you do that, Chrissie?"

The tears come. I can't stop them and they are dragging with them words. I just want to say it, say it to someone, and there no logical reason why Linda is the right choice for this, but I need to say it.

"It's my fault my brother is dead."

I start to hyperventilate and shake the moment I get it out. I've been hiding from the truth for so long, but when I picked up the needles in Alan's bathroom, more fragments appeared and I could remember every part of that night, my part in Sammy's death, from beginning to end in unmerciful clarity. I didn't just find my brother dead. I was with him when he died. I was there in the room, I didn't get Sammy help, and I watched my brother die…

I finally get the courage to look at Linda. She is just sitting there, staring at me, confused and steamed.

She leans back into her seat, making a taut line with her arms from body to steering wheel. Her fingers are curled tightly around it, so tightly they don't have color.

She starts shaking her head. "Jesus Christ, Chrissie. How could you think that? What were you when your brother died? Nine? Ten? How could you possibly believe it was your fault? Whatever you think you did, you are thinking wrong and you have to cut out that burning shit."

I can't begin to reason why I start to tell her every part of that night, the parts that have haunted me, the parts newly remembered, and the most terrible part, my part in this, that I watched him die and never went for help.

Silence. When I can't talk any more there is just silence.

Linda exhales heavily. "Fuck, you were just a little girl." She puts the car in gear and starts to drive. "And you're remembering your brother wrong. I knew your brother, Chrissie. He was brilliant, he was a fuck-up, and a hardcore addict. And he was going to die one way or another eventually because he was on the ledge every fucking minute of his life, and not you or anyone was ever going to stop it." She downshifts the car, shaking her head. "Fuck! You have nothing to do with him dying. He lived on the ledge. He died. End of story, Chrissie."

Shakily wiping my nose with a tissue, I turn to look out the window. "Then why does my father hate me? Ten years. Not one word from Jack about that night. He can barely talk to me. He blames me."

"Fuck, I don't know. Why does my father hate me?" She backs off. "And I'm sure your dad doesn't hate you. I'm sure that's just another thing you've gotten wrong."

She practically slams to a stop in front of the farmhouse, grabs my tissue and starts to dab at my face. "Pull yourself together. We are just going to walk in, Chrissie, and then you just go upstairs to the bedroom and be away from everyone for a while."

I nod, watching Linda climb from the driver's seat. She slams the door and starts walking around the car to me. I feel small, shaky and disoriented, as I listen to her shoes against the gravel drive. She opens my door and gives me one of her *Linda will take care of everything* expressions.

We are almost to the stairs when Bianca storms from the kitchen. "Where the fuck did you go?"

Bianca has her hideously angry face within inches of mine. Linda pulls me close against her. "We went to the village," she snaps.

"Why?"

Linda makes a face and shakes her head. "Because it was there."

Bianca crosses her arms. "I am not cleaning up that breakfast mess. And there is no dinner."

"Deal with it. Call for pizza or something. Just fucking deal with something on your own for change."

The girls start arguing and I'm trapped, shaking and being supported by Linda's steady arm, with the others between me and the stairs. The verbal free-for-all is loud enough to draw Alan and Len from wherever they were in the house, and Len is babbling on that that's enough of the cat fight, and Alan is watching me. I start to tremble more fiercely and the tears come back.

"Shut the fuck up everyone!" Linda silences the room, puncturing the sound barrier.

Alan's face changes and I can see exactly when he realizes I'm crying. "What's wrong? Why are you crying, Chrissie?" I don't answer and his temper explodes. "Goddammit, Linda, what did you do to her?"

Linda shakes her head, they lock eyes and I can see that their closeness is the type of thing where they can communicate without words. Alan's anger vanishes and he's only worried now.

"I'm going to take her upstairs," Linda says in a quiet voice that somehow makes everyone back off except Bianca.

Shaking her head, she exclaims, "Oh, no you're not. You're going to get your ass in there and clean the breakfast mess, Linda, and the little princess is going to make dinner."

Alan grabs Bianca's arm. "Why don't you just shut up for once, you miserable cunt."

Bianca pulls away. "Because I'm sick of everyone falling all over themselves for the little princess. I'm not going to spend another evening all about not upsetting Chrissie."

"Fine. Then I'm done. Gone. Out of here," Alan says, taking me from Linda and picking me up.

"Oh fuck, Bianca," Kenny Jones shouts into the chaos of the room.

Alan starts climbing the stairs and I focus of the sound of the creaks rather than the arguing downstairs. He takes me to the bathroom, undresses me and sets me in the tub.

It is antique porcelain, sitting on legs in the middle of a fifties style black and white tile bathroom. The sink is a square pedestal and the toilet is old. The windows are high in the walls, foggy glass circles that mute the light. It is a room held in another time. Like me.

Alan sinks down beside the tub, reaches for a washcloth and a bottle of bath gel that someone left in here.

"Are you OK?" he asks.

I nod.

"What happened when you were out with Linda?"

I turn until my cheek is resting on my knees. "Nothing happened. We talked. I don't know what it is about Linda. We talked about everything." My eyes focus on him and there are fresh tears. "Everything, Alan. I told her everything."

He continues to wash, but his faces changes and I can see he understands what I mean by everything, and that it hurts him that I opened up to Linda.

He reaches into the tub to pick up the cloth he dropped. "I'm glad you did that, Chrissie. Maybe someday you'll trust me enough to do the same."

He doesn't push, he just kisses me softly on the cheek. He knows when to let there be quiet between us, when not to push me, when to use his meanness, when to use his kindness, when to love me and when to stand back.

I watch Alan wash me. He is gentle and kind. I never expected him to be that kind of guy. Alan was right. I did think he was safe. I did think he was going to prove only to be an asshole.

I start to cry again. He always takes such good care of me, but today I realize it is important to him to take care of me, something more about him than me.

I curl into a tight ball as he washes my back. I am someone Alan loves. And that is something more about him than me.

Chapter Sixteen

The next morning, I wake alone and go to the kitchen to find Alan making breakfast. I feel badly. It must be my turn and he's cooking because I don't know how to.

"Is pancakes all right with you?" he asks.

I nod and drop a kiss on his cheek. There are things I don't like about Alan, but these sweet, thoughtful moments and how he loves me are enough to keep me here with him. I stay with him because I love how he loves me.

I sink at the piano. I start to play. I feel good today. Last night I told Alan I love him, it felt right finally to say the words, they flowed easily and honestly out of me, and those black eyes filled with some expression, something I don't know if I've ever seen before. I love him. He loves me. What could be more wonderful than that?

Kenny Jones enters the room. "What the fuck is she playing?"

"*Jesu, Joy of Man's Desiring*." Alan flips a pancake. "And no, Kenny, it is not the Beatles. It's Bach."

"Are you sure she's Jackson Parker's daughter?"

Alan ignores him.

I feel Kenny too close to me. I continue to play.

"Play Chrissie, Joy of Kenny's Desiring."

Oh crap! I stop playing. There is never any telling what Alan's reaction will be to shit like that. I grab my book of D.H. Lawrence and move to the sofa to read.

I look at Alan. He is pissed, but he isn't exploding today. He continues to cook breakfast.

"You're a fucking piece of shit, Kenny," Alan says quietly easing food onto a plate.

"I know," Kenny says, sinking on a chair at the table. He reaches for the coffee pot. He fills a cup. Kenny looks at me. "Hey, little kitty, what happened to the music? I thought you were going to play Chrissie, Joy of Kenny's Desiring."

I ignore him and turn a page. The Rowans step down the stairs. Linda pats me on the arm. Len drops a kiss on the top of my head. I follow them with my eyes as they go to the breakfast bar to grab pancakes.

The vibe in the room is strange, painfully taut, and then I remember last night during the girl melee, Alan had announced he was leaving and quitting. The strangeness in the room isn't about me. It's about Alan.

Alan brings me my plate and sets it on the coffee table beside me. "Do you at least know how to wash dishes?" he asks.

I make a face and shake my head.

Linda starts to laugh. "She's lying, Manny. I can tell."

He drops a kiss on my nose and those black eyes are shimmering with affection. "I can tell, too."

He sinks down beside me and I ease up, reaching with my fork to grab a bite of my pancake. He turns my book to see what I'm reading.

"Have you read that?" I ask. "I hate it. I would be willing to wash dishes for a week if you could give me a synopsis."

"Chrissie, what's wrong with you? This is great literature. Don't they teach you to appreciate literature in California?"

I toss the book on the table. "Sorry, Alan, that I don't match your highbrow standard. I wasn't raised to appreciate *Lady Chatterley's Lover*. I was raised to appreciate *Rule for Radicals*.

I think Jack gave it to me for Christmas the same year he gave me my Tiffany bracelet. Never philosophically consistent, not even over the holidays."

Alan studies my face. "Do you want to go to the village to call Jack?"

I tense, since I don't know what's in my expression that he would ask me that. "Nope, I want to eat pancakes."

He leaves it alone and goes back to the kitchen.

After we're done cleaning up the dishes, Alan takes me to the barn with him. It is my first time in the rehearsal space. It is empty. The guys aren't here, and I sit on the floor as Alan methodically positions the effect pedals, and I stare at the rafters, the old wood, the spider webs, and the musty, dark world that is the barn.

It is a place before time. A place without time. Alan is playing, adjusting, working through something that is only in his head.

I wander over to look at some kind of rusty, half broken piece of farm equipment. There is the most extraordinary spider web in the wheel spokes. Thick and intricate and swirling. Definitely a mercilessly constructed trap. But no spider. I stare at the floor, wondering if it's near me.

I hear a sound close to me and I look up to find Alan has unplugged and is standing above me.

"This is the most incredible spider web I've ever seen," I exclaim, pointing. "I wonder how longs it's been there."

"I had a little girl," he begins in a soft voice, and every nerve in my body feels a prick. "Molly. She was five. She died fifteen months ago."

Quiet. Alan steps away from me and sits on an old crate. I straighten up and I don't know whether to move toward him or stay where I am. I don't even know why he's telling me this today.

He gives me a rough laugh that has nothing to do with humor. "Don't look so apprehensive, Chrissie. This is just a story."

My heart twists. *Bullshit, Alan. This isn't just "a story" to you.*

"I never wanted her. I didn't want to be bothered having to care about someone and I didn't know her mother. Not at all. I did all the correct things financially, but I didn't want to be bothered, and I made sure everyone knew it."

He stares up at the rafters and runs a hand through his hair. "But Molly was a cute little thing and she wasn't the least bit put off by me. She did what she wanted, smiled and laughed, and eventually she had me, she owned me. I adored her in every way."

I feel a sad smile I can't hold back. *Yes, that's the Alan I know.*

"What happened to her?" I ask.

He rises from the crate and goes back to plug in the guitar. "She got sick. A week later she was dead. Her mother never bothered to call me. She was dead before I found out she was sick."

Oh my. How awful, how absolutely awful. Knowing Alan, I can't imagine any girl doing that to him.

He hesitates at my reaction. "I'm not responsible for her dying. And I am not responsible for not being there. But I regret them both. There is a difference."

The hairs on my body stand up. "Did Linda tell you what we talked about?" I ask nervously.

Alan shakes his head. "No, she wouldn't do that. She's a true friend. You can trust her with anything. Linda is one of the few people on earth I trust completely."

He turns until his back is facing me, starts adjusting things and begins to play. I realize this conversation isn't intended to start or finish anything. It's an Alan truth card. He takes a step forward and will wait until I follow. He's letting it alone until I'm ready.

I sit on the old crate, watching him play, as the barn fills up with the rest of the band. I don't know why I could tell Linda all my messed up shit. I don't know why I can't tell Alan.

Maybe I just can't tell him that worst part of me because I love him.

* * *

Tonight there is something frantic in me. After the guys finished rehearsal for the day, Alan and I went back to the bedroom, made love, and I slept curled into him. When I opened my eyes, Alan was beside me watching me sleep. The world looked the same, but internally I woke different.

I pull on Linda's awful loaner mini dress and I fluff out my hair, brushing the underside, spraying it, in that way that Rene calls the "just been fucked" look of hair. My body is anxious, I feel it my flesh, frantic sensations running loose inside me.

We are on our way to the village, to some sort of bar, where the guys might or might not play before an audience to get a little of the edge back before they go back on the road.

I study my face as I put the finishing touches of makeup on and find something strange about me that I can't identify.

Everyone is already gathered downstairs waiting, by the time I leave the bedroom. The air is filled with cigarette and other smoke, and I can tell by the loudness that quite a bit of drinking and other stuff has gone on while Alan and I slept.

I can feel Alan watching, but he doesn't come to me. God, he is beautiful. Black hair, intense dark eyes, ordinary casual dress, but all Alan. It is still a little mind blowing that he is with me.

Len smiles. "Is that all right with you, little kitty?"

All right? What is Len's talking about? I've not followed any of the conversation since I entered the room.

"The cars," he says with heavier meaning. "We've got to pair off. You're driving with us."

Everyone is moving, getting ready to leave, and I roll forward onto my feet. Len puts his hand on the bare skin of the small of my back.

"You OK?" Len whispers.

"Sure I'm great," I say with an overly bright smile.

He gives me a half smile. "You know, Linda has a dress just like that. I always want to jump her when she's wearing that dress."

I shrug. "Maybe I should take it off."

Len laughs a little too loudly.

Once we are out in front of the farmhouse, everything suddenly feels very weird to me. But then, it's been a weird day.

I can barely see Alan's face in the darkness around the gravel driveway, but I can feel he is studying me closely. The air is chilly, it touches my flesh, and I shiver. I am beginning to feel a dull, persistent sadness mixing with the frantic. Something is off. Is it me or is it him?

"You OK, Chrissie? Cold?"

I shake my head. "I'm fine."

Yes, this definitely feels strange.

The Rowans stop bickering and pile into the car. Alan leans a hand on my door, not opening it.

"Why don't we stay behind tonight," he says quietly. His eyes touch my face softly, gauging my reaction. There is something in his voice I can't quite make out.

Alan turns us until I'm in his arms and his back is against the car. His mouth joins mine and I feel an almost hungry desperation in his need for me. Then it occurs to me in the way he kisses me, in the way he touches me, that he needs to know that we're OK, that I'm OK. I suddenly know he can feel the weirdness, too, and that the weirdness is in me.

He doesn't break the kiss; he intensifies it. His hands move up beneath my dress, to the bare flesh of my thighs and I am lifted and molded into him. He is doing what he does so well, pulling me into him.

"Let's stay, Chrissie," he breathes into my ear.

He is using that voice he uses. The velvet seduction. The voice he uses to get me to do what he wants me to do. For some reason, he doesn't want me going on the dysfunctional outing tonight.

I tip my head back. "No, Alan, you are not using me as an excuse to bail on them. I don't want *them* thinking I'm some uptight bitch who ruins everyone's fun."

He sets me back on my feet. He is studying me again and his eyes are black and totally unrevealing. "Fuck what they think, Chrissie. I think we should stay behind."

He stares at me. God, he can be so frustrating at times. If he has something to say, why doesn't he just say it?

He opens my door and I drop into my seat. I can see that he doesn't want to go, but I climb into my seat and we are going.

The car is strangely quiet as we drive. After the loudness of the house, it is very eerie. Alan doesn't turn on music, and even the Rowans aren't bickering.

The roads are narrow, lined with trees, and without street lamps. Without the mountains and the ocean, I can never tell what direction I'm going. Are we going north, south, east or west? I stare out the window into the smothering darkness. I don't know. I can't feel the direction. It is an unexpectedly disturbing thing.

The rest of the dysfunctional are at the bar by the time we get there, their pretty line of fancy cars tucked into a lot full of less spectacular vehicles. As we pull into a gravel parking space, I look around for something to give an indication as to what amusement this place could hold for them. It is rustic and tucked in a thicket of trees, and I have a feeling we're more likely to find NRA members than the rocker set here.

But this is Alan's choice. Alan's favorite place at the lake. I wonder what he likes here.

Linda is pushing at the back of my seat, and I climb out of the car before Alan can open my door. She springs out of the car and agitatedly begins to adjust her clothing.

Linda shakes in head in irritation. "I hate that backseat."

Len gives his wife a roguish grin. "You didn't last week, love."

"Oh, shut up, Len."

I laugh as the Rowans move ahead of us. Their bickering is part of them. I have a strange feeling they are going to be the only normal, the only constant tonight.

Alan gives me a small smile as he pulls back the heavy wood doors, and I step into a dim, smoky tomb and feel a rush of dread. The bar is packed, pulsing and loud. But this is not a trendy nightspot for the fashionable off on holiday from the city. This is a redneck bar full of locals.

The attention of the entire establishment is trained on us. The guys root out a space in the far end of the bar, away from the stage but near the dancing. They are dragging two tables and putting the chairs together for us.

Linda snakes her arm around my waist and guides me deeper into the room. "Don't worry, Chrissie. They know us here and the UK has a peace treaty with the Beverly Hillbillies. But if the room explodes, run. Our job is to stay clear and bail them out in the morning."

I laugh as Linda sinks into her chair and gestures for the waitress. Alan waits for me to sit and I scoot over in between him and Linda.

"What do you want to drink?" Linda asks.

"What are you drinking?"

"Tequila shooters with a beer chaser."

I look up at the girl. "I'll have the same."

Alan is watching me and somehow staying engaged in the rapid laughter and chatter around the table. The waitress returns with her heavily burdened tray.

Linda does a little *cheers!* motion with her shooter at me. "Pound it, Chrissie."

I copy her move. I bite my lemon, down the shot and then take a fast gulp of beer. Everyone laughs. Alan is watching me quizzically.

"Two more," Linda shouts in that confident way at the retreating waitress. She smiles at me. "We need to go shopping when we are back in New York. We're out on the road in two weeks, Chrissie, and you'll need to get everything."

Out on the road. Alan is going back on tour in two weeks. I hate that Linda assumes, in her all-knowing way, that I'll be leaving with them.

When the band breaks, the guys move to the stage. They all talk and there is a familiarity that tells me they know each other and that they've dropped in to play live to get the edge here before.

The waitress returns, and in a moment I have another shooter.

"Drink now, Chrissie."

I do it simultaneously with Linda and this time the tequila doesn't burn. I'm glad it's rushing into my stomach and soon my veins.

I lean into Linda. "I want to dance."

She takes a deep gulp of her beer. "The UK should be playing soon. We'll need to go find some redneck toys."

Redneck toys? I laugh. Linda has my hand and she is tugging me from my seat. I feel slightly wobbly as I stand. God, how could two shots of tequila make me feel this way?

At the edge of the dance floor I stare.

Linda laughs. "Don't worry, Chrissie. The redneck toys will come to us. You look fucking hot tonight."

Blackpoll starts to play, and we are on the packed floor dancing with two college-type guys who look as out of place here as I do. There is something boyish and pleasantly good natured about my partner. For some reason, he makes me think of Neil and that crazy night at Peppers, and Jesse Harris in the kitchen.

He can't be more than twenty.

Linda's college dude has that bad-boy air about him, the kind of look Rene calls "axe-murderer," but next to Linda he looks harmless and overwhelmed. Linda doesn't dance as if she's married, and her young admirer is very into it and very overt in the use of his body.

I look up at my sweet-fresh-faced guy. "You come here often?"

He laughs. "No. We drove down from Cornell for the weekend. I saw you come in with the band. Which one is yours?"

I can tell by how he says it that he knows who they are. But of course, he would. This is a college age guy.

"Alan Manzone."

He looks impressed.

"For tonight," I add.

Shit, why did I say that? It makes me sound a little too slutty, a little too available, and to my disappointment, a little childishly petty. He's all smiles, since I just suggested an opening that doesn't exist. There is no opening with me for this guy. I should never have let him think it.

"Are you OK?"

I shake my head.

"Do you want some air?"

I look around the bar for Linda. She is across the dance floor, beneath the stage, and her penetrating laugh eclipses the loudness of the music.

I take my college guy's hand and pull him with me out the front door. The cold air hits me like a blast and I feel numb, out of my body, even though every part of me is anxiously churning.

I turn, leaning against the front rail, to find my Cornell boy watching me.

"Are you OK?"

"Stop asking me that," I snap, not at all reasonably. Shit, I don't want to freak out right here and I don't know what's going on inside of me.

He is still, unsure, studying my face in that way guys do when they think there is something wrong with a girl.

"I didn't mean to piss you off," he says cautiously.

"I'm not pissed off at you."

I lean into him and join my mouth with his. I don't know why I do it. Maybe I just want to know how it will feel to kiss someone other than Alan. His mouth moves on mine, deepening the kiss, a pleasant seduction, and I can feel that he is into this. I feel nothing.

I should stop this... the front door swings open, hitting the wall like an explosion. I hear it before I see and understand: Alan rips the boy from my arms and hits him. The guy crumples to the ground like a collapsing house of cards and, in horror, I realize this is my fault.

I try to check and see if he's OK, but Alan harshly grabs my arm. He drags me through the parking lot to the far side where it is dark and our car is parked.

Alan takes me by both arms and holds me beneath his face. "What the fuck is the matter with you?"

"I don't know," I snap, and I really don't know.

I just stare and he becomes more pissed off. He drags me to the car, opens the door and shoves me into my seat. He collapses into the driver's side and every part of him is alive with extreme anger. He is breathing heavily.

"Chrissie, what the fuck is wrong with you?"

I hit him. It feels unexpectedly good. I hit him again and again and again. Alan's entire body freezes, his face stripped of emotion. I hit him and he just lets me. I hit him harder and I start to cry.

He hauls me across the center console until I'm straddling him. His features are tense and unreadable. "Calm down, baby. Whatever it is just talk to me," he demands roughly.

Those black eyes are fixed on me, warm with compassion and so giving. I hit him again. "I hate you," I hiss into face.

I lean in, kiss him, and I start freeing him from his pants. Suddenly, the only thing I want is to fuck him. Like a tramp in a car, fuck him hard and angry, right here. I feel my panties jerked aside and his flesh there, seeking. He gently starts to ease into me and I jam him into me roughly.

My fingers curl in his hair like claws and I move my body up and down frantically on his. I devour him with my lips.

I ease out of him and I slam down. I pause at the tip and then I swallow him. I bite his lower lip. I nip at that pulse in his neck. I push him deep into his seat, using my body to control and consume him.

I start fucking him even harder. He's gentle with me. I get rougher. He tries to kiss me softly. I move my mouth harder and more demanding. He caresses me, lovingly. I resist and twist away from his touch.

I want him angry and he is not. But I am angry and that is all I am sharing with him in this frantic joining of my body to his. My anger and my sorrow and my pain.

I move hard and fast, and I can feel that he is holding back, waiting for me to climax. But I can't climax, I can't quiet, I just rage, and I want to rage until there is nothing left in me.

He pulls down my dress and my breasts are in his face, a nipple held in his teeth. He does those little bites and tugs that usually drive me crazy, but it is not enough. For some reason, I can't release that part of me where pleasure is.

I join his mouth back with mine and I kiss him in a wild way, more tongue, deeper, harder than ever. I take his tongue and give it a tug, a hard suck. All my muscles below clench tightly, yet don't release, and Alan lets go, finishing in me.

I feel a strange sense of triumph, even though I didn't climax. I pushed Alan to cum, and I realize that, for some reason, that was part of what I needed.

I slowly collapse against him, my breathing ragged, and the pulse of my body still alive and awake *there*.

The earth quiets and the car stills. The windows are steamed. The only sound is that of our breathing. I'm still straddling Alan. I am quiet in the flesh. I am not quiet within me.

He doesn't separate us. He doesn't move.

After what seems a monumental amount of time, he lifts his face from the tuck against my neck, beneath my hair.

He stares at me and the gentleness of his expression makes me want to cry. I fight the tears.

His long fingers stroke my bare back in a calming way. "Chrissie, I don't understand what's happening to you," he whispers, frustrated and urgent. "What were you trying to do? What is it you want?"

I shake my head. He folds me in his arms and holds me. Our bodies are both sweaty and damp. Our pulses are racing. "What is it you need me to do for you? Baby, just tell me. Tell me what you need."

I ease back almost to the steering wheel. I can't speak through the spurts of my breathing. The tears are burning tracks on my cheeks. "You are leaving," I choke out.

I start to sob out of control and curl into Alan's chest. His arms are warm and strong and his hands a velvet comfort on my back.

"Why, Alan, does everyone I love leave me?"

Chapter Seventeen

Alan carries me into the farmhouse. He sets me on the bed. He undresses me. He eases me down beneath the covers and tucks me in.

We say nothing, as I watch him move around the room. For some reason, he wants the harshness of incandescent light out of the room, because he takes a Coleman lantern, puts it on a table and then sets it ablaze.

He undresses in the warm glow, and the sight of him naked and perfect and at ease with himself takes my breath away. I love to look at Alan. But tonight it is not a sexual thing, because the fucking in the car I think has left us both depleted.

What's in the room is a quiet, a closeness without touching, and love.

He settles on the bed, fluffing up his pillow against the foot rest, and reclines with an easy grace so we are lying side by side, facing each other. It is an arrangement of our bodies that silently conveys *talk to me*.

I lower my gaze. I finger the pattern of the quilt. I don't know where to start. I don't know what he knows, but I know he feels it. It's in me, he feels it, he is unafraid of it, and I am unafraid of it with Alan.

I crawl down to the foot of the bed, and he surrounds me with his body, and the feel of him is warm and safe.

I start to cry, I don't want to, but the tears are not something I can hold back. "What I want, Alan, is to talk about my brother."

* * *

When I am done telling Alan all the things that haunt me, ev̶
the things I remember that I didn't share with Linda, I stare up
at Alan and cover his mouth with my hand. I don't want him to
say anything. He held me while I cried. Through some parts he
cried with me, and in the end I told him everything. I held back
not a single part, and that is enough for one day.

I stare up at him. "Can I ask you something?"

Alan laughs. He runs a hand through his hair. "Really,
Chrissie? You're worried about asking me something after all
that? You can ask me anything, baby. You should know that by
now."

I laugh. It does seem silly to worry. "How long can we stay
at The Farm?"

He takes me in his arms and rolls until I am on him. "As
long as you want."

"It's just, everyone leaves tomorrow. I don't want to leave
just yet."

"Then we won't leave."

"Tomorrow is Sunday."

"So?"

"Rene comes back to New York. I want Rene here. I want
to stay at The Farm and have Rene here."

Alan frowns, that "Rene not my favorite girl" expression.

"That's no big deal. I'll drive into the village early
tomorrow. Call Colin. Arrange to bring her here."

I curl into his chest. I feel much better. I've given more
parts of me to Alan and it feels so very right. I trace the ink on
his stomach. "I think The Farm will be good for Rene."

* * *

The next morning, we leave early for the village. Alan doesn't
have a car at The Farm so we take the rust bucket Jeep and that's

e dysfunctional will be gone, except for the return from calling Colin and making the inging Rene upstate.

n, fighting with my hair as we whiz down lane. He is a maniac when he drives. There is something about him always on the edge, even in his quiet moments, a certain sense that he silently rages against living and that he isn't fully at peace within himself.

I smile and I watch him and I say nothing. There is no radio in the rust bucket. He starts to hum quietly. I don't think he realizes it, or what the artful lines of his face betray. He is thinking of his own regrets today. My heart squeezes and twists. When does the pain of our mistakes leave us? Maybe never. Maybe that is life, living with the pain of our mistakes.

I stare out the window. Tears prickle my eyes. I've lived with my mistake for ten years and the pain hasn't left me yet. Perhaps Alan can feel it today. Perhaps that is why he's thinking of Molly. Perhaps that is why we are together when we really don't make sense in any way.

I lean into him across the center console and lay my head against his shoulder. It is in this comfortable quiet when we make the most sense to me. This beautiful guy, gifted and brilliant, too often lost inside himself. Just like me, his not so beautiful, gifted or brilliant girlfriend. Too often lost inside myself. Simultaneously opposite from and totally right with one another.

It can be a hopeful thing to find the other perfect half of yourself, someone who gets you, someone to love and be loved by. I never expected the other perfect half of me to be Alan Manzone. He's such a weirdo, but then I'm strange too.

Alan stops singing in mid-verse and looks at me. "Why are you laughing?"

I make a face. "Sometimes I just think funny thoughts. Where are we going?"

"To use a phone."

"But this doesn't look like the same way we went to the redneck bar."

"Back roads, Chrissie. Less traffic. Less people."

His eyes flash a smile toward me, but his mouth has a slightly apparent grim line. Oh, Alan, what is worrying you today?

I sigh. Do I even want to know what is worrying him today? Nope, I don't want to know. We feel good today. Really good.

He pulls into a motel parking lot. The Seven Dwarfs Motel and Cabins. I start to laugh.

"You did say you wanted to bounce a bed in a hotel named after a Disney movie," he murmurs, his voice very sexy.

"How did you remember that bit of stupidity, with everything that's gone on since we got here?"

"I remember everything you say. Always."

The look in his eyes makes me shiver. I smile and hug him, trying to contain my dopey happiness over this.

I watch him climb from the Jeep and go into the lobby. In a moment he's back, room key in hand, grinning.

He drives around to a cabin on the far side of the facility.

"Quite an adventure to use a phone," I whisper.

The cabins look lovely, utterly tranquil, but really tacky. Alan lifts me from the Jeep to carry me, and we are kissing all the way down the short tree-lined path to our door. It is almost like a meadow here, with fresh spring grass and newly blooming wildflowers. Suddenly I imagine lying with Alan in the grass and gazing up at the trees, and seeing the deep, black sky full of stars at night. I wonder what it would be like to make love outdoors. The thought of running away with Alan and getting lost in some rural idyll is very tantalizing, yet it makes me feel sad and a touch homesick, and even a touch lost again.

"Hey, what's wrong?"

I look up to find Alan studying me, key in hand, almost into the lock.

I shake my head. I smile. "Not a thing."

"Good. I have plans for you." He opens the door and points at the bed. "But now you have to sit. Behave. I've got to make my calls first."

I nod, flush, feeling his touch without contact, as I drop in a heavy bounce on the bed. Alan reaches for the phone. He really is going to make the calls first. He sinks on the edge of the bed, takes a slip of paper from his pocket, and begins to dial away, as I try to focus on the room.

The lamp makes me laugh. A Snow White figurine base. I wouldn't be surprised to find Wicked Witch sheets beneath the heavy burgundy bedspread.

The first call is to Rene. His tone is surprisingly cordial as he explains in that imperative guy way that she needs to pack and be ready when Colin arrives to collect her. He hangs up.

I expected the call to be longer. I expected the Spanish Inquisition of questions out of Rene. But for some reason, the questions didn't come, and for some indefinable reason Rene is just rolling with this when Rene never just rolls with anything.

Second call is to Colin. I watch Alan's hand move up and down his thigh as he barks rapid orders to Colin. My breathing spikes as I try to catch the words and ignore my spiking body. He touches himself and I want him to touch me. I stare at those long, tanned fingers. Now would be a really good time, Alan. Touch me. Please touch me now.

Another call. I lie back on the bed and stare at the ceiling. It's so frustrating how quickly he can make me hot without trying. So frustrating that he can concentrate on his conversation when I can hardly concentrate on anything but him when he's near.

I glance at him and then I roll on my side until my face is near his back. I'm done behaving. I pull up his shirt. I make small kisses up his spine until I reach that tattoo across his shoulder blade. I use it as a road map for my traveling lips and tongue. I let my fingers dance from his side to his stomach and then lower, lower—*ah, sharp inhale of breath*. He stops my hand and looks over his shoulder. He gazes at me darkly. It makes me feel so hot when he looks at me like that.

He continues talking as I ease up on my knees to kiss the pulse in his neck. I kiss his shoulder, then the other shoulder. I can hear the voice on the other end of the phone. It sounds male and professional. His lawyers perhaps. I should stop this. This is an important call.

I lie back on the pillows, finding it nearly impossible to behave. What's up with that? There is something carefree and wild in me today that is new. Perhaps it is the calm after the storm of last night and the silliness of where we are. I'm probably the first girl ever to have dragged Alan someplace like The Seven Dwarfs Motel and Cabins.

I make a face, Alan catches it, and I cover it quickly with a smile. I fiddle with my shoelaces and then pull them off. My toes begin to poke at his ear. His warm fingers wrap around my ankle and I make a pout, thinking he's about to push my foot away, but he starts to kiss each toe, a gentle touch of lips, a tantalizing suck. *Oh my*. Desire, thick and pulsing, dances through my flesh. Jeez, he's only kissing my feet. I close my eyes and surrender to the feeling, the touch of his lips on my arch, the feel of his tongue on my ankle.

"Get your clothes off now," he breathes and abruptly lifts me off the bed.

Oh shit, the call ended. I'm not exactly sure where he's going with this, but I undress anyway because Alan is naked and completely hard, and I am totally hot for *whatever*.

"Don't play with me, Chrissie, unless you are ready to play." He hoists me up and turns me on the bed pulling me back until my knees are on the edge.

He kisses my back and then that "wrong" spot, before he hovers at the right spot and then moves to kiss the back of my thighs.

He grabs my hips and fills me so quickly. He is touching me and the feeling of being completely filled makes my body burn and swallow him greedily. I groan and invert my back. The tilt allows him to penetrate more deeply. Slowly, he withdraws and then sinks into me. The tempo builds, harder and faster.

I see the mirror above the desk. He is watching us in it. I watch him watching us and it makes my blood scorch through my veins. The rhythm is quick and intense, and I revel in it, watching him, watching us, watching him watch me watch. And it is all there, in his face, in the reflecting mirror—his passion, his love, his pain and his beauty—and it is us I see, very right even in everything so very messed up about us both.

Quick, rough, and right. We come apart, together, and I explode around him in a chorus of squeaks and high-pitched whimpers.

Alan collapses on the bed, taking me with him until my head is cradled against his chest and we are both struggling to breathe.

He turns his head to look at me. "I'm not finished with you yet."

I smile. "How long do we have the room?"

"Until tomorrow."

"I didn't think they would rent rooms by the hour at a motel named after a Disney movie."

"Actually, they do."

I lift up my face to look at him. "Really?"

He nods. I laugh.

"They couldn't break a hundred and that's all Linda had," Alan says, lightly tracing my arm with his fingertips.

I start to laugh harder. "I forgot you don't carry cash. Why didn't you just charge it?"

He sighs, raking a hand through his hair, and he smiles. It should be a completely comforting kind of smile; it is relaxed, happy and slightly understated. I find it not comforting at all. I tense.

"The last thing you need, Chrissie, is for anyone to know we stayed here by the hour."

* * *

I lie naked, sprawled over Alan's chest, and we've been kissing and touching quietly for hours. I think the sex only ended because I feel drained, or else he would be working toward it again in this quiet after our passion. Alan's sexual energy never wanes. All parts of Alan always rage simultaneously within him and never sleep.

Alan trails his fingers up and down my back. "So, did bouncing a bed in a motel named after a Disney movie work for you?"

I nod. I don't want to talk. I just want to lie in this comfortable calm I feel in us both. I lay my cheek against his damp chest and can see through the window it's late afternoon.

"We should get dressed. We should go," he says. He kisses me, and then turns until we are spooning and I am wrapped in the warmth of his body. "Rene is probably almost to The Farm. Do you want to call Jack before we leave?"

Why did he mention Jack? I don't want to let anything from the real world in yet.

"No. I don't want to talk to him until we are face to face. I don't want to risk accidentally starting anything while I'm on the phone. That wouldn't be right."

"Do you want me there when you talk to Jack?"

Oh jeez, that's a lot to process. The thought of having Alan with me when I'm with Jack is very weird and unsettling. It's one thing to be with Alan and another to try to picture Jack in the mix.

It was a sweet and kind offer, but just too strange to consider today. Still, I don't want to hurt Alan's feelings.

"I think that would be a little hard to do. I go home Sunday and you are out on the road the week after. And this is my shit, Alan. Something I need to take care of on my own."

Alan eases back until he is staring directly into my eyes. "I can be there if you want me there, Chrissie."

"I know. I just don't see how."

"Since you're not going home, Chrissie, we can have Jack fly here before we leave on the road. Solution."

I tense. It is not the first time he's said I'm not going home, but it's not really something we've talked about and I can't tell if he is serious, just being kind, or what exactly he's suggesting.

I pull out of his arms, pull on his shirt, and then sit on my knees staring down at him. "I'm going home, Alan. I have to finish school and go to college. I can't just drop everything and run off with some guy."

"I'm not just 'some guy.' I'm *the* guy you're going to spend the rest of your life with."

My heart does a somersault.

Alan's intense black eyes lock on me. "Why do you have to go back? What difference is finishing school going to make? It is the trap of ordinary people and you are not ordinary. What happened to just being, and being happy, or was that all just bullshit?"

My cheeks grow hot and my body goes cold. "I can't stay, Alan."

"Why?"

"It's not how I'm made and you don't really want me to stay, so why don't we just leave it alone."

Shit! Peaceful Alan evaporates before my eyes, replaced by angry Alan. "Don't ever tell me how I feel. Don't ever tell me what I want. You don't even know what you want."

Alan climbs from the bed and pulls on his jeans.

"You are not going back to Santa Barbara, Chrissie."

He continues to dress, and when he's got everything on except his shirt, he holds out his hand to me. "Give me my shirt. Get dressed. We're getting out of here."

Petulantly, I shrug out of it and toss it at him.

I pull on my panties, bra, and top and realize that my hands are shaking. I feel so sick and disoriented. I don't want to go back to Santa Barbara. I have to. The thought of going home turns me into a cold, nervous wreck. But I can't stay, even if every part of me wants to. I can't stay.

I can feel him watching me. "Rene is probably at The Farm. We need to go."

I nod and climb from the bed. I make clumsy work of trying to pull on my jeans.

"Fuck, Chrissie. Don't cry."

I shake my head. "I hate it when you're mean. You can be so mean."

"You're not going back to Santa Barbara, Chrissie. There is no point in arguing about it. So why don't we just go back to The Farm and be good to each other."

Truce. He is calling a truce and I let him help me with my clothes, but my limbs feel suddenly weak and too heavy. Alan thinks he's gotten his way. Discussion over. He believes I am staying. But I can't. And I don't know how I'm ever going to leave him.

* * *

When we get back to The Farm, all the dysfunctional are gone except the Rowans.

I am just climbing from the rust bucket Jeep when the front door swings open. Rene and Linda spring onto the porch together. Jeez, they are both in too short shorts and tank tops, with some kind of cocktail in hand.

Rene darts down to the driveway and flings her arms around me. We are hugging. We are laughing. God, how I've missed her. We've been through so much together. There is a part of me that will never make sense without Rene.

"I'm so glad to see you, Chrissie. The wedding was a nightmare. Thirty-seven was a nightmare. I don't know how I got through it without going postal, and mother is, of course being mom, and I don't know what to do about that. And jeez, what's up with this farm? Why are we in the middle of nowhere? What the hell are we supposed to do here…?"

* * *

Since Bianca is gone, there is no chore list, and Alan and Len are in the kitchen making dinner.

Rene and I are curled on the downstairs sofa drinking what I think are Mai Tais, but I can't tell for certain. I don't really like it. Too sweet. Maybe rum? I've never liked rum. Rene guzzles hers with enthusiasm.

"So, what's up, Chrissie?" Rene whispers. "You've hardly said a word. Is it all the tabloid shit? You know Eliza is going to die when she sees it. Was Jack really pissed?"

Her questions and comments roll off me. I have so little time left with Alan. I won't let anything—not the world, Rene, not Alan and not me—ruin it.

I let my eyes widen at her in that *back off* way. "I'm happy. Leave it alone."

Rene frowns. I laugh. She is staring at me like she doesn't know what to make of me.

* * *

Our last six days at The Farm whisper away in a comfortable quiet. There is much we do not talk about, the shit is beneath the carpet whether you talk about it or not. You can love whether you talk about it or not.

I've learned so very much about life so quickly from Alan.

After I pack up my things, I look at the old style bedroom, wanting to memorize every part of this space.

I brush at my tears and make my way down the creaking stairs. Out on the porch, I find that everyone is packed up and the Rowans are just waiting to say goodbye to me before they go.

Len drops a kiss on my head before Linda pulls me into her arms in an exuberant hug. "I love you. See ya soon."

"See ya soon, Linda."

It is so hard to hold back the tears, since she thinks I'm going on tour with them. I am really afraid I might never see her again. In a short span of time, she became an important piece of my history.

I wave at Rene as she climbs into the Town Car with Colin. She is going back to Jack's to wait for me. Alan helps me into Jack's old, scarred leather jacket. We are going back to the city on the motorcycle. I don't know why. It looks like it might rain, but Alan said it won't, so I am going downstate the way I got here, sitting behind Alan and letting the world pass us by.

Chapter Eighteen

Something pulls me from sleep. Alan's bedroom is dark and I am alone. Where is Alan? Then I hear the sound of raised voices in the apartment. I reach for Alan's t-shirt and pull on a pair of panties.

I freeze at the terrace doors. *Oh god!* Jack is here and they are arguing.

"You have the nerve to pull my daughter into your fucked up life and you think it's going to be OK?"

Alan's face is calm, emotionless, but I can see how angry and hurt he is.

"You've got it wrong, Jack. I'm willing to explain if you're willing to listen."

Jack's expression is intense and harshly dismissive. "What can you possibly say that will change anything you've done? In three weeks you have made a complete nightmare of my daughter's life. Will it undo dragging her through the rag sheets? Whatever you think you can say or do isn't going to change any of the shit you've done."

"I appreciate—"

Jack cuts him off. "I was you. You can't bullshit someone who has been where you are."

I step out onto the patio. "Stop it, stop it, stop it!" I scream at the top of my voice.

Jack points a finger at me. He's never done that before. I've never seen my dad so angry. "Go pack your things. Be ready to go when I am finished here."

I twist away from the hand that tries to take hold of me. "No!"

"No?!"

"Whether I go home is my decision and it has nothing to do with you."

Jack stares. "I'm done discussing this. Pack your things. We're going back to the apartment. We are flying home tomorrow."

"You are a little late, Jack. I'm eighteen. I don't have to go anywhere with you," the very angry girl inside me screams.

"Yes you do, Chrissie. We are leaving."

"I'm not going anywhere with you. I can't do it anymore. I can't live as if everything is normal because it's not."

In frustration, I push the hair back from my face, and then I hear a sudden silence that sounds loud in my ears. Before I can react, Jack grabs my arm and drags me near a light.

The color drains from Jack's face. "What is this? Chrissie, what happened to you?"

I forgot my Tiffany bracelet in Linda Rowan's car. I shake my arm out of my father's grasp. "It's nothing. It's old. I've had it since I was thirteen."

He looks confused, dismayed, disoriented. "I don't understand." He sinks weakly on the edge of a table and I can see that he's not sure what he's seeing or perhaps he's just trying to lie to himself. "I don't understand. How did that happen? How could you injure yourself badly enough to do that without me knowing?"

Alan's eyes are a strange mix of fury and sympathy. "You don't know your daughter at all. Your daughter did that to herself with candle wax. She burns herself," Alan yells, unleashing truth into the room in a voice loud enough to shake the New York Skyline.

"I don't understand. Why would you do that, Chrissie? Why?" Jack is shaking and horrified, and he moves to take me into his arms, but I back away to the safety of Alan.

"Because you hate me," I scream.

Everything about Jack freezes all at once. "I don't hate you. How can you say that?"

"You never talk to me. You avoid me. You left me in school for eight fucking years just so you didn't have to see me. Why, Daddy? Why do you hate me?"

"I don't avoid you. And we talk all the time."

"When was the last time you ever noticed anything about me? I'm a pretty messed up girl. Did you even notice, Jack? Three weeks with Alan and he knows every messed up part of my fucked up life. Eighteen years with you and you know nothing. You don't want to know me and you sure as hell don't want me close to you."

"You've lost me, Chrissie."

"I lost you ten years ago."

Jack steps toward me, close, but doesn't touch me. He is despondent. "I don't know why you are so angry, but whatever you think I've done wrong it's not because I don't love you."

"Then why do you avoid me?"

"I don't."

"You left me in that school for eight fucking years. You made me someone else's problem just so you didn't have to be near me."

Jack's eyes are frantic and desperate. "No. Never. I didn't know that's how you felt, but you've got it wrong, Chrissie. All wrong. I'm here, baby girl. And I wouldn't be here if I didn't care."

Uncertainty fills my head. "I don't think I have it wrong. I think you blame me and you hate me for it."

Jack rakes a desperate hand through his hair. "I don't hate you. I don't understand what you are talking about. Blame you for what? What could I possibly blame you for?"

I stare at him and the little girl in me starts to shake and hurt. "You stopped being my dad when Sammy died. We dropped him in the ground and never spoke of it, and we really haven't spoken since."

I feel it. All the words bubbling up. I can't stop this.

"I am so tired of hating you," I sob.

Jack is crying. I've made him cry. It should please me, please me that he might hurt even in a small way, as I do, but it makes my internal mess even messier.

I sink against the terrace wall. Alan crosses the patio and eases down behind me, a barrier between me and the cold concrete. His warm arms are rocking me, his lips are in my hair, and I am back in that night. I can't stop it.

"It's going to be OK, Chrissie. Just talk, baby. Jack is listening. Your father is listening."

The words bubble up. I can't stop them and I am back in that night again.

* * *

It is late. Maria lets me stay up late. I think she likes to keep me near her. She is always watching and she is always close. She doesn't play with me very well, but I like that she stays close.

We are in the kitchen and I am watching her wash the foil she used to cover my meal last night. Why does she do that? Why does she wash the foil and add it to the giant ball beneath the sink? I hate that she saves my food and gives it to me a second day. The bowls of cereal are the worst. The charms get soggy in the milk. I don't want to eat it, but Maria expects me to, so I force down the soggy charms and she smiles.

I like Maria. I don't understand what she says, but I like her. She is thin, dark haired, and gentle like Mommy. I don't know what it is about her face, but she has that look that Mommy had before Mommy left. Sammy calls it haunted. No, I think Maria is just sad, so I do as she tells me, pointing and talking to me in fast words I don't understand, so she will smile and look less sad.

The foil ball is very large. When is it finished? What do we do with it when it's finished? I smile. Maria smiles. The foil is put away for another day.

I hear the front door open. The voices. I know the sound. Sammy. I spring from the counter before Maria can stop me and race down the hall.

I know Maria is right behind me, but I am faster. I am into Sammy's arms before she can stop me. I laugh as I'm tossed into the air and then lowered for a kiss from my brother.

"What are you doing still awake, baby girl." He says it in a growl. He is only joking. I smile. Sammy looks good. I think he is well again. That's what Jack calls it because he thinks I don't understand about the drugs. He thinks I don't know that Sammy has problems. But we are very close. My brother and me, even though he is ten years older. He talks to me and he lets me talk to him.

Sammy looks good tonight. I laugh. "Toss me again."

Into the air. He catches me. His friends are in the living room, and quickly the tidy quiet has changed. The music is blaring. Vince has opened the bar. There is laughter, music, and people everywhere in the room.

I stare up at Sammy. "Where did you come from?"

Sammy laughs. "New York this time, squirt." He makes a pouty face. "I'm here only one night, and then we're off to San Francisco."

I hate that he is leaving so soon. Everyone comes and goes except Maria and me. Even Mommy left, but I know that that was different.

The room is quickly filled with smoke. It burns my eyes and throat, and the music is too loud. It hurts my ears. I don't like it. Sammy's parties are not good. But Sammy's parties bring him here so I don't tell Jack.

Maria rushes across the room and tries to grab me away. I avoid her hands and hide behind my brother.

"Maria. Dame un abrazo y un beso. ¡Eres bella."

I don't know what Sammy said. Maria looks unhappy. Rapidly, she fires back. "Llamo Señor Jack. No se permite estar aquí cuando no está página. Las partes. No son buenos para la niña."

Sammy pouts and he is tickling her and trying to hug her and trying to kiss her, and Maria is angry, but she is laughing and shaking her head.

"No esto no es bueno. Llamo Señor Jack," Maria says in a frantic tone.

Sammy sinks on the arm of a couch. "No, Maria. No llame el Señor Jack"

I watch, hidden behind my brother, smiling. Whatever they are arguing about, Sammy is getting his way. But of course he would. Everyone loves Sammy.

Maria holds out her hand for me. "Niña. A la cama."

I take Maria's hand. I look at my brother. "Come later to say goodnight. Don't leave without saying goodnight."

He crosses his heart. He smiles at me. "Never, baby girl."

We are almost to the door. I smile at Vince. He ignores me. To Maria he says, "Llama al Señor Jack. Y llamo la inmigración."

I feel Maria shaking. The color is gone from her face and her fingers are so tight around mine that they hurt. She nods.

"Fuck, Vince! Why did you say that to her? She wasn't going to call Jack."

Maria stares at Sammy. She stares at Vince, and then she quickly pulls me down the hall to my bedroom. She has that look again, afraid and crying without tears. I see it in her eyes, but there are no tears on her cheeks as she tucks me into my bed.

I do not know what the strange look on her face means.

"Los amigos de su hermano. Son diablos."

I don't know what she said. I give her a hug. I watch as she closes the door. I listen to the party.

The minutes pass very slowly and I hate them. Sammy doesn't come and he promised. Even though the house has quieted, his friends have left, Sammy hasn't come as he promised.

I climb from bed and peek out my door. The hallway is dark. Maria has gone to bed. Good. I don't like upsetting Maria. She would be upset that I am not in bed asleep.

I tiptoe down the hall. I am nearly to the living room, but I hear voices from the other part of the house. They are in Daddy's bedroom. I follow the angry voices and I stop in the hallway, peeking in.

Sammy is arguing with Vince. Why are they fighting? I thought they were best friends like me and Rene. I never see Sammy without Vince.

Vince storms out of the room. He brushes past me without a word. I am pushed back into the wall. The front door slams. I look in the room. Sammy is sitting on the bed. He looks so sad. I don't like when my brother is sad.

I tiptoe into the room. Sammy's face snaps up.

"Baby girl, why aren't you in bed?"

I run across the room. I hug my brother. He looks like he needs a hug. I can feel something strange in him. It feels like Sammy is crying, but I don't see tears. He exhales slowly in a jerky way.

"Go to bed, Chrissie!"

I shake my head. I don't like the way my brother looks. I don't want to leave him. He picks me up.

"Don't tell Jack," he says and I know what he is asking. I am not going to tell about the party and the fight.

I nod. I love Sammy. I won't tell Jack.

"Is Maria good to you?"

I nod.

"I miss Mom."

I nod. I miss Mommy too.

"How long is Jack gone this time?"

I stare. I don't know.

Sammy tucks me into bed. He kisses my nose. "I'm glad Maria is here with you. Now go to bed, baby girl."

"Don't leave without saying goodbye."

"Goodbye." Sammy makes a funny face.

I roll my eyes.

I lie in my bed. I can't sleep. I don't know why. The house is very quiet. I climb from bed and tiptoe down the hall. I peek into the room. Sammy is there. I see the drugs. Sammy thinks I don't see and Jack thinks I don't understand, but I do see and I do understand and I don't want to leave my brother.

The floor creaks. Sammy turns. He sees me. "Get the fuck out, Chrissie!"

Why is he angry? Sammy never talks to me that way. I shake my head. I run into the far corner of the room. He was well when he got here. Why is he sick again?

"Go," Sammy growls. He is reaching for me.

I shake my head. I squirm so he can't catch me. Sammy lies back on his bed. There is something wrong. He is sweating and breathing hard. He looks so strange. I am afraid. Should I run and get Maria? Should I call Jack?

I watch. The minutes are slow. Sammy looks so strange. He is getting sicker. It is different. I ease out of my hiding place and cross the room. He is breathing so funny and the look in his eyes is very strange.

His flesh is moist and wet when he touches me. His hand is weak and it trembles. Sammy looks so strange.

* * *

Silence. Dead silence all around me.

"No, Chrissie. No. You are remembering it wrong," Jack says in tortured determination.

"Dammit, you don't remember something like this wrong, Daddy," I scream in long-suppressed frustration. "For a long time I thought it was just a nightmare. I mean, wouldn't we have talked about it if everyone knew I was with my brother when he died? But it's not a nightmare. It's real. Maria found me in the morning next to Sammy's bed. I was with her when she called you. Then Patty Thompson showed up, and the police and they took Sammy away. And Maria kept me in my room. And you showed up, Jack, and you never spoke to me again."

"Chrissie, I didn't know you were with him when he died. Maria…" Jack's voice fades away in a lost way.

"I was there. From the beginning until the end. I didn't find him. I was in the room. I stayed. I saw. I didn't understand. You have to believe me. Please, Daddy. Please. Don't hate me anymore. I didn't understand. I would have gotten help, but I didn't understand. He looked so strange and I watched. I watched it all. I just sat there and watched. Oh god…it's my fault Sammy died. I watched him die and I never got him help. Is that why you hate me? Because it's my fault Sammy is dead?"

Jack sinks in front of me. He takes me in his arms. "No, Chrissie. I don't hate you. It wasn't your fault. It was my fault, baby girl. Sammy had issues. I knew it. I should have been there."

I wipe frantically at my tears. "I didn't find Sammy. I was in the room when he did it. I was with him when he died. And it's been really, really hard because I've been so afraid you hate me."

Chapter Nineteen

Two words. I have never let them out. I've guarded them inside me. It is time to let them out. I can't hold them in any longer. It is time to let them go. To heal. To confront the pain.

"I'm sorry."

Silence.

"Did you hear me, Daddy? I'm sorry."

I curl against my father's chest and I can't stop saying it: I'm sorry. I'm sorry. I'm sorry...

* * *

I thought I would feel better letting it out. I don't. It is only different. A different kind of weirdness. The weirdness of letting truth into the room.

Jack and I talk through the night, until it feels like there are no words left inside either of us. I don't know where we go from here. I don't know if this helps. It doesn't feel better yet. It only feels different.

Different. Not better. Not worse. Just a different kind of weirdness.

* * *

We sit on the terrace on a double chaise lounge waiting for the sunrise. Now that I've grabbed hold of Jack I can't seem to let go. We've finally started the journey we need to finish together.

At some point last night, Alan quietly slipped from the terrace. Light is spreading across the sky and I stare up at Jack. He looks lost in his thoughts, his magnificent blue eyes locked on some indiscernible spot on the horizon. It feels good to hold my dad. It feels good to be held by him. It feels good that we are together.

I see something on his face, a fleeting emotion that is quickly lost behind the usual arrangement of his features. "What are you thinking, Daddy?"

Jack laughs softly and turns to fix his blue eyes on my blue eyes. "I was thinking of Grandpa Walter. How much he hated me."

Mom's dad. And yes, Grandpa Walter always hated Jack. I make a face because it would be pointless to pretend that Grandpa's dislike wasn't obvious. It was blatantly obvious. Jack laughs again.

"Today I don't blame him. Scary thought, today I really get Walter."

I make a pout and then a smile.

"I love you, Daddy."

He drops a kiss on my golden brown hair. "I love you too, baby girl." Jack smiles, stares at the sky and then sighs heavily again. "Our plane leaves at four, Chrissie. We should really get back to the apartment, pack up, and head out."

I feel cold and shaky. I know what I want to do, I know what I need to do, and clarity is not always a peaceful thing.

"I'm not going home today." I say it simply, no bullshit, no drama, no equivocation.

I feel Jack tense. "What are you telling me? You are not staying, Chrissie. You may be eighteen but you are still my little girl."

I ease out of his hold until I am sitting, hugging my legs, my cheeks pressed on my knees. "There are things I'm not finished with here. There are things left for me to do. Things left for us both to do. I will see you in the morning at the apartment.

We are going to clean out Mom's things, and I think that we do it together."

If I didn't know Jack, I wouldn't see the pain whispering through his eyes. It is that subtle a thing. It makes me think of what Alan says he sees in my eyes. I can feel the tears, but I fiercely fight to hold them back.

"You're not staying here, Chrissie."

I kiss Jack on the cheek. "I'll see you in the morning, Daddy. But now you need to go. Alan gave you last night. But I am keeping today for Alan."

The look in Jack's eyes nearly makes me crumble. I want to cry so very badly, because I think I know what I am going to do, but I don't really, and somehow I don't think I will know until I am there at that moment when life forces me to choose right or left.

Right or left. I stare at Jack. Is it really true that the turns we make don't matter and that the journey will end as it should, no matter what turns we take?

I don't think Jack is right about this. I think the turn I make will be the one I can live with, and I don't have a clue which one that will be.

* * *

I find Alan in the bedroom sitting in a chair at the far side of the room before a window, staring out at the city below. I lean quietly back against the door and just gaze at him. He is bathed in the glow of dawn and still dressed in the clothes from last night.

The bed is exactly how I left it, his side perfectly tucked in and my side with twisted and scrunched up blankets. My side. His side. I fight back the tears. In such a short time, he's become everything to me: the mirror I stare at myself in and the other perfect half of me.

"You OK?" he whispers.

I nod.

"Jack still here?"

I shake my head. "I sent him back to the apartment."

Jeez, why am I standing here like a fool against the door?

"Everything OK between you and Jack?"

I shrug. "Things are OK. Sort of good, actually. We've still got a lot to work through."

I wish I hadn't said that Jack and I still have a lot to work through. For some reason I now know what I have to do. Taking in a deep breath, I move across the room until I'm sitting on my knees in the space between his legs.

There is something on his face that makes me anxious and afraid. "Are you OK?" I ask.

He runs a hand through his hair and he shrugs. "I thought I was going to go out there and just find that you'd gone. No goodbye. Just gone with Jack."

"I could never do that."

Suddenly he pulls me into his arms and he is kissing me, kissing me passionately, all across my face, across my tears and cheeks and lips. The fierceness hits me like a tsunami, because I can feel panic and need and love in how he kisses me.

"I love you," I whisper against the warm flesh of his neck.

"Don't leave," he whispers against my lips as I am carried to the bed.

I lock my mouth to his as we frantically shed our clothes, a desperate almost frenzied passion inside of me. Alan's breath begins to quicken in response, but he tries to whisper something.

I stop him with my kisses and the twisting urgency of my body. I don't want to talk. I want to pull him inside of me and to feel that completeness, that total loss of emptiness that I only feel with Alan.

"Love me and be good to me, Alan," I murmur against his skin, and I know he understands what I am asking.

He lifts me and slowly lowers me onto to him, filling me completely. I moan incoherently as I let him move and guide me.

He tilts his pelvis, guiding my hips with his hands as he moves himself in and out of me. I can't imagine not being here with Alan. We feel so right together.

I want to consume this slowly, but I can feel my body building and building, climbing higher even as I resist it. I can't stop myself and I explode around him. He cries out in turn.

We lie as we finish, me draped across his flesh, neither of us saying anything. He holds me and I hold him, and I realize that the tears moistening my cheeks are not only from my eyes.

"I don't want to talk about anything," I whisper.

"Then we won't talk."

I rub my cheek against his chest. I kiss the flesh above the pulse in his neck. I love him so.

* * *

You can't hold the minutes back, no matter how hard you try to. The minutes go only faster when you do not want to let them go. I want to stay here in this perfect quiet with Alan, but Sunday morning is here and I can't do a damn thing about it.

I roll over in Alan's arms. I look at the clock. 9 a.m. Jack and I settled on 10 a.m. after heated negations for the ritual of packing up Lena's things and finally saying goodbye to Mom. I have a little time. Not much. I really should get moving. I can shower after the packing. It will save me a little time now, but not enough. No amount of time will ever be enough, and I still don't know what I am going to do after saying goodbye to Lena.

I turn my face into my pillow to hide my tears. I'm going to lose him. Alan won't want to be with me if I go back to Santa

Barbara. Oh, he'll try. He'll do all those be-kind-type of things. There will be the phone calls and maybe a letter or a present. But that won't last long because the real world exists whether we want it to or not, and the real world made us over from the start.

The bed shifts under his weight as Alan turns me slowly in his arms so I can face him. My head is nestled on his arm. His eyes are black and searching.

I gaze at his beautiful face. It is emotionless, compassionately so, and I hate that he can give nothing away if he wants to. His eyes stare into mine, hardly blinking, calm and smiling, merely because he wants them to. Reaching up, I caress his cheek and run the tip of my fingers across the perfect structure of his jaw. I want to remember each line on his face exactly how he looks at this moment.

Time moves in, hovers and slips away. I can't stop it.

I rummage on the floor for Alan's shirt and pull it over my head. I climb from the bed. "I've got to go, Alan."

I start to gather my clothes, and carelessly I shove them into my duffel, carefully avoiding Alan's eyes. I can feel him watching and I wish he'd just say something, because the faster I get through this the sooner the pain will go away.

"Do you want me to go with you?" he asks.

I shake my head. "No. I'm meeting Jack at the apartment. We're packing up my mother's things today."

Alan sits up. A torturous and heavy pause in the room hits me like a punch. "And then?"

"I catch a plane and go home to Santa Barbara."

More heavy silence. The lump in my throat is strangling and I can't look at him because if I do I don't know what I will do.

"You can't be serious, Chrissie. You're not leaving."

The room is filled with Alan's panic and his need. It moves across my flesh like a chilled nightwalker.

"I have to go, Alan. I'm not ready to be everything you want me to be."

"I don't want you to be anything other than you are," he whispers, his voice raw. He crosses the room and stops my hands in their frantic efforts of packing. "You're not leaving, Chrissie." His thumb traces my lower lip. "I love you."

"I love you, too," I whisper, almost unable to push the words out of me. "But I have to go home."

I step away from him and gather my clothes to wear. I lift his shirt to my face and breathe it in deeply. "Can I keep this shirt?"

"Why?"

"I love the smell of you. I want to smell you until I can't anymore. In a perfect movie lovers would never end they would slowly fade away. I want to smell you until I can't smell you anymore."

He closes his eyes. Oh shit, that was a really shitty thing to say, but I didn't mean it and I wish I hadn't said it.

"You can keep the fucking shirt, Chrissie."

My scalp prickles as every nerve in my body is suddenly blasted by a chill. The earth falls away beneath me. Oh no, this is not how I want this to go between us. What have I done? I don't want us to part angry.

Alan pulls on his jeans and crosses the room to light a cigarette. Finally, he runs a hand through his hair and doesn't look at me. "I'm sorry. You may have the shirt, Chrissie. My reaction to the shirt thing has nothing to do with you. It is an enormous irritant. The shirt thing. But I shouldn't be rude to you. Sorry."

My eyes open to their roundest and it takes everything I have not to cry. That was unkind, Alan. Why do you have to be such a shit at times? A shit who lets me know that girls taking souvenirs after climbing from your bed is a frequent event; a shit who on purpose reduces me to meaningless, when my words were only an accident; a shit because…

"You can stay, Chrissie. You can stay with me in New York. We can get married. Whatever you want. I'll quit now before the tour starts. I don't want you to leave."

I have to get out of the room quickly. Anymore and I'm going to crumble and stay. "I can't stay, Alan. And you don't really want to marry me."

That spikes his anger. "Don't tell me what I want."

Oh jeez, another stupid blunder. I'm going to ruin us if I don't get out of here quickly. I sink my teeth into my lower lip and continue to dress. The words clog in my throat and they are too painful to speak. I hear them in my head: Oh Alan, I've got my own shit to fix.

"I can't stay," I repeat.

"If you leave we are over."

Oh god, I see it and I don't want to. Alan loves me, but right now Alan loving me is more a thing about him than me. He doesn't want me to leave because he's afraid to be alone. That's the fear and desperation I see in his eyes and it is the wrong reason to stay.

We both have so much messed up shit we need to work through. It would be wrong for us both if I stayed. But I don't remember me before Alan and I don't know if I really want to.

I reach for my purse. He flinches as though I hit him.

"At least let me take you home," he says in despair.

"No. I think I want to walk today. Can you have Colin deliver my things to the apartment?"

"You can't walk home, Chrissie. There are at least two dozen photographers at the curb waiting to pounce on you. Don't be unreasonable about this."

How could I have forgotten about the tabloids?

"Then I'll go with Colin alone. Can you call him for me? I want to go to the garage alone."

I rush quickly from the bedroom. I head for the foyer. I listen. I am so relieved that Alan doesn't follow me. I press the elevator button and the doors open. I couldn't leave if he followed me, but that he didn't really hurts me.

I lean back into the icy metal wall and stare at the square mirror images of myself. Oh, please doors close! Close quickly! Then I realize I haven't pushed the garage button. I hit it and I am numb. The metal moves, taking me away.

Oh god—Alan Manzone asked me to marry him and I've walked away. The only guy I've ever loved. The only guy who will ever understand me. The second the door slammed closed I knew it with certainty: Alan is the love of my life. Crippling pain slices through me and I am not at all sure I've made the right decision.

The love of my life...and I walked away. What have I done? The pain is indescribable, but I can't surrender to my grief. I've got to pack up my mother's things with Jack, catch a plane, and somehow return to Santa Barbara and fix my perfectly fucked up life.

Deep down I know I'm doing the right thing. The right thing for Alan. The right thing for me. It just doesn't feel that way today. Alan is right: I never know what I want, but I always know how I feel.

* * *

Everything seems longer and slower and harder. Usually any return home feels faster and easier because it's familiar. There is nothing familiar today. It is just long and slow and hard.

I have survived the first day without Alan and the trip to the airport with Jack. Internally I am still messy, but a different kind of messy. Parts of me have been quieted, new parts of me stirred awake, parts of me I leave behind, and parts of me I take.

I repeat that last part in my head. I want to put it in my journal once we are aboard the plane. There should be something in my journal about Alan.

We are ushered into the VIP wait lounge in the airport terminal, and for today that is more about me than Jack. The tabloids have been our crushing shadow all day. I don't care. They don't know what the last three weeks have been about, and they never will. Let them write what they want. No one other than Alan and I will ever know or understand it.

It is too honest. Too human. Too real. I love Alan and he loves me. That's it. End of story. And I leave New York for the simple reason that that is what girls like me do. We say goodbye. We board the plane. We go home and fix our own shit.

Jack hasn't said a word since we finished clearing out Mom's personal things from the apartment. It never occurred to me until I came to New York that Mom's things were exactly where she left them and Sammy's room remains exactly the same as it was that day. Jack has lockboxes too. I am like him that way: keeping things in little boxes, hurting privately and slow to share my pain.

Jack's silence today is more about him than about me, and I am OK with that. I understand it because I said goodbye to Alan today.

More airport security comes when it is time for us to board the plane, and by how everyone on the plane stares at us I can tell we are the last ones on the plane even though our seats first class.

I laugh. No proletarian seats today.

We are in the air before Jack speaks.

"It's going to be OK, Chrissie. It will all blow over. It always does."

But I don't want it to blow over. I am in love with Alan.

I smile. "Why did Rene leave yesterday?"

I was so consumed with Alan I didn't stop yesterday to wonder why Rene left me.

"The school is graduating you early, Chrissie. They remarked that they would prefer you clear out your things on Sunday so as not to disturb the returning students. Rene and Patty are packing up your things from your dorm room today."

Oh shit.

"Are the Thompsons angry we've been kicked out of school? I know how Rene's mom feels about never having the crap be public."

Jack gives me a small smile. "They didn't kick out Rene. She left in solidarity and the Thompsons are cool with it."

It's awful, but I start to laugh anyway. I can't help it. I was kicked out of school before Rene. What were the odds of that? I laugh harder and Jack laughs, and suddenly we are laughing in a crazed way that doesn't match any of this.

When the laughter quiets, it is a comfortable thing. A comfortable thing, for the first time, in a very long time, between Jack and me.

"I think tomorrow we should go buy you a new car," Jack says somewhere over Colorado. "A Volvo. The safest car on the road, but not flashy. Hopefully, it won't be something anyone wants to steal."

up with that? I expected to be dragged to an
1 therapy center. What's with the car shopping,
ght be better between us, but it doesn't make
any less confusing.

ωιιγ μι. ve buying me a Volvo?"

"You're out of school early, Chrissie. You were planning a
road trip across country this summer with Rene. Leave early.
Get lost for a while. Let it all go. Sometimes it's the only way
you can find yourself."

I smile and think of Alan. Jack is right, but I also think I
might have already found myself, and that returning to Santa
Barbara is a very big mistake.

When Jack falls asleep, I pull out my journal and make my
Alan entry. I stare at the newspaper photo I have tucked there.
I love this photo of Alan and me. Us on the terrace, curled
around each other, waiting for the sunrise. How did they get it?
Telephoto lens? I wonder if you can ever get a real photo from
a newspaper. It just seems to capture us, and everything that was
us, through these unexpected weeks. I start to cry. The caption
is cruel and wrong, those fuckers in the press never get anything
right, but the photo is totally us.

I wish I could see the future. I wish I knew with complete
certainty if my decision were right. I wish I were older, looking
back after having gotten through this.

What if I'd stayed?

I turn to stare out the window. I can't see the earth and I
can't see the sun and I can't see the journey ahead of me.

~THE END ~

Read most of my books FREE in Kindle Unlimited:
Continue Chrissie and Alan's story in the rest of the Half Shell Series:
The Girl on the Half Shell

The Girl of Tokens and Tears

The Girl of Diamonds and Rust

The Girl in the Comfortable Quiet

For new releases and upcoming book signings: http://susanwardbooks.com

Or like me on Facebook:
https://www.facebook.com/susanwardbooks?ref=hl

Or Follow me on Twitter: @susaninlaguna

Continue the Parker Saga with the Sand & Fog Series(Alan Manzone and Kaley Stanton's story. A total of five stand-alone novels) and The Affair without End Series(Jackson Parker's story)

Broken Crown(Sand & Fog Series)

The Girl of Sand & Fog(Sand & Fog Series)

The Girl in the Mirror(Summer 2016)

One Last Kiss(Affair without End Series)

One More Kiss(Affair without End Series)

One Long Kiss(Affair without End Series)

One Forever Kiss(Releasing Spring 2016)

Or enjoy on of my stand-alone contemporary romance releases:
The Signature

Rewind

Or enjoy one of my new bodyguard series, Locked & Loaded:
Graham Carson Books:
The Manny(Available for Preorder)
His Man(Releasing Summer 2016)
For the Love of Ella(Releasing Fall 2016)

Dillon Warrick:

Pistol Whipped(Releasing April 26, 2016)
Take Down, (Releasing Summer 2016)

Skyler Mathews:
No is the New Yes(Releasing Summer 2016)

PREVIEW THE GIRL OF TOKENS & TEARS

I find vacant my favorite spot with a view of the Berkeley

Campanile and the giant concrete slabs with sculptures of bears atop them in a grassy and shaded area of the campus. I sink down, curl into a ball hugging my knees, and fight to stop the tears.

I can't believe I chose this over marrying Alan...

"Here, you look like you could use this," says a quiet, male voice above me.

I look up only far enough to see the carry-size pack of tissue held out to me in long, tan fingers. I take one and anxiously dab at my tears. On the concrete walkway below there's a pair of some kind of work shoe and dark blue pant legs that look like they belong to a jumpsuit or something. Oh God, it's the janitor I barreled into. How humiliating is this? To be the girl alone on a concrete slab, crying, and being consoled by the janitor.

I don't look up, praying he'll go away.

"Can I sit on your bench?" he asks politely.

"It's not my bench and it's a free country."

I cringe. That sounded childish and snooty. No wonder I haven't made a single friend here.

"I'm sorry," I add.

"No problem. You're upset. I get it. I just want to eat my lunch. No harm, no foul."

He makes a small laugh over his own comments. I avoid looking straight at him, inhale another sniffle, and touch my nose with the tissue.

"Thank you. You've been very nice," I whisper.

He settles near me, copying my posture: feet on the bench, his legs bent, and facing me.

"You know, Lambert will only bully you if you let

him," he advises kindly. "And he only bullies the students he thinks have potential."

How would you know? You're the janitor, I say to myself. "Thanks. I'll try to remember that. He doesn't hate me. I have potential."

He laughs and, from a pack on the ground, he takes a brown lunch bag and sets it beside him. So he really did just come out here to eat his lunch. The janitor suddenly popping up here has nothing to do with the sorry sight I must have been running out of Lambert's classroom. A small measure of calm returns to me.

"Rough year?" He's carefully unwrapping some kind of minimart precooked burrito thing.

Jeez, is he going to eat that cold?

He holds it out to me. "Do you want a bite? It isn't as terrible as it looks."

I start to laugh, even though I really don't want to. "Thanks, but no thanks!"

"Come on. What's not to love? Week-old beans. Week-old rice and I'm not even sure what the sauce is. Be bold. Be brave. Eat a minimart burrito from yesterday."

OK, that was funny. I look at him then, locking onto his green eyes. There's a really sweet, teasing glint in them. His eyes are large, brightly colored, and filled with a smile. Shoulder-length blond-streaked brown hair peeks out from beneath an army green bandana, and the face of the janitor is tanned, really good looking...and really familiar.

Why does it feel like I know him?

"Are you homesick? Is that why you mope around campus all day?"

I lift my chin. "I don't mope. And how would you know what I do all day?"

He takes the keys hanging from his belt and shakes them. "There's not much to do when you push a broom in the music department except listen and watch everything." He takes a bite of his burrito. "You have Lambert's class from 10 until 11. You sit on this bench until noon. You have a practice room from 1 until 2. You sit on this bench until 3. You have your lab with Jared the TA—who's hot for you, would really like to date you, and is afraid to ask— that's at 3:30. And then sometimes you do another hour in a practice room, but most of the time you disappear from campus. You're back at 7 for symphony. That's your Tuesday/Thursday schedule."

My eyes widen and I tense. Jeez, maybe he's not just the janitor. Maybe he's a stalker or something.

"How do you know all that?" I ask anxiously.

"I push a broom, remember?" he replies casually.

I start to gather my things.

"Hey," he says, putting his hand on my arm. "You don't have to run for security, Chrissie. I would never hurt a hometown girl. The rest of the girls I stalk are in big trouble, but you're pretty much safe from me. We've got that whole SB thing going on. We're hometown bonded."

His boyish eyes start to twinkle above an endearing smile. I stare at him. Chrissie—he knows my name. SB thing? He's from Santa Barbara, too. I study him more closely and I just can't place the face. I know the face, but I'm not connecting the dots, and I'm not tapping into that instinct thing telling me if I used to like him or if I should run.

He frowns. "Now I'm hurt."

Crap, he can see I'm not remembering him.

He tosses his unfinished burrito into the bag. "Do you forget every really, really cool guy who does you a really, really big favor?"

I feel my heart drop to my knees. *Really, really cool guy...* Oh crap! This day just keeps getting worse. Neil Stanton. Yep, I definitely remember him. The jerk from that night Rene and I went clubbing at Peppers before leaving for spring break in Manhattan. The guy who thought he needed to give me life advice after making a fool out of me. In my memory I can hear him say *Didn't Daddy teach you anything about how the world works?*

I do my best imitation Rene rich-girl-put-down face. "Sorry! It's just that Daddy taught me not to speak to the janitor."

He rolls his eyes and shakes his head. "And here I was just trying to be nice to you. Why is it girls only remember the parts of everything you don't want them to? Never the nice parts. Just the parts you want them to forget."

PREVIEW THE GIRL OF DIAMONDS AND RUST

I can't breathe. I can't feel my legs, I can't feel my arms, but somehow my body rises from the chair and moves toward the door.

"It doesn't matter, Alan. If you had called me I wouldn't have changed my decision," I whisper with more injury in my voice than I want to show. "I don't want to talk about this with you. Not now. It's too late."

I'm almost to the door when he stops me. He whirls me around to face him. Those potent black eyes lock on mine directly and the lockbox breaks open. It all tumbles out. My hurt. My regrets. My love for him. In leveling waves, real and present and consuming me.

He takes my face in the palms of his hands. "Please, stop hurting yourself because you hate me. I can't bear knowing that all this has happened because you hate me."

I say it before I can stop myself. "I don't hate you, Alan. I love you."

"Then don't marry Neil. It's in all the trades. It's why I came here today. Don't marry Neil because you hate me. Don't hurt yourself again because you hate me. I couldn't live with that. I swallowed my pride to come here. I couldn't let *you* hurt *you* again."

He pulls me against him, surrounding me with his flesh, and he is trembling with his emotions, as frantic and despondent and in pain as I am.

I don't know why I do it. Maybe it's because this is goodbye. Maybe it's because I want to stop this. Maybe it's because Alan is crying.

I lean into him and join my mouth with his. His mouth moves on mine tentatively at first, only gentle contact. Then it deepens on its own, and I can feel it changing, that we are both changing what this is.

I pour all my hurt and heartbreak of the last year into

our kiss, and it happens as it always did—the second I touch him, I am lost in him and we are lost in each other.

I shouldn't do this... And then the words in my head are silenced as Alan puts me on the bed.

PREVIEW THE GIRL IN THE COMFORTABLE QUIET

I can't stop shaking. God, I wish my body would be still. But nothing in my life could have prepared me for this. Maybe there are some shocks so severe that they reverberate through you, and you can't do anything except wait until they quiet on their own.

I stare down into my wine. This is definitely one of those shocks.

Rene sinks to sit on her knees across the coffee table. She just stares and I can see this has leveled her as much as me. She doesn't know what to say. It is as if this crisis is so enormous she's afraid to speak. A Rene first.

My eyes fix on her, stricken and wounded. "I can't believe this. How could it be true? Shouldn't I have known? How could I not know? I'm married to the man."

Rene flushes, something flashes in her eyes and then she looks away.

Oh my God.

"You knew!" I accuse harshly. "You knew and you didn't tell me. How could you do that, Rene? How could you do that to me?"

"No, no, no. I didn't know, Chrissie. I swear. I had suspicions and you were so certain about Neil. I ended up thinking I was wrong. Crazy. I thought I was wrong so I didn't say anything because I didn't want to hurt you."

"Why didn't you tell me? What kind of friend are you?"

She eases forward in a posture simultaneously

aggressive and defensive. "I did try to tell you, Chrissie. When we lived together in Berkeley. I told you I didn't like Neil. I told you there was something about him I didn't like. You just didn't hear me."

Flashing snippets of old memories soar through my head. Oh God, she did tell me. I just didn't understand. I refused to see what Rene could see, but deep down, I think I always knew.

I jump to my feet and run to the bathroom, slamming the door behind me. Everything is running loose and frantic in me and I can't bear to look at Rene, not for another moment. I haven't gotten a single thing in my life right. Every decision I've made *hasn't* been right or left turns. It's been right or *wrong* turns, and the wrong path is the one I invariably take.

I let Alan go, over and over again, and he's the only man I've ever truly loved. That is the truth. Why do I hide from it?

I married Neil and I shouldn't have. That is the truth and I hid from that as well. That nagging voice deep inside me told me not to do it, I ignored it, and I refused to listen. My life is in shambles, I have no one to blame but me, and I don't know how to fix any of it.

PREVIEW BROKEN CROWN

I shut off the shower, deciding not to call Chrissie. I dress for an excursion on my bike. Traveling the rural splendor of the United States on a Harley is one of the few things left in my life I still enjoy. The decision this time has nothing to do with savoring the scenery. The days it will take to travel from New York to California will give me a chance to back out if sanity decides to return. The call ahead of time will do neither of us any good if I decide not to see her.

I sink down onto my bed to make two phone calls. I tell my assistant to clear my calendar for the next month, and hang up as she bellows every reason why that isn't possible. Then I call the garage to get my bike ready.

I tuck into a backpack only what I need for the journey to Los Angeles. I almost leave the bedroom when I recall the lump in my sheets. Tucking the bracelet into my pocket, I reach out a hand and shake the body in my bed.

"You need to get dressed and get the hell out of here, love. I'm going to California. If you're a whore, I'd like to pay you first. If you're a nice girl, leave me your number."

The brown-eyed beauty sits up, pulling with her the blankets to cover her naked flesh. Morning-after modesty, another farce since my memory isn't so dim that I forgot what we did last night. Those pouting red lips smile.

Ah, Boston bred. The girl isn't ruffled by any of it.

Smoothly charming, she says, "I'll bill you. Though it's often considered a blurry difference, I'm not a whore. I'm your attorney. One of your divorce attorneys. I brought the finalized settlement contracts, and though you missed our meeting, I waited ten hours in this apartment for you to return to sign them since your ex-wife has an irritating proclivity to change her mind. I thought it best we jump on the offer and settle it fast since you didn't have a pre-nuptial agreement.

"When I tried to explain, you jumped on me. I thought what the hell, it's been a slow day and I'm earning five hundred bucks an hour for this. Why shouldn't my job have an occasional perk? You have been interesting. I've never been laid by a man who holds an infinity band while he fucks me. I think it's better I don't tell you the things you mumbled. I'll only warn you that you should be relieved it's covered under attorney/client privilege since my meter ticks until you sign those documents.

"The contracts are on the dresser. Please sign them so I can shower, dress and go. It's Saturday, in case you don't know what day it is, and I play racquetball at six. *That* I didn't expect you to know. It was a subtle attempt to speed you up in the signing."

I laugh softly. My attorney is charming. I go to the dresser and do a quick study of the contracts. "Thank you for not boring me with whatever I mumbled and thank you for promising to bill me so it's privileged. You can, however, bore me by letting me know how much this is costing me."

Panties and bra in place, my attorney scrambles from my bed gathering her clothes, then snatches the signed contracts from my hand.

"Me, I cost you seventy-two hundred for this meeting. Your ex-wife cost you one-hundred-sixteen million two hundred-twenty-seven thousand, a combination of cash, future cash, and an interesting assortment of personal property. You did, however, manage to retain the Malibu house that, against my advice, you battled her over, the bill from me five-hundred thousand over the value of it."

I clutch her chin a little roughly and give her a hard kiss. "You, love, were a bargain."

I leave her, half dressed, staring at me from my bathroom doorway. It sounded theatrical even to me. Chrissie would have given me such shit for those theatrics, but the girl seemed to be expecting something like that so I played along.

Thank you for reading. You might enjoy a sneak peek into Chrissie and Alan's future, with <u>Rewind</u> **A Perfect Forever Novella.**

He doesn't laugh. Instead, his gaze sharpens on my face. "I am being nice, Kaley. I came to you. I got tired of waiting."

What? Did I just hear what I think I heard?

Before I can respond, he says, "How's your afternoon looking? Do you have time to take off and come see something with me?"

My afternoon? There is something. I'm sure of that, but I suddenly can't remember a single thing.

"What do you have in mind?"

"I want to show you where I've been living. What I've been doing. I think you'll find it interesting."

Interesting? Why would I find it interesting?

"So do you think you can cut out for a few hours?" he asks, watching me expectantly.

I focus my gaze on the table, wondering if I should go, wondering why I debate this, and what the heck I have on the calendar that I can't remember. God, this is weird, familiar and distant at once, and I haven't a clue what I should do here.

I stare at his hand, so close to mine, on the table. Whoever thought it would be so uncomfortable *not* to touch a guy? It doesn't feel natural, this space we hold between us, spiced with the kind of talk people have who know each other intimately. What would he do if I touched him?

His fingers cover mine and he gives me a friendly squeeze. The feel of him runs through my body with remembered sweetness.

Suddenly, nothing in my life is as important as spending the afternoon with Bobby, and for the first time in a very long time, I don't feel like a disjointed collection of uncomfortably fitting parts. I feel at ease inside myself being with Bobby.

I stop trying to access my mental calendar, and smile up at Bobby. "I've got as much time as you need."

Bobby chuckles and his hand slips back from me. He rises and tosses some bills on the table. "Just a few hours, Kaley. I'll have you back before the end of the day."

I rise from my chair and think *not if I figure out fast how not to blow this.*

Or enjoy the first novel in the Perfect Forever Collection: The Signature. **Available Now. Please enjoy the following excerpt from The Signature:**

She became aware all at once how utterly delightful it felt to be here with him, alone on the quay, with the erotic nearness of his body.

She closed her eyes. "Listen to the quiet. There are times when I lie here and it feels like there is no one else in the world."

"No one else in the world? Would that be a good thing?" he asked thoughtfully.

"No. But the illusion is grand, don't you think?" she whispered.

Krystal turned her head to the side, lifting her lids to find Devon's gaze sparkling as he studied her. He shook his head lazily. "No. The illusion wouldn't be grand at all. It would mean I wasn't here with you."

It all changed at once, yet again, and so quickly that Krystal couldn't stop it. The ticklish feeling stirred in her limbs. Devon's words, as well as the closeness of their bodies, should have sent her into active retreat, and instead she felt herself wanting to curl into him. *What would it feel like if kissed me? Would I still feel this delicious inside? Or would that old panic and fear return?*

Laughing softly, Devon said, "I'm not used to relaxing. Can you tell?"

"I wasn't used to it before Coos Bay either. There is a

different pace of life here. At first I thought there was no sound. That's how quiet it seemed to me. Then I realized that there is music, beautiful music in this quiet."

After a long pause, he murmured, "You'll have to bring me here every Saturday until I learn to hear music in the quiet."

Krystal smiled. "Once you hear the music it's perfect."

"It's perfect now to me." His voice was a husky, sensual whisper.

He was on his side facing her. *When had that happened?* An inadvertent thrill ran through her flesh, and she could see it in his eyes—the supplication, the want, and an unexplainable reluctance to indulge either.

Devon was no longer smiling, his eyes had become brighter and more diffuse. His fingertips started to trace her face with such exquisite lightness that her insides shook. For the first time in a very long time, she felt completely a woman, and wanting.

Was it possible? Had she finally healed internally as her flesh had done so long ago? Was she finally past the legacy of Nick? Was what she was now feeling real? Should she seek the answer with Devon? Or was it better to leave it unexplored?

"You are a very beautiful woman," he whispered.

She watched with sleepy movements as his mouth lowered to her. It came first as a touch on her cheek, feather soft between the play of his fingers. Her breath caught, followed by a pleasant quickening of her pulse. She was unprepared for the sweetness of his lips and the rushing sensations that ran through her body. His thumb traced the lines of her mouth as his kiss moved sweetly, gently there.

His breath became rapid in a way that matched her own, and his mouth grew fuller and more searching. The fingertips curving her chin were like a gentle embrace, but their mouths were eager and demanding. Flashes of desire rocketed through her powerfully. Urgency sang through her flesh, a forgotten melody, now in vibrant notes. She found herself wanting to twist into him. Reality begged her to twist back.

ABOUT THE AUTHOR

Susan Ward is a #1 Amazon bestselling author in LGBT Erotica, #2 Amazon bestselling author in the Rock genre, and an Amazon Top 100 bestselling author in Erotica Humorous, Coming-of-age, Contemporary Romance, Historical Romance, Regency Romance, Women's Fiction, and Romance Sagas.

Her hometown is the inspiration for the Parker Saga which includes the Half Shell Series, Affair without End Series, and Sand & Fog Series. She has 15 romance releases available on Amazon and all her books are free in Kindle Unlimited.

Spare a tree. Be good to the earth. Donate or share her books with a friend.

Printed in Great Britain
by Amazon

42978356R00244